LEGACY
FOR THE
YOUNG PISTOLERO

Young Pistolero Series Book 4
by
Robert J. Alvarado

OTHER WORKS

Robert J. Alvarado
www.youngpistolero.com

Non Fiction

Elfego Baca Destined to Survive
2013 Sunstone Press, Santa Fe, NM, First Printing
2016 Sierra Press, Albuquerque, NM, Second Printing

Fiction
Award Winning Young Pistolero Series

The saga follows Rafael Ortega de Estrada, a seventeen-year-old Mexican peón on the run, riding a stolen Appaloosa stallion. After shooting the haciendero who raped his younger sister, Rafael heads north and enters the United States in 1866 and finds life on the other side of the border holds new dangers along with the promise of a new life.

This gritty tale is set in the American Southwest as Americans and Mexicans struggle after the Mexican-American War. In this tumultuous era in the late 1800s, Rafael (Rafe) grows into a man who respects both his heritage and embraces life in his new country.

Young Pistolero (Book 1) 2013 Sierra Press
2018 Finalist for Drama TV Series category, by the Latino Books into Movies Awards sponsored by Latino Literacy Now.
#1 Fiction Book for 2015; by The Latino Author, by Corina Martinez Chaudhry

Star of the Young Pistolero (Book 2) 2014 Sierra Press

Death Stalks the Young Pistolero (Book 3) 2015 Sierra Press #1 Fiction Book for 2016; by The Latino Author
Legacy for the Young Pistolero (Book 4) 2017 Sierra Press #3 Fiction Book for 2017; by The Latino Author
A Reckoning for the Young Pistolero (Book 5) 2018 Sierra Press
Dangerous Venture (Book 6) 2019 Sierra Press
Justified Vengeance (Book 7) 2019 Sierra Press
The Black Phantom (Book 8) 2020 Sierra Press
Lost Treasure (Book 9) 2024 Sierra Press

Other Fiction
The Jalapeño Republic 2020 Sierra Press
2021 International Latino Book Award Medalist. Insights from the ILBA judges, "It was an interesting book, quite different from most futuristic novels I have read."

Jake Flores Mystery
Just Vanished –2020 Sierra Press
2021 International Latino Book Award Medalist. Insights from the ILBA judges, "From the moment you start reading it, you imagine an action TV series that keeps you involved."

Zia Westerns
Set in the New Mexico and Arizona territories of the Southwest, these westerns draw from the Southwest's unique flavor. Originally part of New Spain and then Mexico, the Spanish settlers and native Indians forged an informal peace until the years after the Mexican-American War brought them into the Wild West. These stories are set during this chaotic time and attempt to paint a realistic picture of the meaning of the Zia symbol.

The Spanish Sword 2020 Sierra Press
2021 International Latino Book Award Medalist. Insights from the ILBA judges, "This book is carefully crafted and felt thoroughly researched."

Valentina 2022 Sierra Press

Spanish Language Books

Este libro constituye la traducción de una obra de ficción realizada por su propio autor. La serie original, galardonada y titulada Young Pistolero, fue escrita en inglés estadounidense y posteriormente vertida al español mexicano por el autor con el apoyo de la herramienta de inteligencia artificial ChatGPT. Cualquier error o imprecisión que pudiera encontrarse en la traducción es fortuito y responde únicamente al uso de dicha herramienta.

Publicación en español de Sierra Press:

Joven Pistolero (Libro 1)
Estrella del Joven Pistolero (Libro 2)
Muerte Acecha al Joven Pistolero (Libro 3)
Legado para el Joven Pistolero (Libro 4)
Ajuste de Cuentas para el Joven Pistolero (Libro 5)
Aventura Peligrosa (Libro 6)
Venganza Justificada (Libro 7)
El Fantasma Negro (Libro 8)
Tesoro Perdido (Libro 9)

PRAISES AND AWARDS

Young Pistolero, Young Pistolero Series
2018 Finalist for Drama TV Series category.

The Latino Books into Movies Awards are conducted by Latino Literacy Now, a 501c3 nonprofit co-founded by Edward James Olmos and Kirk Whisler. The judges for these awards are screenwriters, directors, producers, and others from the entertainment industry. They have deemed these books worthy of consideration for future television and movie production.

Young Pistolero, Young Pistolero Series
#1 Fiction Book for 2015; by The Latino Author
Death Stalks the Young Pistolero, Young Pistolero Series
#1 Fiction Book for 2016; by The Latino Author
Legacy for the Young Pistolero, Young Pistolero Series
#3 Fiction Book for 2017; by The Latino Author

Young Pistolero Series is a great fiction story that incorporates both history and a great story plot of a young man whose life spirals after avenging the rape of his younger sister. It has all the muster of a good western including gun fights, murder, and survival. The author does a fantastic job of incorporating the history of the United States and Mexico during a time when the Wild West was in full swing and struggles occurred on both sides of the border. The descriptions of history add much to the story and make the life of Rafael, the protagonist, really interesting.

Mr. Alvarado weaves a plausible plot and his setting descriptions and actions are right on. His graphic scenarios of land and territories make you feel as if you are right there alongside the rider as he heads through some rough terrain. His characters were exactly what you might expect of people living in the 'rough' west trying to survive the elements and mayhem of that time.

The writer incorporates Spanish words, which allows the reader to identify with the characters; however, he brilliantly illustrates the meaning after each and every word so non-Spanish speaking readers don't miss a beat. The book is filled with so much action that you can't put the book down. It has all the earmarks of a great western series. If you are looking for a good book to read, then this is one to put on your list this year. An excellent read! – Corina Martinez Chaudhry

I know this series will earn many more awards. A wonderful contribution to Southwest Hispano history and culture. - **Rudolfo Anaya, acclaimed novelist, poet, playwright, professor emeritus, 2015 National Humanities Medal Award recipient**

I just completed reading *A Reckoning For The Young Pistolero*. Great book. I've read the entire series and I'm looking forward to the next book. Mr. Alvarado is very skilled at utilizing historical knowledge as well his own personal experiences to keep you captivated from beginning to end. Being from New Mexico, I can personally relate to the language and setting so appropriately used in the book. I highly recommend the entire series. You won't be disappointed. - **Sammy Soto, retired high school educator/administrator Albuquerque, NM**

I am impressed by the historical detail and fast-moving plots. I also like the way he incorporates two very different young men and follows their lives. The author does a good job of developing these contrasting characters so that readers can walk in their boots and see how fate has shaped them. My father was a screenwriter for television when I was growing up in California and he wrote many westerns, including Wagon Train and Gunsmoke. Alvarado's novel could be the basis for one of those television westerns because of its engrossing plot and its clear depiction of heroes and villains. - **Dr. Jennie Nelson, PhD in Rhetoric and Writing, Carnegie Mellon University, post-graduate professor of writing, University of Idaho**

Mr. Alvarado vividly illustrates many rugged times after the Civil and Mexican American Wars through the eyes of a 17 year old peon who comes to the U.S. and adapts and grows into a hero. The Young Pistolero is a great new historical western series!
– **by Richard Golenda, post Secondary and College History Teacher post Chairman of the Pueblo Economic Development Corporation.**

LEGACY
FOR THE
YOUNG PISTOLERO

A glossary of *italicized* Spanish words is provided at the end of this book, with the exception of words which are equivalent in both languages, such as *importante* = important, *Mamá* = Mama, or words of Latin origin found in the English dictionary. Other words, phrases, and sentences written in Spanish are immediately explained within the text itself.

Printed in the United State of America

ISBN-13: 978-0991477746

SIERRA
PRESS

Published by Sierra Press
Phoenix, Arizona
First Printing, July 2017

Cover art and design by John Flinn
Graphic art by Daniel Alvarado and Lina Luna

DEDICATION

This book is dedicated to my mother. At 95 she is still an inspiration to me and everyone in our family.

The oldest of a family of ten, my mother grew up in the Chandler, Arizona area. She lived through the depression and married during World War II. She is part of the great generation, which gave more than they took. She always encouraged me to work hard and follow my dreams. Thanks mom.

ACKNOWLEDGEMENT

First and always, I owe more than thanks to my wife for her unending hours of critique, review, and clarity. She always keeps me honest in my writing and helps me find and keep each character's vision.

My thanks to my brother Dan for his creative talents in designing a unique cover and to my friends and family who encouraged me to continue the saga of the Young Pistolero Series, thank you.

I would like to acknowledge the wealth of historical information which is weaved into this work to depict the places and events of this saga's time period. As a work of historical fiction, where real-life historical figures or actual locations are used, the situations, incidents, or dialogues concerning those persons or places are entirely fictional and are not intended to depict actual events or to change the entirely fictional nature of the work.

DISCLAIMER

In an effort to accurately describe the social fabric of New Mexico during the timeframe of this book, readers should consider the author's transitions from the use of the terms, Spaniards and Mexicans. After the discovery of South America in 1492, New Spain, considered to encompass Mexico and much of central America, was under the control of Spanish Kings and Queens.

Over the next several hundred years, Spaniards emigrated north into what is now the American Southwest. Legions of settlers traveled to spread the Catholic religion and to seek fortunes in gold and silver. For their efforts, the Spanish royalty bestowed land and titles to the adventurous settlers. In New Mexico, Spaniards founded Santa Fe as the capital of the Kingdom of New Mexico in 1610. Industrious, the Spanish settlers created a robust economy and raised their families for generations. Rather isolated, New Mexico remained an extension of New Spain until the Mexican Revolution began in 1820.

After the Mexican Revolution ended in 1821, the country now known as Mexico emerged from under Spanish control. After the Mexican-American War ended in 1848, the border between Mexico and the American Southwest was in dispute. Finally, the Treaty of Guadalupe Hildalgo created the border as we know it today. In the treaty, Articles VIII and IX ensured the safety of existing property rights of Spaniard/Mexican citizens living in the Southwestern territories. Despite the treaty's assurances to the contrary, land grants owned in New Mexico were often not honored by the United States because of interpretations of the treaty and U.S. legal decisions. Fraud and greed by powerful American lawyers and politicians stripped many descendants of original land grant owners of their land.

Because this book is set after the Treaty of Guadalupe Hildalgo, the terms Spaniards and Mexicans are often intertwined. Even today, the descendants of the original

Spanish settlers maintain their heritage as Spaniards. However, Americans who began settling in New Mexico at that time used the term Mexicans for the local population living in the territories.

In today's world, the term Hispanic is often used to describe a diverse population of Spanish-speaking peoples. However, this book attempts to be true to the fundamental use of the terms, Spaniards and Mexicans, as it might have been used by the different characters in the story. In no way does it intend to disparage the people described by the usage of the terms.

CHAPTER 1

On an early evening in July of 1871, Rodolfo Guerrero urged the old and tired mules along a rutted cattle trail in the hills northeast of Torreón, Mexico. María Ortega sat on the seat of the rickety wagon by his side, her long dark hair whipping around her face in the wind. They had been on the trail from El Paso, Texas, for over two weeks, slowly winding their way south toward Torreón on forgotten dirt paths through the rural countryside.

Almost a month ago they left a ragtag band of *bandidos* in the hills not far from the abandoned Reyes *hacienda,* while they traveled to El Paso to buy guns. On this return trip, tucked safely under other supplies, the guns and ammunition were a precious cargo. Discovery by the authorities would mean immediate arrest, if not execution.

Despite the danger and long hours bumping along on the broken down wagon, the last month with María renewed Rodolfo's spirit. He loved to watch her genuine excitement of each blazing orange, pink, and gray sunrise as they lay in each other's arms waking to glorious mornings. Her strength and practical ways amazed him and made him proud. Though raised a *peón* on *don* Bernardo Reyes' *hacienda,* she was smart and knew of plants and herbs in this part of Mexico using them for both cooking and healing.

Rodolfo, the leader of a loosely bound band of *peón* outlaws, left Javier in charge of the group when they left for El Paso, without any specific plan as to how to find them on his return. He found himself fretting, wondering if he would be able to locate his amigos. Although he knew the hilly escarpment was a safe location with a view of the valley below and a rock overhang for protection from the weather, it was not normally possible for the band to stay put for any length of time. Slowly he drove the wagon on, hoping he could find the campsite before nightfall.

About an hour later, Hector, one of the lookouts for the *bandidos,* came running down the path from the abandoned logging road waving to Javier. "A wagon is coming," he yelled. "A wagon with two people."

At Javier's signal, several men picked up heavy clubs. Women and children scurried under the overhang, leaving the cooking fires unattended. Javier hoped it was Rodolfo and María returning, but learned how to protect the group over the last month. He wanted to show Rodolfo he was a responsible man who followed orders and had kept the group safe, though worried what Rodolfo would say about the new people who joined the group in his absence.

Winding up the trail, Rodolfo's nose caught the scent of roasting beef in the wind. He let out a big sigh of relief knowing they were almost home. María was half asleep and leaning on his shoulder when they pulled into the campsite. "María, wake up. We're here." Rodolfo nudged her awake as he stopped the wagon.

"Jefe, bienvenidos," Javier shouted out a welcome, recognizing Rodolfo driving the old wagon. *"Muchachos,* help Rodolfo put the mules away," he bellowed to the other men.

"Gracias Javier, help María get down," Rodolfo told him. Exhausted from the last leg of the trip, Rodolfo climbed down from the seat. Behind him he heard giggling and a woman's voice. Turning around he watched in amazement as six women and a group of children ran out from under the overhang of rock. The women smiled at him and walked to the cooking fire. The children happily ran off playing with sticks. Walking out of the dim light of the overhang, Rodolfo saw more than ten men standing quietly.

"Jefe, today is a good day. We have a calf on the spit and we will all eat well tonight," Javier said puffing his chest out proudly hoping the man he considered the boss was pleased.

"I smelled it coming up the road, Javier. María and I need a good meal and rest," Rodolfo told him noticing his friend's pride.

"Sí, jefe. You look tired. I hope all went well in El Paso," Javier commented. He led Rodolfo and María to a large rock where he told them to sit.

"Benita, bring food and water," Javier ordered one of

the women.

A woman, unknown to Rodolfo, brought them each a large tortilla stuffed with meat mixed with wild onions and peppers, while another woman brought cups of water. Rodolfo and María nodded to the women with thanks and hungrily ravished the meal. Over the long weeks on the trail, they had eaten mostly meager rations. The tortilla and meat was a feast.

Javier sat beside them eating a stuffed tortilla. "Javier, what are all these people doing here?" Rodolfo asked.

"I was going to ask you the same," María chimed in. When they left, she was the only woman of the group of thirteen men.

"*Jefe,* this is your doing," Javier answered.

"My doing! Why do you say that?" Rodolfo asked.

"Yes, you shared what we stole with the poor people and word got around. They found us and want to be here. Now, we have many mouths to feed. I have done the best I can, but the *hacienderos* are watching their stock more carefully and it is harder to steal a steer now. Today we got lucky," Javier told him. Though proud of how he had managed, Javier was glad Rodolfo was back to take the responsibility of these people off his back.

María looked around and asked, "How many new people are here?"

"Fourteen men, six with wives and children. Just this morning a man and his woman with two children found us. She is pregnant. All total we are twenty-seven men, six women and eight children," Javier explained.

"What, what the hell are we going to do with all those people?" Rodolfo tried hard not to shout.

"*Cálmate mi amor,*" María said trying to calm him.

"I will not calm down. I cannot be responsible for the women and children," Rodolfo huffed.

"I am a woman, Rodolfo," María reminded him, "and we have the guns. We can take what we want from the *hacienderos,*" she spoke of the rich landowners.

"Look at them María, do they look like fighters?"

María looked around and saw men in dirty cotton

peasant clothing wearing leather sandals and well-worn straw sombreros. The women wore simple shirts and skirts with their long black hair braided down to their lower backs. The children ran around barefooted, some half naked. They were not fighters; they were *peóns,* simple peasants, people who never owned anything in their lives. *Peóns* worked like slaves for *haciendaros,* the land owners of the large estates, as both she and Rodolfo had on *don* Bernardo's *hacienda.* These were simple working people, who needed much and asked for little.

"How are they able to find us when *la policía* and the *haciendaros* cannot?" Rodolfo asked wondering how it was possible.

"I was as curious as you," Javier said. "I asked some of them how they knew where to find our campsite. They told me *peóns* know about us and the word has spread that we are the only *bandidos* who help them. You know how *peóns* pass information, but they keep our whereabouts a secret, *jefe.*"

"It is as you dream," María said to Rodolfo. "The *peóns* will rebel against the *haciendaros* for their freedom."

"They say there are many other *bandido* gangs around who only take for themselves and kill anyone who gets in their way. They report those *bandidos* to *la policía.* We are the only ones who help them and they will do what they can to help us," Javier informed Rodolfo as he finished his tortilla. "Did you get the guns in El Paso?" he asked changing the subject.

"Yes we got the guns. I will show them to you in the morning. María and I are tired and need rest." Rodolfo took María by the hand and led her to the spot where their bedrolls and belongings had been placed away from the main campsite. On the way the people looked at them and smiled. Some bowed and some of the children ran alongside of them and giggled and screeched as they touched them before they ran back nearer the fire.

Exhausted from the trip Rodolfo lay down and María curled up in his arm. Around them the night critters resounded in the monotonous symphony with no conductor, the natural rhythm of the shadow of night.

"María, what are we going to do with these people?" Rodolfo whispered to her and in his voice she heard an uncertainty she had not heard before.

"I do not know, *querido*. You are the *jefe,* and you will figure it out. Sleep now my love, things will look better in the morning," María said before falling asleep in his arm.

CHAPTER 2

Alvaro Gutierrez, Vicente Vargas, Benjamin Pacheco, and Oscar Peralta, four young Spanish gentlemen of Santa Fe, sat on horseback at the top of a knoll overlooking Rafael Ortega's new house which was under construction. The four young *caballeros* were Diego de la Torre's trusted friends and had been looking for the *mestizo* from Mexico who killed him. They considered Rafael a *mestizo,* a Mexican of mixed Spanish and native Indian blood, who was not acceptable by Spanish society in Santa Fe.

Last month, Diego attacked Rafael on the plaza in Santa Fe and they fought with swords on horseback until Diego's horse fell on him and killed him. The young *caballeros* were there at the plaza and powerless to help Diego because Carlos Zuniga, Rafael's friend, held them at gunpoint to make it a fair fight.

"Are you sure it is the *mestizo's casa?*" Oscar asked Alvaro. "How could a *mestizo* own such a big house?"

"They say he is a businessman, a horse breeder, and the *Americano* laws here in Santa Fe do not care he is a *peón.* Such a thing would never have been allowed by our ancestors."

"*El pinche* sheriff is protecting him. Says it was self-defense. We have to show Santa Fe we Spaniards are still in charge," Alvaro cursed the sheriff.

New Mexico became a United States Territory in 1850 after Mexico lost the Mexican-American War and the citizens of New Mexico now lived under the new American laws. The previous ruling class, the Spanish elites, detested the change. They had ruled this land for almost three hundred years and no treaty was going to change their ways.

These four young *caballeros* were toddlers when the territory was established as American, but their fathers and grandfathers, the ruling *dons,* raised them in the Spanish traditions. Like their ancestors, they continued to dress in Spanish *trajes,* with ruffled bell-bottomed pants and silver-studded waist jackets and flat crowned hats. According to Spanish tradition, they were destined to control Santa Fe by the power of their families. Their friend Diego was the son and heir apparent of one of the larger *haciendas*. Rafael Ortega, a *peón mestizo* from Mexico, killed him and it was their right to make him pay.

"We could burn the house," Benjamin said.

"We should burn his horse barn and kill all his horses, including the big Appaloosa," Vicente added. Oscar nodded his agreement.

"*Culóns,*" Alvaro retorted calling them chickenshits. "We must kill him, not burn down his house and barn or kill his horses."

"He is not an easy man to kill and he is an American. We could get our necks stretched if we kill him," Benjamin protested. Of the four dandies, he was always the least likely to start a fight or finish one. Rafael had bested him twice and Benjamin knew the *mestizo* was dangerous with both a sword and a gun.

"What about the Spaniard, Carlos Zuniga. He is betrothed to Bibiana de Soto, but he befriends the *mestizo* dog. He held us at gunpoint so we could not help Diego. He too should pay," Vicente grumbled.

"*Don* Pedro does not want Carlos killed. I heard him say so. He only wants the *mestizo* killed for violating his niece. He sent her away to protect her from the *desgraciado* who pretended to be a *caballero,*" Benjamin replied calling Rafael a despicable wretch who had pretended to be a Spanish gentleman at the de Soto fiesta.

"How can *don* Pedro allow Bibiana to marry Carlos. His family lost their land grant in Los Lunas and he has nothing to offer. I hear he will teach school in the fall. How can *don* Pedro accept him?" Alvaro asked thinking he would love the chance to marry the lovely and rich Bibiana. As one of the bachelor aristocrats of Santa Fe, it should have been someone like him betrothed to *don* Pedro's eldest daughter.

"*Don* Pedro is a fool and will rue the day he allowed this marriage. Bibiana should marry a Spaniard in our tradition," Vicente agreed.

"Carlos is a Spaniard," Benjamin interjected. "Many of us have lost land grants to the *Americanos*. It is not his fault."

"He may be a *caballero,* but he has no money or power," Alvaro said. "I know *don* Pedro talked to Diego about marrying Bibiana before that *pinche mestizo* killed him." Alvaro cursed about Rafe's heritage, while knowing Diego had only toyed with the idea of marriage. Diego had loved the bachelor life and was not ready to settle down to run the family *hacienda* and have children.

As the four young *caballeros* watched Rafael's property, a young Appaloosa mare ran freely up the fenced hillside near them. The young mare raced like the wind with a short mane blowing in the breeze. Behind the mare two older colts grazed on the soft green grass. Rafael had started his breeding business with Rayo, a magnificent Appaloosa from *don* Bernardo's *hacienda* in Torreón, Mexico. His RO brand had been garnering praise in Santa Fe.

"Look at his horses," Alvaro said pointing to the pony sired by the big Appaloosa. "No *mestizo* should have such blooded animals. It is not right."

The three other dandies nodded in agreement. The Appaloosa was the superior horse, rearing and battling Diego's smaller black stallion. Though Diego was a superior swordsman and could have easily bested Rafael at the sword, the Appaloosa altered the odds. In the minds of the four young *caballeros,* pure-blooded Spaniards were always superior to mixed-blood *mestizos.*

"Is that him?" Oscar asked as a man on horseback rode up toward the house. They studied the rider as he came into view, but the horse was brown and the man older.

Since the killing, Diego's friends had argued on how to seek their revenge. In the old days it would have been easy. They would have found the *mestizo,* dragged him in public humiliation, and killed him in public. The Spanish law gave them that right. The new American laws would have them jailed or hanged for such an action. They knew their revenge must be done in secret. Everyone would know they were to blame, but the deed must be untraceable to their hands.

"Come on. He's not here. Let's go to the cantina,"

Alvaro said. They turned their horses heading down the east side of the hilltop toward the town of Santa Fe, Alvaro taking the lead. Since Diego's death, Alvaro had become the most prominent *caballero* of the younger generation. His family had more land than the others. A part of Alvaro relished Diego's death, because it propelled him to the top and he now held authority over his companions. It would be his call to determine how the *mestizo* would die.

CHAPTER 3

When the four young *caballeros* reached Santa Fe, they rode into the *barrio* toward de Vargas Street. Strands of red chili *ristras* hung from the *vigas* jutting from thick adobe walls of the houses. Graceful archways covered sidewalks running in front of several buildings in this older part of the city. Alvaro led them around a corner and rode down the street to Burro Alley. Taking the narrow alley, they rode to the cantina's corral.

The Palacio Cantina proudly catered to *caballeros* from families of pure Spanish ancestry since it had been established in the early 1800s. When the four *compañeros* pushed the door to the cantina open, the man playing a Spanish guitar hesitated momentarily while several sets of eyes assessed them, and then the music continued.

The smooth stucco walls of the cantina were decorated with conquistador weapons and large murals of Spanish explorers and conquistadors graced the walls depicting a once glorious past. The cantina, owned by Virginia Barceló Verdugo, was a bastion for the local Spaniards – a place *Americanos* were not welcome and would be run off at the tip of a sword. The floors of the Palacio were covered with fine, thick European carpets. Elegantly etched mirrors reflected the paintings. Crystal chandeliers, rich draperies, and imported furniture from Spain made the Palacio feel more like Spain than Santa Fe. Although most of the furnishings were old, they sparkled from the laborious care given to polishing and preserving them.

"Hola caballeros," the bartender welcomed them as they walked up. Without asking he poured four glasses of brandy. The Palacio Cantina catered to Santa Fe's Spanish aristocrats serving only the finest liquors from Mexico.

At a back table, several older *dons* were drinking and playing Monte. It was a simple card game, played with forty cards after eliminating the 8's, 9's and 10's from a full deck. After the cards were shuffled and cut, the Monte dealer pulled the bottom two cards, called the bottom layout, and placed them face-up. Next the top two cards, called the top layout, were placed face-up. Players chose which layout to bet, top or bottom, and made their bets accordingly. Once the bets were placed, the dealer turned the deck face-up. The card showing was called the 'gate.' Players won if the gate was of the same suit of either card in the layout they bet on.

Alvaro took his brandy and sat at a table away from where the older *dons* were playing the card game. Frustrated by the recent events and the death of Diego, Alvaro fumed. The old *dons* hardly seemed annoyed. He heard all they had done about Diego's death was to pressure Sheriff Johnson to arrest Rafael. The *dons* cowardice inaction made Alvaro's blood boil. He blamed them for allowing the *Americanos* to take over New Mexico. It was their paunchy-bellied generation who did not fight. Now, Alvaro and his friends did not have their birthright.

Sipping his brandy, Alvaro rolled plans to kill the *mestizo* around in his brain. Over the last several weeks they learned the man calling himself Rafe was Rafael Ortega de Estrada. He was a peasant who grew up on a *hacienda* in Torreón, Mexico. Through a coincidence a number of years ago, he was taken on as an adopted son by George Summers, a prominent gun maker here in Santa Fe. An *anglo,* George Summers raised Rafe as an American, giving him respect and an education. It did not matter to Alvaro. The *bastardo* was still a *mestizo* and no better than a dog.

The fight had been over Ana Teresa de Soto, the beautiful *señorita* from California. She was Bibiana's cousin. She and Bibiana had been riding the *paseo* around the plaza in their carriage on the warm summer evenings. It was a courting ritual by Spaniards, where unattached young men and women flirted. Both Diego and Rafe were courting her, though at the time *don* Pedro de Soto thought Rafe was a *caballero.* Had *don* Pedro known Rafe was a *mestizo,* he would never have been allowed to step a foot near Ana Teresa.

Benjamin, Vicente, and Oscar joined Alvaro at the table. Virginia Verdugo followed the three young *caballeros* holding a deck of cards. "Monte?" she asked. Alvaro stood, bowed, and kissed her hand inviting her to sit next to him.

"You look lovely tonight, madame. Come, take some of our money and we will drink the night to our ancestors," Alvaro said.

Virginia sat beside Alvaro. Usually she dealt Monte to the old *dons* sitting at the back table, but since Diego's death she found it hard to hold her tongue against them. Diego de la Torre was not just a prominent son of Santa Fe's elite Spaniards, he was her lover. Now he was dead and the old *dons* drank, laughed, and wanted her to act as if nothing had happened.

"Leave it to the sheriff," *don* Mateo had told her. "The American law will take care of it."

Virginia spit on the American laws. The sheriff would hassle her from time to time for not allowing Americans into her establishment. She told him it was her cantina and only her friends could come in. He did not press the point, but she knew someday it would be different.

When her mother, *la doña Tules,* started this cantina her reputation spread all around Santa Fe. It catered to the aristocrats every wish for imported Spanish liquor and beautiful *putas. La doña Tules* ran the finest whores in Santa Fe. Her *putas* were blonds, redheads, blacks, Spanish, *Indias* and *mestizas* catering to all *caballero* desires. When her mother died, Virginia took her place running the cantina in the same manner.

In the old days, the *dons* would have handled the *mestizo* and made sure he died a horrible death. Now the *dons,* the Spanish gentlemen with over-stuffed waists and gray hair, cared little for tradition. They did not care if Diego died from his horse falling on him or by the *mestizo's* sword, but Virginia cared.

She placed the top and bottom layers up for the Monte game and said, "Place your bets."

Virginia had heard Alvaro grumbling about Diego's death and he talked of revenge. She had heard him urging the others to take the matter into their own hands and kill the *mestizo.* Virginia wanted to know more and wanted to fuel Alvaro's fire. Now when he came to the Palacio, Virginia flirted with him. She gave him her obvious attention and thought he was flattered. Alvaro knew she and Diego were lovers and she wanted to leave him with the impression she might consider him as a suitor.

They placed their bets and Virginia turned the top card. Alvaro and Vicente won. The simple game was pure luck. Virginia ran clean gambling tables, though the house still won more than half the time.

After about an hour of playing Virginia asked, "What are you going to do about the *mestizo* dog who killed my Diego? The old *dons* over there have lost their *cojones* for such tradition."

"The bastard must die," Alvaro snarled.

"*Sí,* you must avenge my Diego. The *Americanos* will do nothing and those *dons* are *culóns,*" she whispered into his ear. Calling the old *dons* chickenshits would be considered an insult, but Virginia was feeling brazen.

Virginia poured another round of brandy for the young *caballeros* at her table. They were all from prominent families, but she knew Alvaro would be the leader. He was tall and cut an imposing figure in his brown *traje.* The suit's ruffled pants stopped atop highly polished boots with silver toes. Around his trim middle, the *traje's* sash was made of blood orange satin. His brown hair had a slight curl and his eyes were a gray blue. An ornate sword hung from a sheath at his side.

Alvaro turned to her and smiled, "Do not worry madame, Diego will be avenged by my sword. I am sure you are missing him greatly and I am here to help ease your suffering."

Virginia coyly placed her hand on Alvaro's thigh. "I knew you would not fail to follow the traditions." Virginia's advances only made Alvaro more determined to kill Rafael, avenging Diego and claiming Virginia as a prize.

CHAPTER 4

Several long dark weeks had passed since Rafe found out the truth from his mother about his illegitimate birth. She told him the night he came home battered, after he and Diego de la Torre fought on horseback in the Santa Fe plaza. Diego, a local Spanish aristocrat, detested Rafe because he was a *mestizo* of a lower Spanish caste status. Diego was compelled by his pretentious nature to ostracize Rafe for his attention to the beautiful *señorita,* Ana Teresa de Soto.

Rafael Ortega, known now by his American nickname Rafe, was a *mestizo,* born a *peón* in Mexico. He was a peasant of mixed-blood heritage and Diego was a pure-blooded Spaniard from the old bastion of Spaniards here in Santa Fe. The Spaniards still believed in the *casta* system and believed *mestizos* should not be allowed to marry a Spanish woman.

Rafe had been fighting to shed the stigma of his birth since coming to Santa Fe over five years ago. Yes he had been born a *peón* on *don* Bernardo *hacienda,* but now he was an educated man and horse breeder of significant wealth and here in New Mexico had all the rights and freedoms afforded by the United States Constitution and laws. New Mexico was a territory of the United States and those new laws ruled, but the Spanish aristocrats held onto their power through intimidation and the sword.

Diego had taken out a personal vendetta against Rafe for his courtship of Ana Teresa de Soto. When Diego affronted him in the plaza wielding his rapier, Rafe defended himself. Had it not been for Rayo, Rafe's superior horse, Diego might have killed him, though Death had other ideas. Diego's unbounded loathing cost him his life that day on the plaza. Rafe and Rayo were bruised and battered from the fight, but now the fight seemed inconsequential to the revelation from his mother.

The weight of his mother's shocking disclosure pressed on Rafe and in this dark world he was Rafael Reyes de Estrada. He was the bastard son of *don* Bernardo Reyes, the tyrant *haciendero* of his youth in Torreón, Mexico, and the *desgraciado* who raped his fifteen-year old sister María and continued to force her to bear his bastard children. His mother's revelation – the *don* had also raped her when she was young and he, Rafael, was his bastard son. He was the son of the man he spent his entire life hating.

Standing in Rayo's stall working on the horse's hoof, a sinister growl came out of the dark side of his soul and he chuckled at how Death took *don* Bernardo to his master in hell. Rafe had intended on killing the *desgraciado,* but the wizened old devil dropped dead from a heart attack when Rafe confronted him. Rafe rode away from Torreón vowing never to go back. Santa Fe was his home now. In Santa Fe he was a businessman, a horse breeder, and he was planning on marrying Ana Teresa.

Pablo, the horse master from the Reyes *hacienda* brought news from Torreón after *don* Bernardo's death. The laws of Mexico had changed and Rafe could inherit the large estate even though he was a bastard. Pablo and the priest in Torreón had proof of Rafe's true identity. He would not care about the inheritance, if it were not for his sister, María, and the *bandido* Rodolfo. Pablo also brought the news from Torreón about how María took off with the bandit. Rodolfo had been Rafe's best friend in Torreón, and Rafe knew him to be a good man, but life had turned him into an outlaw.

Rafe learned from Pablo, María and Rodolfo headed for the hills of Mexico living as *bandidos,* fighting for the rights of the *peóns.* She left her two children, Antonio and Alicia, here in Santa Fe with their grandmother and in Rafe's charge. Both Rafe's mother and Pablo were pressing him to go to Mexico City to claim his legacy and take ownership of the Reyes *hacienda.* Pablo reasoned it was the only way to protect María. Inherit the *hacienda* and let her and Rodolfo live on it. His mother implored him to save his sister from the life of an outlaw. "Think of the children," she told him.

To do what his mother asked, he must take his rightful name, Rafael Reyes de Estrada. He must accept his birthright as the son of the man he hated the most in the world. The thought hurt him to his core.

For a couple weeks after the fight with Diego, Ana Teresa's uncle and guardian, *don* Pedro, kept her sequestered refusing to allow Rafe to see her. Rafe's only hope to speak to her was through Carlos' fiancée, Bibiana. Ana Teresa was living with her cousin, Bibiana, under the hospitality of Bibiana's father after her family lost their ranch in California. A week ago Carlos told Rafe *don* Pedro sent his beloved Ana Teresa away. No one knew where. The days of waiting and wondered were driving him crazy.

When Rafe thought about Ana Teresa, his thoughts were about the memory of dancing the bolero with her. He could vividly see her golden eyes looking at him and her red dress trimmed in black swaying as she moved gracefully. Since that night he was smitten and she returned his affection. It was their love, which caused so much turmoil from the old Spanish aristocracy of Santa Fe. Her uncle wanted to maintain control over the purity of the caste system and against the American laws which would allow them to marry.

Yesterday, Carlos told him Bibiana overheard her father tell someone he sent Ana Teresa away to be with her parents in Spain. Once again Rafe felt the brunt of the old Spanish caste system. Ana Teresa had been sent to Spain all because she was interested in him, a *mestizo*. Rafe riled believing the caste system had no place here in New Mexico in 1871, but the law was conflicted. He and Ana Teresa had rights, but no one would stand up to the Santa Fe Spanish aristocrats who lived by the old ways.

He did not even have a chance to see Ana Teresa to tell her how much he loved her and now she was gone. She had professed her love for him and agreed to marriage and they clung together in a few brief moments. He tried to keep those few minutes in his heart and he swore he would find her as soon as he finished his business in Mexico.

Rafe heard hoofbeats near the barn and looking up saw Carlos ride into the barn on Santiago. Carlos had accompanied Bibiana de Soto, his fiancée, to Mass this morning at the San Miguel Church. It was the church where they would be wed in September. Rafe raised his hand to signal Carlos. He did not call out a greeting and instead took Santiago to the stall and started to unsaddle the black horse. Rafe thought Carlos' lack of response unusual and wondered if he and Bibiana had a fight.

"*¿Cómo estás?*" Rafe asked Carlos if all was well when he walked to the door of Santiago's stall. When Carlos turned, there was blood on his shirt collar.

"What happened to you?" Rafe asked.

"Diego's friends caught me near the stream and surrounded me on the way back here. They pulled their swords on me." Rafe knew Carlos rarely wore his sword and never on Sunday to Mass. He was a master swordsman and quite good with a gun, though used his faith for God's protection. Carlos was a devout Catholic and had been educated at a seminary in Madrid, Spain. He looked at life through the lens of God's plan and did not believe in killing.

"Why? They have no quarrel with you. Surely they blame me for Diego's death," Rafe fumed.

"Oh yes, they blame you. They told me to tell you this is a warning, a warning for us both. They are coming to avenge Diego and will make us pay."

"Us? Why are they blaming you?" Rafe asked. "Let them come after me if they want. I would gladly show them how these work," he grumbled patting the GSW pistols on his hips.

"Alvaro said I stopped them from helping Diego and also I am a disgrace as a Spaniard for having a *mestizo* as a friend," Carlos said. "The first part is true."

"You only made it a fair fight."

"I don't think they care at this point. There was hate in their eyes, especially Alvaro."

Carlos was Rafe's best friend and confidant, more like a brother than a friend. Rafe saved Carlos' life and though he had reciprocated in return, the events created a special bond between the two.

"You need to be very careful. They are emboldened and I don't think they fear the American laws. They could easily have killed me today and no one could hang the blame on them," Carlos said.

Rafe assumed the initial furor over Diego's death had dissipated. The sheriff ruled it self-defense and had brought no charges against him.

"I must put a stop to them," Rafe said. "I will not live my life here in Santa Fe in fear and your wedding is coming up soon. Tell me, who was it?"

"Rafe, you cannot take on the entire Spanish aristocracy. They will lose their *bravado* after awhile. Perhaps you should go to Mexico to see about the *hacienda* and get out of town for a few weeks," Carlos suggested.

Yesterday, after Carlos told Rafe the latest news about Ana Teresa, he and Rafe talked for many hours. Carlos understood Rafe's conflict. His heart was with Ana Teresa, but his family responsibility lay with María. He had to go to Mexico City to prove his birthright from *don* Bernardo Reyes and to claim his legacy. After securing the inheritance, he knew Rafe planned to come back to Santa Fe and continue his horse breeding business. Carlos was to begin teaching at the San Miguel Catholic Diocese School starting in September and he and Bibiana were to be married several weeks later. Carlos hated to tell his friend he wondered if both plans were in jeopardy.

"No, I will not run away. I have done nothing wrong. Diego attacked me and I am not a *peón* anymore. I had every right to court Ana Teresa and we should be allowed to marry. It is time for the *dons* to realize they do not rule the world anymore. Even *peóns* in Mexico have been given rights by the new president." Rafe's frustration over the Spanish caste system burned in his soul. He had lived it and like shedding a skin now enjoyed the fruits of his own hard work. The United States Constitution gave him those rights here in New Mexico.

"You know the Spaniards are living in the past. Change will take time," Carlos said with a sigh. He knew Rafe was right and he felt sorry for his friend who was caught between the two worlds of the American laws and the Spanish elite's caste system.

CHAPTER 5

It was mid-afternoon several days later when George Summers walked into the sheriff's office for the third and hopefully the last meeting regarding his adopted son Rafe's involvement with the death of Diego de la Torre. George was acting as a character reference on Rafe's behalf and most of all staying on top of the ongoing investigation of the death of Diego. There was no doubt Rafe acted in self-defense and many witnesses testified to that fact. However, the Spanish elites in Santa Fe were outraged over the killing and wanted justice. George did not call it justice, but revenge.

"Thanks for coming George," the sheriff held out his hand and George shook it. George sat down across from him placing his hat on top of the desk.

"The Spaniards are threatening to take matters into their own hands, pressing me to look into what led up to the confrontation. Even though Diego's horse killed him in the fall, they believe Rafe is to blame. I'm worried an all out war is brewing."

George assured him it all had to do with girls and explained the social class as defined by Santa Fe's Spanish aristocrats. At first the sheriff, a man from Kansas, did not grasp what George meant about Spanish traditions and the caste system. George pointed out it was similar to how black slaves were often unfairly regarded in the United States.

"You know Rafe is innocent. Yes they were fighting, but Diego attacked Rafe and it was Diego's horse, not Rafe, which killed him. Everyone saw it. The American laws should protect my son."

"The law protects him and I won't bring any charges, but I can't protect him from a stray bullet or the sword of Spanish revenge. Innocent or not, Rafe could pay the price."

In a way George blamed himself for the troubles Rafe encountered here in Santa Fe. After Rafe saved his life in west Texas, George brought seventeen-year-old Rafe to Santa Fe and raised him as he would his own son. At the

time, Rafe was an uneducated *peón* on the run after shooting
a *haciendero* for raping his sister. Regardless of his social
status, George sensed Rafe's true nature. He was both
intelligent and honorable.

George taught him gun making and was impressed
how Rafe learned to operate the machines used in the
foundry to make the various parts. Rafe was not afraid of
hard work. Besides working in the machine shop, George
found tutors to teach him English, history, and mathematics
and Rafe thrived. What he did not teach Rafe were the social
practices followed by the Spanish elite in Santa Fe. Instead,
George educated Rafe as a New Mexican man, an American
man, free to follow his dreams and his heart.

Now Rafe was involved in the accidental killing of
Diego de la Torre, one of Santa Fe's aristocratic sons.
Finding out Rafe was a *peón* from Mexico, they believed Rafe
did not fit in their world nor allowed to marry Ana Teresa, a
Spanish *señorita* from California.

"I think Rafe should leave town for awhile until this
fiasco settles down some," the sheriff broke into George's
thoughts.

"Perhaps you are right," George responded. "Rafe
needs to go to Mexico to see about his sister. I'll talk to him."

As George left the sheriff's office, he pondered his
adopted son's actions. What George could not understand
was why Rafe pretended to be a Spanish *caballero,* attending
a fiesta at the de Soto *hacienda.* Rafe told him, Carlos had
been invited to the Easter fiesta by Bibiana, now his fiancée,
and Carlos invited Rafe to go along for moral support.
Dressed in *trajes* and riding Rafe's blooded horses, the two
attended the party. Carlos was a gentleman, but Rafe should
not have pretended to be one. At the fiesta, *don* Pedro de
Soto accepted him into his home and Rafe met Ana Teresa.

George did not anticipate the Spanish caste
distinctions would affect his adopted son here in Santa Fe.
Josefina had brought it up from time to time, but he ignored
his wife's warnings. George believed he was raising an
American not a Mexican or Spaniard, so he gave no credence
to her warnings. Now, he was sorry he did not listen to his

wife when she tried to tell him what would happen if Rafe mingled with Santa Fe's Spanish upper class and they found out about his heritage.

To George, Rafe's life was a never ending seesaw of accomplishments and tragedies. George gave Rafe a new life in Santa Fe along with an education and helped him acquire land adjacent to the GSW ranch and foundry to start a horse breeding business. Rafe now had eleven blooded horses and had sold three colts of his RO brand. To see him flourish filled George with pride.

However, Rafe's past did not want to let him go. George could not help his adopted son with the upsetting tragedy from Torreón – Rafe was in truth the bastard son of the *haciendero*. Actually, George was proud of how Rafe handled the news and knew he was planning a trip to Mexico City to secure his inheritance.

As if Rafe did not have enough to occupy him, this business with the Spanish aristocrats here in Santa Fe was disturbing and George could not think of an easy solution. He knew their ways and they would want blood. They might not be satisfied until they had Rafe's blood on their swords and George felt helpless to protect him.

George decided to stop at the Santa Fe Saloon for a drink to drown the disturbing thoughts about Rafe before he headed home. He pushed in the doors and headed to the bar.

"Hello George. Haven't seen you for a while," the bartender said with a surprised look.

"Hey Pete, give me a bottle of rye and a glass." George said to the bartender.

"Sure thing."

The bartender placed a glass and a bottle on the bar and George replaced them with a silver dollar. Walking outside George sat down on the patio facing the main Santa Fe plaza. Cool shade covered most of the patio from the lattice ceiling intertwined with sweet honeysuckle. The air was fragrant with the honeysuckle blossoms and bees hummed while flitting from flower to flower. He pulled off his hat and sat back on a wicker chair. Pouring a shot of rye, he took sips of the smooth liquor and tried to relax.

"George," he heard Mayor Billy Thornton call out from the plaza. George was on his second shot of rye when the mayor walked up to him. "I haven't seen you round lately."

"Hello Billy."

"Mind if I sit and have a drink with you?" the mayor asked.

"Please, come and sit. I got this bottle and I can't possible drink it all," George said and waved the mayor to a chair at the table.

"How you been, Billy?" he asked as the mayor sat down. The bartender saw the mayor sit and came quickly with a second glass.

"Been doin jes fine," Mayor Thornton replied in his southern drawl. William, Billy, Thornton was born in Missouri and was a Confederate Veteran of the Civil War. Thornton was a no-nonsense politician who took particular pains to suppress crime and disorder in his town of Santa Fe. George thought he was doing a good job.

"How's the family? Heard your wife and children are back in Missouri," George asked.

"Shur nuff. Elsie took the boys to visit her family back east. They kin have that hot and sticky place. Me, I like it rat heah," the mayor said with a laugh.

"I hear you Billy. Can't beat the summer weather here in Santa Fe," George said and clinked glasses with the mayor before downing the rye.

"Say George, the sheriff tells me yer dopted son Rafe got hisself tangled up with the Spanish uppity-ups and one of them young uppity-ups got kilt," the mayor said hoping George would fill him in on more of what he knew about the situation.

"That's right Billy. Rafe is smitten on a *señorita* from California who was visiting her uncle's *hacienda* and Diego de la Torre had his eyes on her too. Several weeks ago Diego attacked Rafe in the plaza and in the battle Diego was killed by his horse. It was self-defense and the horse killed Diego, but the Spanish elite want revenge."

"That so, them Spanish ristrocrats are sayin that a low-life mes'tiso was fooling round a *senorita*. I heard they are a sayin your boy attacked the man named Diego and killed him," the mayor said before he downed another shot of rye. "What the hell is a mes'tiso anyway?"

Calmly George tried to explain hundreds of years of Spanish heritage in a simple way. "The Spanish pride themselves on tracing their blood lines and believe anyone not of pure Spanish blood is a lower class. When the Spanish conquered and colonized the Americas, the settlers began to intermix with native people. A *mestizo* is a person of part Spanish and part native Mexican Indian blood. The aristocrats believe themselves a superior race and treat the mixed-blood people as inferior."

"So your son is one of these mixed-blood types?"

"Yes," George replied. "Here in New Mexico it should no longer matter, but the *dons* are trying to cling to the past."

"The sheriff is investigating and witnesses say Diego attacked Rafe on horseback wielding a rapier. Rafe was defending himself. Fortunately, Rafe's horse was taller and stronger than the black stallion Diego rode. The Appaloosa knocked Diego's horse over and it crushed him to death. Rafe is a *mestizo*, but he is my son and a good man," George told him.

"You be right bout the Spanish and how they worry their daughters gettin on with non-Spanish men. Why, they don't even like us 'mercans too much neither," the mayor said and laughed while he poured another shot.

"You know how it is with the whites and blacks in the south, Billy. The Spanish are the same way here in the territory," George added.

"I surely do." Billy poured himself another drink from the bottle and downed the shot in one gulp.

"Well, the sheriff will sort it all out. One thing for shur, things are a changin here. Now we's all 'mercans and them Spanish won't be able to control the territory much longer. I hears there's a big push to make us a state."

"Yes, I believe the Territorial delegates are putting up a proposal for statehood. I can only believe New Mexico will become a state soon," George said.

The mayor stood up and stretched. "I bess be gettin along. You tell Rafe I'm a comin out to have a look at buying one of his fine horses real soon. Thank you for the rye old friend," the mayor said and downed the sip of rye in his glass. He stuck out a hand and George shook it.

CHAPTER 6

It was several weeks since Rodolfo and María arrived back to the hills near Torreón, Mexico. The long and dangerous trip to El Paso to buy guns had been exhausting, but now Rodolfo realized he had bigger problems. Almost two months ago, he and María left a rag-tag group of thirteen men in the hills not far from the Reyes *hacienda.*

They were free *peóns,* men free of servitude to a *haciendero.* In the world Rodolfo wanted, they would be free to farm their own land and graze their own cattle. The Mexican ruling class made that all but impossible for *peóns.* It was not a crime in Mexico to be a free *peón,* but with no work, money, or food it meant starvation. Rodolfo knew the dream he had been painting to these *peóns* was just that, a dream.

Living off the land and often making raids on the local *haciendas,* they lived a perilous lifestyle. They were *bandidos* or criminals in the eyes of the law and only escaped capture by continuing to move and hide in the desolate hills. He and María returned to find the small band of thirteen had swelled to twenty-three and seven more joined them over the past week. Word of his exploits and generosity for poor people was spreading throughout the countryside.

"You shared what we stole with the peasants and word got around. They found us and want to be here," Javier explained when Rodolfo and María returned home. Rodolfo's vision, his dream to help *peóns* create a better life, now seemed a crushing responsibility.

The past week since returning home to Mexico and rejoining the *bandidos,* Rodolfo Guerrero fretted about how to protect all the new people, especially the women and children. For her part, María spent her time getting to know the people and worked with the women to feed the children and see what was needed to clothe them.

At night when the fire burned low and Rodolfo held María in his arms were the few moments he could try to forget the chaos and danger. More than anything else, he worried about María being caught and imprisoned or even worse, killed.

"It is too dangerous, María. If we cannot be on the move it is only a matter of time before *la policía* find us. I love you. You are my life, but you must go back to El Paso," Rodolfo implored her several days ago. María loved him and he loved her, but what kind of life could he give her as the leader of *bandidos* on the run.

It amused María to see Rodolfo fret and wonder what he would do with his new responsibilities. Rodolfo's vision, the one he grandly told her at the lake the day they made love for the first time, was coming true.

"Querido, we have guns and ammunition. You have more than twenty men to defend us and the women will fight too. If *la policía* finds us, they will not live to tell anyone," María said vehemently.

Her words shocked Rodolfo. He was trying his best to accept the fact he was now the leader of a growing rag-tag and hungry group of *peóns.* He took stock of the new men to learn if any had experience handling guns. *Peóns* were not allowed to own or carry guns in Mexico, but he was pleased most of the men had a general knowledge and a few were decent shots. He gave his most trusted man, Javier, the responsibility to begin training the new men.

With the guns bought in El Paso, Javier was training them on how to handle the rifles and pistols. Rodolfo knew it was necessary to teach them to shoot, but worried about the valuable wasted ammunition. Each day Javier did the training several miles away in a small isolated canyon for fear the gunshots might be heard. Each night the men returned with smiles and stories about their improving abilities.

"We need more guns and especially bullets. I underestimated how much we would need," Rodolfo complained to María after seeing how the training was reducing their stockpile of bullets.

"I still have a few gold coins," she reminded him they had not spent their entire fortune in El Paso.

"Even with the money we cannot buy ammunition here in Mexico, María. More people are arriving every day.

We need more bullets to hunt for food as well as to defend ourselves. We will need a lot of money and another trip to El Paso."

In the past, Rodolfo and his gang lived off small game, like snared rabbits or doves. Now it took much larger game to feed the hungry lot. Kiko and Pancho took the best of the *bandidos* and raided nearby *haciendas* for food to feed the band of people. They raided the fields and gardens returning with sacks of corn, potatoes, and vegetables. When they could, they stole a pig or a young calf for slaughter. More often it was a few chickens, which were easier to carry.

The people never complained even when food rations were meager. *Peóns* were used to having little to eat and little control over their lives. It was the children who really bothered Rodolfo. They needed meat in the bellies to be healthy and grow.

Tonight with María tucked under his arm as they lay under the starry night sky, Rodolfo wanted to talk to her. The weight of his responsibility for these people was becoming more clear. They looked to him for guidance and protection. What had seemed simple in the past was fast becoming a complex situation.

"María, I have a plan. Paco, the miner from Zacatecas, has been telling me about the silver mines there and he says we can rob one of the smaller mule trains carrying ingots to the mint in Mexico City," Rodolfo told her feeling uncomfortable even thinking about this desperate and foolish plan.

"*¿Estás loco?*" she asked if he was crazy.

"*Tal vez lo soy,*" perhaps I am he said. "Paco told me he worked for a small mine operation and only a small guard unit escorted it to the mint in Mexico City. I will question him more before I decide. I think if we are able to rob a silver wagon we can go to El Paso and buy more guns and ammunition," he continued.

"No. I don't like it. It is too dangerous. *Don* Bernardo talked about the silver mines in Zacatecas. I heard him say the government protected them with many soldiers," she warned him pulling up and away from him. Looking into his eyes she said, "It is too risky. We must find another way."

Rodolfo saw the concern in her eyes and knew she was probably right. Unfortunately he saw no other solution. Robbing a *haciendera* in a coach for her rings or a few coins would not feed this group. Eventually the ammunition would run out and then they would not even be able to kill game, much less defend themselves.

"Paco says the same thing, but he says the smaller mines don't get the protection the big mines get. He believes the smaller escorts will be easy to take. He says the soldiers protecting the small mine shipments are mostly drunks and only care about where they get their next drink," he added.

"No *querido,* you will be killed," she implored him to give up the idea. He pulled her in closer to him and stroked her hair to calm her fears.

"Mi amor, Paco and I will go to Zacatecas. I will see for myself if what Paco says is true, before I decide if we could rob such a mule train," he assured her.

"I will go with you," she said.

"No my love, you must stay here. Paco and I are only going to see if it can be done. There will be no trouble."

"The people need you here. I need you here. Zacatecas is a far ride and you may be gone for some time. We are outgrowing this small cave. Many of the children are sleeping outside and one of the women is pregnant."

"I know. Tomorrow I will send Kiko and Hector on a scouting trip. There are caves and cliffs all over these canyons. Besides it is time for us to move on. When they find a better location with a larger cavern, we will move and resettle the people. Then Paco and I will go to Zacatecas."

María did not like the plan, though she knew she could not stop Rodolfo from pursuing it. She too saw the hungry look in the children's eyes and the skinniness of their limbs. No one complained, but she understood the weight of responsibility which rested on Rodolfo's shoulders. The people looked to him for guidance. They were here because they believed in him. They believed he could provide them a better life than living like dogs on a *hacienda,* slaving for a master.

María nestled in Rodolfo's arms. Her love for him seemed unbounded. She could not get enough of his body and making love to him made her feel alive. She had only known the way of the old *don,* how he mounted her and pushed her away when he was spent. Rodolfo was a tender lover and she was learning about herself as she tried to please him. Tonight he seemed worried about the problems of the people and she knew he was probably exhausted. Wrapping her arm around him tightly, they fell asleep under the stars.

CHAPTER 7

When George Summers arrived home at his GSW Ranch, Rafe was not at the foundry. In fact neither Carlos nor Rafe were about. Esteban said he saw them a little while ago. George walked across the expansive yard from the foundry to the house and stepped into the kitchen of his home.

His wife Josefina and Rafe's mother Celiá were busy working and talking in the kitchen when he came in. María's young daughter, Alicia, was sitting on the floor with one of the cats in her lap.

"Hello George," Josefina greeted him. "How was your meeting in town with the sheriff?"

Josefina could see the deepening worry line across George's forehead. Ever since Rafe's fight with Diego, she pressed her husband to keep abreast of any developments. Having grown up in Spain, Josefina understood the traditions of the Spanish caste system. She knew the anger of the Spaniards here in Santa Fe, over a *mestizo* killing one of their own, would fuel their vengeance directly at their adopted son.

Josefina blamed herself for not educating Rafe better in the Spanish *casta* distinctions and warning him to keep away from the Spanish elite here in Santa Fe. Josefina had brought it up from time to time to George, but he ignored her warnings, telling her they were raising an American not a Mexican or Spaniard. Everything would have been fine had Rafe not fallen in love with the niece of a prominent *don,* one of the old bastions of the Spanish ruling class here in Santa Fe.

"Sheriff Johnson knows Rafe is innocent and not responsible for Diego's death, but he thinks Rafe is in danger from friends of the de la Torre family. He suggested Rafe should leave town for awhile until things calm down," George said.

Celiá gasped and clutched at her chest. *"Madre de Dios."*

"What do you think George?" Josefina asked.

"I think he may be right. Rafe is an excellent shot and if confronted can defend himself, though not if caught alone by a group of *caballeros*. Diego has many friends."

George shook his head and wondered if the danger would ever end for his adopted son here in Santa Fe. Revenge was a fickle adversary and George worried Rafe might never again be safe here. Rafe worked so hard to shed the stigma of his peasant heritage to become an American man, and yet the past haunted him.

"He was not in the foundry. Have you seen him lately?"

"No, we have not seen either he or Carlos for hours. Did you look in the barn?"

George turned and walked out of the kitchen and back across the mostly barren expanse between the house and the outbuildings. The GSW horse barn was behind the foundry and Rafe had an even larger barn built for his budding horse breeding business many yards behind the other with a large pasture heading up the hill behind it. George headed to Rafe's barn.

The large double doors stood open as George walked into the barn. It smelled of horses and clean hay. Pablo's head was visible near one of the stalls.

"Hello Pablo. Is Rafe here about?" George asked.

"No se Señor Summers. He and Carlos rode off just a little while ago. I think they were going to the ranchhouse."

George could see Rayo's and Santiago's stalls were empty. Rayo and Santiago were two of Rafe's prized Mexican blooded horses, which were the foundation of his horse breeding business. Rayo was Rafe's personal horse and he had given Santiago to Carlos for saving his life.

"Do you want me to saddle a horse for you?"

"Yes, thank you Pablo."

Pablo deftly saddled one of the horses and George was soon riding toward the spot Rafe had picked for his ranchhouse. Three years ago George helped Rafe purchase a large acreage adjacent to the GSW ranch to start his horse breeding operation. Rafe had repaid him in little over a year.

When Rafe's family joined him here, Rafe funneled the profit from the business to contract a large home to be built for them. It did not surprise George how Rafe always put others ahead of himself. It was the same honor seventeen-year-old Rafe displayed when he found George dying in the Texas desert. He could have ransacked the wagon and left George, a stranger and a gringo, to die. George owed Rafe his life.

The peak of the roof of the unfinished ranchhouse popped into George's view. As he got closer, two horses stood quietly near the front of the house, one was Rayo, an Appaloosa, and the other the tall black horse named Santiago.

Rafe and Carlos walked onto the veranda as George rode up.

"*Don* Jorge, come and see the progress they have made," Rafe called to him using his personal name for his adopted father, George. Sliding off the horse George walked up the veranda steps and followed Rafe into the house.

The walls were framed and lathed, with most completely covered in new plaster. The stone fireplaces in the two front rooms were complete and looked ready to use. A stairway led to a second floor.

"Come see the kitchen," Rafe said enthusiastically. His son acted as if everything was right in the world and George hated the thought he needed to tether his gusto. George followed Rafe into the large kitchen, which looked completed. The only missing piece was a large stove, which George knew was on order.

"Your mother will love it," George told him. "In fact I think Josefina will be jealous," he said jokingly. Rafe was sparing no expense in furnishing the home with all the latest modern conveniences.

"Rafe, we need to talk," George said.

"I'll get the pistols completed tonight, I promise," Rafe said thinking George was talking about work at the foundry. Rafe had been slack on his duties lately. "I just wanted to show Carlos the progress on the house before it got dark."

"That's not what we need to talk about. I met with Sheriff Johnson again today. He says the Spanish nobles are pressuring him to give them justice against you for killing Diego."

"Rafe didn't kill Diego. The sheriff knows that," Carlos interrupted. Carlos had watched the entire fight and testified how Diego's horse fell over on him crushing Diego to death.

"That is true, but they still want revenge. I fear it is not safe here for you," George said to Rafe. "I think you should leave town for awhile until things simmer down."

Rafe had made Carlos hide the cut on his neck from George. Rafe thought it was his problem and he did not want his adopted father or Carlos involved. Even though Diego's friends had accosted him, Carlos felt he was not in real danger. He did not believe they would mortally harm another Spaniard. It was Rafe they wanted and they only used Carlos as the messenger.

"I plan on leaving for Mexico City as soon as the house is done and I get mother and the children settled. Joaquin told me the house should be finished in about a month," Rafe said.

"I mean, you need to go now. Sooner than a month from now. The sheriff cannot protect you and neither can I." George made the statement as a demand and not a suggestion.

Rafe stood quietly pondering the comments and knew George was worried. He could see it in his face.

"What if I stay close to the ranch and foundry?" Rafe finally asked.

"Look around," George said. "Diego's friends could be anywhere even watching us now. If they are bent on revenge as the sheriff believes, you are not safe anywhere, not even here."

"But, the house needs finished and . . . " Rafe started to protest.

"I will make sure the house is completed and Josefina and I will see your mother and the children get settled. What plans have you made for your trip to Mexico?" George asked.

"I want to take two of the young horses, a mare and a

stallion with me. The stallion is for Chief Letoc and the mare is for the Healer, Xihuitl," Rafe said. I owe them both so much. "Pablo will go ahead and make the appointments with *don* Bernardo's lawyer in Torreón. Pablo and the priest will verify my birthright. We will start from there," Rafe said.

CHAPTER 8

Later after the evening meal, Rafe, Carlos, and George sat in the parlor discussing the trip to Mexico in depth. A feeling of déjà vu nagged George as he remembered the last trip Rafe and Carlos planned to Torreón. That trip was to rescue Rafe's mother, sister, and children from the *hacienda* where *don* Bernardo continued to father María's bastard children. Rafe almost did not return when the plans went awry. The old *don* shot him and without the help and caring of a traveling healer, Rafe would be dead.

"Rafe, are you certain you can inherit the Reyes *hacienda* in Torreón?" George asked skeptical about politics in Mexico. There was too much turmoil and inequality in Mexico and George worried Rafe would be in danger wanting to claim property belonging to Mexico's upper class, laws or no laws. It seemed to him Rafe had legal trouble both here and there.

"Pablo told me President Benito Juárez has changed the laws regarding *mestizos*. He said they now are entitled to inherit, if they are the first-born male of the *haciendero,* as long as there are no other heirs. If you are thinking this might be difficult, you may be correct father, but I have to try for the sake of María and Rodolfo. If it was not for them, I would let the *hacienda* rot or let the government take it," Rafe expressed his views adamantly.

"Mexico City is not like Torreón or Santa Fe for that matter. It is a huge city and you have little experience in such a place. You will need proper introductions and you do not have the credentials to get them. It will be dangerous," George warned him.

"Carlos and I have talked about it. He has family in Mexico City and has written to them. He is sure they will help me and have connections there. I will try to get the lawyer from Torreón to go with me to Mexico City. Pablo says he is a tough lawyer and knows the new laws well enough to defend my case," Rafe told George.

"Yes, my uncle is well connected in Mexico City. I have already sent him a letter explaining the situation. I will write again and give him a better idea of when to expect Rafe," Carlos added.

"Having connections will help, but you are headed to a world you know nothing about. Look at what happened to you here in Santa Fe. I fear the Spaniards in Mexico are more clever and fearsome than you might expect," George said to Rafe.

"You worry too much. This is a legal matter. It is not like the last time when we went to rescue my mother pretending to be horse buyers," Rafe responded.

George was torn. He wanted Rafe to get out of town, but worried sending him to Mexico City might be fraught with new dangers. He was *mestizo* and the bastard son of a *haciendero*. George feared Mexico was more entrenched in the ways of the Spanish elites than Santa Fe.

"I hear you, but I don't like it. Perhaps I should go with you," George protested.

"Father, you know they don't like gringos down there. At least I can hide easier than you, if there is trouble," Rafe responded and chuckled.

"You can hide, yes, but you are *mestizo* and cannot even wear your pistols."

"I am going as an *Americano,* not a *peón.* I will be wearing my pistols."

George sensed trouble was waiting in Mexico. Regardless of any new laws, the caste system was even more in play there. *Don* Bernardo's ex-wife Carmela could contest the inheritance to get the valuable property, of that he was certain. Tired, George went to bed leaving Rafe and Carlos in the parlor talking about the trip.

"Rafe, what George says is true. The Spaniards in Mexico City will be many times more entrenched in the *casta* system than the Spaniards here. The nobility detests President Juárez and his liberal ways toward the under classes. Your task may not be as easy as we think, regardless of the new laws," Carlos said after George went to bed.

"I will not live like a scared *peón.* I am an American and

will demand respect. Besides it is possible Carmela will not even want the old *hacienda* or have a claim. Pablo says she and *don* Bernardo were officially divorced before his death."

Rafe decided to be ready to leave in two days. He would tell Pablo tomorrow, to ride ahead and start making the arrangements in Torreón. While Rafe wanted Pablo, the horse master and his boyhood mentor from *don* Bernardo's *hacienda* to stay here in Santa Fe, even Pablo agreed he would rather return to Torreón. After Rafe inherited the estate, Pablo would help to find María and would stay to help run the *hacienda*.

After he climbed the stairs to his second story bedroom, Rafe took off his boots and hung his pants and shirt on the rack. He looked around his bedroom in the glow of the lamp. His gunbelt with his GSW pistols hung from the bedpost. The quiver Chiwiwi made him hung on the other side along with the remnant of the silver amulet that saved his life. In a drawer of the chest, a small leather pouch held the pieces of the turquoise stone, which had been shattered when *don* Bernardo shot him point-blank in the chest.

He knew George's worries were not unfounded. Lying back on the bed, he stretched out his six-foot frame and stared at the ceiling. He brought Chiwiwi's face to his mind and tried to keep it in his subconscious as he fell asleep.

Rafe heard a loud bell in his dream. It was ringing loudly and then he heard shouting in the courtyard. He and Carlos stayed up late in the parlor planning the trip and he woke foggy-headed. He heard the bell again and then heard a loud clang as a door slammed down the hallway.

An orange glow filtered around the edges of the curtains. Stumbling from bed, Rafe pulled the curtain open. High up behind his barn a steady orange glare filled the sky. The glare came from the direction of his new house. His groggy brain tried to fathom what he was looking at until it registered – fire. His new ranchhouse was on fire.

He grabbed his pants and boots, jumping into them as he made his way down the hallway. By the time he reached the bottom of the stairs, George was already at the backdoor talking to Enrique and Pablo. The horses had alerted them to the danger. At first they checked the barns and then suspected a fire in the foundry. It was only a few minutes ago they started to see the orange plume rising on the far hillside.

"Pablo, secure the horses and the barn. Keep a sharp eye," Rafe yelled as he ran to the barn. Pulling Rayo from his stall, Rafe jumped aboard bareback. "Yeahh!"

Rayo jerked his head and took off at a gallop. Rafe covered the distance of almost a mile quickly. As he crested the field approaching the house, flames were licking high into the sky. Smoke and flame curled under the veranda roof and out the window openings. The house was completely engulfed in fire. As Rafe watched helplessly, he heard the crack of one of the larger timbers as the fire weakened it and part of the roof collapsed in a loud roar.

The well was dug, but the pump system was not installed. Rafe could only sit on Rayo and grieve. The house was a present for his mother and the start of a place to raise his own family. A place he planned to bring Ana Teresa after they married. A place his own son would someday be born. The rage inside him was burning as bright as the fire.

As George and Carlos rode up the hill, they could see Rafe's silhouette in the orange glow of the fire. They heard a loud crack and a roar as the roof collapsed. Riding up beside Rafe, they silently watched the house burn. Soon the second floor roof collapsed onto the first floor and the flames began dying away.

Turning their horses, they rode down the hill. When they reached the horse barn, Rafe noticed Pablo standing near the door. He was holding a sword.

"Where did you get that?" Rafe asked jumping off Rayo's back and taking the sword.

"We heard horses. When we came outside to check if it was you, we found this sword sticking out of the barn's wall. It is a sign," Pablo told him.

It was Spanish, though not overly ornate. Rage flared in Rafe's gut. Diego's friends burned his house and left this sign for him.

"They must pay for this. Tomorrow I'll ride to the de la Torre *hacienda* and make this right," Rafe growled. Sure of his abilities with his GSW pistols, Rafe had no fear to confront the scoundrels. Either they backed off or they died.

"Do you not see? That is what they want. It would give them the chance to kill you without legal recourse," George said taking Rafe's arm.

Rafe shook away from his adopted father seething in a rage. "Then I'll go to the sheriff and file a complaint."

"Against who?" George asked.

"Against the *dons,* against Diego's comrades, against the Spanish aristocrats who did this," Rafe raged on.

"You have no proof. No one saw anyone or anything. They will say it was just bad luck or a coincidence."

"What about this sword?"

"There are many swords. It will prove nothing."

"You know my house did not just catch fire, *don* Jorge. This was Diego's friends getting revenge. Carlos and I know who they are. I have done nothing wrong. Diego came after me at the plaza." Rafe's anger was dripping in his words. George and Carlos knew he was right, but revenge was double-edged.

"They have enacted their revenge," Carlos said. "Perhaps it will be enough."

"It will never be enough. They will continue until I put a stop to them. I know how these Spaniards think. They will not stop until I stop them or die trying."

"You have to calm down," George said. "Thankfully it was only your house and not your horses. We will put extra guards on duty here at the barn."

"Just my house! What about you? What if they come after you and Josefina and the girls like they attacked Carlos? What then?" Rafe blurted out.

"What do you mean they attacked Carlos?"

"Diego's friends confronted me on my way home from Bibiana's on Sunday. They were trying to scare me and send a message to Rafe," Carlos said.

George pondered a few moments before he said. "You need to leave town as soon as you can. I will tell the sheriff you are gone and make a claim for your property. I'll make sure the word spreads you are not here and they have no quarrel with me. I'll get Joaquin to start rebuilding the house."

CHAPTER 9

Rodolfo guided María away from the camp toward a clear pool in the deepest part of the nearby stream where they stripped and got in. She splashed his face and swam away and he chased and caught her. She pushed his head under water where he buried his face on her breasts. She screamed a laugh and pushed him away. They played and chased each other for a while, before they found a secluded grassy spot to make love.

It had been many days since they slept together. Privacy was at a premium in the campsite and while some of the couples seemed less concerned, Rodolfo felt it was his duty to set a good example and show respect. He made it clear to the men, sex was only allowed for couples or when the women allowed it. The poor women in the camp were not *putas*.

"Mi amor," María expressed her love touching Rodolfo's face. She had begged him several times to take her to Zacatecas. "You and I could pose as a young couple and Paco our friend," she begged him again.

"No my love, you must stay here. I have no idea what we will find in Zacatecas and need to be ready to flee, if necessary."

Since first thinking about the plan, Rodolfo decided to take three men with him to Zacatecas. He thought perhaps they could rob the silver and return in a fortnight, even though he told María they were only going to see if what Paco said was true.

"You are worried? Stay here or take me with you," María said. She sensed tension in him growing over the last several days. She pulled Rodolfo on top of her nakedness and spread her legs wrapping them around him pushing her hips in a playful manner.

"María, you cannot change my mind even if you entice me. I love you too much to put you in even more danger." Rodolfo pulled her body toward him and they intertwined their bodies. María's skin felt like warm velvet, though she shivered at his touch. He never thought he could love someone so much. He thought life would not give him the pleasure. When he started in the *bandido* life, Rodolfo cared little if he lived or died. Now he cared deeply for María and for a life with her.

Sometimes he even thought living as *peóns* on a *hacienda* would be a better life than this. At least they could be together and safe. They could have children playing in the yard with food in their bellies. The life he was giving her now was fraught with peril. As he pondered robbing the silver mines, he wondered how they could use the silver to buy a small piece of land. *Peóns* could own property and farm, if they could afford it. Keeping *peóns* destitute was how the *haciendervs* kept their power.

That evening, Kiko and Hector returned from their scouting trip saying they found a location about twenty miles from here with all the necessary requirements. A stream ran in the canyon for water. There was a much larger cave and several smaller caves along an overhanging escarpment of rocks. The overhang would provide a natural camouflage for their campfires. Kiko said he saw many rabbits and a few deer higher up the canyon.

Rodolfo explained the move to the people at supper as they gathered around the fires. He told the women to pack their belongings and for everyone to be ready to move in the morning.

The next morning, Javier loaded two horses with a few provisions and took them to where Rodolfo was rolling his blankets. The rest of the camp was in chaos. María was directing the women to pack and prepare for the move.

"Good luck amigo," Javier said.

"We will be back as soon as we can," Rodolfo told him. "If you have to move again, leave me some sign which direction, so I can find you." Javier nodded.

Rodolfo slapped the reins of his horse to a walk down the dusty path away from the campsite with Paco, Hector, and Pepe following him. Looking back María was watching them go. Her dark hair flowed beneath the colorful scarf she wore. She wore a simple white peasant blouse and a checkered skirt of blue and red. She looked radiant in the morning sun. Rodolfo's heart ached. They had said their goodbyes yesterday near the stream, clinging together after they made love.

Rodolfo used the old cattle trails, which crisscrossed the terrain, using the sun as his guide. He felt they were in little danger and it was unlikely *la policía* would bother them, though he kept scanning the horizon. They each had a pistol and some ammunition buried inside their saddlebags. If stopped, they would say they were just a group of *peóns* heading for the mines in Zacatecas to look for work.

Along the way Rodolfo pressed Paco for as much information as the young miner could relate. Paco said his family lived in Zacatecas and worked as miners for generations. It was the only available work for *peóns*. Paco had been twelve when he started working in the mines after his father has hurt and could no longer work.

"At first I liked the work. It was hard digging at the rock and carrying loads through the mines, but at least inside the mine you were not slaving in the burning sun all day," Paco explained. After several years, the backbreaking work was already taking a toll on his young body and he did not like how the mine masters treated the men. Once a man's body was broken and bent and could no longer pull his share, he was cast out.

"Few men last past their mid thirties and they look like old men, bent and useless. Like with my family, once my father could no longer work, it was my turn to feed my brothers and sisters. It is so with many in Zacatecas. Mining is the only work. If you are not mining, you are not eating," Paco explained.

"Why did you leave?" Rodolfo asked him.

"I worked for several mines, but they all treat the *peóns* like slaves," Paco told him. "The mine *jefes* are mean and use whips to keep the *peóns* working. I finally left and worked on a large *hacienda* south of San Luis. I sent *pesos* back to my family," Paco said.

"Now you are living with us so what about your

family?" Rodolfo asked.

"I have been saving some *pesos* you have given me and I will give them to my mother when we get to my house," he said.

Anxious to get to Zacatecas, they started at sunup each day and rode until it was dark. They were making good time and on the fifth day Paco told Rodolfo they were getting close. As they approached Zacatecas, Paco took the lead. He headed east of the city to an area dotted with small *jacals*. They were no better than the mud and stick shacks where the *peóns* lived on *haciendas* in Torreón. Paco stopped in front of a small shack and ducked his head inside. Rodolfo heard a loud joyous shout.

Paco's family was ecstatic to see their son and brother. Though the furnishings inside the home were sparse, it was clean and it reminded Rodolfo of his family's *jacal*. Paco's mother cooked tortillas and beans with chili and the family talked excitedly. Paco told his parents they were on their way to Mexico City and would like to stay for a few days. It made Rodolfo smile and he thought it a good explanation of their trip.

On the many long hours of riding, they decided Rodolfo should spend time at several *pulquerias* in town, while Paco would ride the roads leading in and out of town looking for mule trails. Paco explained mules were loaded with packs of silver ingots at the smaller mines instead of using wagons. Mules were able to traverse the steep remote mountains, going where wagons could not go.

"Where are these small mines? Do you know?"

"There are many mines all over the small canyons. The terrain is rugged," Paco replied.

Later that evening Rodolfo walked the several miles into town from Paco's home. Like many Mexican towns, Zacatecas had both a vibrant well-kept part, where the mine owners and soldiers lived, and an older run-down side where the peasants lived. The difference in the two worlds was striking. In the rich part of town, lovely two-story adobe houses lined both sides of the cobblestone streets. Iron railings surrounded the second story balconies and flowers cascaded down in colors of red, yellow, and purple. Tall iron gates and high fences surrounded the elaborate homes and protected them from *bandidos*. Along the street in this part of town, ornate carriages stood ready to take the occupants from one place to another.

As Rodolfo walked, he kept his head bowed in respect. As long as he played the part, no one took notice of a dusty, ragged *peón*. Passing the upper class area, Rodolfo entered a different world. It was the world he knew well. Shabby houses were made of sticks and mud. Some had only canvas covering the open roof for protection from the sun and rain. Where the same road had been smooth and embedded with stones, it was now uneven and rutted. The few horses standing along the railings looked tired and dirty.

Seeing a *pulqueria*, Rodolfo pushed open a flap of canvas and walked inside. *Pulque* was a poor man's drink and it suited *peóns* who could not afford wine or beer. Made by fermenting the sap of the agave plant, *pulque* was the color of milk and a somewhat bitter yeasty taste.

Miners sat at small tables drinking the milky liquor. They wore simple *camisas* and *pantalones* covered in dust and dirt smeared their tired faces. All of the faces were *Indios* and *mestizos*. Rodolfo noticed under the dust and dirt their faces looked like young men, and yet when they stood up they stooped like old men. The talk was of the mine, the work, and after having their fill of *pulque* they drifted home.

He ordered a *pulque* and sat at a table by himself near the back. A few men stared at him, probably wondered why he was clean, but none said anything to him. They knew he was a stranger and peasant or not, they were wary of strangers. He knew *peóns* were friendly by nature, but also suspicious. They were used to being spied upon by their masters. Rodolfo understood their stares, because *don* Bernardo had many spies, even other *peóns* at the *hacienda,* who would keep the *haciendero* abreast of any infraction. Rodolfo suspected it was the same here at the mines.

CHAPTER 10

Each night after Rodolfo returned to Paco's house, he and the *bandidos* excused themselves and walked up a hill behind the house. There they could talk in private. Paco found several well used trails with mule droppings leading away from Zacatecas. Rodolfo learned little at the *pulquerias,* other than listening to miners complain about the condition of the mines and singing sad songs.

On the third night at a *pulqueria* called La Pasadita, Rodolfo heard an old *Indio* brag about being the master muleteer for a small silver mine just south of Zacatecas. He heard him brag how the mines hired him because he was the best muleteer in these parts. Most of the tired miners at the *pulqueria* ignored the *Indio's* ranting, but Rodolfo worked his way closer and listened attentively to the old man.

When Rodolfo returned that evening to the *jacal,* he told the *bandidos* about the old muleteer. They talked into the night about how to approach the old *Indio* for information.

For two nights Rodolfo returned to the La Pasadita Pulqueria, taking stock and listening to the muleteer tell his stories. Tonight the muleteer sat at a table by himself, sipping at a tall clay cup of the bitter, milky *pulque.* The old braggart sat quietly, seeming lost in his thoughts.

"I have heard you say you are an expert on training mules?" Rodolfo stepped near him and asked the old Indian politely. "I have a young stubborn mule. This one needs to be trained by an expert on how to pull a cargo wagon." Rodolfo stood with his ragged hat in his hands, looking at the old *Indio* with respect. "You are such a man?" he asked.

"Es la verdad," he responded it was true. Rodolfo hoped his praise of the old man would make him friendly.

The old Indian stared up at Rodolfo. Judging by his clean *pantalones,* the young man was no miner. After sizing up the young man standing next to his table he said, "I don't train mules to pull cargo wagons. I train them to haul loads of silver ingots on their backs out of very steep canyons," the old man bragged taking another swig of *pulque*. "My services are wanted by all the mines around here," the old man continued bragging.

"Certainly you know much more than I about mules. May I buy you a *pulque* and perhaps you would be kind enough to give me a few tips on training my stubborn mule." Rodolfo knew the old muleteer might dismiss him. The wizened old *Indio* would not talk easily to a stranger, especially one not a local miner. However, Rodolfo had watched for three nights as the man was mostly ignored by the miners and he hoped the man would want to engage in conversation. After a few long moments, the old man waved his hand to the other chair at the table. Rodolfo sat and signaled to a young girl to bring another *pulque*.

"My name is Rodolfo. I come from Torreón. My *haciendero* has died and I am here looking for work to support my young wife." Most of the story was not true.

"I have a wagon and several mules. I was hoping perhaps I could find work here hauling supplies for the mines," Rodolfo continued his lies to engage the muleteer.

The old man sipped the *pulque* as they continued to talk. The young man, named Rodolfo, treated him with respect, listening intently to what he was saying. It was unusual. Most of the *peón* mine workers here in Zacatecas treated him with disdain. They were either jealous or thought he made deals with the mine *jefes*. The young man looked strong and spoke in a manner showing he had some limited education. His eyes were clear and bright with eagerness.

"There are a few supply wagoneers. They run their wagons like trains, in large convoys using the main road into Zacatecas. You could try to get a job loading and unloading the wagons, but it is not steady work."

"I need steady work. Who takes the supplies from Zacatecas to the mines?" Rodolfo asked.

"The *jefes* send mules to pick up supplies or sometimes I take a load on my mules on the way to pick up the loads of silver."

Rodolfo bought the old man another *pulque* hoping to keep him interested in talking. He decided to change the subject back to mules.

"How did you learn to train mules? It is obvious you are enjoying the health and wealth of your profession. I suspect your services are very important to the mine owners." Rodolfo's compliments seem to have the desired effect.

"It is in my blood," the old *Indio* winked at him. "I am a Cazcanes Indian. My name is Maxorro, after the great chief who fought in the Mixton rebellion in 1541, repelling several Spanish attacks. My people killed Hernan Cortés' top general, Pedro de Alvarado, when his horse fell on him during the retreat. It was the Spaniards who first brought horses and mules to this land. We Cazcanes learned the ways of the Spanish *conquistadores* and how they trained their horses and mules."

Maxorro smiled when Rodolfo wanted to know more about his ancestry and he began to talk freely. Most *peón* miners tired of his stories quickly or thought him just an old senile Indian when he bragged about his ancestry. Maxorro was used to being mostly ignored by the miners, however this young man showed an interest in him and treated him with respect.

"My mules are like children. You must treat them with care and attention. It takes years to raise a good mule that will work for you."

As their discussion continued Rodolfo said, "Perhaps I should just try my hand at mining."

"Look young man, you won't last long swinging a pick or shoveling ore into buckets or carrying the buckets to the smelter. You should go back to a large *hacienda* and be a farmer. You will live longer and in better health," the old man advised Rodolfo with a serious tone in his voice. He meant it as good advice. Working in the mines was a dismal life. He had been lucky to learn about mules, but still his old body was starting to feel each bumpy mile.

"Did you start as a miner?" Rodolfo asked him trying to keep Maxorro talking.

"No, I was never no *pinche* miner. No Cazcanes would do such work. Miners are filthy and don't live too long.

When they can no longer work, the mine owners throw them out. Look at these poor souls. They break their backs all day, then come here and get drunk before they go home. They will die young," he went on with a disgusted look on his face.

The *pulqueria* was slowly emptying as the miners had their fill and headed home. Rodolfo bought the old muleteer three *pulques* and the old man was starting to nod off.

"Perhaps we could continue this discussion another evening, tomorrow perhaps?" Rodolfo asked him.

"I will not be here. My mules and I will be heading on our next trip. I have enjoyed talking to you and wish you well, but remember do not become a miner. It is only a life a misery," Maxorro said.

"Gracias," Rodolfo replied. "I will remember your warnings. *Buenas noches,"* he wished him good night.

Rodolfo was elated as he walked back to Paco's house. The old muleteer had given him the information he needed. In the morning, he and his *bandidos* could follow Maxorro to the mine and plot a way to steal the silver.

CHAPTER 11

Very early in the morning two days after the fire, Rafe made ready to ride south. Before he left, Josefina made him promise to wire whenever possible. Rafe knew his adopted mother was worried. She made him a large food sack and told him to go with God's blessing. It was Celiá, his mother, who broke down in tears.

"It's alright, *Mamá*. I will not take any chances."

"You almost did not come back from Mexico the last time," she said.

"And *don* Bernardo is dead, *Mamá*. I have no enemies in Mexico now."

"Find María," she implored him. "Tell her the children and I send our love."

Carlos and George insisted on riding with him until he was well south of the city. Pablo left yesterday so he would reach Torreón ahead of Rafe. Pablo would check on the *hacienda* and setup a meeting with the lawyer. As they rode through the streets of Santa Fe, they kept a sharp lookout. They were armed even though Rafe doubted any of Diego's friends were up this early.

As they neared the La Cienega Stage stop, George pulled up. "I guess this is far enough," he said. "I have been watching and I'm sure we have not been followed."

Rafe took the reins of the packhorse from George and the colt from Carlos. Rafe insisted on taking the young horses with him even though it would slow him down. "I have debts to pay," he claimed. The young black stallion sired by Santiago was for Letoc and the young Appaloosa mare sired by Rayo was for Xihuitl, the Healer in Mexico. Rafe strung the two young horses behind the packhorse.

George and Carlos watched him head south on the road to Albuquerque before they turned and headed back the way they came. When they reached Santa Fe George said, "You go on ahead. I must find the sheriff and tell him Rafe is gone. He will make sure the word gets spread around town to the Spaniards."

"I told Bibiana and told her to tell her father the same thing. He will make it known to the other *dons,*" Carlos replied.

Rafe did not look back after he rode away from George and Carlos. Keeping his anger at bay over the last several days had been exhausting. He knew it was Benjamin, Alvaro, and Vicente who attacked Carlos and they also burnt his house. He wanted revenge and would have gone to kill them, but George and Carlos convinced him to leave town instead.

The three had attacked him at the abandoned *hacienda* the day he met with Ana Teresa last spring. They would have killed him that day if Ana Teresa had not defended him wielding a sword. The three were Diego's best friends and were elite Spanish dandies of Santa Fe.

He stopped near the river and let the horses drink, while he rested under a willow. After a night in Algodones at the Stage Inn, Rafe left early and was almost to Albuquerque. He planned on making the Isleta pueblo by early afternoon. The task he planned there today was weighing heavy on his mind. The young stallion was a gift for Letoc, Chiwiwi's uncle and chief of the Isleta Tiwa tribe. Chiwiwi was Rafe's first love. She was buried at the Isleta Mission after Carlos' brother killed her.

Rafe remembered the battle at the Anaya *hacienda* vividly. Carlos' out of control brother, Benicío, had kidnapped Chiwiwi and another young maiden from the pueblo. Letoc's braves surrounded the gated compound in an attempt to rescue the girls. He, Carlos, and George Summers were also there. After the Indian warriors burned down the gate, Rafe rushed the entryway and found Chiwiwi. As they stood in an embrace, Benicío screamed from the burning porch of the house. Even now Rafe could clearly see Benicío raise the rifle and shoot in their direction. Behind him Carlos fired several rounds at his brother. Benicío fell in a heap on the porch, but Chiwiwi lay dead in Rafe's arms.

For almost a year Rafe had nightmares reliving her death. In the dreams Benicío often mocked and scoffed at him. The dreams always ended when Benicío killed Chiwiwi and Rafe was helpless to save her. He had not seen Letoc since the day she was killed. The chief held no blame against him. Regardless, he brought the young colt as a gift for the chief. It would never replace Chiwiwi, but he meant it as a token of respect.

South of Albuquerque he spotted the dirt path which led to the pueblo. Rafe turned left across the river. In the distance, Isleta's bell tower was visible in the teal blue sky. As he neared the pueblo, adrenaline flushed Rafe's body and soured his stomach. The memories were still so fresh in his mind, he expected to see Chiwiwi running up the path to greet him.

He took several deep breaths trying to calm down and trying to think what to say to Chief Letoc. Because of several unfortunate actions Chiwiwi and two other young maidens from the village were dead. Though Rafe risked his life to save her, he also felt responsible. Had he not brought Benicío's brother Carlos to the pueblo to save his life, Benicío would never have kidnapped the girls.

The July noon heat smothered Rafe as he neared the pueblo. He rode in slowly towing the horses. From the north road into the pueblo, the twin bell towers of the whitewashed Saint Augustine chapel stood tall over the low buildings of the pueblo. He crossed the dry arroyo on the small wooden bridge, the same arroyo which ran wild with a flashflood one day in June two years ago. It was one of those central New Mexico thunderstorms causing flashflood havoc and carrying desert debris downstream at torrent speeds. Rafe was traveling nearby and heard a small child screaming and Rayo's ears had perked toward the cry.

In the rush of chocolate colored water, Rafe spotted a young Indian boy bobbing up and down while being flushed downstream along with juniper branches and tumbleweeds. Rafe rushed Rayo along the bank of the arroyo and managed to throw a lasso and catch the boy before he drowned. He pulled the boy from the arroyo and took him to a nearby clump of squatty juniper trees where they were somewhat shielded from the rain. Rafe would never forget the joyous look on the mother's face when she saw her son was safe.

The distraught mother invited Rafe to follow her to the pueblo. There he met Chiwiwi, who became the love of his young life. The young boy he saved, Baqito, was Chief Letoc's only son. Chiwiwi, sister to the boy's mother, was Letoc's niece. The pueblo celebrated in his honor.

Rafe rode the dusty path directly to Chief Letoc's house. He could feel the sting of the people's dark eyes as they watched him, though no one stopped him. He dismounted and tied the horses to a hitching post outside the house and walked through the cloth-covered door. Inside, Shuren, Chief Letoc's wife, was sitting folding clothes. She was humming a tune he heard her hum before.

"Hello," Rafe said softly.

Shuren turned to look and her eyes widened as she stood up and grabbed him, "Rafael!" she said as tears welled up and flowed down her cheeks and on to his shoulder. Rafe held onto her in a tight embrace.

"You welcome," she finally said in broken English when she pulled back and looked into Rafe's eyes.

"Thank you Shuren," he answered. "Is Letoc here?"

"No, he come soon," she said. "We find Baqito."

Rafe was surprised how much English Shuren could now speak. Letoc, a strong leader who looked to the future and not to the past, wanted his people to learn English. He built a school and was educating all the children. Shuren led Rafe out of the house and they walked to the school next to the chapel. Some children were out playing, chasing each other, but most were huddled in the shade of a large cottonwood tree trying to stay cool.

"Baqito, Baqito, come," she called to her son. Rafe was amazed as a young boy ran toward them on tall spindly legs. Baqito appeared to have grown a foot since Rafe had saved him from the rushing water.

As the boy neared them, he recognized Rafe. "Rafael!" Baqito ran to his arms and Rafe held him. He spoke rapidly to his mother in their native Tiwa language.

"Baqito is happy you have come," Shuren said.

"Yes, I am very happy," Baqito said. He grabbed

Rafe's hand and pulled him toward the chapel. Seeing Baqito's excitement and acceptance toward the stranger, the children mobbed him pulling at his pants and laughing. Hearing the commotion, a young woman walked out the chapel clapping her hands.

Rafe strode toward her with the children circling him. As he reached her she said, "Hello, I'm Katherine Baxter, the teacher here and who might you be?"

Rafe bowed slightly. "My name is Rafael Ortega de Estrada. I saved this young man's life a couple years ago," he said putting his arm around Baqito.

"Ah yes, I have heard the stories. Letoc and the elders hold you in high esteem." She clapped her hands several times and spoke loudly, "Children, children, please return to your desks. Playtime is over."

As the children began to stream back into the chapel, Shuren spoke to the teacher in Tiwa. Miss Baxter nodded. "Shuren wishes to tell you that you are very welcome. Letoc is away in the hills with the braves. She wants you to stay until he returns."

"I cannot. I am on my way to Mexico City. Tell Shuren I brought a young stallion for Letoc. He will be a fine horse. I will stop again on my way home, but I must be going."

The teacher related the message in Tiwa. Shuren nodded.

"How did you learn Tiwa?" Rafe asked.

"I know enough to make simple sentences. Like the children learning English, we teach each other."

"Please tell Letoc when he returns I am sorry I missed him. I will come again."

"I will," she replied.

As Rafe turned away, he caught a view of the small cemetery beside the chapel. Shuren seemed to understand his need. She led him to Chiwiwi's grave. It was adorned with fresh flowers. Rafe knelt beside it. She was his first love. Their love was pure and bottomless. For more than a year after her death, he dreamed of her. The dream always ended with Benicío killing her and Rafe unable to save her. The dreams no longer haunted him, but her memory still lived in his heart.

He thought he could never love again. Then Ana Teresa came into his life reawakening his heart. He said a prayer over Chiwiwi's grave and stood. Shuren and Rafe walked back to the plaza and he took the reins of the black stallion and handed them to her. "For Letoc," he said.

"Thank you. I will tell him of you."

As Rafe stepped up and onto Rayo's back, he looked over the plaza. Several of the Tiwa women stopped their work and stared at him. Shuren stood quietly nearby. He turned Rayo and headed across the plaza and toward to dirt path. Rayo stepped across the wooden bridge over the arroyo and Rafe walked the horse until he was well away from the village. When he reached the main road south, he turned his horse left and kicked Rayo to a gallop.

CHAPTER 12

Doña Carmela Reyes, ex-wife of deceased *don* Bernardo Reyes, screamed at her *abogado,* "What do you mean the *bastardo* can inherit the *hacienda?* What nonsense are you telling me!" she screamed at Alirio Mansano, her lawyer.

"Lo siento señora," the lawyer replied he was sorry. "I was told by the government land official, the laws have changed and now the first born male of a *haciendero* may inherit all properties and assets as well as debts pertaining to the *hacienda.* This is true, even if the first born is a *mestizo* and illegitimate, if there are no legitimate heirs."

"How can that be? Who was stupid enough to come up with a ludicrous law like that?" she continued screaming.

"Our *presidente,* Benito Juárez," the lawyer said simply.

Carmela learned of Bernardo's death months ago after his regular payments to her stopped coming. She assumed she would have rights to the land as recompense for money he still owed as specified by their divorce. In her usual manner, Carmela demanded her lawyer determine the necessary legal filings to get her money from the estate.

During her last visit, Alirio Mansano questioned her about Bernardo's bastard children. Somehow her stooped and bent ex-husband had managed to fuck the young *peón* girl, María, and got her pregnant. It was the final blow to the marriage and Carmela had left him for his indiscretion. Everyone at the *hacienda* knew María's young son, Antonio, was Bernardo's.

"That *pinche Indio* has gone too far. First, he executed our Emperor Maximilian and now as *presidente* he is giving rights to *peóns*. What can we do to stop the *bastardo?"* she continued cursing.

"There are new laws, Carmela. We will make our filings, but I cannot promise you anything," Alirio told her.

"But that boy is only a child, maybe five or six. Surely he cannot inherit such a vast property."

"He can if his mother acts as his guardian until he is of

age."

"That *peón* bitch. I will kill her if she tries."

"*Cálmate,* Carmela. You are getting excited over something which has not happened yet. I have made inquires at the land office and no paperwork has been filed. The *hacienda* is deserted and all the *peóns* are gone. We do not even know where the mother and boy are and if she even knows about the new inheritance laws."

Alirio Mansano looked at Carmela Reyes who sat across his desk. In her fifties she was still an attractive woman. A few wisps of gray hair did not detract from her beauty. Her deep set blue eyes smoldered with anger, only making her more striking. Alirio had been helping her fight her ex-husband, *don* Bernardo Reyes, for many years and had executed the final divorce papers over a year ago.

Carmela sat fuming. The *peón* bitch would not inherit her *hacienda.* She would not allow it. It was bad enough her husband wandered from bed to bed while they were married. When they were first married, he was hers and hers alone. He adored her and showered her with anything she wanted. He had even killed her first husband to obtain her hand in marriage.

She had loved him then. He was tall, brash, and full of pride. He swept her away from Mexico City and the dull life as *don* Leonardo Bustamante's wife. *Don* Leonardo was an older successful silver mine owner, a good provider, and a lousy lover. He used her as he would a trophy, smiling and holding her arm at parties and then would get drunk and grope her. Bernardo's lust for her brought out a passion in her beyond compare. She gladly helped him orchestrate the killing of *don* Leonardo outside of Zacatecas on one of his many trips to the silver mines. They took her first husband's money and Bernardo used it to purchase the extensive lands of the *hacienda* in Torreón and to start a successful horse breeding business.

Bernardo allowed her to build and furnish the home in elaborate imported furniture and tapestries. She ran the *peón* staff with an iron fist forcing them to cater to her every whim. They hosted sophisticated and grand parties and became an admired couple in Torreón. Carmela stopped at little expense to make her life comfortable and luxurious. Bernardo raised blooded horses and the *hacienda* was more and more successful each year.

They were rich and they were happy. Only one thing escaped her. She was barren. After several years, they began arguing about it. He blamed her. The lust they once shared for each other began to dim. She knew he lusted after some of the prettier *peón* girls and tried to ignore it. She was the mistress of the *hacienda* and the girls only provided him with relief of his manly needs from time to time.

Then the crazy *peón* boy shot Bernardo and left him crippled. He almost died. It would have better if he had, but he lived to be bent and bedridden. Then she learned the truth; the boy shot Bernardo because he had raped his sister. When the news spread around the *hacienda* that the young girl, María, was pregnant, Carmela decided to leave and returned to Mexico City.

For years her lawyer had been helping Carmela milk Bernardo for money. Blood money for the knowledge he killed her first husband as well as his indiscretion. She used her power wisely and assumed someday the *hacienda* would again be hers. Finally, when she found out the *hacienda* was in ill repair and most of the prized horses gone, Carmela consented to a divorce.

Carmela used Bernardo's money to rebuild a glamorous life in Mexico City. She lived in the socially connected Colonia Roma neighborhood, where Spaniards maintained their elite way of life. She engaged in social events and parties. Several years ago she met *don* Luis Orozco at just such a party.

Don Luis owned a large *hacienda* located in the southeast corner of the state of Jalisco where he planted tobacco, coffee, sugarcane and was also experimenting with the blue agave plant. He reminded her of Bernardo when he was younger and like Bernardo was completely infatuated with her. *Don* Luis showered her with gifts, jewels, and money and wanted her to marry him. She would marry him someday soon, however not before she extracted what was rightfully hers from her ex-husband's estate.

"What about the money he still owes me. Surely that gives me claim to the land?" she asked. "I deserve compensation and now that the old *bastardo* is dead, I will take the payment in land."

"Carmela," Alirio began trying to sooth her. "The money owed to you from the divorce died with Bernardo. I have told you that. I made the claim, but doubt it will be executed. We can only wait to see if the young boy's mother files for the inheritance. Regardless, the government may deny your claim. You are divorced and not his legal wife."

"All this legal rhetoric is ridiculous. I was his wife for twenty years and it was my money which originally purchased the land. Surely that counts for something more than him sticking his *pene* in some *peón* girl and getting her pregnant."

"I understand how you feel, Carmela. I can only suggest we wait and see what happens."

"File the claim anyway. I want the money *don* Bernardo owes no matter where it comes from. Do it Alirio," she demanded. Carmela stood in a huff and without saying goodbye swept out of the lawyer's office.

Don Luis Orozco and his trusted bodyguard, who sat quietly in chairs on the far wall of the office listening. They stood and followed her out the door. Alirio thought it interesting that a man such as *don* Luis would allow Carmela to speak with him about the *hacienda* in Torreón without intervention. Normally men handled affairs such as these, though Alirio handled Carmela's divorce from *don* Bernardo and knew she was a formidable foe in her own right.

Don Luis took Carmela's arm as they left the lawyer's office. *"Mi amor,* do not trouble yourself so. I have more money than you will ever need. Come let us forget this foolishness and retire to my *hacienda* in Jalisco. I will make you the richest woman, beyond all others."

Carmela allowed *don* Luis to woo her. She liked leading the rich widower along and would marry him, however she had no intention of allowing a stupid *peón* girl to best her. Especially since it was her horrible brother who shot

Bernardo and left him crippled. She would like nothing better than to see both of them dead. No, Rafael Ortega de Estrada's sister and her bastard son would never inherit the *hacienda*.

CHAPTER 13

"No te preocupes querida, let the lawyer handle the problem and do not fret so. It does not become you. If the young bastard's mother tries to claim the *hacienda,* I will have Buck kill her and the boy too," *don* Luis assured Carmela not to worry. They arrived home after meeting with the lawyer in the city and Carmela had pouted the entire way, fuming over her conversation about the inheritance.

Located in an affluent neighborhood called Colonia San Ángel, Luis' mansion was in keeping with Carmela's idea of style and opulence. About five miles south of the city center, it had once been owned by a nobleman. *Don* Luis enjoyed the luxury, but would rather be at his *hacienda* in Jalisco tending to his business. The only thing keeping him here was Carmela.

Don Luis Orozco became acquainted with Carmela Reyes through social friends in Mexico City. He had hosted a large fiesta at his Mexico City mansion, as a farewell party for his eldest son who was leaving for the military academy in Madrid, Spain. Socially connected in the city, *don* Luis invited most of the city's elite and Carmela came with friends. Luis was smitten with her immediately.

Carmela still had the body of a much younger woman, though Luis knew she was only about ten years younger than he. Her skin was almost alabaster and her eyes a clear bright blue. There was no doubt she was of pure Spanish blood. Luis spent the entire evening courting her attention. At first she was aloof and rebuffed him. Her voice said no, but her eyes told him otherwise. She finally allowed him to lead her onto the dance floor.

Luis, widowed for four years, found Carmela both lovely and a challenge. He found her headstrong ways enchanting, rather than annoying. He had asked for her hand and though she had put him off, she spent most nights here at his mansion and in his bed.

Carmela looked at Luis's bodyguard, Buck, and said,

"Tell him to go. We do not need him tonight." She hated the nasty *Americano* and wished Luis would send him back to the *hacienda*. She did not understand Luis' need for protection in Mexico City, especially here at the mansion and disliked his constant presence.

Samuel S. Buckner, who liked to be called Buck, stood beside *don* Luis slowly spinning his hat with his right hand watching Carmela climb the stairs. Now at twenty-nine, Buck was a handsome young man with dark brown hair and deep blue eyes under heavy eyebrows. A well trimmed mustache above full lips accented his boyish looking face. Five foot ten inches tall, he had not lost his lean muscular build.

The afternoon was boring. He was disinterested in the dealings of his *patrón's* woman and her problems. Employed by *don* Luis for the old man's protection – a hired gun. The hours he with the old man were boring and *don* Luis treated him not with contempt, but not with gratitude either.

The rich *haciendero* hired him as a bodyguard because of the unrest plaguing the city. *Peóns* were more brazen these days since President Benito Juárez had given them more rights and wealthy landowners were their targets. Buck only found the job exciting when *don* Luis had been accosted by *peóns* and Buck wasted no time in killing them.

"That is all, Buck," *don* Luis said in a dismissive voice, standing on the staircase leaving Buck standing in the foyer. "I will be taking siesta with my *doña.*"

Buck was a twenty-three-year-old captain in the Confederate Army when he came to Mexico with General 'Fighting Joe' Shelby in 1865. General Shelby refused to surrender to the Union forces and instead his Iron Brigade fought all the way to the Mexican border for what they hoped would be a new life. They made it to Mexico City in the fall of 1865. When the South finally lost the Civil War, some Confederates wandered home, while others fled to Brazil. Another group including Buck took residence on land southeast of Mexico City where Emperor Maximilian gave each of them 640 lots at one dollar per acre. There they began planting cotton, coffee, cocoa, and tobacco. The farms flourished, but they constantly had to fight off attacks by Indians, *bandidos,* and *guerrilleros,* as well as disease.

Buck and his fellow Confederates had grand visions of the town Carlota, named after Maximilian's wife, located in the New Virginia colony. Now, Benito Juárez was president and things were changing rapidly. Buck chose to remain in Mexico City, instead of returning to his home in Kentucky, not wanting anything to do with a country led by 'the Butcher', General Ulysses S. Grant.

Deciding to stay in Mexico, Buck knew farming was not in his soldier heart. He and some of his friends headed for Mexico City and hired themselves out as gunslingers. He found Mexico controlled by the decedents of Spanish aristocrats, much like his home in Lexington, Kentucky, where southern gentlemen controlled the prosperity of the state. In Lexington it had been black slaves who did the farming, household chores, and any menial task. Mexico did not have slaves, as such, *peóns* did all the work.

His life in Mexico City entailed everything he enjoyed – horses, guns, and women. Life as a hired gun fit his demeanor well. Some men killed only out of necessity, Buck killed both for need and pleasure. His only complaint was how his boss expected a subservient attitude from him, treating him in a dismissive manner, which grated him.

"Patrón, me necesitará esta noche?" Buck asked if the *don* would need his services tonight. Buck made it a priority to learn the language and in the almost five years here in Mexico City he had become fairly proficient in speaking Spanish.

Don Luis stopped halfway up the staircase and turned back. "No, Buck. Carmela and I have a few guests coming for supper here at the house. You are free until morning. We will return to my *hacienda* tomorrow or perhaps the next day. I must meet with *don* Cenobio to discuss some business. Be back here for breakfast, sometime before noon," Luis replied.

Recently Luis was contacted by a man named *don* Cenobio Sauza. Cenobio was a young *tequilero,* a distiller of tequila. He was looking for large plantation owners who would agree to grow the blue agave plants for distillation into a smooth liquor. Cenobio explained the plant needed large expanses of land and time to grow, but needed little tending. The altitude and weather in Jalisco provided the perfect environment for the blue agave plants to flourish. Luis was contemplating the idea, but the young man told him little that would convince him to commit his land to the agave.

When Luis pushed in the doors to their bedroom, Carmela had removed her dress and sat in her slip brushing her hair. He walked behind her and placed his hands on the back of her shoulders.

"Querida, my love, come with me to the *hacienda* tomorrow. Do not worry so about the old property in Torreón. Your old life is done and I can offer you the world. Come and share my riches. It does not become you to be so stressed," he lovingly said while he massaged her shoulders.

"I know *querido,* but I cannot let Bernardo's *peón puta* take what is rightfully mine. I will not give it up." Carmela was determined to get the property and sell it for a handsome profit. The blood money from the death of her first husband had financed it, something Luis did not understand and would never know.

Luis tolerated Carmela's tantrums over the *hacienda* in Torreón, not caring one way other. He was rich beyond his needs. After his first wife's death, Luis engaged all of his efforts in his *hacienda* located in the southeast corner of the state of Jalisco. The large plantation successfully produced tobacco, coffee, and sugarcane making him a very wealthy man. Though he wanted and needed to return to his plantation, Luis wanted and needed Carmela more.

"Come to bed my love. You are tired and upset. I will make it right." He bent his head and began to caress and kiss her shoulders. Though the bent of her shoulder indicated she was still angry, he knew she was full of lust. Her need for sexual pleasure abounded, which was so unlike most women he bedded. Not having had any children, Carmela's treasure was as tight as any young woman's and Luis craved making love to her.

Carmela felt his tender lips seeking a response. She wanted to rebuff him, still full of hate in her heart for the possibility of losing the *hacienda* to the bastard son of Bernardo. *"Ahh mi amor,"* she responded to his advances, raising her hand to touch his cheek. *"Mi amor,* without you I could not endure this wretched affair. Take me to bed and erase these bad feelings tearing at my heart."

Carmela took Luis' hand as he led her to the bed. He was older than she, but he could more than satisfy her carnal desires. Slowly he removed her slip and undergarments, leaving her standing naked. His eyes and hands caressed her. As his hands tenderly moved down to her belly, she could feel her passion growing. He gently pushed her to the bed and stroked her nakedness with wonton abandon. For Carmela, Luis was the man she thought Bernardo would become – rich, powerful, and full of passion.

He stood above her and removed his shirt and pants, his *pene* already hard for her. Perhaps he was right and she should not care about the past and only the future. She did not need the old deserted *hacienda* in Torreón and it would probably be a pain to sell. She could marry Luis and he would give her the lavish lifestyle she deserved. After putting up with a crippled, *desgraciado* ex-husband, Carmela knew she should embrace the future Luis offered her.

As he stroked between her legs, Carmela groaned in pleasure. Her hips responded in kind. This was all she wanted and needed in life. As her body succumbed to the sexual frenzy, her last thought about the *hacienda* in Torreón was that she would go to Jalisco with Luis in the morning.

CHAPTER 14

Four days after crossing the border, Rafe arrived in Torreón. It was just past noon and the town was busy with shoppers and wagons. Rafe rode down the central plaza to a few stares. At the Hotel Bilbao he walked up to the desk clerk.

"May I help you?" he asked looking up to see a man dressed as an *Americano.*

"I am Señor Rafael Ortega de Estrada from Santa Fe, New Mexico. I will need one of your best rooms," Rafe spoke with authority in perfect Spanish.

"Certainly *señor,* is there anything else?"

"Send a boy to the Reyes *hacienda* to alert *don* Pablo to meet me here." Rafe placed two *pesos* on the counter.

The young clerk looked quite confused by Rafe's request, muttered an acknowledgement to the *Norte Americano,* and handed Rafe a key.

After cleaning up, Rafe walked downstairs and out to the plaza. For the first time in his life, Rafe walked tall in his hometown. He was no longer a peasant. He was an American and Rafe had his holster belt with his double action GSW pistols strapped around his waist.

Unlike the last time he came here, Rafe had no misgivings about returning. This time he was on a mission to acquire his legacy. It was a legacy he did not really want, but would take so he could give it to his sister María and Rodolfo. This time he did not have to pretend to be a lowly *vaquero,* averting his eyes lest he be recognized. He was Rafael Ortega de Estrada, an American man, and soon to be the new owner of *don* Bernardo's *hacienda.*

As Rafe sat drinking and enjoying a small meal, his eyes explored the plaza. The town of Torreón probably looked much as it had last year when he and Carlos came, but it was as if he was seeing it for the first time. The plaza in Torreón was larger than Albuquerque or Santa Fe. Graceful stucco, two-story homes surrounded the plaza on two sides. From the second story iron balconies, heavy baskets hanging with flowers burst with color. The Catedral stood at the east end. The center of the plaza had many large trees and several fountains. Rafe remembered when fiestas filled the plaza with music, treats, and dancing. Shops and small cafes surrounded the plaza and wagons and carriages were moving along the *paseo*.

As he ate, three *vaqueros* rode down the street. He saw two *peóns* lower their heads and scurry along the sidewalk as they approached. Two *Indios,* with wood strapped to their backs slowly walked with the heavy bundles. A carriage with a *doña* and a young girl clacked on the cobblestones toward the cathedral. The *doña* sat under a parasol. Rafe tried not to react to the obvious disparity.

Pablo arrived at the restaurant just as Rafe finished his meal. He saw the one horse buggy drive up and went out to meet the old horse master. With him in the buggy, Pablo carried the painting of *don* Bernardo's grandfather and an envelope containing Rafe's secreted Catholic birth certificate and a letter – the items which would prove Rafe's claim.

Rafe ordered two beers and signaled Pablo to join him at the restaurant's patio.

"We have a meeting with *don* Bernardo's lawyer in about an hour," Pablo said to him. His name is Nicolás Jiménez."

"Pablo, have you ever met this lawyer?" Rafe asked.

"No, but he is a good *abogado*. He works for all people, *peóns* and the rich. He fought the Mexico City lawyer when *doña* Carmela sued the *don* for civil divorce. I have heard he is a man to be trusted," Pablo said.

Pablo carried the documents to the table, leaving the picture in the buggy. He pulled out the paperwork and handed it to Rafe.

"It looks very official," Rafe said. "It shows I was born to Celiá Ortega de Estrada and *don* Bernardo Reyes de Cordoba and it shows my birthday, December 16, 1849."

"There is also a letter from Padre Andres. He swears the certificate is true," Pablo said and handed another piece of paper to Rafe.

"Is he willing to testify in person?" Rafe asked.

"Well, he is old and I am not sure he can travel, especially to Mexico City."

Rafe pursed his lips. He wondered if a written letter from the padre would have enough weight in court. "What about the painting? Do you think it looks like me?"

"You will see," Pablo replied.

"Maybe they will say it is a coincidence. You know, like in Santa Fe they say all Mexicans look alike." Pablo grinned at Rafe's joke. When it was time to go to the lawyer's office, Rafe and Pablo finished the beers and Rafe left several *pesos* on the table.

"*Bueno, vamos,*" Rafe said let's go and picked up the birth certificate and letter.

They rode the buggy the few blocks to the lawyer's office and the assistant immediately showed them into his office. "*Buenas tardes señores,*" the lawyer Nicolás Jiménez greeted them graciously.

"*Señor, somos Rafael Ortega de Estrada de Santa Fe, Nuevo México y Pablo Contreras de Torreón.*" Rafe introduced himself in the formal customary manner of a Spanish gentleman with a slight bow, then introduced Pablo.

Nicolás Jiménez shook their hands and completed the introductory greetings. "*Por favor sientate.* How can I be of service to you here in Torreón?" the lawyer asked them to sit.

"*Señor,* we have heard the new property laws of Mexico allow a bastard son to inherit property, if the son is the first born and only heir?" Rafe spoke up.

"*Sí,* some of the inheritance laws have changed. I believe that is one of them, but I hear it is very hard to prove. One must have hard evidence and even if you do, it will be a battle with any other heirs," the lawyer said as he sat back on his chair. He looked directly at Rafe with a skeptical eye. "What do you have as proof?"

Rafe handed him the envelope with the birth certificate and the padre's letter. "I have this."

The lawyer studied the birth certificate. "Reyes? *Don* Bernardo Reyes?" The lawyer asked shocked with a sudden recognition at Rafe's name.

"*Sí,*" Rafe simply replied, yes.

Jiménez knew *don* Bernardo well for many years. The lawyer had orchestrated many dealings for the old *don,* including his divorce from Carmela. He was well aware of the *don's* other bastard children by the young *peón* woman named María, but *don* Bernardo never mentioned he sired an older son. So, the striking young man standing in front of him, who looked like a gentleman, was Rafael Ortega de Estrada, María's older brother – the young *peón* boy who shot *don* Bernardo for raping María. The lawyer knew the story well. *Don* Bernardo had grumbled about the shooting many times, swearing revenge upon this young man.

"I know Padre Andres and Sister Isabel Garza. The padre is an honorable man. Is this the only proof you have?" the lawyer asked trying to collect himself.

"We have this," Pablo said and pulled the blanket off the painting and lifted it up onto the lawyer's desk. "The painting is *don* Bernardo's grandfather, *don* Rafael. It hung in the stairwell at the *hacienda* for all the years I was there, with the other paintings of the Reyes men. I saved the paintings from vandals after the *don* died," Pablo explained.

When Pablo unwrapped the blanket protecting the painting of *don* Rafael Reyes de Zamora, Rafe's great-grandfather, the lawyer gasped.

"It could be you," he said to Rafe. "The resemblance is uncanny." Even Rafe could see his face in the painting, especially now as he trimmed his mustache and beard in the Spanish manner of a small triangle beard under his lip and a thin mustache. "How is this true? *Don* Bernardo never told me about you," the lawyer said.

"*Don* Bernardo raped my mother. As soon as she knew she was pregnant, she told Pablo. Three weeks later she married my father and he raised me as his own and gave me his name. My mother kept the secret of my birth from me until recently. I believe *don* Bernardo knew the truth." Rafe told the lawyer.

"Come closer," the lawyer waved his hand. Rafe stood up and moved closer to the painting where the lawyer could look at him and the image on the painting. After scrutiny, a slight smile curled on the lawyer's face. "This may be enough proof to convince the government for your inheritance, but I will tell you now, *doña* Carmela could fight you because *don* Bernardo still owes her money from the divorce." Jiménez replied.

"But they are divorced. Would she still have a claim on the property?" Pablo asked.

"Not a legal claim, no. However the court may lean toward her social status to overrule the inheritance of a bastard. The laws are new and somewhat untested in complex situations. I know *doña* Carmela and she will demand restitution in some manner."

"Do you think I have a case?" Rafe asked.

Nicolás quietly pondered and studied the birth certificate and letter. He looked closely again at the picture. "Yes I believe you have enough evidence to make a claim. Of course, I have no control over the outcome."

"Will you go to Mexico City and plead my case?"

"*Sí,* I would be happy to go. I can leave in a few days and I will prepare the claim and file it with the land office." In truth Nicolás wanted this case. He would relish beating *doña* Carmela and her arrogant lawyer from Mexico City. They had won the divorce case against *don* Bernardo. After the proceedings, *doña* Carmela belittled him saying, "You are *criollo,* I am *gachupín.* You can never win against me." Her aloof manner just because she was born in Spain offended him. Nicolás Jiménez might have been born in Torreón, but knew Carmela was more of a *puta* than a fine *gachupín* lady. He heard she was living with a *don* in Mexico City and they were not even married.

"Very well, get started and keep an account of your charges," Rafe said and shook the lawyer's hand. He provided the lawyer an address where he could be located in Mexico City when the lawyer arrived.

CHAPTER 15

Buck saddled his horse after his boss dismissed him for the night. He named the horse Bala, meaning bullet in Spanish. Bala was a Spanish Andalusia with a long thick mane and a tail of silver gray. Andalusians were descendents of the original horses brought from Spain by the conquistadors. Typically Andalusians were compact in size, but strong and docile by nature making them easy to train. Bala was anything but docile, more tough and mean like his master.

Buck rode away from *don* Luis' home. He looked forward to a free night at El Tío Pepe's Cantina. It was a bar where he and some of his friends frequented to eat, drink, and gamble in the heart of Mexico City. The *don* said they would leave for his plantation in Jalisco tomorrow. Buck disliked living at the isolated region where the *hacienda* was located. From there, it was a far ride to any cantina or brothel and he knew he needed to get his fill of *putas* tonight.

Near the cantina was La Ruiseñor, the Nightingale brothel. Madam Lucia ran the house with prostitutes of all types, some imported from France, Spain, and some beautiful Aztec *Indias*. Buck planned to partake of several tonight after carousing at Tío Pepe's.

Before he left for the cantina, Buck donned his best black *traje* with small silver stars sewn on the outside seams of the bellbottomed pants. Red silk ruffles at the bottom of his pants met his highly polished boots. He began wearing the attire of a *caballero* when he moved permanently to Mexico City a number of years ago, giving up his Kentuckian soft deerskin pants and jacket. He thought the ruffled Mexican suit frivolous at best, ridiculous at worst.

His black boots which he had custom-made in Texas shone brightly from frequent polishing. The boots were unique with a red Protestant Cross embroidered on the outside of each boot. It was his only obvious protest against this almost completely Catholic nation. He sported a black flat crowned hat with a plain, highly polished silver band about a half-inch wide.

In his high school years, Buck was sent to a military preparatory school, where he excelled in weapons but did poorly in academics. He was only accepted to West Point Military Academy because his father pressed a prominent congressman from Lexington. At West Point, he again excelled in weapons and did better with his studies. During his graduating year the Civil War broke out, with the first shot fired at Fort Sumter in the Charleston harbor.

A few days after the incident at Fort Sumter, the cadets and their commanders gathered at the West Point parade ground where the Southern cadets ceremoniously separated themselves from their counterparts from the North. Buck was only too happy to go to war, especially against the uppity Yankee boys from New York and Boston.

When the south lost the Civil War and the rebellion was in disarray, he followed General Shelby with his 'Iron Brigade' as they fought their way to the Mexican border. Buck would have rather stayed north fighting Yankees, but trusted Shelby, who told them they could continue the fight from Mexico. Shelby's efforts collapsed after Emperor Maximilian refused to finance Shelby's offer to build an army of Mexican, French, and Confederate forces to fight the growing forces of Benito Juárez.

Buck then joined up with Brigadier General James E. Slaughter, another Confederate, commanding troops here in Mexico. Like Shelby, Slaughter also offered his army to Maximilian. In the end, the pompous Mexican Emperor denied the Confederates help and all the pretentious plans were just dreams. Eventually Shelby, Slaughter, and many Confederates gave up and went home leaving others, like Buck, stranded in Mexico. Good with a gun, he offered himself as a *pistolero,* which suited him just fine.

Arriving at the livery in the central part of the city, Buck walked the short distance from the livery to the cantina. He left his horse at the stable to be brushed and corralled for the night, knowing tomorrow he might be riding to Jalisco.

Entering the smoky El Tío Pepe's Cantina the bartender greeted him. *"Hola Buck,* tequila?" In the bartenders thick Spanish accent his name sounded more like *'Buk.'*

"Sí. Bring me a bottle" Buck told the bartender in return.

The small cantina served many liquors, especially many fine tequilas. Buck had acquired a taste for the musky liquor made from agave, but he missed a fine Kentucky bourbon. He took a shot of tequila and walked over to the Spanish Monte table. A beautiful *mestiza* woman was dealing and flashed her dark brown eyes at him. *"¿Quieres apostar, señor?"* she asked him if he wanted to place a bet.

Buck downed another shot of tequila and placed a silver five *peso* coin on the top layout which was showing a spade and a heart. Buck liked those suites because the spade reminded him of death and the heart was love. Turning the bottom card, the gate showed a spade and Buck won. He continued playing as the cantina began to fill. He noticed a few of his friends were strolling in and gathering at the bar.

A little while later, Salvador Perez de Aguilar walked in. Like Buck, Salvador was a *pistolero* for hire. Salvador joined Buck at the Monte table and they played the mindless game. Salvador suggested adding a shot of tequila to the bets, with the loser downing a shot. After numerous rounds, both men drank plenty of shots between them.

Buck tired of the stupid game, wishing these Spaniards knew how to play poker or faro. *"Eh Salvador, vamos a coger algunas putas!"* Buck said to Salvador asking if he was ready to go fuck some whores.

"Sí absolutamente, vamos," Salvador replied and they tipped the Monte dealer and headed out the door.

They strolled down the street to La Ruiseñor brothel. It was well after midnight and the cool of the July morning hung delightfully in the city's air. It was one of the things Buck loved about the beautiful city. It never snowed in Mexico City and it had a temperate climate year round. Kentucky was cold in the winter, hot and humid in the summer. He especially detested his years at West Point in the frigid winters of New York.

"Señores, no pistolas," a large muscular doorman demanded they check in their guns at the brothel's door. They gladly hung their gunbelts on a hook knowing the strict rules of the popular brothel. However, Buck kept a derringer in a secret pouch just inside his right boot. Buck and Salvador frequented the Ruiseñor often and knew the routine. They seated themselves in the opulent parlor and waited.

"Buenas noches señores, what is your pleasure?" Madam Lucia asked as she walked in the room. A well endowed older woman, she was dressed in a low cut red and black satin dress. Her black hair with some white streaks was pulled back, gathered, and tied with red roses.

"Buenas noches doña Lucia. You know what we like. Bring us your new ones," Buck answered.

"Ah, today is your lucky day. I have several young *señoritas* fresh off the ship from Acapulco. They are from *China y Japón y Las Filipinas.* Here is a bottle of the finest tequila in all of Mexico. I will bring the *señoritas* out shortly." She placed the bottle and glasses on the table and left.

"Eh Salvador, chicas from the Orient. You better get your *garrancha* sharpened. I bet their treasure spot is very small," Buck blurted out and they both laughed. Buck knew Salvador would be interested in the Oriental delights, but he loved beautiful, hot-blooded Spanish women. He found Asians too formal and steeped in traditional lovemaking, which meant the man did all the work while the woman yielded herself timidly. Buck loved rowdy hot sex with a fiery Spanish woman. The Spanish *putas* engaged in rough sex, biting, slapping, and teasing their man.

Madam Lucia emerged from the curtained door leading a young Japanese woman. Her face was painted white with bright red lips and a light shade of red on her cheekbones and just above her eyelashes to the corner of her black eyes. Jet black hair was pulled back into a tight bun atop her head with thin white sticks crisscrossed through it. A small string of pearls hung to the side from one of the sticks. She wore a colorful kimono with a red sash around her waist. The beautiful Japanese angel floated as she walked with her head slightly to one side and her eyes looking to the floor.

The madam clapped and the curtain parted again. Another young girl stood halfway through the curtain when a large explosion blew in the front door of the brothel. She screamed. The house became alive with screaming women. Upstairs Buck heard the thump of feet as *caballeros* scrambled to get their weapons. Buck slapped Salvador, who was mesmerized by the beauty of the Japanese *puta*. Jumping up Salvador grabbed the Japanese whore and helped her hide behind the sofa before joining Buck near the door.

They retrieved their guns as chaos erupted around them. Buck heard gunfire and bullets hitting the exterior of the brothel. Both Buck and Salvador were gunslingers and had been under fire many times, so they knew to keep their wits about them before taking action. The brothel's bodyguard deserted his post when the shooting started and the Spanish *caballeros* upstairs in the rooms would probably try to save their *gachupín* necks.

"¡Muerte a la gachupíns!" a man in a white cotton shirt and pants and large sombrero yelled as he rushed into the brothel with a gun pointed in front of him. Across his chest crisscrossed bandoliers were stuffed with bullets. Outside Buck and Salvador could hear more voices yelling and more shots were fired.

Buck aimed at the *peón* fighter in the doorway and put a bullet in his chest. He fell dying in the doorway. Another *peón* was behind the dying man and turned to run, but was pushed forward by the men behind him. Salvador yelled to Buck, aimed at the man and took his shot. The rebel went down in a heap cross the doorway.

"Matalos a todos," a voice screamed to kill them all, urging the rebels into action.

Bullets began to riddle the interior of the brothel through the broken glass windows forcing Buck and Salvador to seek cover toward the back of the main room.

"I thought *peóns* couldn't have guns here in Mexico?" Buck asked.

"They get them somehow. They are the scourge of Mexico City."

A bullet hit the wall just above Buck's head. He saw two *peóns* coming through the blown out doorway. Buck jumped up and fired, hitting each in the chest. Blood spurted through their dirty white *camisas* as they fell. Beside him, Salvador aimed and fired through the shattered front window. They heard a painful scream outside.

"Buck, vamonos! There are too many of them," Salvador hissed to Buck not wanting to give away their position.

"What about Madam Lucia and the *putas?"* Buck could hear screaming from the upstairs rooms.

"I don't think they will hurt the women. They are after *caballeros."*

"Sí, we may have to fight our way out the back door. Make sure your guns are fully loaded," Buck answered.

"Listo, vamos," Salvador yelled out he was ready to go.

When they reached the backdoor to the brothel, a loud voice from outside was yelling and it stopped them in their tracks. The voice was ordering the door to be broken down.

"Señores vengan por aquí," Madam Lucia yelled at them from the top of the stairs to follow her. No sooner did they reach the second floor than the backdoor flew open and the fighters rushed in with guns blasting.

The madame led them to a window on the side of the building where they crawled out onto a small ledge and hugged the wall until they could jump down to the roof of the building next door. From there they hunched low and ran from the brothel until they could jump to the roof of another building. As a soldier it was not in Buck's heart to run. He would rather be fighting, but this was not his fight.

Buck and Salvador crouched on the roof, peeking occasionally at the activity below them. Several other *caballeros* from the brothel were hiding on another rooftop, one without his pants. The morning sun was lightening the eastern sky a bit before Mexican Army soldiers finally surrounded the rebellion below.

Once the soldiers calmed the situation, Buck and Salvador found a way to get off the rooftop. Buck headed for the livery. Saddling his horse, he rode straight to *don* Luis' house, tired after spending hours crouched on the roof near the brothel. The many shots of tequila he and Salvador downed at the cantina left his stomach churning for food. He hoped the *don* would not want to begin the long ride early this morning for Jalisco, for he needed a few hours of sleep and some food in his belly.

CHAPTER 16

The streets of Mexico City were empty and quiet until he approached the upscale neighborhood of Colonia San Ángel. Suddenly he heard yelling and gunshots in the distance. Buck urged his horse faster toward the sound. The yelling became distinct as he rounded a corner near *don* Luis' mansion.

"*¡Muerte a la hacienderos!* Death to the robbers of our land!" voices yelled.

The *peóns* were everywhere, brazenly yelling and in large numbers. He knew their anger was fueled by years of servitude and directed toward the ruling class. Dressed as a *caballero*, Buck knew he could be a target.

He found the caste system here in Mexico confusing, though not dissimilar from the United States. The *hacienderos* and business owners needed labor, cheap labor to work the fields and mines. Like in Kentucky, landowners clearly needed the black labor force on their cotton and tobacco plantations. Here in Mexico the labor was a mixture of Indians, Negros, and a class of people of mixed origin the Mexicans called *mestizos*. The upper class Spaniards called the workers *peóns* and treated them with contempt, especially the *mestizos*.

In Mexico the ruling class were pure-blooded Spanish, with the top nobility Spaniards born in Spain. Full-blooded Spaniards, such as *don* Luis and his mistress Carmela, enjoyed the privileges and spoils of the ruling class. Buck found it interesting the Mexican hierarchy had less to do with money and everything to do with heritage. Here if a nobleman squandered all his money, he was still treated with the utmost respect, simply due to his birthright. In the United States a man with money was treated with respect, regardless of his upbringing, except for blacks and Indians, of course.

Reaching *don* Luis' neighborhood, Colonia San Ángel, Buck heard gunfire nearby. Spurring Bala to a gallop on the cobblestone streets, he rode toward his *patrón's* mansion.

Ahead of him, he saw a band of *peóns* with rifles terrorizing the upscale neighborhood. Pulling up Bala, he studied the situation. The *peóns* were running in the streets, shooting at windows and yelling. He could see a small band near *don* Luis' mansion. Pulling his pistol, he checked the loads.

Buck relished a fight and never backed down. Kicking Bala in the flanks, he screamed a Confederate battle cry and rode directly at the *peóns* in front of *don* Luis' house. All six rounds hit their mark, as he rode through the peasants. They dropped like flies as he rode by, one screaming in pain. Another took a shot at him before slumping to the ground, but the bullet was way off mark.

The adrenaline rush made him feel alive, especially the killing. He turned Bala around at the end of the street and inspected the carnage he left behind. Four *peóns* lay on the street not moving, one was crawling slowly for cover leaving a trail of blood. The dead *peón's* friends had scattered and were nowhere in sight.

He wound his way through the back alleys finding the back of *don* Luis' two-story colonial house. Tethering his horse, he grabbed his rifle, and climbed to the roof using a hardy honeysuckle vine. When he reached the top, a volley of gunfire and screams erupted from the street below him. He crouched, ducking under the edge of the parapet, and peeked over with his rifle ready to fire. Below him government troops surrounded the protestors and were firing at will toward the *peóns.*

Some of the ragtag peasants threw rocks and carried stiff pieces of wood, while others carried old rifles, but they were no match for the soldiers. Soon they were overwhelmed by the government troops and scattered in all directions or were arrested. Buck watched as the ruckus dissipated, then hurried down off the roof and into the house. He found *don* Luis and *doña* Carmela hiding in the wine cellar.

"*Patrón,* it is safe to come out now," he called down to his boss.

"*Buck, ¿dónde has estado? Nos querían matar,*" *don* Luis asked Buck where he had been with anger in his voice. The *peóns* wanted to kill them and Buck should have been here to protect them. It was so like *don* Luis. Last night he felt safe here at the house and dismissed Buck. This morning it was Buck's fault the *peóns* threatened the couple.

"I am here now *patrón,* come out. It is safe," he replied.

"The *pinche peóns* are getting more brazen, *patrón,*" Buck reminded him.

"Yes, it is because that *pinche Indio Presidente Juárez* has fueled their anger. Now, they want our money. Buck, get my carriage ready. We leave for Jalisco immediately," *don* Luis said as he held onto a visibly shaken Carmela.

"Come my dear, let us get our things packed quickly," *don* Luis said leading Carmela to the door.

By mid-morning Buck rode behind *don* Luis' covered carriage. The *don* and Carmela packed hastily and the carriage was already well out of the city. Buck packed a few necessities in his saddlebags and tied a small valise on the back of the carriage.

Away from the city, Buck relaxed somewhat. It was less likely they would be attacked here on the road. Still he kept a sharp eye on the surrounding countryside. As the day dragged, Buck's tired body began to feel every jolt. He pulled his hat lower to shade his eyes from the setting sun. Finally the *don* called to the driver to stop at the next stage stop.

Six days later *don* Luis' carriage arrived at his *hacienda* in Jalisco. Luis was happy to be home and away from the madness in Mexico City. The trip was uneventful, though Carmela complained about the bumpy roads and hot dusty trail. It was noon and Luis expected *don* Cenobio later in the day. To his surprise, the young Cenobio was sitting on the veranda having lunch.

He stood up and walked out to the carriage to greet the *don*. *"Don* Luis, I took the liberty to get here early, no disrespect to you *señor. Buenos días, señora,"* Cenobio bowed and greeted Carmela as he approached the carriage and Carmela stepped out.

"Ah, bienvenidos a me casa," *don* Luis welcomed him. "Finish your lunch. I will have a much needed bath and we can sit and talk." Luis and Carmela disappeared into the

house, while servants unloaded the carriage.

About an hour later after Luis was refreshed, he ordered lunch for himself and found Cenobio on the veranda. "Looks like rain is coming," Luis started with small talk, pointing toward the southwest sky.

"Yes, it has come in everyday before sunset now for the past two weeks. It is good for the crops, no," Cenobio added.

"*Sí*, my crops enjoy a good rain."

After pleasantries, Cenobio took an unlabeled bottle out of a leather briefcase and poured the liquid into two small glasses. "I want you to taste this."

Luis picked up the glass, looked at it holding it up to the sun, before he sniffed into the glass. He then took a sip and held it on the tip of his tongue.

"*Esto es magnífico,*" he declared delighted with the taste. "What is this?" he asked. The drink was smooth without any bite. It tasted like tequila, but with a delightful taste and no bitterness.

"Tequila."

"*No, no puede ser,*" Luis responded not believing it was tequila. He often drank what was considered to be good tequila and this was much smoother than any he had ever tasted.

"*Sí*, it is tequila and that is why I am here *señor,*" Cenobio responded in a calm voice. "I am looking for land owners in Jalisco who could grow the blue agave. Men who are willing to take a risk with me for this new product."

Luis swirled the slightly amber liquid in the glass and took another sip.

Cenobio had been warned *don* Luis was a shrewd businessman. Regardless, the young entrepreneur pressed on hoping he might be a man to take a risk.

"This fine tequila comes from only blue agave. I have experimented with many trials and formulated a method to cook and extract the liquor. Only the blue agave can produce this taste. You have many acres of land perfect for growing the blue agave on your *hacienda,*" Cenobio continued explaining his methods to make the tequila.

"Tell me more. How do you know how to make this, when others can't?" Luis asked.

"I worked for the Cuervo family distillery and I learned everything I could about fermenting agave. They make a good tequila, but I believed it could be better. I setup a small distillery in a shack at my house and in my experiments discovered the blue agave is the best for fermenting quality tequila. It requires a longer cooking time and must be aged for over one year," he answered. Cenobio held his breath waiting for the *don's* response. He was young and though spirited, untested. He needed someone like *don* Luis to believe in him.

"Agave grows wild here in Jalisco. Even I have some growing wild on my untilled acres. Is it all blue agave?" Luis asked.

"*Señor,* as you know agave grows wild all over Mexico. Blue agave grows wild here in Jalisco. It likes the red volcanic soil and cooler weather," Cenobio said.

Luis drained his glass and Cenobio refilled it. Luis downed the shot in one long sip. "What do you want from me?" he asked.

Cenobio wanted to rebuke *don* Luis for downing the shot. Most men drank a shot of tequila in one gulp to overcome the bitter taste. Cenobio's tequila was smooth and a man could sip the liquor, much like a fine bourbon or cognac.

"I am currently leasing La Gallardeña distillery from *don* Lazaro Gallardo, but it is small and mostly outdated. I will need a bigger and more modern distillery. For now the distillery I have is sufficient to get started, but I have big dreams. From you, I need any blue agave you have growing on your fields and want you to consider expanding your fields to cultivate only the blue agave."

Cenobio could see the old *don* contemplating his request and said an internal prayer. "Also, I need funding to buy wagons and mules to haul the agave to the distillery and the tequila to market," Cenobio told him.

Luis leaned back in his chair and pondered what Cenobio said, thinking of the possibilities. He appreciated the younger man's enthusiasm and liked the taste of the tequila sample. Most of all Luis was an adventurous man like his ancestors who braved the arduous ocean trip from Spain to the New World. He liked taking risks and this one intrigued him. He owned many acres of untilled land. Growing the blue agave could utilize those acres for a profit with little effort.

"Very well, Cenobio. I have an interest in this project of yours. What is the offer you propose?" Luis asked sitting forward in his chair. Normally, he did not like showing his emotions while doing business, but this young man impressed him with his passion.

"I will guarantee to buy all your blue agave at a price better then the going market price. If you can loan me money for wagons and a new distillery, I will give you ten percent interest and pay back the initial loans in two years," he stated and waited for a counter.

Luis leaned forward and spoke quietly. "I want to be a partner. I have many acres and can buy more. I will buy the wagons you need and buy or build a larger distillery. For that I want twenty percent of all your profits."

Cenobio was elated. It was more than his dreams could imagine. *Don* Luis owned extensive lands in Jalisco and was willing to buy more. With wagons and a distillery, Cenobio could begin to make the fine tequila. It was everything he hoped for and more.

"Agreed. The only thing I demand is that I control the quality of the tequila. I have spent too many years at Cuervo where they make cheap inferior tequila. I want a quality product."

Luis stuck out his hand to Cenobio. "We are partners then," he replied. "I will have my attorney draw up a contract, but in the meantime how much do you need to acquire the wagons and mules?"

CHAPTER 17

Outside the lawyer's office Rafe put a plan in motion, "Pablo you stay here in Torreón until the lawyer leaves for Mexico City. I will take the young Appaloosa to my friend the Healer and then go to Carlos' uncle's home in Mexico City. Pablo, find my sister and Rodolfo. Tell them about the *hacienda* and tell them to wait for me there until I get back."

The next morning Rafe rode along the foothills of the Sierra Madre mountain range, riding Rayo while trailing the packhorse and the young Appaloosa for Xihuitl. He owed Xihuitl his life after the Healer nursed him when *don* Bernardo shot him in the chest last year. Xihuitl and the silver star amulet from Chiwiwi's uncle, Chief Letoc, had saved him from certain death.

Rafe estimated it was late July or early August. Since he left Santa Fe, the days had begun to blur. Out here in the wilderness, his only compass and timepiece was the sun. He purposely avoided the Indian villages along the way as he remembered how these remote Indians disliked outsiders. When he was traveling with Xihuitl, he had dressed as a *peón* and acted as the healer's apprentice, otherwise it was likely he would have been shunned.

He had left Xihuitl in a hidden village called Tenochtitlán at the bottom of a deep canyon inhabited by descendants of the Aztec people. The people's Aztec ancestors fled from the Spanish invaders and they lived in the remote village for their safety. Outsiders were not allowed.

It was a problem he pondered as he rode along. How could he make contact with Xihuitl, when the people did not allow outsiders? Though he was dressed in a simple shirt and *pantalones,* there was no mistake he was not an Indian. Besides the inhabitants, only the Tarahumara Indians were allowed access to Tenochtitlán.

Rafe decided his only option was to stop at the Tarahumara village where he and the Healer visited on their travels. He hoped Chief Tepórame would remember him. He and Xihuitl saved the baby of the chief's niece. Rafe hoped the chief would agree to send a runner to Tenochtitlán to ask the Healer to come out to meet with him. As Rafe neared the Tarahumara village, he had a sense of being watched and at times glimpsed runners on the high ridges. He kept the horse to a slow cantor toward the village.

Long shadows of the canyons shaded the village as night started early in this part of the Sierra Madre mountain range. It was almost dark when Rafe entered the village and no one stopped him. At the center of the village an old man with white hair and stooped shoulders emerged from a large hut. He wore the typical white loincloth and a bright orange shirt. A band of the same color wound around his head and was adorned with a crest of short turkey feathers. He raised his hand in greeting.

"Cualli tonalli cacique Tepórame," Rafe greeted the chief in the Nahuatl language. Rafe had learned a few words of the old language while traveling with Xihuitl.

To Rafe's surprise the chief replied, "Ah Citlalin welcome back to my village. I knew you were coming," Chief Tepórame replied in Spanish. "Come sit and rest yourself." Rafe smiled as the Chief used the name the Healer gave him when Rafe had no memory. Citlalin meant star in Nahuatl and the Healer used the name because Rafe's silver star amulet saved his life. Rafe decided to use the name here in the Tarahumara village rather than explaining his true identity.

Rafe dismounted and two young boys led his horses away as he followed the chief into a large hut. Inside a fire glowed brightly. The chief motioned for Rafe to sit near the fire while he took his usual place on soft animal furs.

"What brings you here my young friend?"

"Chief Tepórame, I came to see my friend Xihuitl. I believe he is in the hidden city of Tenochtitlán, but I am not allowed to enter. I came to ask if you would send one of your runners there to ask Xihuitl to come out and meet me. Would I be asking you too much for this favor?"

"I will send a runner to Tenochtitlán in the morning,"

the chief assured him.

"You are most gracious. You said you knew I was coming. How is it possible?"

"My runners informed me of an intruder coming to the village. They have been watching you for many miles and one of them recognized you. Eat and rest. You are welcome here."

The flap on the door parted and the aroma of roasted turkey filled the room when two women brought a platter of food and cups of a strong drink. Rafe and the chief talked for several hours sitting beside the fire.

"Tepórame, I brought a gift for you." Rafe reached into his saddlebag and took out a black velvet pouch. He pulled the string to open it and pulled out a magnifying glass. It was three inches in diameter, set in a metal ring with a small stem. At the end of the stem, a long leather string was attached through a small loop. Rafe put the string around the Chief's neck and put the glass in his hand.

"Take the glass and place it above your hand and move it up and down until you can see your hand clearly. It will get bigger so you can see your hand more clearly," Rafe told him while helping to move the magnifying glass.

"Aye!" the Chief cried out and dropped the glass, his eyes widening in surprise. Rafe chuckled.

"Don't be frightened. It is not magic. It is only a glass which makes things larger to help you see better," Rafe tried to assure the Chief. "Here, try it again. I brought this glass for you, because I remember how you have trouble seeing up close," Rafe continued. He put the magnifying glass back into the Chief's hand. He picked up a small clay figurine with colored detail on its face and held it up. He showed the Chief how to use the glass to focus on the object.

This time a huge smile spread on Tepórame's face. "Aye, it is a wonder! I can see it completely. Thank you my son, thank you." The Chief kept looking through the glass and took the figurine away from Rafe turning it in his hand to view all of its detail. Tepórame used the magnifying glass as he moved about the room. He sighed and laughed at using the glass.

"Tomorrow I will show you how to start a fire with it using the sun," Rafe told him.

"I do not believe it. Truly it would be magic."

A little while later, a woman came and escorted Rafe to a sleeping hut leaving a dish of cool water near him on the floor. He woke the next morning to the sound of yells and shuffling feet outside the sleeping hut. It was early sunrise and deep shadows still filled the canyons. Eagerly he got up and dressed, and when he pulled the curtain to the outside door he saw twelve young Tarahumara children chasing a hard brown ball, kicking it from one runner to another. He remembered learning about the ball game, which trained the young men of the village to become hearty runners.

The morning shadows from the canyon walls held the cool mountain air even in early August. He walked to the central plaza where he sat on a large rock waiting for daylight to reach the center of the village. Women started gathering at the communal kitchen. Some brought firewood and some carried baskets of various foods balanced on their heads.

Before long, Chief Tepórame appeared out of his hut led by one of the women who brought food last night. She spotted Rafe sitting on the rock at the central plaza and slowly walked the Chief to the same spot. Rafe noticed how frail Chief Tepórame appeared, not only because of his poor eyesight, but he walked slowly leaning on the woman for support. He wore the magnifying glass around his neck.

"*Kuira-bá,*" the Chief greeted Rafe a good morning in Tarahumara.

"*Kuira,*" Rafe replied with the customary shortened greeting.

"I sent runners to Tenochtitlán early this morning. They will soon return with word from our friend Xihuitl. Come, we will have our meal now, then you will show me how to start a fire with the magic glass," the Chief said. Rafe walked with him to the communal eating area.

A heaping wooden bowl of *pinole* was handed to him by a young girl, who bowed and backed away. The Chief was served first and was already spooning the oatmeal-like paste. Rafe ate *pinole* when he and the Healer visited the village. It was a Tarahumara staple made of ground roasted corn combined with water and ground cinnamon, sweetened with honey or agave nectar. Sometimes they mixed *chia* seeds into the gruel. Xihuitl had told him *pinole* was a main source of energy for the runners. Though somewhat thick and pasty, Rafe knew he would not be hungry for many hours.

After the morning meal, Rafe led the Chief to a spot of dirt where the sunlight hit brightly. On the way he gathered dry grass and some small twigs. He arranged the twigs crosswise atop the dry grass and asked the Chief for the magnifying glass. He asked the Chief to sit on a nearby stump where he had a clear view. Carefully, Rafe tilted the glass until he found the sun's rays and pinpointed the light at the dry grass. Before long a small wisp of smoke trailed up from the dry grass. Rafe blew on the grass bringing the small pile to a steady flame.

"*Naik'*," the Chief yelled jumping up as if he was young and grabbed the magnifying glass out of Rafe's hand. He turned it upside down looking for the fire. "*¿Chi? ¿Chi?*" he asked Rafe how?

Rafe laughed and tried to take the glass from him, but the Chief would not let go.

"*El fuego viene del sol*," he told the Chief the fire came from the sun. "Here, give me your hand." Rafe held the Chief's hand with the glass and pointed it so as to send the concentrated sunlight onto the top of the Chief's other hand. In a few seconds the intensified sunlight made the Chief's hand hot.

"*Aye*," the Chief yelled and quickly pulled his hand away.

Rafe handed the glass to the Chief and went to gather dry grass and some twigs. He returned and arranged the grass and twigs as before. By the time he returned a small group of villagers were surrounding the area. He took the Chief's hand and moved the magnifying glass over the spot until the sunlight concentrated a beam directly on the dry grass.

"*Concentrar el punto brillante*," Rafe told the Chief to focus the bright spot on the dry grass. After a few tries, the grass started to smoke and burst into a small flame.

Some of the villagers backed away in fright, while a tall man moved in closer toward where his chief was standing.

"What magic have you brought our Chief? You are a witch," the man said to Rafe.

Chief Tepórame put up a hand and said something which calmed the man.

Rafe backed away from the crowd surrounding the old chief letting him show off his newly found magic. Cries of joy and laughter began to fill the area as they took turns starting a fire with the glass. Rafe noticed the tall man was now completely enthralled, showing others how to aim the glass.

A pair of runners dressed only in white loin cloths and leather sandals, ran across the plaza and stopped near the Chief. He motioned them to approach and listened to them nodding his head. He looked toward Rafe and signaled to him.

"Xihuitl will meet you, my son. I will have your horses readied and you will follow these runners. They will take you to him," the Chief said.

Chapter 18

The morning following Rodolfo's conversation with Maxorro at the *pulqueria,* he and his *bandidos* packed supplies on their horses and headed south away from Zacatecas. In this desolate area it was not hard to pickup Maxorro's trail. The mules left deep imprints in the soft sandy soil. By mid morning, the four *bandidos* were following the mules, but keeping well out of sight.

Every several hours, Maxorro stopped and rested. It was obvious the muleteer knew every inch and resting place along the path. The old muleteer seemed in no hurry. In the evening he built a small campfire and cooked a meal.

From Rodolfo's vantage point, he saw the old man check each mule's legs and give them fresh grain, which he carried on one of the mules. Rodolfo and his men ate jerky and did not start a fire. They did nothing to give themselves away.

Maxorro was up early and continued on his way up the steep path. He arrived at the mine in the early afternoon on the second day. A man carrying a long whip appeared and walked out to greet Maxorro.

"Oye gilipollas, ya es hora de que llegaras," the mine superintendent yelled out calling Maxorro an asshole and demanding to know why it took so long to arrive. Maxorro lowered his head as if waiting to be whipped.

He took off his sombrero and humbling himself said, *"Perdóname Sancho, pero las mulas eran tercos esta mañana."* He asked the man with the whip, named Sancho, to forgive him. He blamed the tardiness on the stubborn mules.

"We have no time to waste, get your mules in place. The ingots are ready to be loaded." Sancho waved his hand. *"¡Apúrense muchachos!"* Sancho yelled out at the loaders to hurry up. Six tired looking Indians worked in pairs, lifting the heavy packs on either side of each mule. Sancho snapped his whip at the Indians. Rodolfo saw him use it on an old stooped man. Rodolfo could see the older Indian struggling to lift the heavy pack. The superintendent's whip cracked again.

Rodolfo seethed inside wanting to kill the abusive *bastardo,* but knew in his heart it would do no good for these people. It was not Sancho, it was the caste system. As long as *peóns* had no rights, they would continue to be abused.

When the Indians were done loading, ten mules carried two leather packs, one on each flank with heavy leather straps binding them in place. Two mules carried supplies. The heavily loaded mules started back down the mountainous path. Sancho and six men with rifles rode behind them. The six men wore shabby military uniforms and Rodolfo knew without asking, they were Army soldiers who were assigned to the mine to protect the shipment. Behind Sancho, four ragged *Indios* followed the little train.

The trip down the mountain path was more treacherous and the heavily laden mules moved slower. Rodolfo noticed Maxorro rested the mules more often. The superintendent would become agitated with the slow pace and yelled at Maxorro and tried to whip the mules into movement. Rodolfo saw Maxorro respond vehemently, stopping Sancho from touching the mules. Surprisingly, the angry superintendent backed off.

Rodolfo sent Hector and Pepe to scout the surrounding countryside for places to hide and several alternative ways for them to escape. When they took the silver, Rodolfo knew the government would send troops. He felt his advantage was a knowledge of how to live off the land. After all, he and his *bandidos* had been avoiding capture for years.

In the evening, two of the *Indios* unloaded the packs of silver from the mules. The other two *Indios* prepared a meal for the superintendent and the soldiers. Maxorro ate jerky and stale tortillas from his supplies. Rodolfo could see the *Indios* ate little. He and Paco watched as the soldiers sat near a small fire and drank *pulque.* The man named Sancho sat with them for awhile, then retired to a nearby tree stump. The Indians sat without a fire in a group far away from both the soldiers and Sancho. Rodolfo surmised they sat far from

Sancho's whip. Maxorro stayed near the mules.

The diverse groupings made an attack more difficult. Paco and Rodolfo spent the first night watching the group sleep. The soldiers, apparently feeling little danger, stacked their rifles in a pile and drank *pulque* until they passed out. One was assigned guard duty and Rodolfo watched as he waited until the others were asleep before he snuck down and helped himself to the *pulque*. Sancho drank some, but not as much as the soldiers. He finally fell asleep leaning against a tree stump with his rifle across his lap.

Rodolfo knew the mule train was headed for Mexico City. Sizing up options, he decided hitting the miners while they were still in the treacherous mountain canyons was to his advantage. The closer they were to Mexico City, the further he was from the relative safety of Torreón.

In the morning, Rodolfo watched the Indians reload the mules. The packs looked extremely heavy, requiring the Indians to work in teams to lift them. Rodolfo wondered how many bars were in each pack and how heavy. The mules obviously struggled carrying a pack balanced on each of their flanks.

The four *bandidos* kept the mule train in sight all throughout the next day and night. The nightly ritual was replayed. The mules were unloaded, the soldiers got drunk and fell asleep. Sancho fell asleep near the fire with his whip and pistol close by. Rodolfo was not worried about the Indians. They were not armed and would probably cheer if he sliced Sancho's neck. He was concerned with Maxorro. Though the man was old and unarmed, Rodolfo could tell he was strong and treated his mules with care.

The silver mule train was camped just south of Aguascalientes. They traveled nearly forty miles in three days and Rodolfo heard Maxorro complaining. Sancho raised his whip to the old man, cracking it near him. "They are just stupid mules. They will work or you will not get hired again," the mine superintendent screamed at him.

Rodolfo watched the mine superintendent go through the usual ritual, feeding the four *Indios* the minimum, before he went to eat and drink with the soldiers. Maxorro pulled food in his packs. Rodolfo crouched behind bushy trees and watched. He heard the soldiers brag about how many *putas* they would get when they got to Mexico City. Sancho bragged he would be able to pay for more and better *putas* beyond the soldier's dreams.

Later, the four *bandidos* plotted the heist on a knoll not far away. It was a clear night and the stars popped out brightly in the sky. A part of a moon hung on the horizon. It would give them enough light to make their escape. Rodolfo laid out the plan.

"I will take Sancho. Paco, you subdue Maxorro, but do not hurt him. Pepe, you and Hector load one sack of silver on the each of our horses. Do not fire your gun unless you have to. I think the soldiers will stay asleep and we do not want to waken them.

"What about the *Indios?*" Pepe asked. "What if they start shouting?"

"I will grab the whip when I kill Sancho. They will behave, thinking I am the new *jefe.*"

The *bandidos* had their assignments. Rodolfo waited until long after dark. The soldiers were dead drunk, including the soldier who was supposed to be on watch. Sancho slept against a tree. Rodolfo waved to his friends and then headed into the camp.

As Rodolfo approached, he heard snoring from one of the soldiers. All was quiet. Rodolfo walked to where the mine superintendent slept. He planned on killing him, but it was not his way to be a murderer. If the man was awake and they were fighting, then he would gladly kill him. Rodolfo reached down and picked up Sancho's whip and rifle. Raising the rifle he brought the rifle's butt end down on Sancho's head. The man groaned and slumped. He ripped the tyrant's shirt and put a wad in his mouth and used a long strip to tie the wad firmly around his head. He grabbed a rope and bound him securely. Before he walked off, he gave Sancho a mighty kick. The man did not respond.

Turning from Sancho, Rodolfo saw Paco had bound and gagged Maxorro. The old man was struggling, but secure. He walked to where the silver bags were piled. Pepe and Hector were struggling to lift a single bag.

"Our horses cannot carry us and this load," Pepe whispered. "It's just too heavy."

"How many bars are in each bag?" Rodolfo whispered back.

"Three."

"Load two of the mules as we saw the *Indios* do, a bag on each side," Rodolfo told them changing the plan. "Tie the straps tight."

Pepe and Hector struggled to load the mules when the scrawny Indians seemed able to do it. Rodolfo pondered whether to rouse the Indians to load the silver, but thought better of it. They were pretending to be asleep. Rodolfo saw two of them open their eyes and then roll over and face the other way. They did not want any part of this robbery, nor would they raise an alarm. In the morning they would say they saw or heard nothing.

Finally two mules were loaded and Rodolfo led them to where the horses were picketed. He had watched Maxorro over the past few days and saw several things the old muleteer did to keep them moving. To get them started he flicked the lead mule's front legs just above the hoof.

Blue moonlight illuminated the countryside helping Rodolfo and his *bandidos* escape north toward the foothills of the Sierra Madre. The night swallowed them up quickly, though the traveling speed with the mules was slower than Rodolfo planned. He kept the group moving, wanting to get as far as they could before daylight and the soldiers woke up.

It was near daylight when the group got to the first hideout south of Zacatecas. They would stay in this protected canyon during daylight and travel only at night, taking turns posting a guard to watch for the soldiers who would surely come after them.

CHAPTER 19

Rafe followed the Tarahumara runners from the village. Even on horseback, Rafe struggled to keep up with the swift Indians. When he and Xihuitl went to the Tarahumara village last year, Rafe learned the Indians could run all day without stopping to rest or for water. It was a survival technique. Watching them again brought joy to his heart as he remembered his days with the Healer. Though at the time he had lost his memory of his past life, the adventures with Xihuitl were clear in his mind.

It took several hours of following the runners as they traversed the narrow trails. Rafe strung the young Appaloosa and packhorse behind him. At the mouth to a large canyon, the runners told Rafe to stop, rest, and wait for Xihuitl. Picketing the horses, he rested against a fallen log at the mouth of the canyon.

The view across the canyon was spectacular. The sun caught the colors of the soil and rock in shades of reds and oranges. The deep blue sky painted a backdrop for green trees and shrubs. Judging by the sun's angle and heat, it was early afternoon.

In the quiet he suddenly heard the Healer's voice say his special name, "Citlalin!" It startled him and he looked expecting to see Xihuitl standing nearby. All he could see was emptiness. "Citlalin!" He heard the voice again and focused on a tiny dot in the distance. He was sure he was hearing the Healer's voice, though the form was quite a distance away.

Rafe stood up and shaded his eyes watching the tiny image moving toward him. As it got closer, he recognized a familiar form riding an old shabby horse. Rafe watched the silhouette as it came into focus and the Healer rode toward him. Confused, Rafe thought the Healer appeared much younger than the old man he left in the hidden village a year ago.

The Healer was dressed in a white loincloth with a red

cape tied to his neck. On his chest he wore a gold breastplate with intricate artwork carved into it. Around his head he wore a headband with short golden feathers thickly spread to cover the top of his head. Leather sandals laced up past his ankles circled his bronzed legs.

"Do not look so shocked Citlalin. It is me, your friend Xihuitl," the Healer said as he arrived and jumped from the horse with a mischievous grin.

"But, you look so much younger. How can that be?" Rafe asked.

"All in due time Citlalin. What brings you back to me?"

"Healer, I brought this young Appaloosa mare for you to replace that old horse. I owe you my life and never had a chance to repay you," Rafe said as he untied the tether and pulled the young Appaloosa to stand beside the Healer.

"Citlalin, she is a magnificent horse! I saw you riding her in my visions. I heard you talking to her and calling her Star."

"Yes I named her Star. I trained her myself at my horse ranch in Santa Fe. How do you know these things?" Rafe asked him.

"Have you forgotten so quickly my young apprentice? The Gods show me wonders."

The Healer stroked the young Appaloosa and patted her neck and face. The horse reacted to him by rubbing her face on his chest and pawed the ground with her right hoof. By the twinkle in the Healer's eyes, Rafe could tell he was pleased with the young mare.

"Star is a good name for a good horse. Come let us sit and rest. We have much to talk about. Did you hear me calling to you?"

"Yes I heard your voice, but you were too far away. I must have been dreaming."

"No, you heard me using my friend the wind to call to you." Though surprised by his words, this time Rafe accepted the Healer's statement and did not question it.

"I have learned many things living in the hidden village. The ancient Aztec ancestors come to me in visions and teach me the old ways," Xihuitl tried to explain.

"You look healthy and happy. Your new life is obviously agreeing with you," Rafe said.

"Yes. The ancestors have been adding years to my life. My visions tell me I have more work to do. I thought I knew enough about medicine and healing, but now I know I have more yet to learn."

Though what the Healer was saying seemed impossible, Rafe believed the old Healer had powers beyond this world. He followed the customs of his parents and a shaman named Tonauac, who practiced the Aztec healing methods and traditions. Xihuitl believed in the power of the ancient Aztec Gods.

"I have been wanting to go to my home in Teotihuacán for some time. The ancestors told me to wait until you came for me. I need to arrange for my property to be given to my nephew and to collect a few of my belongings. I have no need for my old life any longer. We will travel to Mexico City together. Teotihuacán is only a short distance northeast of the city," the Healer said.

"How do you know I am going to Mexico City?" Rafe asked.

"You have a destiny to fulfill there. You have to complete your circle, but it will not be easy," Xihuitl warned. "I will return in one hour, then we will go."

While the Healer returned to the hidden village to gather his things, Rafe pondered the Healer's strange explanations and warnings about Mexico City. As he lay back against a fallen log he scanned the canyon around him. Above him were tall ponderosa pine trees. Near ground level green oak grew amongst the blooming Amapa trees painting the canyons a pinkish purple. In and around the trees night-blooming Cereus cactus created strange shapes with their large arms twisting in all directions. On the ground around him the yellow marigolds attracted honeybees creating a soothing melodic tune which put him to sleep.

"Citlalin, wake up. I am ready to travel." The Healer shook Rafe's shoulder. Stirring, he felt completely rested. The Healer was dressed in traveling clothes and wore an old straw hat Rafe remembered him wearing when they traveled in the hills south of Torreón. The old gray donkey was packed with leather pouches and traveling gear.

Rafe saddled the young mare and adjusted the reins. The young horse had not been ridden for several weeks, so Rafe worried she might shy. Xihuitl stroked the young horse gently patting her neck. When he stepped into the saddle, Star adjusted to Xihuitl's weight and stood patiently.

Rafe climbed up on Rayo and took the reins of the packhorse, while Xihuitl strung the donkey behind him.

They rode side by side across the canyon floor heading south. "Tell me about your business in Mexico City," he asked Rafe. Rafe pondered a minute trying to decide where to start.

"You remember the day the two Chichimeca boys found me shot in the canyon. The man who shot me was *don* Bernardo. I grew up on his *hacienda* as a *peón*. When I was seventeen, he raped my fifteen-year-old sister. In a rage I grabbed my father's flintlock pistol and shot him. I fled north taking this Appaloosa." He paused collecting his thoughts and Xihuitl waited without comment for him to continue.

"Through a number of events, I ended up in Santa Fe with my adopted parents, George and Josefina Summers. My mother and sister were alone at the *hacienda* to fend for themselves. Not a day went by I did not ache for them, but I feared coming back to Mexico. I believed I had murdered the *haciendero* and was a wanted man in Mexico."

"But he was not dead," Xihuitl said.

"Yes, I had only crippled him. He continued to rape my sister in revenge for my actions. When I learned the truth, my friend Carlos and I came to Mexico to rescue my mother and sister and her two children. It was on that trip *don* Bernardo shot me and you saved my life."

"The Goddess Coatlicue, the preserver of life, saved your life. I just gave you food and shelter," Xihuitl said humbly. Rafe understood the Healer's beliefs having spent many hours like this on horseback traveling from village to village in the mountains of Mexico.

"Well, as you know Healer, the lady of fortune

sometimes throws a blow at you and knocks you toward a different path. My mother finally admitted to me the *haciendero* raped her when she was a young girl and I was the result of her terrible tragedy. So the man I hated most in this world is my real father. My mother kept the secret all these years until *don* Bernardo died."

"You killed him?" the Healer asked.

"I wanted to, I planned to, but he died of a heart attack."

"The Gods kept you from that terrible act."

"The laws in Mexico have changed so now the first born of a land holder can inherit his legacy, even if he is a bastard. I am going to Mexico City to claim the *hacienda* and give it to my sister and her man, a childhood friend of mine named, Rodolfo. They are living as *bandidos* in the hills. I believe they are in much danger. If the inheritance goes as planned, I will give them the *hacienda* so they can live in peace."

"Will you stay in Mexico?" the Healer asked.

"No, I will return to Santa Fe. I have a growing horse breeding business there and a woman I love. I will make my life there."

"Citlalin, I wish I could help you in your endeavor, but it is not of my world, but I will ask the Gods for their help on your quest."

Chapter 20

As morning broke, one of the soldiers riding with the silver mule train went to relieve his full bladder behind some shrubs. Stumbling back toward the burnt fire, he saw the superintendent tied to a tree. The soldier ran to wake the sergeant.

"Despertarse, despertarse," the soldier shook the sergeant's shoulder. As usual he was hungover, groggy, and slow to wake up.

"Mira," he hissed pointing to the mine superintendent tied and gagged. Sancho's head lolled to one side, with a piece of his shirt wrapped around his mouth as a gag.

"¿Está muerto?" he asked the soldier if Sancho was dead. The sleepy sergeant was now fully awake and concerned. He knew he would be to blame if Sancho was dead and the silver stolen. It would be his neck in a noose for this. Glancing to where the silver pouches were stacked, he breathed a sigh of relief to see the sacks still piled on top of each other.

"See if he is alive," the sergeant ordered the soldier. *"Lvántate,"* the sergeant kicked the boots of the other four soldiers to waken them.

The first soldier knelt beside Sancho and rocked his shoulder. Sancho groaned and slowly came around. Quickly removing the gag and untying his hands, the soldier asked him what happened. *"Oye, ¿qué te ha pasado?"*

"El bandido me asaltó," Sancho told him bandits assaulted him. "Go check on the silver," he ordered the sergeant as he struggled to stand up on wobbly knees.

It was only then, Sancho noticed Maxorro gagged and tied near the mules. "Untie him," he shouted at a soldier.

"Oye, four sacks of silver bars are missing," the sergeant reported.

"Hijo de puta," Sancho cursed. "This is your fault. Where was the guard?"

Chaos reigned at the campsite. Sancho yelled at the

Indians. They shook their heads and said they saw nothing in the night. Sancho knew he would get blamed for this and he would go to jail if he did not recover the silver. It was his duty to get the entirety of the silver load to the mint in Mexico City. His brain swirled with the problem before him – he could not trust these soldiers to deliver the silver and he could not leave it here with them and go off after the *bandidos*. One thing he knew for sure, he probably would no longer have a job, even if he did recover the silver. He would blame it on the soldiers, but he doubted it would make much difference. He would get blamed as well.

"Señor, ¿qué hacemos ahora?" the sergeant startled him when he asked him what they should do now.

Sancho made his decision. "Send one of your men back to the mine and report the robbery and tell them to send someone to escort the silver to the mint. Tell them I will go after the robbers."

Maxorro stepped to where the mine superintendent was talking to the soldiers. "They took two of my mules. I saw their faces. I recognized one of them. I will go with you and I will track them. Tell them to send another muleteer," he said to Sancho.

Sancho pondered Maxorro's words. He forgot about the old Cazcanes Indian muleteer and the mules. "You saw their faces? You could recognize them?" he asked.

"Sí. I believe they will head north. I am a good tracker. You want to find the silver and I want to find my mules, no?"

"Tell them to send someone to drive the mules and two more soldiers. Tell them to hurry," he barked at the soldier and sent him back to the mine.

For the rest of the day, Sancho either sat by himself or screamed at the soldiers. He blamed them for this mess. They were barely passable as soldiers, the dregs of the military. As usual, they were drunk and passed out. He would be blamed for that. It was his responsibility to run the mule train in a manner to provide protection and he was charged with getting the silver to the mint. In seventeen years, though he had contemplated being robbed he never felt threatened.

He questioned the Indians and Maxorro again for any information. The Indians saw nothing and Maxorro only said he thought he recognized one of the *bandidos* as a stranger who was at the *pulqueria* in Zacatecas. A young man who said he was from Torreón.

Sancho posted a soldier as a guard throughout the day and into the night. No *pulque* was passed around the campfire. Maxorro tended to his mules and the Indians enjoyed a day of rest. As night fell, Sancho decided on a new plan.

Late that night after all the others were asleep, Sancho quietly crept over to the silver bags. Earlier in the day he located some rocks about the same size and weight as a bar of the silver. In silence he opened two of the pouches and removed a bar of silver from each, replacing them with the rocks. The heavy bars he took to his saddlebags and buried them at the bottom. Then he curled by the fire and went to sleep.

In the morning, the soldiers returned with a mine representative and a new mule master. The mine representative interrogated Sancho about the events of the robbery.

"Where were you when they took it," he was asked.

"I was asleep. The soldiers posted a guard. Do I not get time to sleep?" he retorted angrily.

"What about the soldiers, why did they not help you?"

"As usual, they were drunk and passed out," Sancho admitted.

"You are responsible for this silver mule train. Why did you let the soldiers get drunk?"

"I cannot watch them every minute. They hid the *pulque* amongst them," he answered. He knew the mine representative knew the ways of the slovenly soldiers, but in this instance Sancho was to blame.

"Are you going after them?"

"Yes, Maxorro and I will leave immediately. I will take two soldiers with me. I will bring the silver back to the mine along with the heads of the *bandidos*. I promise you that!" His eyes narrowed as he said it, hiding the uncertainty he could find the *bandidos*.

Even as he said it, Sancho thought the plan ridiculous. The *bandidos* could be anywhere. His chances of actually finding them and recovering the silver were slim. He would give it a week, then kill Maxorro and the two soldiers and escape with the silver in his saddlebags. He could go north to Texas or New Mexico and live out his days in luxury.

Chapter 21

Doña Carmela adjusted to the boring life at *don* Luis' Jalisco *hacienda*. After the ruckus in Mexico City, at least she felt safe here. She spent her time ordering the servants to make special meals and to rearrange the furniture to her liking. Each morning a young girl helped her bathe and dress and in the evening a servant washed her feet and brushed her hair. It was the type of treatment she expected and relished. At night, she and Luis lay wrapped in each other's arms. Like the old days with Bernardo, Luis was an ardent and lustful lover, even more attentive to her every whim.

She decided Luis was right and she should give up any claim to the *hacienda* in Torreón. She did not need it, nor did she really want it. She gave Luis her answer and told him she would marry him. He had enough money to keep her happy. They would make a life here in Jalisco until the unrest in Mexico City died down, then they would spend time in both places.

She just finished her bath and dressed when she heard hoof beats in the courtyard. Carmela was sitting at her vanity table trying to decide on her jewelry for the day when a servant delivered a letter to her. It was sealed with the crest of her lawyer, Alirio Mansano. She read it quickly.

Señora,
I have received word a claim has been made on the Reyes hacienda. I will dissuade the officials from making a formal decision on the claim until you have returned. The claimant's name is Rafael Reyes de Estrada. He is claiming his right as the first born male of don Bernardo Reyes.
Please advise me of your wishes.
My most sincere regards,
Alirio Mansano

The letter floated from her hand to the floor as a rage built inside her. Rafael was María's brother and the *peón* who shot Bernardo. At first she could not believe the words on the paper. Surely there was a mistake. How could Bernardo have kept this secret all these years?

After her disbelief dissipated, anger swelled in her bosom. The face staring back at her from the mirror scowled, showing the crinkly lines around the eyes and near the mouth. Rafael must be in his early twenties. It meant Bernardo could not even keep his *pene* buttoned in his *pantalones* in their early days of marriage when she was young and full of lust. Carmela picked up her hairbrush and angrily ran it through her hair. How could he humiliate her this way?

"Desgraciado," she cursed her wretched dead ex-husband. "Rot in hell."

Finally calming herself a bit, Carmela gathered herself went to find Luis.

"Ah querida, did you rest well?" he said as she floated into the parlor.

Holding the letter in her hand, she waved it toward him. "The *pinche baboso* who shot Bernardo is his bastard. He has made a claim on the land."

"¿Qué?" he asked what she meant.

"Alirio sent this letter saying the *peón* has made a claim on the *hacienda* in Torreón. He claims to be the legal heir of Bernardo and he has proof."

"Do not distress yourself so, my love. We have decided our future and you do not need the money," Luis told her wondering why she was suddenly upset again over the property.

"This is not about the money. I will never allow that *peón* to inherit the Reyes property. I will not allow him to disgrace me so."

"It is no disgrace. So the boy is a bastard. He will always be *mestizo*. Let him have the worthless piece of land. I will give you this and so much more," Luis stood and took Carmela in his arms, but she pushed him away.

"No, I will not let him have it. Never! I'm returning to Mexico City." Carmela turned leaving the room with Luis staring at her back. No man could understand her anger. Spanish *dons* felt it their right to take a mistress. She could barely abide Bernardo's violation of María. He was older then, she less in love with him, and they made love only occasionally. She almost understood Rafael's rage when he shot Bernardo for his sister's rape. She too was livid when she found out María was pregnant and Bernardo the father.

María's mother was a different story. Carmela was young and beautiful and in her prime. She and Bernardo made love regularly, sometimes more than once a day. Still he violated Celiá and now Rafael was making a claim for the land. This could never have happened when *gachupíns* ruled the country. She cursed President Juárez for giving *peóns* rights as she stormed up to her bedroom.

"Pack my things," she screamed at the maid.

"Sí señora."

Hearing Carmela screaming at the maid, Luis knew her mind was made up. She was not a timid woman and not one to be controlled. Perhaps it was why she was such a passionate lover. Resigned to her wishes, he sent a servant to find Buck, his bodyguard. When Buck walked into the parlor, Luis explained the situation.

"Buck, you are taking *doña* Carmela to my house in Mexico City and you are to stay with her and keep her safe," he ordered his gunman. "I will return as soon as I finish my business with *don* Cenobio. Do not let anything happen to my beloved or I will feed your *cojones* to the dogs," he warned.

"Do not worry *patrón* she will be safe," Buck assured him.

"If I am not back, go with her to the Land Management hearing. We shall see how the judge rules. If he rules against Carmela, I will deal with the *peón* with money."

"Why don't I just kill him before he shows up for the hearing?" Buck asked thinking it an easy solution.

"I agree, why not just kill him and save me a lot of grief?" Carmela sneered. The men had not heard her return to the parlor. The maid was following her down the stairs carrying two large traveling bags.

"No mi querida, I want no trouble for you. I would rather buy him out. The poor ignorant *peón* will take the money and drink himself to death. You know how they are

when they get a little money in their pockets," Luis said smirking as he said it.

Luis called for his carriage and helped Carmela into the coach. Her bags were loaded on top and Buck mounted his horse. After Luis kissed Carmela and closed the coach door, he walked back to Buck. "If a hair on her head is harmed, you are a dead man," the *don* hissed at him.

"*Sí patrón.*"

CHAPTER 22

Rafe and the Healer had been traveling south for four days from the canyons of the Sierra Madre. In every direction yucca and scrubby bushes eked out an existence in the arid soil. They filled the days talking, remembering, and enjoying their time together. Rafe found the Healer to be a wealth of knowledge about the history of Mexico and of the land and people. He had answers to all of Rafe's questions.

"Look up ahead. There is Mexico City," the Healer said pointing to the distant horizon.

At first Rafe thought it was a mirage in the early morning clouds, until the shapes came into better focus. As they approached a huge mountain range came into view. It rimmed a valley containing a vast lake. Mexico City sat in the middle of the huge lake, bigger than any city Rafe had ever seen. Causeways over the water connected the city to the valley from four main directions. Rafe never imagined such a sight. Arriving at the top of a knoll overlooking the city, Rafe was speechless. He had traveled to Chicago and other large cities with George Summers, but none of those cities were as beautiful as this.

The lake surrounding the city was teeming with small boats. People on foot and in wagons, carts, and carriages traversed the causeways in and out of the city. The peaks of large red rooftops jutted several stories above the flat-topped roofs of most of the city. From his vantage point he noticed the city streets were organized in a grid, except, one main road ran diagonal from the northwest to the southeast across the city. Beyond the city and to the southeast, Rafe saw two huge snow capped mountains.

As if reading his mind the Healer explained, "Many, many years ago this vast mountain range of volcanoes created the lake you see around the city. The remnants of the volcanoes are usually snowcapped all throughout the year. The Aztecs built their capital city here for the natural protection it provided. Citlalin, imagine what this would have looked like before the Spaniards rebuilt the city. You would be looking at Tenochtitlán – the center of the Aztec world. Come let us go into what is left of the old Aztec city," the Healer said.

They entered from the northern causeway teeming with *Indios* and *mestizos* hauling or carrying vegetables, baskets, pottery, sheep, firewood and countless other goods to be sold in the city. The *peóns* quickly moved aside for ornate carriages carrying the nobles. Rafe watched as a carriage driver struck a *peón* carrying a bundle of firewood on his back for not moving quickly enough and forcing the driver to slow down. The action triggered his instinctive anger over the *peón's* treatment.

Rafe and the Healer struggled to stay together amongst the busy traffic crossing the causeway. As they approached the center of the city, the houses became more ornate with iron railings forming small balconies on the second story windows of the houses. It reminded him of Santa Fe and Torreón, only on an immense scale.

"Chile verde!" a man yelled he had green chili to sell on one side of the street.

On the other side a man with a large stack of wood called out, *"Leña!"*

All around him people with carts were selling their wares of watermelon, vegetables, pastries and flowers. *"Sandía!" "Verduras!" "Pasteles!" "Flores!"* The calls of the vendors filled the air.

They rode past houses finally reaching an area with huge buildings. The buildings stretched in all directions, starting as single story and some as tall as four stories high. Made of quarried stone, the big buildings were ornately decorated by carved murals and pointed stone cupolas trimming the roofs. The Healer led Rafe to the Zócalo, the main plaza of the city's center. Rafe estimated it was ten times larger than Santa Fe's plaza, maybe bigger.

The plaza was alive with activity. People strolled, rode horseback or in carriages or carts. The center of the Zócalo was lush with cobblestone paths crisscrossing through the gardens. The lush gardens struck a sharp contrast to the brown cobblestone roads of the city.

"This is the heart of Mexico City. Over there is the Cathedral," the Healer pointed it out to Rafe. "It was built on top of Templo Mayor, one of the Aztec's major temples of Tenochtitlán. The Spaniards tore it down and used the stones to build the Cathedral," Xihuitl explained.

The Cathedral's architecture was elaborate. The huge church had two square towers on either side of the massive front entrance. Rafe estimated the towers were over ten stories tall with what looked like round bell spires at the top. The main portions of the building had enormous domed roofs. Carvings of stone and buttresses decorated the rooflines.

As they rode along, two-story government buildings with tall windows covered by iron railings and balconies stretched the entire length of the block. The Healer explained the front walls were really a fortress facade. The actual buildings were within the wall's protection.

They rode around the plaza seeing it from all angles. Xihuitl tried to describe the city as it was in the glorious days of the Aztec Empire. "What you see now are Mexico City's government buildings. In the time of the Aztecs this was the center of all religious activity. Here stood the main temples dedicated to the Aztec Gods – Huitzilopochtli, Tlaloc, and Quetzalcóatl. Also in this area you would have found schools and quarters for the priests along with a court for the ritual ballgame. Around the city is where the common people lived and grew crops. I cannot even describe how grandiose Tenochtitlán must have been in the days of the Aztecs. I can only imagine it a vision of grandeur."

They finally stopped and dismounted near a part of the plaza where vendors used makeshift booths to sell their wares. Everything from saddles, baskets, meat, fish, vegetables, fruit, flowers, goats, pigs, and hot food were available. The Healer headed to a booth where an Indian woman was serving a group of men waiting in line. He ordered two bowls of *atole,* which was a thin gruel made of maize flour flavored with fruits and chilies and two clay cups of hot chocolate.

"Enjoy Citlalin. This is a meal which would have been served to your Aztec ancestors," he said. Rafe found it intriguing how Xihuitl assumed he had Aztec ancestors.

They sat on a stone bench and watched the busy plaza as they ate. Rafe first took a small taste of the *atole*. The sweetness of the fruit and spice of the chili exploded on his tongue in an unusual combination of flavors. The hot chocolate was spun into a frothy sweet drink.

Rafe's eyes took in the sights, his ears took in the sounds, and his nose took in the many aromas of the plaza. It was 1871 and the people around him were descendents of Aztecs and Spaniards. The horse, brought by Spanish conquistadors to the New World, was now commonplace. Carts and carriages traversed the large plaza's roads. Soldiers in Army uniforms patrolled the streets with rifles hung over their backs. The ladies wore fancy dresses of the latest European styles, more stylish than most in Santa Fe. He thought Ana Teresa would be stunning in one of the elaborate gowns.

Children ran around the plaza in glee. They chased balls with sticks and chased one another in the carefree joy of children. The vendors, dressed in simple *camisas* and *pantalones,* were Indian or *mestizo,* though were not shabby. Rafe thought the life of a *peón* here in Mexico City was probably better than in the rural areas.

He let his imagination take him to a time before the Spanish conquistadors, when the city was known as Tenochtitlán. The Healer had told him stories of the glorious reign of the Aztec Empire as well as how they performed the rituals of human sacrifice to the Aztec Gods. He tried to picture the Templo Mayor, the major pyramid, where the Aztecs practiced these sacrifices. Xihuitl described it as having two grand staircases leading up to a tall temple on top. One side was for Huitzilopochtli, the God of War and the other for Tlaloc, the God of Rain. At the time of the Aztecs, it would have been the tallest structure in the city.

Rafe watched in fascination as a group of young boys played a game with a wooden ball. Tall wooden poles stood on either side and the object was obviously to get the ball through the hoop hanging from the pole. The Healer explained it was a game which had been played for hundreds of years. In the time of the Aztecs, the ball and hoop were made of stone.

"Citlalin, I must be on my way," the Healer said bringing him back to the moment, as Rafe was spellbound watching all the sights and sounds of the city.

"Yes, I have much to do myself. Tell me where to find a hotel so I can clean up and rest," Rafe said.

"Come, follow me. Over there on the west side is the Portal de Mercaderes building. On the upper floors are hotel rooms overlooking the plaza." The Healer took the reins of the young Appaloosa mare and walked it across the plaza toward the Portal Hotel. Rafe followed pulling Rayo and the packhorse.

Arriving in front of a four-story building the Healer turned to Rafe and said, "Citlalin, I must leave you here. If you need me for anything, I will be at my home in Teotihuacán for several weeks. Just ask for the Healer, Xihuitl. Everyone knows me there. *Ma cualli ohtli,"* he wished him good luck in his native Nahuatl language.

"Gracias Xihuitl, I will remember." Rafe thanked him and said goodbye with an *abrazo.*

As the Healer rode off, Rafe asked the doorman to look after Rayo and the packhorse while he checked in at the front desk. Though the outside of the building was rather plain in comparison to some of the ornate buildings on the plaza, the opulence of the interior stunned him. The lobby opened four stories high. The rooms opened onto a balcony surrounded by ornate iron railings. The highly polished wood railings were trimmed with gold. Huge chandeliers with hundreds of candles hung from thick chains. Rich burgundy and beige tapestries hung on the windows.

As he crossed the large foyer, he felt the stares of several eyes. Dressed in dusty traveling clothes and not his suit, Rafe suddenly felt out of place. The thought they might not even let him stay here bothered him. Taking a deep breath and squaring his shoulders, he strode across the highly polished marble to the hotel's desk.

"¿A su servicio?" the clerk greeted him in a tradition manner asking how he could be of service.

"Soy Rafael Reyes de Estrada de Santa Fe, Nuevo México" Rafe introduced himself in a formal customary Spanish manner. "I require a room and stabling for my horses."

"Por supuesto," certainly, the clerk replied turning the guest book toward Rafe.

Rafe gave the desk clerk several *pesos* and instructed him to send a runner to fetch his belongings and take the horses to the Portal's stables.

"I have been traveling from Torreón and require a bath and a shave. Is there someplace I can go?" Rafe asked.

"Señor, hot water will be brought up to your room. I will send our barber to your room in an hour," the desk clerk told him.

Rafe walked up the stairs and found his room. The elegance of the decor in the room was equal to the lobby. A large vase of fresh flowers had been placed on a table. Two large doors stood open allowing a slight breeze to stir. Each door opened to a balcony, one facing north and another facing east. He could see the Zócalo plaza in both directions.

After a long, hot bath, Rafe felt refreshed from the days on horseback. He tried to forget why he was here and concentrated on the sights and sounds of the city. Music floating from the plaza through the open doors of the balcony drew his attention. Below him, strolling groups of musicians played guitars and sang. The sun was dipping over the mountains to the west. He dressed and walked outside on the plaza level. Mexico City's temperate climate and a slight breeze was intoxicating when mixed with the smell of the flowering bushes which lined the plaza. It was near dusk and the plaza was beginning to come alive with some festivities.

More street vendors selling food had their carts parked along the *paseo.* Children carried paper cones of roasted nuts or other sweets. Rafe stopped and bought two meat *empanadas.* The Plaza was starting to come alive with carriages circling the *paseo,* carrying *señoritas* and their chaperones as the gaslights began to illuminate the night.

Young *caballeros* dressed in their best *trajes* on their blooded horses strutted alongside the carriages flirting with the *señoritas* who were hiding behind their fluttering silk fans. The chaperones did their best to discourage the dandies, but the ritual continued.

Rafe tried to watch the Spanish ritual without emotion. It brought back the memory of the terrible incident with Diego de la Torre at the plaza in Santa Fe. Diego wanted to kill him, because Rafe was not a pure-blooded Spaniard, but a *mestizo*. Diego thought it was only a Spaniard's right to engage in the procession and to charm Ana Teresa. A man such as Rafe, a *mestizo* and *peón,* was not allowed. Though he tried to forget, tried not to let the image bother him, the nagging feeling of inferiority persisted. Even though Diego was dead for his pompous actions, Rafe's love, Ana Teresa, had been sent away. She was sent to her family in Spain because of him, because a *mestizo* was not good enough for a Spanish woman. The nagging feeling turned into anger and then a seething rage. Rafe turned and walked back to the hotel wondering when the world would change.

CHAPTER 23

Rodolfo and his gang of *bandidos* rode by night and rested by day after they robbed the silver muletrain. They were making good time on an obscure trail heading north. They took turns scouting ahead and behind waiting for a posse of soldiers to come looking for them.

"*Jefe,* I saw a few Indios trailing six scrawny cattle some miles back," Pepe reported on the afternoon of the third day. "Do you want Hector and me to go take one of the cows? We have not had meat since we left Zacatecas."

They had been on the trail for three days and everyone was hungry. "No, let the Indians keep their cattle. You know we cannot burn a fire. It could be seen for miles and we cannot take that chance," he told Pepe.

Pepe grumbled at him, but not with much fervor. His friends, these *bandidos,* were used to living without. They believed in their right to be free men and knew with that right came danger and hardship. Like Rodolfo, they did not want a *hacendero's* whip on their back.

They lived on stale tortillas and chewed on jerky. Rodolfo's stomach growled like the rest of his friends. The twelve bars of heavy silver were strapped to the backs of the mules. Each time they stopped, Rodolfo unloaded the mules as he had seen the muleteer do.

He pondered the value of what they stole. He was sure it was a fortune. On the many long hours of trekking though the wilderness on their way north, Rodolfo pondered a bigger problem than his current hunger. The plan to steal the silver had been at first a dream. Paco painted the lure of the silver trains and he let the dream entice him. Surprisingly they actually executed the plan and with the exception he underestimated the weight of the silver, things had gone well.

What he failed to contemplate was there seemed no way to exchange the silver bars for food or ammunition. The first day they stopped and unloaded the mules, he and the men inspected their booty. Much to his dismay, each bar was stamped with the mine's mark. Any attempt to exchange the bars for money could easily identify the bars as stolen.

As his *bandidos* celebrated their exploits, Rodolfo grew more and more worried. He and his men had a fortune in their grasp and yet it might as well be a burden of worthless rocks. He did not have the heart to tell them, when they laughed and cajoled each other reliving the robbery.

As the sun began to grow low in the western sky, Rodolfo told Hector and Paco to get the mules loaded. He told Pepe to cut a branch of mesquite. At each stop they wiped away the evidence of their campsite.

Paco and Hector loaded the first mule and were working on the second one. The mule brayed loudly and he heard Paco curse. Rodolfo looked up at the sudden sound. Paco slapped the stubborn mule and in a swift move, the mule kicked Hector squarely in the chest knocking him to the ground with a thud.

"¡Mierda!" Paco cursed trying to steady the mule.

"¿Estás bien?" Walking toward him, Rodolfo asked Hector if he was okay.

All Hector could do was move his head back and forth. His eyes stung in pain. His chest burned.

"Can you move?" Rodolfo asked him.

"No se. No puedo respirar," Hector whispered telling Rodolfo he could barely breathe.

Rocking back on his haunches, Rodolfo did not know what to do, but he knew he would not leave Hector to die.

"Unload the mules," he barked at Paco and Pepe. Rodolfo continued to bark orders and about an hour later Hector was lying on two blankets under the shade of a mesquite tree. Pepe was off trying to snare a rabbit for dinner. With all precautions put aside, if Pepe came back with a rabbit, they would cook it over a fire tonight. Hector needed the food to keep strong.

Rodolfo was unsure about Hector's injury. He said it hurt to breathe and he cried out when they moved him onto the blankets. He certainly could not ride in this condition. A large purple bruise covered the right side of his chest. Rodolfo wished María were here. She knew about medicine and about treating wounds. She had helped a man gored by a bull by using fire to cauterize the gash. Hector's wound, however, was not external. His insides were damaged.

Pepe returned with two small rabbits. Quickly starting a fire, Paco and Pepe skinned and cooked the meat. Pepe also gathered some tuberous cactus, which he chopped and simmered in the juices of the rabbits. The moon had already risen by the time the meal was ready. Dividing up the meal, Rodolfo cut two extra portions for Hector, which he wrapped in a cloth. Hector would need the extra food later.

"*Gracias* Hector. I guess that old mule wanted us to eat," Paco teased Hector for his injury.

"*Sí amigo*. You can get better now. Our bellies are full and we should be on our way," Pepe said.

Hector grunted in reply. Rodolfo smiled knowing Pepe and Paco were concerned for Hector, but it was the way with these *bandidos* to tease each other.

Rodolfo stamped out the fire after the meal and told the men to get some sleep. He sent no one to check their backtrail. If the soldiers were after them and saw the fire, they would not travel at night.

As he lay staring at the stars in the night sky, he wondered why they had not seen any soldiers and no one seemed to be chasing them. He knew once the theft was discovered, the mine superintendent would mount a posse. Paco asked him why he did not kill the abusive *jefe*. Rodolfo replied it was not necessary, but in truth Rodolfo had never killed a man. To his friends, he bragged about killing *haciendemos* and *vaqueros*. All the *bandidos* talked of killing. Few probably had shot or maybe even killed someone in a fair fight.

For the most part, the gang used their pistols for protection and for hunting. These *peóns* had been farmers, not *vaqueros*. They were not violent by nature. If they robbed a carriage, they would brandish their gun to intimidate, not to kill. The *señoritas* and *señoras* would scream and quickly hand over their jewelry and coin.

Over the past two days, Rodolfo kept to little used trails and open wilderness, though he thought a tracker could pick up their trail without much difficulty. Perhaps something had drawn them off in the wrong direction. This part of Mexico was mostly uninhabited wilderness. If the mine superintendent thought they went south, perhaps they had a chance to escape.

Rodolfo finally fell asleep to the sounds of the nighttime insects. In the morning he would have to make a decision about Hector.

Chapter 24

In the morning, Rafe woke to a light cool breeze blowing through the open balcony doors. Last night he was overwhelmed by the sights and sounds of Mexico City, especially the ritualistic courting procession on the Zócalo. It brought back bad memories. It was a similar ritual on the *paseo* in Santa Fe where Diego became offended and said Rafe was inferior and not allowed. It was the reason he and Diego fought in the street and why Diego was dead.

This morning he committed himself to forget the past and stand tall. He was an American, not a *peón,* and he vowed to remember it, no matter what happened.

When he walked downstairs for breakfast, he asked the desk clerk to send a message to *Señor David Salazar de Rosas de Colonia Coyoacán. Don* David was Carlos' uncle and Carlos had written to him about Rafe's trip. His uncle replied to say he would be welcome.

After breakfast he strolled the plaza. A few stores were just opening, and he purchased two silk scarves, one for Josefina and another for his mother Celiá. By ten in the morning, people were filtering onto the plaza for the day's activities. By Mexico City standards, the plaza was practically empty, but it would have been a busy morning in Santa Fe.

When he returned to the hotel, the desk clerk motioned to him.

"The man waiting outside in the carriage is here to take you to the *Salazar* home. I have taken the liberty to have your horses readied," the clerk said.

"*Gracias.* Tell the driver I will pack quickly and be ready to go."

Up in his room Rafe packed. Carrying his own satchel, he strode down the stairs and walked outside to the parked carriage. Rayo and the packhorse stood quietly tied to the rear and the coach's door stood open.

"*Señor Reyes, por favor,*" the driver greeted him and took his bag.

As they traveled southwest of the Zócalo to Colonia Coyoacán, Rafe noticed how the neighborhood had narrow cobblestone streets and small plazas. The homes were exquisite old colonials of purely Spanish architecture. Each window was covered by intricate iron bars with hanging flowers dripping over the railing. The walls were made of smooth stucco, with carved stone facades around the windows and doorways. Each home was built around a large front courtyard surrounded by a dense hedge or wall.

The driver pulled to a stop in front of a two-story large home built in a U-shape around the lush interior gardens. Fragrant flowers permeated the afternoon from the large garden courtyard. A servant ran out the front door to the carriage. He bowed to Rafe, as he stepped to the ground. A middle-aged man walked briskly down the front steps and greeted Rafe.

"Soy David Salazar de Rosas a su servicio," don David stuck out his hand saying he was at his service and Rafe took it. He wondered how this man and his family would receive him. Carlos had told him, "Do not worry. My family in Mexico City are a mix of *criollo* and *mestizos.* You will be welcome."

"Soy Rafael Reyes de Estrada," Rafe said to Carlos' uncle and bowed slightly.

"Come, we have been expecting you. The family is anxious to meet Carlos' *Americano* friend. As they walked into the main door of the home, music and a woman's voice filled the hallway, though it was a song Rafe did not recognize. The woman's voice pleased his ears.

Don David walked to a door on the left side of the grand stairway and pushed in the doors.

"Carlota, Carlos' *Americano* friend has arrived. Stop your practicing." The young woman at the piano stopped playing and rose walking toward her father. She stopped in front of Rafe and *don* David and bowed.

"Encantada de conocerte señor," she said.

"Igualmente, señorita," Rafe replied he was equally happy to meet her.

"May I finish my practicing later *Papá?"*

"Sí mijita."

Don David led Rafe to large chairs in front of a dark fireplace. No fire was necessary today in this temperate Mexico City weather. *Don* David motioned for Rafe to sit and he sat across from him.

"Carlos wrote to me when he killed Benicío and followed you and *Señor* Summers to Santa Fe. He said you saved his life. I understand he is to be married soon?" *don* David asked after he lit a cigar and offered one to Rafe.

"Yes, in September to Bibiana de Soto. They are very much in love. I hope I will be able to return to Santa Fe in time for the wedding. It is taking me more time here in Mexico than I expected."

"Carlos wrote to me about your inheritance in Torreón. Tell me more."

Rafe leaned forward in the plush chair and explained the situation concerning the inheritance. It was difficult to admit his mother's rape and the circumstances of his birth, but *don* David did not react negatively to the information. Rafe explained how he hoped to inherit the land and property and give it to his sister and Rodolfo. *Don* David's only response was to nod his head in understanding.

"I am not a lawyer, but the new laws of President Benito Juárez are benefiting *mestizos*. It is about time my country started to treat all its people with respect."

"You support the new president's reforms then?" Rafe asked a bit surprised.

"Yes. My family and I are typical of many here in Mexico. My ancestors arrived from Spain in the 1500s. They landed in Veracruz, but later made their way to Mexico City. One of my early ancestors married an Aztec woman of royalty. Later more of the family made the journey from Spain and joined the family here. They were wool merchants. Later they also grew and exported cocoa to Spain." It was now *don* David's turn to discuss his family's dark secrets.

"Since arriving to New Spain our linage is *criollo* and *mestizo;* we have all been born here. The ruling *gachupíns* instituted the *casta* system to persecute the Indians and to discourage Spanish colonists from inter-marrying with the natives. The Catholic Church believed the Indians were pagans and therefore inferior. Over the many generations, it was impossible to stop Spaniards from marrying natives. There were many in my family who married native Indians. I carry Indian blood in my body," *don* David admitted.

"But you live here in Colonia Coyoacán as a Spaniard and not a *mestizo?*" Rafe asked.

"Yes. Like so many here in Mexico, my ancestors were able to pay the local church to falsify birth certificates. The *casta* system is governed by two things, a person's status according to their birth certificate and their physical appearance. If a person looked Spanish, they could pass freely in Mexican society. Later, in the early 1700s some of our family went to the Kingdom of New Mexico. Carlos is from that group of our family."

Don David's explanation left Rafe confused. *Don* David lived well in Mexico City, a respected man, while Rafe was raised a *peón* on *don* Bernardo's *hacienda,* but they were both *mestizo.* It made him think of the day he and Carlos rode to the de Soto ranch for the fiesta. It was the day he met Ana Teresa. Rafe worried about pretending to be a *caballero* and Carlos told him, "You can be whatever they believe you are."

A servant entered the room. *"Señor,* supper has been served in the dining room and the *señora* is waiting for you."

"Come let us join the family," *don* David said. "While you are here, you are our honored guest. Whatever you require, just ask and one of the servants will serve you."

Rafe followed his host to a huge dining room lit by candelabras with multiple candles. The table seated sixteen and four spots were empty. They took two of the empty spots, *don* David at the head of the table. After all were seated, *don* David clinked a silver spoon on a crystal glass. *"Por favor, atención a todos,"* he called for everyone's attention. "I want to introduce Rafael Reyes de Estrada. He is here from Santa Fe, New Mexico in the United States on personal government business. Please make him feel at home."

Rafe was sitting across from Carlota. She smiled coyly at him and then looked away. A young man sitting next to Carlota asked Rafe about Santa Fe. Rafe explained he was a horse breeder and many questions followed.

Huge platters of spiced meat and potatoes were served with fresh tortillas. Baked squash and fresh tomatoes were offered. Everyone at the table was talking and laughing. It was a family of all ages, some young, some old and they all greeted him warmly and made him feel welcome. For the first time in his life, he felt truly welcome in his homeland of Mexico.

CHAPTER 25

Buck sipped black coffee in the garden courtyard of *don* Luis' house in the affluent neighborhood called Colonia San Ángel about five miles south of the city center. He was not a happy man. The *don* gave him strict orders to guard his mistress. For the six day coach trip from Jalisco, Carmela complained about every bump, the heat, and the dust as if it was his fault. She acted as if Buck was her personal servant. She insisted on him calling her *patróna,* meaning she was his boss, bowing and helping her in and out of the carriage. Once he did not respond *"Sí, patróna,"* and the woman hissed at him. She was not *don* Luis' wife, at least not yet, and she certainly was not his boss. In fact, Buck thought her not much better than a high priced *puta.*

Since they arrived two days ago, he enjoyed a bit more freedom from her venom as there were servants here at the house. The city was quiet and it seemed as if the *peón* uprisings were under control. Buck stayed all day and all night at the house, even though *doña* Carmela told him he could go. The *don* had explicitly threatened to kill Buck if anything happened to her, and Buck took the *don* at his word.

"Buck, estoy lista para ir," *doña* Carmela called out saying she was ready to go, startling him out of his thoughts.

He helped her to the carriage and asked where she wanted to go, *"Bueno patróna, para donde?"* She handed him a small traveling bag and stepped up and into the coach.

"En primer lugar, quiero visitar a mi amiga Mariana y segundo que me llevara a casa de mi madre. Voy a pasar la noche. Se llega por mí mañana por la tarde," she told him first he was to take her to visit her friend, Mariana. Then he was to drive her to her mother's house. She would be spending the night there and then he could pick her up tomorrow afternoon.

"Sí, patróna," Buck replied and closed the carriage door.

Buck waited for Carmela at her friend's home for over four hours in the hot sun. The nasty woman treated him like a servant and not a bodyguard. Finally she floated out of the front door and down the steps to the courtyard where he and the carriage waited.

"Deja ir a la casa de mi madre," she said. Buck refused to acknowledge her command verbally, though helped her into the carriage and closed the door. When they reached her mother's home, Buck asked, "The *don* said I was to protect you at all times."

"Do not be silly, Buck. I am safe at my mother's house. Be here at noon tomorrow. I will be ready to go."

After Buck drove the carriage back to the *don's* house, he saddled his horse, Bala. He knew exactly where he wanted to go. First, El Tío Pepe's Cantina for drinks and gambling, then La Ruiseñor, the Nightingale brothel, for a young *puta* or maybe two.

When he pushed in the door at Tío Pepe's, his friend Salvador Perez de Aguilar was already playing roulette. He had just won a big pot.

"Hola Salvador," Back said. Judging by the pile of chips in front of Salvador, he was on a winning streak. "Looks like you are having a good night."

"Buck. Where have you been?"

"Jalisco, then guarding my *jefe's puta.*" Buck called Carmela exactly what he thought she was, a whore.

"La policía have been keeping the *peóns* from roving the streets and causing trouble. Remember the last time I saw you, we had to escape to the roof." The two *caballeros* laughed and Buck laid down a bet on Red 14. The croupier spun the wheel and both Buck and Salvador lost. Buck played three spins, losing all three, before he headed to the bar to get a drink.

"Tequila, a bottle," Buck told the bartender. "Not that rot gut stuff either."

The bartender put a bottle of Cuervo on the bar and Buck put down two *pesos*. "Do you want a glass, Buk?" the bartender asked in a thick Spanish accent.

"No, no glass." Buck replied.

He wandered to a table where a man was dealing Monte. He never had much luck at the roulette wheel, but with Monte he usually at least broke even. Buck had been at the Monte table and drank more than half of the bottle of tequila when Salvador pushed his shoulder.

"Eh Buck, ever since you got here my luck has soured. I'm ready for a *puta*," Salvador complained. Buck had a small winning streak going at the Monte table, but he rose to join his friend. Grabbing the bottle, they walked out the door and down the street to the Nightingale.

Arriving at the brothel, Madam Lucia greeted them. *"Buenas noches, señores,"* she purred. As usual they waited in the parlor for the madame to parade the available women.

The first woman was Juanita. She was *mestizo* with tan skin and dark eyes. Though she was probably only thirty, Buck thought she was too old and wornout to be interesting.

Next Lucia brought out a red headed and freckled woman who called herself Bridgette. Salvador quickly jumped up and paid the madame for her, leaving Buck sitting alone, waiting. As minutes ticked by, he wondered what was taking so long. He stood and began to pace in the small waiting area.

Finally, the curtain parted and Madam Lucia walked in front of a young Japanese girl.

"This is Sayuri," Lucia said. "She is from Japan. Is she not pretty?"

Sayuri's colorful silk fan spread in front of her face with only her night black eyes looking out as she came through the parlor entrance. She was dressed in a traditional Japanese kimono of pink silk with colorful birds embroidered into the arms and sides. A wide band of black and pink silk was wrapped around her thin waist. She took tiny steps, closed her fan, and stood with her hands folded in front of her.

She bowed to Buck. *"Konbanwa,"* she greeted him saying good evening in Japanese.

Generally Buck liked Spanish *putas*. They were hot blooded and allowed him rough sex. Sayuri was small and fragile, looking like she would break into pieces if he held her too tight.

"Buenas noches Sayuri," he politely replied in Spanish. Her exotic features were enough to arouse his desires, which

he could already feel responding. Never, not here in Mexico City nor at his home in Lexington, Kentucky, had he met such an alluring feminine creature.

He and Madam Lucia negotiated her price for an hour of her time. *"Vamos,"* he said and Sayuri motioned toward her room. She shuffled behind Buck on her wooden platform shoes, as was the Japanese custom to respectfully follow the man. Opening the door, she removed her shoes before she entered and pointed for him to sit on the bed.

Sayuri knelt before him and removed his boots. She fingered the red Protestant Cross embroidered on the outside and just above the ankle on each boot. The smell from his socks almost knocked her off her feet. Next she stood up and removed his waist length jacket and ruffled white shirt. His chest was covered in a thick tangle of sandy hair a bit darker than the curls on his head.

She unbuttoned his ruffled trousers and pulled them off. She carefully folded the *traje* and placed it over a small chair. Buck grabbed at her, but she shook her head from side to side and pushed him back to stretch out on the bed. Walking to the dresser she rinsed a washcloth in a basin. Carefully she washed his face and shoulders and arms, then his chest and stomach and his legs all the way down to his toes. Buck closed his eyes and relaxed. No *puta* ever treated him this way.

Sayuri rinsed the washcloth often. She turned Buck over and washed his neck, back, buttocks and the back of his legs. Buck found the washing both sexual and relaxing. She seemed in no hurry to finish, taking her time to thoroughly wash each part of him.

She turned him again on his back and took his penis in her hand. Gently washing it, her stroking made it hard. He tried to grab at her, but she pushed him back onto the bed. Finishing his bath, Buck lay on the bed watching Sayuri carefully undress.

She unwrapped the wide sash holding her kimono and let it drop. Under the beautiful dress, Sayuri wore simple white undergarments. Carefully she folded the kimono and hung it over a screen.

The white top was wrapped around her slender body and tied with a silk cord. Slowly unwinding the top, it gaped open and exposed her petite lightly tan body. She had small firm breasts and long brown nipples. Laying the top aside, she washed her breasts and arms with the washcloth.

Buck found himself lost in her image. She was so different than any *puta* he ever bedded. As he watched, she removed the dangling red beads and black sticks from her hair. With her fingers she untangled her almost waist length shiny black hair and fluffed it out to drape over her shoulders.

Sayuri found this *Amerikano gaijin* offensive, but she was paid well to service him. Only by bathing him could she tolerate his offensive odor. Japanese men were fastidious and usually the Mexican *caballeros* were clean. She slowly worked at her bathing ritual while he lay quietly on the bed looking at her. He paid for an hour of her time and she planned on extending the bath as long as possible.

Buck waited for her to remove the white pants. Under them tight stockings covered her legs and feet. The stockings were split at the big toes to fit the wooden Geta platform shoes. Finally naked, Buck looked longingly at her smooth slender body. Between her legs wispy dark hair barely covered the triangle of her pelvic bone. She walked to the bed and crawled onto it on her hands and knees toward Buck.

CHAPTER 26

It was two days after the theft when Sancho, Maxorro, and two soldiers left the silver mule train, while their replacements restarted the silver load to the Mexico City mint. Sancho fumed knowing he was not going to make his normal salary and bonus for the trip. He also raged at the delay knowing the chance to find the thieves grew slimmer with each passing hour. Sancho and the two soldiers traveled on horseback, while Maxorro drove a wagon pulled by two mules. Sancho required the wagon and mules saying it might be the only way to carry back the stolen silver and prisoners. For now, it carried water and food supplies for the small posse.

Maxorro spent the time scouting and found the *bandido's* tracks heading north as he suspected. He recognized his mule's hoof prints. Maxorro hated leaving the rest of his mules in the hands of another man, but he hoped finding the silver thieves might get him a reward from the mine. He was not getting any younger and wondered how many years he could continue being a muleteer. Though not as hard as mining, the long and arduous trip between Zacatecas and Mexico City had taken a toll on his body. Sleeping on the hard ground did not help.

The terrain was rugged and Maxorro hoped whoever stole his two mules was giving them adequate rest and water.

"Are you sure they went this way?" Sancho yelled at Maxorro. He was grouchy and becoming more belligerent with each passing mile.

"*Sí.* They are ahead of us."

"How far? How much ahead?" Sancho asked.

"I cannot tell. They are not lighting fires at night and the wind is erasing the hoof prints quickly," Maxorro responded.

"This is your fault," Sancho said. "You should have been guarding your mules. You let them take the mules and brought this shame on me."

Sancho groused at him since the robbery forgetting Maxorro had also been gagged and bound. He bristled at the mine superintendent's complaints, but felt uneasy to rebuke him.

When they stopped the first evening, the two soldiers asked for *pulque*. "Do you take me for a fool?" Sancho growled. "If you had not been so drunk on *pulque,* we would not have been robbed. You should be glad I did not have you shot!" They grumbled, but did not press the point further.

By the fourth day, Maxorro could tell the mule hoof prints were deeper and fresher. It surprised him, as it meant the *bandidos* were not making the same distance as they had in previous days. Maxorro hoped it was not because his mules were ailing.

Miles ahead of the small posse, Rodolfo built a campsite where Hector lay seriously injured. For two days Hector lay comatose with fever. Pepe argued they should leave him. *"El va a morir,"* Pepe said he was going to die anyway. "We should leave him or shoot him," Pepe whispered out of Hector's earshot.

"No. What if it was you lying on the blanket Pepe? Would you want me to leave you to the buzzards?" Rodolfo asked. Pepe did not ask him again.

Rodolfo ordered a small fire to be kept burning near Hector's blanket and they roasted small rabbits and a dove to provide food for the group. Paco made a creosote broth and dropped small amounts between Hector's lips and wrapped cloths soaked in the creosote broth on his injured chest. The injuries were internal and Rodolfo wondered if the warm creosote cloths would do any good, but agreed with Paco to try everything. Late this afternoon, Hector groaned in pain. Rodolfo hoped it was a good sign.

After five days of following the mule hoof prints, Maxorro noticed a thin smoke plume rising up ahead. Sancho ordered the soldiers to make camp and ordered Maxorro to investigate.

Rodolfo sat high up on a dirt knoll leaning against a mesquite tree watching the back trail. Tired and weary, all he had on his mind and heart was María. She was right; he should not have attempted this robbery. He blamed himself for their situation. He did not have the heart to kill or leave Hector. His injured friend had been with him since Rodolfo began living as a free *peón*. Hector worked on a *hacienda* north of Torreón and watched the *haciendero* whip his father for stealing potatoes from the main garden. Hector said his mother was sick and they had no food.

Rodolfo used his few solitary moments to ask God for help. As he meditated in prayer, he spotted an old Indian in a sombrero below him on the trail. At first the old man appeared feeble, wandering alone out in the wilderness, lost. Rodolfo watched him carefully. At this point he trusted no one, not even an old man. He hoped the man did not see the smoke from the fire, but knew it was exactly what drew the old man to their campsite.

Maxorro approached the *bandido's* camp pretending to be wandering and stumbling from hunger. For the last two days he pondered his fate. If Sancho and the soldiers found the *bandidos,* Maxorro wondered about Sancho's motives. Out in this wilderness anything was possible. Sancho could kill or arrest the *bandidos* as he bragged he was going to do, or let the soldiers kill the *bandidos* and then steal the silver himself. Maxorro knew the mine superintendent would be reprimanded or probably lose his job even if the silver was returned. Maxorro began to think his chances of returning with Sancho to the mine and continuing his life, slim.

Rodolfo scrambled to the campsite just ahead of the old man to warn his friends. "Be friendly, perhaps he will be on his way after a few bites of food." Rodolfo knew the silver sacks were well hidden under dirt and bushes not too far from the camp. Their pistols were hidden under Hector's blanket and they would pretend to be a group of traveling *peóns* with an injured man.

Walking slowly into the *bandido's* camp, Maxorro said a prayer. He prayed they did not kill him on sight. *"Hola,"* he raised a hand in greeting. Maxorro was pleased to see his mules appeared to be well tended. They were tethered to a tree where they stood in the shade.

"Hola, come and rest a few moments. Are you hungry? We have a little bit of food we can share," Rodolfo said. He noticed the old man carried no weapons, or at least not any he could see.

Maxorro kept his head bowed, keeping his face shadowed under his sombrero. He could see an injured man lying on a blanket and saw enough of the speaker's face to recognize it was the young man he met at the *pulqueria,* who called himself Rodolfo.

"You have an injured man. What happened?" Maxorro asked.

"One of the mules kicked him in the chest. It is difficult for him to breathe," Rodolfo replied.

"Ah, stubborn beasts. You have no wagon? Why do you have mules with no wagon?" Rodolfo was surprised by the old man's question and his voice triggered a vague memory. He knew he had heard that voice before.

"Ah . . . we are taking them to my uncle's house. He has a wagon and no mules," Rodolfo lied.

"And the silver? Where are you taking the silver, amigo," Maxorro asked taking off his sombrero and looking at Rodolfo.

"¿Qué estás haciendo aquí?" Rodolfo asked what he was doing here, recognizing the muleteer Maxorro's voice.

"We followed your trail. Sancho and two soldiers are waiting for me back on the trail. We saw the fire and I was sent to investigate. You said you had some food. I am hungry. Perhaps I can eat and we can talk."

Knowing he had no other choice, Rodolfo waved a hand and asked Maxorro to sit. "How did you know it was me?" he asked after he handed him a piece of cooked rabbit.

"I recognized your face during the robbery. I thank you for taking care of my mules. Who are you? Is your name really Rodolfo?"

"Yes, I am Rodolfo Guerrero. These are a few of my friends. We are free *peóns.*"

Rodolfo explained about his *bandidos* and how they lived freely in the hills south of Torreón. *Peóns* and *Indios* should not be treated like slaves. Rodolfo explained his dream, his fight to get rights for *mestizos.*

"They beat us and take what they want. Without a way to defend ourselves we are always at their mercy." Rodolfo told him how he and his woman, María, bought guns and ammunition in El Paso. He described how his small band was now a large group of men, women, and children looking for a better life. Silver would provide that better life for everyone. With silver, he could go to El Paso and get more guns and ammunition. With silver the *peóns* could demand better treatment and live on their own land.

"You took a big chance staying here with your injured friend?"

"Yes, I will not leave him."

Rodolfo knew he was taking a huge chance telling Maxorro about the plan. The old man was a scout for Sancho and the soldiers, but something about his manner made him wonder.

As Maxorro listened, he was surprised to find he agreed with Rodolfo. Many times he pondered similar plans. This *bandido* could be the answer to his dreams, the dream of killing Sancho and better yet, taking the silver and living out the rest of his life in luxury.

"The silver is very heavy," Maxorro said. "You have an injured man. We will need Sancho's wagon." Maxorro knew the risks and the results if they were caught, yet the idea intrigued him. Alone it would be impossible, but with this small group of men, it could be done.

"You are with us?" Rodolfo asked him shocked at Maxorro's words.

"I am with you," Maxorro said. "Men like Sancho have been kicking me and my mules all of my life. I believe he might steal the silver from you and leave us all to die. He is a very evil man."

"We need a plan," Rodolfo said.

Paco, Pepe, Maxorro, and Rodolfo discussed several plans. About two hours later, Maxorro headed back down the trail to where Sancho and the soldiers waited.

CHAPTER 27

Buck collected *doña* Carmela the following morning at her mother's house. At least she seemed in better spirits this morning. As for him, Buck was still savoring his time with Sayuri last night. After the first hour, he paid for a second hour and luxuriated in her tenderness. It was an experience he hoped to repeat tonight. She was not cheap and Madam Lucia would no doubt raise her price, knowing Buck wanted the Japanese beauty.

This morning a letter was delivered from the mistress' lawyer, Alirio Mansano. Buck saw the maid place it on the foyer table awaiting Carmela's return. As soon as they arrived back at the house, a servant handed it to Carmela and she tore it open.

> *Señora,*
> *A hearing date has been set for the Reyes property for the 28 day of August at 10 o'clock in the morning. I would like to meet with you to discuss your claim as soon as it is convenient.*
> *Saludos,*
> *Alirio Mansano*

Buck heard Carmela growl as she tossed the note on the floor.

"Be ready to go in an hour," she grumbled at him. He watched as she climbed the wide staircase and heard her yelling to her maids.

A little more than an hour later, Carmela came down the stairs and flowed past Buck to the waiting carriage.

Buck mounted his horse and trotted behind the carriage to the lawyer's office. They traveled north until they reached the main boulevard called Paseo de la Reforma. Once on the boulevard they continued north until they reached Avenida Hidalgo located near the Zócalo, Mexico City's main plaza.

"Buenos días Señora," Alirio greeted Carmela. "You are

looking well. I hope this warm Mexico City weather is agreeing with you. I understand you were in Jalisco."

"I am not here to discuss my health or the weather," Carmela retorted hotly. "I want to know how a *pinche peón* without any birthright can claim my inheritance?"

Alirio Mansano tried not to visibly sigh. He explained numerous times to Carmela, as formally divorced from *don* Bernardo before his death, she had no legal claim to the *hacienda*. She insisted he file the paperwork ignoring that fact and Alirio doubted she would get a ruling in her favor.

"Ah yes, I understand *señora*. The bastard claims to have proof. I have not been given information about his proof, so I wanted to discuss how we can prove otherwise. Were you aware of your husband's, shall we call it an indiscretion?"

Carmela rose and screamed into Alirio's face, "That *pinche bastardo* shot my husband for raping his sister. He probably has provided fake proof to extract more revenge from me. It is your job to deny him his revenge."

"Cálmese señora," Alirio said trying to calm her. "It would be helpful if we could prove his documents false. Were you familiar with this *peón* before the shooting? Could we prove he was not Bernardo's child, but in fact the child of another. Did he have a father?"

Carmela calmed trying to remember Rafael. She remembered he worked in the horse barn with Pablo. His mother and sister worked in the gardens and sometimes in the kitchen. She rarely took an interest in the *peón* families. Why should she? It was Bernardo's responsibility to manage the *hacienda*.

"Probably, I don't remember. They lived on the estate, like all of our *peóns.*"

"His name is Rafael Reyes de Estrada and he is twenty-two years old. Perhaps you could swear Bernardo was incapable of siring the child? After all, you had no children together."

"Are you a fool?" she hissed at Alirio. "He sired the two children by the *pinche bastardo's* sister, María. Am I to swear his *pene* did not work for me, but worked for her?"

    Alirio looked at the floor and mumbled an apology. Sitting near the door, Buck felt sorry for the lawyer. Carmela's venom was obvious.

    Before they left Carmela groused at Alirio, "You better not let that *peón* cheat me out of my property."

CHAPTER 28

Nicolás Jiménez received a formal notice from the Oficina de Administración de Tierras about the Reyes *hacienda* several days ago. Since he had not heard from Rafael, he sent a communication to *don* David Salazar de Rosas' residence. It was the address Rafael gave to him when they met in Torreón. This morning he received a reply from Rafael asking him to come.

"Bienvenidos, gracias por venir" Rafe greeted Nicolás when he rode into the courtyard and thanked him for coming.

"Ah, Rafael," the lawyer replied.

When Rafe showed Nicolás to the parlor, *don* David joined them.

"Este es don David Salazar de Rosas," Rafe introduced his host. The lawyer shook *don* David's hand and bowed slightly.

"As you know I filed your claim with the Land Commission on your behalf. They reviewed the birth certificate and agreed to process the claim," the lawyer began.

"Is that it? It is accepted then?" Rafe asked excited.

"No. It is only the beginning. They may have accepted your claim, but it will be up to the judge to decide. I have been studying the new inheritance laws decreed by President Juárez and to me it seems clear, you are entitled to inherit *don* Bernardo's estate. However, the official warned me about *doña* Carmela, *don* Bernardo's ex-wife. Her lawyer has submitted an application to take the estate."

"Doña Carmela? Why should she want the estate? Pablo said after she left *don* Bernardo she wanted nothing to do with the *hacienda,"* Rafe responded surprised by this turn of events.

"I know. I was *don* Bernardo's lawyer during those years. She tried to fleece him in every way."

"Does she have any legal grounds to make the claim?" *don* David interjected.

"On the grounds she was *doña* of the property for

twenty years. She claims *don* Bernardo used her money to purchase it. The claim is well constructed by her lawyer, Alirio Mansano. He is a well-known lawyer in Mexico City and will have connections. She also claims she is owed money by the estate, because *don* Bernardo failed to meet his obligations of the divorce. Fortunately for you, that part of the claim has nothing to do with the inheritance laws."

"Do you think she has a chance to win?" Rafe asked.

"One never knows about these things. Is there anyone who can vouch for you besides the padre?" the lawyer asked Rafe.

"Just my mother and Pablo."

"The hearing is next Friday. They would not accept your mother's testimony, but they might listen to Pablo, though I don't believe he could arrive in time."

"It sounds like you could be a witness," *don* David said. "You were *don* Bernardo's lawyer for many years and you know what Carmela has been up to."

"It would not be permitted, besides I had no knowledge of Rafael's true identity until he came to my office last month. However, I am fully aware of Bernardo's siring of your sister's children, the young boy and girl," Nicolás said looking at Rafe. "If you are denied, then I could provide expert testimony that your sister's son is the rightful heir."

"The children are in Santa Fe and my sister, well my sister is somewhere here in Mexico but I don't know where," Rafe replied.

"If I lose, can I make a claim on my nephew's behalf?" Rafe asked. "My sister left the children in my care."

"I will have to study more about that. Normally it would be the mother who would make such a claim," Nicolás explained.

Outside in the courtyard, Nicolás shook hands with Rafe and *don* David. He gave them the date and time for the meeting and explained he would meet Rafe one hour prior to the hearing at the Oficina de Administración de Tierras.

As he left *don* David said, "I am worried about Carmela. She has a powerful lawyer working for her and it would not take much to bribe a lowly government official."

"I thought you said President Benito Juárez had put a stop to most of the government corruption?" Rafe asked remembering an earlier conversation.

"Most, not all," *don* David replied.

CHAPTER 29

Maxorro returned to Sancho's campsite in the late afternoon after spending several hours with the *bandidos*.

"What took you so long?" Sancho hissed.

"It is hot and I am on foot. I found their camp and they are treating a sick man. I watched them for some time before I returned to tell you," Maxorro replied.

"You are sure it is them?" Sancho asked.

"*Sí jefe*, I recognize the man I met at the *pulqueria* and he is the same man I saw taking my mules. My two mules are tied to a tree nearby."

"How many men?"

"There are two, *jefe*, and the one who is hurt. That one will not give us any trouble," Maxorro lied as he and Rodolfo planned. They decided it was unlikely Sancho knew how many men attacked the silver train. It was dark and Rodolfo had hit him over the head with his rifle.

"Ha, they will be easy to eliminate," Sancho said.

"They are camped near a small spring and they appear to be waiting for the injured man to die," Maxorro told Sancho. "We should attack at first light in the morning."

"No we will attack now," Sancho replied anxious to get the silver and be on his way.

"It will be dark before we get there and the trail is treacherous."

"I said now," Sancho barked at the soldiers and they jumped up. "Saddle your horses you lazy fools," he said to them.

"Did you see the sacks of silver?" Sancho asked Maxorro.

"No *jefe*. They were not anywhere I could see. Perhaps they buried or hid them," Maxorro said.

"They are *bandidos* and probably not that smart," Sancho said with a sneer.

"Perhaps, but did they not rob our mule train?"

Sancho grumbled at Maxorro to prepare the wagon.

The mine superintendent was reacting as Maxorro suspected. He and Rodolfo thought Sancho would want to attack, rather than wait until the next day, especially if Maxorro suggested to wait. It would be dark by the time they arrived at the *bandidos* campsite, giving Rodolfo an edge.

Rodolfo and Pepe moved Hector to a sheltered location under a scrubby mesquite. As they carried him Hector asked, "Are we going home *jefe?*"

"Soon. You rest and keep quiet," Rodolfo told him.

Paco was assigned lookout duty to watch the back trail for the soldiers. Maxorro told them he would make sure to come down the same trail.

Rodolfo and Pepe gathered more wood and built the fire a bit bigger, so it could be easily seen, hoping the fire would draw Sancho directly into their trap. Both Paco and Pepe carried a pistol and rifle loaded and more ammunition in their pockets. With everything ready, Rodolfo sat and waited for Paco's whistle.

Sancho rode in front with the two soldiers behind him. Maxorro trailed behind with the wagon. When the fire could be clearly seen, Sancho pulled up.

"Maxorro, you stay here with the wagon. I will send one of the soldiers back to get you when we are finished with these *pendejos.*"

Paco saw a head pop up on the trail leading to their campsite. Then two more. Scrambling down from his lookout position, he gave a low signal. Pepe and Rodolfo perked at the sound. Pepe crouched behind a boulder and Paco got into position behind a clump of scrubby bushes across from Pepe. Rodolfo stayed sitting by the fire. His pistol was tucked behind his *pantalones,* covered by his loose *camisa.*

Rodolfo knew he was taking the biggest chance. It was possible Sancho would ride into the camp and immediately shoot him without asking questions. As he waited, his stomach churned and he said a quick prayer to Mary the mother of God.

Sancho rode toward the fire in the almost dark of the evening. He pondered Maxorro's words as he came up the trail. If the *bandido* buried or hid the silver, killing him made Sancho's job harder. A dead *bandido* did not help him; only the silver bars paved his way north.

He pulled up and the two soldiers stopped beside him.

"What is your plan?" one asked.

"You stay with me and we will ride in," Sancho said to the soldier on his right. "Do not kill the *bandido* until we get the silver. Maxorro said there are two of them. I only see one near the fire. You, stay hidden over there," he pointed to his left, "and keep a sharp lookout for the other one."

Paco saw one of the soldiers turn off toward his left, while the other soldier and the mine superintendent slowly rode into the camp.

Rodolfo appeared to be startled by the two men. Sancho pulled his pistol and aimed it directly at Rodolfo.

"Where is the silver?" Sancho said. "I will trade you your life for the silver."

"Silver? I am a simple *peón,* traveling to my uncle's home near Torreón. Come warm yourselves by my fire." Rodolfo breathed a sigh of relief when Sancho came into the campsite talking and not shooting. One of the soldiers rode behind him, his pistol drawn, but the other was not in sight.

"Do you take me for a fool?" Sancho hissed. "We have been tracking you for days from where you robbed the silver train. Those mules over there prove it." Sancho dismounted and walked toward Rodolfo with his pistol aimed at Rodolfo's heart.

"Did you really think you could get away with it?"

"*Señor* you are wrong. I am a simple peasant. Who told you such lies? You, sergeant?" Rodolfo spoke to the soldier. "Do you recognize me as the *bandido?*"

"No, I . . . I did not see you," the soldier replied.

"Shut up Padilla," Sancho growled at the soldier. "Maxorro said those mules are his and he saw you that night at our camp," Sancho said pointing to the mules.

"Maxorro? Where is this Maxorro? Let him accuse me directly. Those are my mules I am taking to my uncle's house. He has a wagon he will let me borrow to move my wife and children to our new home," Rodolfo continued lying making up stories to satisfy each of Sancho's questions.

Sancho shifted his weight from one foot to the other. The *bandido* was smart or Maxorro was lying.

Paco waited as Rodolfo instructed. "Do not show our hand." They assumed Sancho would ride in with both soldiers in a show of strength, but one had veered left toward Pepe's position. As the two men talked to Rodolfo near the fire, Paco circled behind them. The night completely descended upon them, and he could only see the men silhouetted by the fire.

Maxorro waited with the wagon. He heard nothing except the night beginning to come alive. He pulled an old pistol from his pack, which he had kept hidden from Sancho. He hoped tonight would end as he and Rodolfo planned, but if not he had the pistol ready by his side. Perhaps Sancho would return the silver to the mine, and then again perhaps Sancho would kill them all. The twelve bars of stolen silver was a small fortune.

Pepe was crouched behind a small mesquite bush about fifty yards from the campfire. He could see one soldier and the mine superintendent talking to Rodolfo with their guns drawn. Engrossed in the scene at the fire, he was not thinking about the second soldier until he heard a twig snap nearby.

"Oye gilipollas, drop the rifle and back away. Spread your arms wide where I can see your hands," the soldier ordered Pepe, calling him a shithead.

Surprised at the voice behind him, Pepe turned quickly and without thinking fired at the shadow. The sound of the pistol shot echoed in the quiet night.

"Hijo de puta," the soldier cursed as he felt a sting in his arm and fired at Pepe in return.

Sancho, the sergeant, and Rodolfo all jerked at the sound of pistol shots ringing off to their left in the night air. In an instant Rodolfo knew it came from Pepe's direction. In one quick move he kicked one of the burning logs from the fire toward Sancho. Though the log missed him, tiny embers of fire sparked up at the mine superintendent and backed up the soldier's horse. Rodolfo grabbed for his pistol from behind his back and took aim.

Recovering, Sancho raised his pistol to fire, but Rodolfo's gun barked in the night and Sancho fell backward.

From the darkness of the night, Rodolfo heard Paco's voice. "Put down the gun *soldado* or I will put a bullet in your back."

"Sergeant, tell the other soldier to drop his gun and come out or I will kill you," Rodolfo said to the sergeant.

"Roberto," the sergeant called out. "Are you hit?"

"*Sí*, I am hit but I got one of the *bandidos.*"

Rodolfo's heart sank. He prayed Pepe was not hurt badly.

"Roberto," the sergeant called out again. "Walk to the fire without your gun. If you do not, they will kill me. Sancho is dead."

Pepe lay on the ground and could hear the voices. His head felt funny and at first his chest screamed in excruciating pain, but now he felt as if he was floating. He lay listening to the voices as they got further and further away from him. *"Here I am. Don't leave me,"* he thought. Then he heard the voice of his mother calling him for lunch.

Roberto pondered the situation. His sergeant was telling him to drop his gun and walk to the campfire. He said Sancho was dead. He heard a groan from the man he shot and then quiet. He was a soldier, but no hero. The stupid Army put him and the other soldiers on this shitty duty because they were old. He was only forty-three, but in the Army he was considered useless.

"I am coming *sargento.* Tell them not to shoot."

As he approached the fire, Roberto held up his arms to show he held no gun.

"Where is my man?" Rodolfo growled at him.

"He shot me first and I shot back. He is lying back there."

In the night air, Maxorro heard three gunshots, then all was quiet. He pondered the outcome. Getting the mules started, Maxorro walked the mules pulling the small wagon slowly toward the camp.

Paco held the two soldiers at bay while Rodolfo walked to find Pepe. It was dark and he stumbled on a rock and almost fell. "Pepe," he called out. "Pepe answer me." The only noise he heard was the night cicadas buzzing in the bushes. Finally he saw a dark lump on the ground.

"Pepe," he said reaching his friend. He rolled Pepe over. Just the way Pepe's body moved told Rodolfo he was dead. "I'm sorry my friend." He crossed himself and said a prayer.

"He is dead," Rodolfo said to no one and to everyone as he returned to the camp.

"Please, don't kill me. He shot at me first and I shot back," the soldier begged.

Rodolfo killed Sancho knowing Sancho would have killed him in a heartbeat, but killing this soldier in cold blood was something else.

As they stood near the fire, a creaking in the dark was followed by Maxorro's voice. "It is only I, Maxorro. Don't shoot." Maxorro was relieved to see Rodolfo standing and Sancho lying still on the ground. The other *bandido* had the two soldiers covered with their arms in the air.

He drove the wagon into the small campsite and pulled the mules to a stop.

"That one killed my friend," Rodolfo said pointing to the soldier named Roberto.

"Sancho?" Maxorro asked.

"I shot him when he drew his pistol," Rodolfo said.

"He was a bad man," the sergeant said.

"¿Cómo te llamas?" Rodolfo asked the sergeant his name.

"Sergeant Agustin Padilla. He is Corporal Roberto Avila. We mean you no harm. We have not reported our status to the Army for too long now and when the mine reports the theft, we will probably be considered deserters or misfits. In either case our lives are worthless. Let us go, we will not follow you," Agustin begged thinking the *bandido* would probably kill them.

"Yes you can keep the silver, too," Roberto added.

"First, you must know this, we are poor *peóns,* not *bandidos,"* Rodolfo told him. "That is why we stole the silver. It is to buy guns and ammunition to hunt and protect the group of *peóns* living back in the hills near Torreón. I want to buy some land and find a place we can farm for ourselves, not under a *haciendero's* whip."

Maxorro and Paco were carrying Pepe's body to the campsite. They gently laid him near Sancho and Maxorro retrieved a shovel from the wagon.

"Should I bury both of them?" he asked.

"No we will take Pepe and bury him behind that mesquite tree. He would like that. Leave Sancho for the buzzards and coyotes. They probably need a good meal."

While Paco and Maxorro buried Pepe, Rodolfo tied the two guards together. He had no idea what to do with them. It was not in his nature to kill them, but they knew too much to let them go free. Rodolfo found Hector awake and sitting up against a tree.

"Hola jefe, I am getting better. I heard shots. It woke me," Hector said. He was still weak, but Rodolfo was happy to see him moving.

"I killed the mine superintendent. We have been camped for three days waiting for you to get better and they found us." With Rodolfo's help Hector limped slowly to the campsite and sat on the wagon.

"Who are they?" he asked looking at the men tied together.

"The two soldiers who came with Sancho."

CHAPTER 30

Two days before the hearing, *don* Luis arrived back in Mexico City to find Carmela safe, but in a frenzied mood. Nothing he said seemed to calm her temper. She yelled at the servants, raging at her maid's slightest perceived misbehavior and refused his advances.

Don Luis found Buck in the stable brushing his horse.

"Thank you for staying with her," he told Buck. "Go, take some time off, but be here early on Friday morning. We go to the land office for the hearing and . . . " *don* Luis' voice trailed off not finishing his sentence. He dreaded Friday and the hearing for the property in Torreón. If Carmela lost the case, he shuttered to think of her reaction.

"*Gracias patrón.* I will be here Friday," Buck replied. When the *don* walked from the stable, Buck quickly saddled his horse Bala and climbed aboard. There was only one place he wanted to be and only one person he wanted to see – Sayuri.

On Friday morning, *don* David's buggy was readied and Rayo and the packhorse were tied to the back. Rafe insisted he must ride immediately to Torreón, regardless of the outcome. He said his farewells to *don* David's family last night at supper, thanking them for their hospitality. *Don* David slapped the buggy horse and exited the courtyard.

Don David watched Rafael fiddle with his hat. "You are nervous?" he asked.

"*Sí.*" Rafe fretted all morning worrying about meeting with the government officials. Rafe's experience with the Mexican government was *peóns* never won, and Mexico's aristocracy made sure *peóns* stayed in their place. When they discussed it, *don* David told him several times to use his new identity proudly. For his entire life Rafe thought of himself as Rafael Ortega de Estrada. Now he must use his new name, Rafael Reyes de Estrada. He almost choked on the name every time he used it.

He had no idea how today would end. He decided if the judge ruled against him, he would go to Torreón to find his sister and have her file a claim for Antonio. His lawyer and several others could vouch for Antonio's linage as it was well known he was *don* Bernardo's bastard son.

Trying not to think about what might happen today, Rafe looked out from the buggy. The streets were busy with carriages and vendor carts. As they traveled the neighborhood heading into the city center he saw *peóns* with carts trying to sell their wares. *"Chile!" "Sandía!" "Verduras!" "Pasteles!" "Flores!"* At several homes he watched as the servants of the house negotiated with the vendors for their merchandise.

Two *Indios* carried bundles of firewood strapped to their backs and held in place by a tumpline stretched across their foreheads. Two women walked beside them carrying clay jugs in the same way. The Indians stooped with their heavy bundles.

They rode past houses until finally reaching the Zócalo with its huge buildings. They drove several more blocks stopping in front of the Oficina de Administración de Tierras.

"There he is," Rafe said seeing the lawyer waiting for them. He was carrying the painting of *don* Rafael under his arm.

"Buenos días señores," Nicolás Jiménez greeted them. *"Doña* Carmela's lawyer and I met with the government officials yesterday and presented our arguments. The only thing left to do is present the portrait of *don* Rafael to the judge. I cannot tell you how this will all turn out, but when we show him the portrait as compared to Rafael, I hope our arguments will sway him in your favor," Nicolás told Rafe as he led them down the hallway.

A short time later, *doña* Carmela and *don* Luis Orozco rode up to the government building in a carriage. Buck rode alongside on his horse as was his duty as bodyguard. As he rode, he daydreamed of Sayuri and her tenderness. He was almost broke paying for hour after hour of her time. Each hour, Madam Lucia raised the price.

As they rode up, the driver stopped the carriage behind *don* David's. Buck quickly jumped off his horse and helped Carmela out of the carriage to the street. As Carmela stepped to the street, she smoothed her dress and then looked up. Seeing Rayo tied to the back of the carriage parked in front of them, she recognized the distinctive Appaloosa as one raised on Bernardo's *hacienda*.

"*Aiyaa*, look there! That Appaloosa belonged to *don* Bernardo. The *peón* stole it the day he shot my husband. It is mine. Buck, take the horse and hide it," she spoke out excitedly.

"*Patróna*, you want me to steal the horse?" Buck asked his mistress, though he was looking at *don* Luis. Horse thieving was a capital offense in Mexico and could cost him his neck.

Don Luis did not like the idea, even if she claimed it was stolen from her *hacienda*. However, raising Carmela's ire today was not something he wished to do. "Yes, take the horse Buck, take it to the stables at my house. When we finish our business here we will take it to my *hacienda* in Jalisco." Taking Carmela's arm, *don* Luis led her up the steps and into the building.

Buck did not like taking the Appaloosa, but orders were orders. The Appaloosa snorted and shifted side to side protesting the intrusion. His ears flexed forward as his head jerked up and down against the reins tied to the buggy as Buck worked to untie him. He stripped the saddle and threw it into the back of the buggy. Stealing the horse was one thing, stealing another man's saddle was something else. Buck worked quickly hoping no one was watching. Jumping onto Bala, he pulled at the reins and led the stubborn Appaloosa away from the buggy and down the street.

Nicolás Jiménez, *don* David, and Rafe were standing outside the judge's office. They watched as Carmela holding onto *don* Luis' arm walked up to them.

"*Buenos días*," Nicolás Jiménez greeted them and bowed slightly.

"That is him," Carmela sneered pointing to Rafe. "That *peón* shot my husband and should have been hanged." Venom dripped from her words and the scowl on her face bore into Rafe.

Before anyone could respond, the door to the judge's chamber opened and they were ushered inside. Nicolás Jiménez bristled seeing Alirio Mansano, Carmela's lawyer, already sitting across from the judge. Nicolás thought he probably got here early to bribe the judge in Carmela's favor.

"Buenos días señora y señores. Soy Felipe Aragón," the judge introduced himself. I am sorry I do not have enough chairs for everyone to sit. Alirio stood and offered his chair to Carmela.

"This is a hearing regarding the property owned by *don* Bernardo Reyes de Cordoba located in Torreón, Coahuila, Mexico. I believe you are all familiar with one another and I have reviewed the evidence presented to me yesterday by your *abogados*. I understand you have another piece of evidence *Señor* Jiménez?"

"Sí. It is a painting of *don* Bernardo's grandfather, *don* Rafael Reyes de Zamora, this young man's great-grandfather. We believe it shows the bloodline of Rafael Reyes de Estrada and corroborates the authenticity of the birth certificate. Nicolás unwrapped the painting and placed the portrait on the judge's desk telling Rafe to stand nearby.

Carmela stifled a gasp seeing the painting of *don* Rafael, one she had walked by thousands of times. Looking at Rafael was like seeing *don* Bernardo's grandfather standing right there before her.

"Yes I see. It is a very strong resemblance," the judge said looking from the portrait to Rafe's face.

"The painting proves nothing," Carmela sneered regaining her composure. "Any *Mexicano* could shave their beard and look like that. I was the *doña* of the *hacienda* and he is a *peón,* just a horse-stealing *peón* born to a *puta* of a mother. Anyone could have been his father."

Don Luis sized up the young man using the name Rafael Reyes de Estrada. He was dressed like an *Americano* and was not wearing a Spanish *traje*. Regardless, *don* Luis was shocked when he saw the likeness of the young man in the painting. It could have been a painting of him, except Rafael had a slightly darker complexion than the *caballero* in the painting.

"*Señora y Señores,* I have heard the arguments from your lawyers and have studied the documents supporting the arguments. From your side *señora,* I see you were divorced from *don* Bernardo at the time of his death, in which case you no longer have legal rights to his properties," the judge stated.

"But *señor,* my ex-husband owes me restitution, some ten-thousand *pesos!*" Carmela protested.

"*Señora,* alimony is a separate issue. It has nothing to do with who inherits the property in question. I do not know what to tell you about that. What I do know is this man Rafael Reyes de Estrada has a birth certificate and baptismal record naming him the son of *don* Bernardo Reyes. Look at this portrait of *don* Bernardo's grandfather and compare it to this young man," Judge Aragón said.

Doña Carmela forced herself to look at the painting. It hung in the stairway of the *hacienda* in Torreón her entire married life. When she looked at Rafael, the indiscretion of her husband screamed back at her. There could be little doubt the *pinche peón* was Bernardo's son. Tears full of hatred stung her cheeks. *Don* Luis pulled Carmela to him and held her by the shoulders.

"Unless you have any proof which refutes his claim, I have no choice but to rule in the favor of Rafael Reyes de Estrada," Judge Aragón said looking at Carmela.

"No, you cannot. I am the one who paid for the *hacienda* with my own money. Bernardo was penniless when he and I got married," she screamed at the judge, then turning to her lawyer, "Do something to fix this," she yelled at Alirio Mansano.

"*Lo siento señora,* it is all we can do here," the lawyer told her he was sorry.

"I would like a word with you; come outside the office with me," *don* Luis spoke to Rafael, leaving Carmela arguing with the lawyer. Rafe followed the *don* to the hallway.

"How much will you take for the worthless *hacienda* in Torreón?"

"*Señor*, I have no plans to sell the *hacienda*," Rafe responded politely.

"What do you mean you will not sell that worthless place? You cannot afford to rebuild it. I will pay you handsomely. Think about what a person like you can do with all that money," *don* Luis said in a stern voice thinking he could intimidate the *Americano*.

"*Señor*, I do not need your money. The property is but a small payment for what the *desgraciado don* Bernardo did to my mother and sister. My sister has two of his young children she has to raise. You could not pay me enough to make up for what he did. I will keep the property, *señor*," Rafe answered defiantly.

"Be reasonable young man. Everyone needs money. You can help your sister get a good place to live and raise her children," the *don* continued trying to convince Rafe to sell.

"*No señor*, it is not for sale." Rafe turned and walked away from the *don* toward the door of the judge's chamber.

"You will regret your decision, *peón*," *don* Luis hissed. "You will regret it very much."

Rafe wanted to turn around and smack the old *don* for calling him a *peón*, but restrained himself and instead opened the door and left him standing in the hall.

Chapter 31

Buck arrived at *don* Luis' house with the Appaloosa in tow. He worried, knowing he would be seen and the remarkable horse remembered by anyone who saw him trailing it through the streets. He cursed the stupid woman for demanding he steal it. She forced him to put his neck on the line and he had no doubt she would deny instigating the theft, if he were caught.

Tying the horse to the stall gate, Buck took a good look at the Appaloosa. Rayo stared back at him with ears perked forward, snorted, and pulled trying to get away. Buck knew a quality horse and this was one. He heard Carmela talk several times about the blooded horses raised by her late husband in Torreón.

"I would not mind owning you. You are one fine horse," he spoke to the Appaloosa stroking the horse's flank trying to calm him. Rayo responded by kicking the stall with a force which shook the ground.

Buck struggled to get the big Appaloosa into a stall at *don* Luis' stable and narrowly missed getting kicked. It took several lashes from a leather *riata* to force the horse into a stall. When Buck was removing the halter, he barely avoided being bitten by the angry Appaloosa. Shutting the stall door the angry horse kicked and whinnied loudly.

"Come Carmela, we must go now," *don* Luis said after he reentered the judge's chambers. She was fuming and her cheeks stained by tears, but reluctantly she got up and followed the *don* out of the office with her lawyer following them.

"Rafael, please be seated. There is much paperwork to be completed. You and your lawyer may read each page then you must sign. The property is officially yours as of today, but will not be processed for several weeks. I suggest you take claim to the property in Torreón to show your ownership," the judge said.

"Gracias señor," Rafe said and shook his hand. The judge left *don* David, Nicolás Jiménez, and Rafe in the office to review the documents. It took almost an hour for Rafe to complete the transaction for the inheritance. He thanked Nicolás profusely as they were leaving.

"Can you take the painting with you when you return to Torreón? I am on horseback and plan to go immediately to the *hacienda,"* he asked the lawyer.

"Of course. I will get it to Pablo as soon as I return."

They walked out the front doors of the building and into the noontime sunlight. At first Rafe was so euphoric he did not notice Rayo was gone. He shook Nicolás' hand again and wished him a good journey. As the lawyer mounted his horse and rode off down the street, *don* David patted Rafe on his shoulder.

"Congratulations. I had my doubts about the new laws, but I guess change is possible."

The two turned back toward the building. The buggy stood exactly where they left it, but only the packhorse was tied to the back. Rafe stared at the scene for several moments trying to realize what was wrong.

"Desgraciados, they took Rayo!" Rafe yelled out.

"¿Qué?" don David asked what was wrong, not realizing the Appaloosa was missing.

"They stole Rayo, my Appaloosa. Look they left the saddle in the buggy."

"We must call the police," *don* David said.

Rafe's mind was spinning. Wildly he looked up and down the street, but knew Carmela and his horse were long gone. He was in the judge's chambers signing papers for more than an hour.

"I will summon the police," *don* David said again.

Beating his fist against the side of the buggy Rafe said, "No, we cannot. Five years ago I stole Rayo from the *hacienda* when I shot *don* Bernardo. She will attest to that," Rafe admitted. "I will have to find him and take him back."

Don David quietly pondered Rafe's words. Over the course of the last week, they talked about Rafe's life at the *hacienda* and how he shot the *don*. Rafe had not mentioned he stole the magnificent Appaloosa.

"That's very dangerous Rafael. You do not know the city and they will call you a horse thief if you are caught," *don* David warned him. "He was a good horse, but you told me of the others you have in Santa Fe. Leave Carmela to her revenge. You got the property and she only got a horse," *don* David tried to convince him.

Rafe heard *don* David's words and knew he had bigger issues to manage, like finding his sister and Rodolfo and taking possession of the *hacienda,* but Rayo was his horse and his friend. Letting Carmela steal him back negated much of the good done here today.

"Come back with me to the house. I have several good horses in my stable. I will give you one so you can go to Torreón," *don* David advised him.

Don David convinced Rafe to stay until morning before leaving for Torreón. Rafe picked a brown mare from the horses in the *don's* stables and they took her to the livery for new horseshoes. While they were in town, Rafe sent a cable to George and Josefina Summers. It was the fifth telegram he sent keeping them updated as to his efforts. This one was supposed to be a joyous telegram.

> *Father.*
> *Land assigned in my favor.*
> *Carmela stole Rayo. Not sure what I will do.*
> *Love to everyone.*
> *Rafe.*

Rafe sent a shorter telegram to Pablo in Torreón.

> *Pablo.*
> *Land assigned in my favor. Find María and Rodolfo.*
> *Protect property.*
> *Rafael.*

After sending the telegrams and having the mare shod, *don* David convinced Rafe to extend his stay until the morning. He was happy when Rafe agreed it was probably for the best.

No one slept well during the night at *don* Luis' home. The angry Appaloosa squealed, snorted, and kicked the stall all night long. By morning *don* Luis said to Carmela, "I will send the horse back to *don* David's house for the *peón*. It was not right to steal it and now the horse is our problem."

"You are soft, Luis. The *pinche peón* has no rights to the horse.

"Perhaps we should sell it then. It should fetch you a good price."

"You will do no such thing. That horse was one of the best *don* Bernardo ever bred. He is mine," she retorted.

At *don* David's house, Rafe was awake when he heard a rooster announce its presence somewhere nearby. Daylight was just starting to glow through the window. For hours while sleep evaded him, Rafe thought about Rayo. The horse was more like his friend, than a horse. Rafe was with Pablo in *don* Bernardo's barn and named him Rayo after a loud thunderbolt struck near the barn the night he was born. He spent many hours in his youth training the young colt and teaching him to respond to verbal commands. The day *don* Bernardo raped his sister María, Rafe took his dead father's flintlock pistol and shot the *don,* fleeing on Rayo. That was more than five years ago in March of 1866.

Rayo was the foundation of his horse breeding business in Santa Fe. He already sired at least six or seven yearlings and one of the mares was pregnant again. Rafe trained and then sold the blooded stock in Santa Fe for a good price. Yet business and money was not at the forefront of Rafe's thoughts.

Rayo protected him many times and no doubt saved his life on several occasions. Both smart and powerful, last June it was Rayo who killed Diego de la Torre, saving Rafe's life once again. He knew he should take *don* David's mare and ride for Torreón. He needed to take possession of his inheritance in order to defend the claim. He wondered if Pablo had found Rodolfo and María. Maybe they were already living at the *hacienda*.

The mixture of feelings nagged him throughout the night robbing him of sleep. By the time the rooster crowed, Rafe knew he was not leaving Mexico without Rayo.

The Appaloosa kicked through a stall wall and Buck was forced to tie him tightly to the stable gate. The horse continued with the racket of kicking and snorting all day long. He upended his water and refused to eat. *Don* Luis ordered Buck to sleep in the barn and keep the angry horse quiet. Buck slept little and groused about it in the morning.

All day the servants complained to Buck about the wild Appaloosa keeping them awake all night long. When *don* Luis and Carmela arrived back home after visiting friends, Buck went to speak to the *don*.

"We need to do something with that horse. He is upsetting the others in the barn and now they are all making noise. They follow his lead. Do you want I should kill him?" Buck asked.

"No Buck. We will take the horse to my *hacienda* in Jalisco Monday morning. In the meantime, try to keep him quiet," he said helping Carmela out of the carriage.

"If anything happens to that horse, Buck will pay," Buck heard Carmela tell *don* Luis as they walked away and up the steps to the house. Yeah Buck would pay, he thought. The damn *patróna* turned him into a horse thief and now she thought it was his fault the stupid horse was so wild.

CHAPTER 32

George Summers received Rafe's telegram late on Friday afternoon. Sitting at his desk in the foundry, he read the short sentences several times. This was the fifth telegram since Rafe left for Mexico and knowing Rafe was safe brought joy to the household.

The day Rafe left town, George reported the burning of Rafe's house to the sheriff, taking the sword as evidence. Sheriff Johnson agreed the Spaniards had gone too far, but the sword was not enough proof to arrest anyone in particular. George asked the sheriff to make sure word was spread around town that Rafe had gone to Mexico.

Since Pablo also went back to Torreón, George hired a new man to work with Rafe's horses. He stayed in the small room in the back of the barn during the night to protect the horses and building. So far there was no more trouble and the last time he spoke to the sheriff, the Spanish *dons* were not been harassing him about Rafe. Unfortunately, George suspected the issues with the Spaniards were only suspended and not resolved.

George worked with the builder who removed the burned timbers of Rafe's house and a new frame was now in progress. Only the stone fireplace had been salvaged. The builder told him it would likely be next summer before the house could be finished. He would try to get the walls and roof completed before the winter snow began to fly and all work would then cease until at least March.

At supper, George read the telegram to the family.

"Gracias a Dios," Celiá thanked God as was her usual response to good news. Though Celiá was thankful to God for protecting her son, she would not sleep well until her daughter María was safe as well.

George's wife Josefina agreed and said to Rafe's mother, "Now María and Rodolfo will have a place to be safe. It is such wonderful news." The two women clasped hands in joy.

The dinner conversation was happy and elated. Besides talking about the telegram, George's two teenage daughters chatted about an upcoming dance at the church and the two older women discussed the vegetables and tomatoes in the garden. The summer was mild and rainy in Santa Fe and the vegetable garden was producing a bumper crop. Josefina bought extra jars for the canning, which was to start in several weeks. María's two children, Antonio and Alicia quickly ate their supper and asked to be excused so they could go outside and play before it got dark.

"Yes you may. Do not leave the courtyard," Celiá said to them.

George noticed Carlos verbalized less joy about Rafe's telegram and was more subdued. After supper he and Carlos retired to the parlor, while the women went to the kitchen.

"Cigar?" George extended the cigar box to Carlos, who responded by shaking his head no.

"Rafe will not give up Rayo," Carlos said.

"I have been feeling the same way. He will confront Carmela or worse steal him back." They both knew Rafe's bond with Rayo and knew Rafe would not just walk away. "Carmela no doubt recognized Rayo and felt it was her property," George added.

"I should have foreseen something like this," Carlos grumbled. "I should have made him take Santiago instead of Rayo."

George kicked himself for not thinking more about Rafe's choice to ride Rayo to Mexico. Five years ago he stole the horse from *don* Bernardo's *hacienda*. With *don* Bernardo dead, none of them contemplated Carmela's position. The horse was rightfully hers. Rafe stole it when Carmela was *don* Bernardo's wife.

"I should go to Mexico City and stop him from doing anything foolish," Carlos said. "He will listen to me."

"You are getting married in two weeks and you start your teaching job on Monday," George responded looking at Carlos and shaking his head in disagreement.

"Hopefully Rafe is still at your uncle's home. I will send Rafe a response and ask him to give up Rayo for his own safety," George said.

Early the following morning George drove the buggy to Santa Fe and sent the wire to Mexico City. As an extra precaution he also sent a wire to Torreón. Not knowing where Rafe would be, both wires asked Rafe to send a response.

After sending the telegrams, George headed to the General Mercantile. Josefina sent him to town with a list of items she needed.

"Be about an hour Mr. Summers before I can get this all ready," the mercantile clerk said. "You want me to have it delivered?"

"No. I'll go to the cafe and have a bite and come back," George responded.

When George walked into the cafe, Sheriff Johnson saw him arrive and flagged him over to his table.

"Good morning George," Sheriff Johnson greeted him. "Sit down."

"Nice to see you," George responded. George ordered a cup of coffee and a plate of bacon and eggs.

"I heard that boy of yours is still in Mexico," the sheriff said.

"Who did you hear that from?"

"Jim over at the telegraph office said you got another wire from Mexico City." George should have known where the sheriff got the information.

"Yes, he's still there."

"Hope it stays that way for awhile. Couple days ago Fred at the livery heard one of the dandies bragging about burning Rafe's house down. Heard them say he better not show his face around here again."

George was not happy with the news. He hoped the issues between Diego's friends and Rafe would cease over the weeks Rafe was gone. It sounded as if the young Spaniards would still be ready for a fight if Rafe came home.

"How about the older *dons?*" George asked.

"I saw *don* Mateo last week. He didn't say anything about it and I didn't ask."

George's breakfast came and the sheriff got up to go.

"I'll leave you to your breakfast, George. Keep me posted of any news."

"Sure will. Let me know if you hear anything else about Rafe or the fire."

George sat in the cafe trying to swallow the bacon and eggs. Suddenly his mouth was dry and the food tasteless. He wondered if Rafe would ever be able to return to Santa Fe. It was not fair or legal, but it was reality. Now Rafe was in trouble in Mexico and he pondered if he needed to find Rafe in Mexico City and keep him from harm. He knew Carlos was right. Rafe would not let Carmela have Rayo, at least not without a fight.

Chapter 33

When Maxorro stripped the saddle off Sancho's horse, he thought the saddlebags were extremely heavy. Investigating, he found a bar of silver in each bag. The discovery confirmed to Maxorro, the mine superintendent had not planned to return the stolen silver to the mine. Hefting the saddle and saddlebags, Maxorro placed them into the wagon. He and Paco loaded the other silver sacks on the two mules.

Maxorro and the *bandidos* discussed how to hide the silver on the trip back to Torreón, but they devised no plan except to keep a sharp lookout for *la policía* or soldiers as they traveled.

Rodolfo and Paco took turns driving the wagon. When they were not driving, they rode their horses scouting ahead of the small procession. Hector, though in much less pain, rested in the back of the wagon. He felt each bump deep in his chest, but riding was much better than on horseback.

The first day Rodolfo kept the soldiers tied on their horses and tied together at night, but they did not seem anxious to run away. In fact they asked to go with them.

"Roberto and I could be a great help teaching your *bandidos* how to shoot. We can train them how to fight," Agustin told Rodolfo.

"I told you we are not *bandidos,* not like you think. There are women and children. We are free *peóns* looking for a better life."

"And we are no longer soldiers. The Army will shoot us as deserters if we are identified."

By the second day on the trail Rodolfo only tied the two soldiers at night. During the day, he let them walk or help drive the wagon. At night they camped with only a small fire and whatever they could gather to eat.

Rodolfo walked over to where Maxorro was inspecting the mules as was his routine. "Maxorro, what do you think about those two soldiers? Do you think we can trust them?"

"I cannot say for sure. They told me they have no family. Sergeant Padilla told me he was married once, but his wife left him because he drank too much and he could not give her any children. The corporal told me he never married and he comes from the south in the Yucatan and has nothing to go back to. They told me they are glad to get away from the Army, but we must be vigilant and watch them," Maxorro answered.

Rodolfo was conflicted concerning the two soldiers. Perhaps he should have left them to fend for themselves instead of taking them along. In a few days they would be back to the camp near Torreón and he worried he was leading two wolves into his flock of sheep.

When they stopped on the third night, Rodolfo gave each soldier a rifle against Paco's concerns. "We might all starve if we do not get something to eat," Rodolfo said. In reality he was more interested in how the soldiers reacted with a rifle in their hand. If they were planning on killing them and stealing the silver themselves, Rodolfo wanted that conflict now and not at the larger camp where women and children might get hurt.

Hector and Maxorro stayed tending the fire, while Paco, Rodolfo, and the two soldiers went hunting for something large to eat."

It was Agustin who spotted a small antelope. Bringing the rifle to his eye, he killed the animal with one shot. "I told you *jefe,* I am a good shot," he said and grinned at Rodolfo.

Hector and Paco skinned and dressed the antelope and hung it over the fire until the meat sizzled. Sitting around the fire, the *bandidos* and the soldiers sat together and talked about many things. Agustin told them how he and his brother had been volunteered into the Army by his father. He said the family had too many mouths to feed and at least in the Army he had clothes, a horse, and food in his belly. Roberto had been a plantation worker before he joined the Army.

Hector and Paco talked about their lives growing up on a *hacienda* in Durango. As the stars popped in the sky, Rodolfo put another log on the fire. It crackled and tiny embers flew high into the night sky.

"Maxorro, entertain us with some of your stories about those stubborn mules and the *pinche* miners whose silver we stole," Rodolfo asked. Rodolfo leaned back on his elbow listening to Maxorro's stories. His mind wandered to María and to her body wrapped in a warm blanket beside him. When he closed his eyes, he could picture her standing in the morning sun watching him leave. His heart and body ached for her. He had been gone almost a month and prayed every night she was safe. With his rifle held firmly in his hand, he fell asleep.

At the *bandido's* camp south of Torreón, María walked toward the stream with a basket of dirty baby cloths. Two babies were born in the *bandido's* camp just since Rodolfo left. Both were little girls. The tiny one cried a lot. It reminded María of her own baby Bernardo. Though it seemed so long ago, it was only last winter when she buried her son under the tree in Santa Fe. Baby Bernardo cried incessantly and did not want her breast. Her mother and Rafael tried to find something to calm him. Her mother even called in a gringo doctor, but nothing saved him.

When María held the tiny crying girl her heart ached and her nipples tingled in response. Before Rodolfo left, she was suspicious of her condition, but now she was sure she was pregnant with his child. Her belly swelled slightly and she guessed she was almost three months along. Unlike her pregnancy with Bernardo, María felt wonderful, full of life and was not sick in the morning.

She walked toward the stream carrying her bundle engrossed in her thoughts. She did not see a man sitting under the shade of a large mesquite tree until she almost tripped on him.

"*Hola María,*" Pablo spoke and María dropped the basket. The old man laughed and said, "It is only me, Pablo. You are looking well my child."

"Pablo, why are you here? How did you find us?"

"It was not that hard. Many *peóns* know of you and where you are," he responded.

"You went to Santa Fe. Why didn't you stay?"

"That is why I am here. Rafael sent me to find you."

"You can tell him I won't go back. I am a free woman and my place is here with Rodolfo." María spoke with conviction and determination. Though she no longer blamed her brother for taking her and the children to Santa Fe, she did not belong there. Mexico was her home.

"No mija, Rafael does not want you to return to Santa Fe. He told me to find you and Rodolfo and take you to the *hacienda,"* he said.

"What are you talking about? I never want to go to that *hacienda,* never again!" she blurted out.

"No mija, you do not understand. He only wants to help you and Rodolfo. Come sit and hear me out," Pablo said. María picked up the basket and reluctantly sat down beside him.

"You were not the first woman *don* Bernardo raped. Like you, *don* Bernardo raped your mother when she was young and she became pregnant with Rafael."

"What! How can it be?"

"Your mother told me to keep her secret and she quickly married your father. She named him Rafael, after the *don's* grandfather. When Rafael was born, I made sure the priest made a birth certificate naming *don* Bernardo as the father. Did you never wonder why Rafael's skin was lighter than yours and his face more angular like Antonio's?" Pablo asked her.

María sat stunned hearing Pablo's news. Her brother was a bastard to *don* Bernardo just like her own children. Her mother kept the secret from her, even after Rafael shot the *don* and fled. Suddenly she understood her mother's resentment against the *don.*

"My poor mother. How are my children? Are they happy in Santa Fe?"

"Your mother and the children are all well. Antonio follows *Señor* Summers around and he is learning to ride a horse. He will start school this fall. Alicia is growing up quickly."

"I miss them," she said softly, "but this is no place for

them."

"That is why Rafael wanted me to find you. President Juárez has made new laws. Now, a bastard can inherit land, if he is the only heir and first born son. It is so, even if the bastard is a *mestizo*. Rafael inherited the *hacienda* and wants you and Rodolfo to live there," Pablo told her.

"What? It is not possible."

"Yes, it is possible. Rafael inherited the *hacienda*. He filed the official papers in Mexico City. He wants to give the *hacienda* to you and Rodolfo," he continued.

María's mind spun confused by the news. She barely dared to believe it was possible.

"Yes, Rafael sent me to find you. He is worried about you being killed or put in prison and wants you and Rodolfo to have the *hacienda* so you can live in peace. When Rafael and the lawyer return from Mexico City, they will file land documents with the state government here in Torreón," Pablo told her.

"What about all the others?" she asked. She suddenly remembered the enormous responsibility she and Rodolfo had with the families living with them at the camp.

"There are plenty of decent jacals at the *hacienda*. You will need help planting and running the land. All of the people can live there, even I can stay if you want. Perhaps you will need a horse trainer," Pablo said with a twinkle in his eye.

María threw her arms around Pablo and hugged him tight, though she still did not believe it could be true.

"Are you sure? This is not a dream?"

"*No mija,* you are not dreaming. Come back with me and see that it is true."

"I need to wait until Rodolfo gets back. He will expect to find us here at the camp. I will send someone to tell you when we are coming," she told him.

Chapter 34

Rafe found *don* David at the breakfast table sipping coffee and reading the newspaper.

"Buenos dias," he greeted him. "Have some breakfast before you leave for Torreón."

"I'm not going to Torreón until I find Rayo. Carmela has done this for spite. She has no more right to him than I do," Rafe responded.

"No Rafael. She will not give him up willingly. Horse stealing is a capital offense. You could be hanged."

"She is the one who should be hanged."

"Not in this city. Give up this mad idea."

"Rayo is more than a horse to me. He is my friend and has saved my life several times. He is my property now and I'm afraid they will not treat him well."

"I understand your concern for him, but it is you who could get killed here. Let them have him. You said you have some very fine horses in Santa Fe, some of them his offspring. Your life is not worth giving up for Rayo," *don* David told him and Rafe saw the worry in his eyes.

"You don't understand. *Don* Bernardo and *doña* Carmela treated us like dirt when we lived at the *hacienda*. They consigned my father to fight the French and he died at Puebla. The *don* raped both my mother and sister. This is not only about Rayo."

Don David sighed and folded the newspaper. He knew this mission was dangerous and might end badly for Rafael. He had grown to respect the young man over the days he lived under his roof. "They could have taken him anywhere. How can you find him?"

"Nicolás Jiménez has had many dealings with Carmela. He probably knows where she lives. Unfortunately, I don't know if he has left yet for Torreón, nor where he may be staying if he is still in the city."

"Yes that is unfortunate. Let me think on that for a while. Come have some breakfast."

By then end of breakfast, *don* David convinced Rafe to think carefully about his plans to find Rayo. "I have some connections here in Mexico City. There may be other ways to find the horse. In the meantime, you may remain as my guest."

Rafe spent most of the morning pacing the courtyard. Around midday he saddled the mare and rode the streets of Mexico City. It was large and foreign to him. People on the streets stared at his *Americano* clothes. By the time he arrived back, he decided *don* David was right. He was going to need help finding the horse.

Later in the afternoon, Rafe heard hoof beats in the courtyard and a short time later a servant summoned him to the parlor.

"Rafael, meet Ricardo. I have hired him to help you find Rayo. He's a traveling blacksmith who works all around the city. There is hardly a horse in the city he has not seen over the years," *don* David said introducing Ricardo. A middle-aged man stood quietly beside him holding his hat in his hand.

"*Gracias don* David. I very much appreciate your help Ricardo," Rafe greeted the man.

"I've asked him if he knows where *doña* Carmela lives," *don* David explained.

"A woman named Carmela lives in Colonia Condesa which is near Colonia Roma. I remember her well. I have shod her horses occasionally over the years," Ricardo responded. "I remember she did not treat her horses well."

Rafe bristled at his comment. Carmela would not treat Rayo with the care and attention the spirited horse required.

"Do you remember where the house is located?" Rafe asked him.

"*Sí.*"

"Come let us go," Rafe said.

The sun was hanging brightly in the sky when Rafe and Ricardo reached the house where Carmela lived. Sitting on their horses across from the courtyard entrance, Rafe pulled up. The home was modest, though well kept. For some reason Rafe was expecting something more sophisticated. In the back of the courtyard, the small carriage house's doors were open.

"Rayo would be in the carriage house," Rafe said. Unexpectedly Rafe realized finding the horse was only the first of his problems. Retrieving him would be much more difficult.

Ricardo jumped down from his horse and walked into the courtyard with his hat in his hands. He walked to the front door and rang the bell. Rafe watched a maid answer and she spoke to Ricardo for a minute or so. Ricardo walked down the front steps and into the carriage house. In several minutes he returned to say something to the maid who waited on the veranda and then walked back to where Rafe waited.

"What did you say?"

"I told her I was a traveling blacksmith and asked if any of their horses needed shoeing. She told me to talk to the carriage driver. There is no Appaloosa in the barn, but the carriage driver said he was taking his *jefe* to the city for the evening."

Rafe was still not convinced. If this was *doña* Carmela's house then he needed to follow her. Perhaps the horse was being kept somewhere else. They steered their horses to a spot less conspicuous and waited.

About an hour later the carriage driver pulled to the front of the house and Rafe saw a man and a woman step onto the carriage. The woman was not *doña* Carmela. "It is not her," he said to Ricardo.

Dejected, Rafe told Ricardo to make inquires for a *señora* named Carmela Reyes. If he located her, he should come immediately to *don* David's home, otherwise come in the morning. As they parted, Rafe rode to the Zócalo. The plaza was teeming with activity. People, horses, carts, and vendors were busily engaged in life. Rafe rode the plaza and methodically stopped at each hotel.

"*Por favor Señor Nicolás Jiménez?*" he asked each desk clerk for the lawyer.

"*Nadie por ese nombre,*" was the answer that no one by that name was staying there.

It was dark by the time Rafe returned to *don* David's home. Ricardo was also not there indicating he too had no luck. What was waiting for him was a telegram from George Summers.

Rafe.
Do not seek Rayo. Leave him and seek María.
Go to Torreón. Please respond.
Father.

Rafe put the telegram in his pocket. His adopted father was worried and Rafe knew he was rightfully so. Walking to his bedroom, Rafe closed the door behind him and sighed. It was Saturday night and the telegraph office would be closed on Sunday. He promised himself to reply on Monday, though he was not sure what he would say.

The following morning Rafe found *don* David on the patio eating breakfast. Rafe joined him and related the events of yesterday's fruitless search. Hoofbeats sounded in the courtyard and Ricardo was ushered onto the patio a few minutes later.

"*Buenos días,*" he said and bowed slightly toward *don* David.

"Come, please sit with us and have some *café.*"

"Did you find anything?" Rafe asked.

"*No señor.* I have been asking for Carmela Reyes but none of my contacts know the name. I also asked about the Appaloosa. A carriage driver said he thought he saw a *caballero* with such a horse on Friday afternoon, but it may not be the same horse," Ricardo reported.

Rafe's chest heaved. Even finding Carmela in this large city was difficult, let alone a horse which could be anywhere.

"Tomorrow I will go to Alirio Mansano's office and talk to him. I've been thinking he is probably not a part of this scheme. I will see if he will tell me how to contact Carmela," *don* David told them. "I'm sorry Rafael, I should have thought of this sooner."

"I could go," Rafe said.

"No, I think it is best if I do this. Alirio is Carmela's

lawyer and as such sworn to her duty. He might refuse to tell you anything as her advisor in this matter."

Ricardo finished his *café* and Rafe told him to go home. Much to Rafe's torment, they would not start the search again until the morning.

"We must go to Mass this morning, Rafael. We will ask God for his help," *don* David said.

CHAPTER 35

Buck cautiously roped the Appaloosa Carmela called Rayo. He mused Rayo, meaning thunderbolt, was a fitting name for the wild stallion. Buck kept careful watch on the angry horse's hoofs, though it was restricted by the tight bit and bridle. It was the only way Buck had been able to contain the horse. Part of the backside of the stall was kicked down with splintered boards in the gate. Buck thought of himself as an expert horseman, though he could not control the crazy Appaloosa.

Don Luis and *doña* Carmela were leaving for Jalisco early this morning. Last night the *don* gave Buck an uncharacteristic night off before the trip.

"Be here by eight in the morning ready to go," the *don* told him. It gave Buck one more night with Sayuri at the Nightingale brothel and he willingly paid Madam Lucia extra for the entire night with the lovely Japanese *puta*.

During the night, gunfire erupted nearby and woke him. Sayuri lay sleeping near him. He grabbed his pistol and waited. The gunfire moved away from the brothel and only faint shots could be heard in the far distance. He returned to bed and woke Sayuri. Willingly she gave herself to him.

Now as he readied the Appaloosa, his only thoughts were of last night with Sayuri. He pondered how he could find excuses to return to Mexico City to see her again.

Rayo snorted and pulled at the tether side to side wanting to tear away from his new master, but Buck held him securely. Buck could tell the horse was tiring. He had welts on his haunches and his legs from kicking at the wooden stall. Buck hoped he was growing tired of resisting and the trip to Jalisco would not be made impossible by the spirited Appaloosa.

"*Cálmese,*" Buck spoke at Rayo. The horse stood patiently staring at Buck with large dark eyes. Buck could almost see his reflection in them. The more he studied the Appaloosa, the more he was impressed with the blooded horse and surmised *doña* Carmela's ex-husband was an expert horse breeder. When tamed, Buck knew the horse would be superior to anything he ever owned and he planned to make the *patróna* beg him to get rid of the horse.

For the past several months, Buck had been thinking of heading back home to Lexington, Kentucky. He was tired of Mexico and with the threat of another revolution about to break out, it seemed a good time to leave. The only thing keeping him here now was Sayuri. He wondered if Madam Lucia would sell her and how much that might cost. Looking back at the magnificent Appaloosa he wondered if the horse might be an acceptable trade to the madame at the brothel for a Japanese *puta*.

When the carriage was loaded, Buck tied the Appaloosa tight to the rear. He mounted his horse Bala and followed behind. The Appaloosa tugged and pulled the tie rope. Each time it jerked the carriage he could hear Carmela complain.

Before they were out of the city, *don* Luis stopped the carriage and called to Buck. "Get that crazy horse untied from this carriage. He is too wild and his jerking is upsetting the *patróna*. You need to string him," the *don* ordered.

Buck dutifully untied Rayo from the carriage. His plan worked perfectly and the tight tetherline pulled at the horse's head and he responded just as Buck hoped. He would let the Appaloosa be wild and untamable and even encourage it. Eventually Carmela would want to be rid of the wild horse.

The *don* pushed the carriage taking five instead of six days for the trip. Buck heard Carmela whining and complaining often. Finally they reached Las Lomas, a small town not far from the isolated site of the *hacienda*.

Don Luis stopped the carriage at the general mercantile and let Carmela buy supplies and rest before the final leg of their journey. Buck tied the Appaloosa and his horse to a hitching post and wandered into the cantina.

"Hola Buck. You have returned. Tequila?"

"Give me a bottle. Seems quiet today," Buck said to the bartender.

"Oh sí, we had a big ruckus with some *Indios* and

hacienderos. The *Indios* are unhappy about the hard work to harvest the agave. They tried to quit and the *hacienderos* killed a few of them. Things are calmer now."

Buck had drunk more than a third of the bottle passing the time with the bartender when he heard the cantina's door open.

"Buck, the *patróna* is ready to go," *don* Luis called out to him.

Buck threw five pesos on the counter top for the bartender, grabbed the bottle, and headed outside. Carmela sat in the carriage waiting. Deliberately, Buck jerked the Appaloosa's bit causing him to screech and whinny loudly. Buck was hurting him on purpose and the big horse did not like it. Buck made sure Carmela was watching. He pretended to be unable to control the horse and was encouraging its wild nature. *Don* Luis and Carmela were watching Buck struggle.

"*¡Bruto!*" Buck loudly called the horse stupid.

Finally he backed off the tight grip on the bit and Rayo calmed. He mounted his horse and put the Appaloosa in tow. *Don* Luis drove the carriage in front of him.

Buck could hear Carmela grousing at *don* Luis. "He is no horse trainer. Look how he cannot even manage to control the Appaloosa."

"*Querida,* he is my bodyguard not a horse master. I did not hire him to control a wild stallion. You will see when we get to the *hacienda,* the horse will be happier. I have a large field where he will be able to roam free."

"You better make sure Buck watches that horse. Nothing must to happen to him," *doña* Carmela responded.

Buck heard her grumble to the *don*. He did not like the woman and sensed something about her, something he could not put a finger on, but he knew for sure he could not trust her.

CHAPTER 36

Monday morning *don* David saddled his horse and rode to Alirio Mansano's office on Avenida Hidalgo located near the Zócalo. He pondered how to approach the lawyer, who had a reputation as being extremely shrewd. If the lawyer knew about the horse theft, he might be suspicious of any attempt to locate *doña* Carmela.

When he arrived he was surprised to find the lawyer alone in his office.

"Buenos días, soy David Salazar de Rosas. We met on Friday at the land office," *don* David introduced himself and extended his hand.

Alirio shook it and replied, "Ah yes. Please be seated. How may I be of service to you?"

"After the hearing, *don* Luis spoke to young Rafael on behalf of Carmela about buying the *hacienda*. At the time Rafael was not agreeable. It is understandable as he is young and not aware of the huge responsibility of running a large estate. However on further contemplation, Rafael may be more agreeable if terms can be arranged."

Alirio twirled a pen in his fingers as he listened to *don* David. Carmela was livid at losing the property and though he was not aware *don* Luis approached Rafael about a sale, he was not surprised.

"I am acting as a neutral negotiator and would like to speak to *doña* Carmela on his behalf," *don* David explained further.

"I was not aware of any such offer, but it could be arranged," Alirio said. "I can organize a meeting here."

Don David was afraid the lawyer would respond in such a manner. It would be in his best interest to be part of the negotiations.

"You are most kind, *señor*. However, Rafael does not have a lawyer available here in town as *Señor* Jiménez has departed for Torreón. I would like to approach Carmela directly to see if the offer is still an option. Perhaps she has had time to think and is no longer interested. I will have a short conversation with her and if she still wants to buy the *hacienda,* Rafael will have Nicolás Jiménez contact you to negotiate the deal." *Don* David waited for the lawyer to respond.

Several long moments seemed to hang in the air as Alirio pondered what *don* David proposed.

"Her home is in Colonia Roma, not far from here," he answered.

"Gracias señor. I will call on her and you will be hearing from us."

Don David found Rafe and Ricardo waiting impatiently for him when he arrived back at the house. Rafe bounded down the veranda steps upon hearing hoof beats in the courtyard. *Don* David related his conversation with the lawyer.

Ricardo said he knew the Colonia Roma area well. As he and Rafe mounted to leave, *don* David grabbed Rafe's bridle.

"Use caution. This is no small matter and regardless of whether she stole the horse from you, she can have you shot on the spot for trying to steal it back," *don* David cautioned.

It was mid afternoon by the time Rafe and Ricardo reached *doña* Carmela's house and the city was taking siesta. It was the time of day when most activity stopped and life waited for the heat of the day to pass. At Carmela's house they saw very little activity of any kind.

Once again it was Ricardo who jumped down from his horse and walked through the courtyard gate. He knocked on the front door.

"Buenas tardes," he greeted a maid who opened the door. "I am the blacksmith the *señora* said was needed for a new horse she has acquired."

"No, señor, we have no horses here," the maid replied somewhat confused.

"Is this not the house of *doña* Carmela Reyes?" he asked.

"Sí señor, but you must be mistaken. We have no horses here," she answered.

"She contacted the livery and asked for a blacksmith. May I speak with the *señora,*" he persisted.

The maid was puzzled, though if her *patróna* needed a blacksmith she could not turn the man away.

"I told you we have no horses here. Her carriage is with *don* Luis. Perhaps she contacted you from there," she said.

"Ah yes, perhaps I was given the wrong location. Where can I find *don* Luis' home? I will go there and speak with the *señora* about her horses," he continued.

"*Don* Luis Orozco lives in the neighborhood called Colonia San Ángel," she told him.

"*Gracias,*" Ricardo tipped his hat before she slammed the door. Ricardo walked back to where Rafe was waiting.

"Rafael, they have no horses at this house and *doña* Carmela has gone to *don* Luis Orozco's house. He lives in Colonia San Ángel. I know the neighborhood and most of the houses there have stables," he reported.

"*Bueno.* Let's go see if Rayo is there," Rafe told him.

It was a short ride to *don* Luis' home in the Colonia San Ángel area. Rafe was not surprised by the opulence of the houses. *Don* Luis' house was surrounded by a high wall and the gate was closed. Rafe knew *don* Luis and Carmela would recognize him and stayed far down the street while Ricardo walked toward the closed gate and pulled the chain to sound the bell. Rafe was impressed how calmly Ricardo approached the house. The gate opened slightly and Rafe could see Ricardo speaking to someone, then the gate was closed, and Ricardo returned.

"The *don* and his *doña* are not at home. I asked about horses and the servant was very suspicious and would not give me much information. We will have to think of another idea."

Rafe sat his horse and pondered if he could scale the wall of the courtyard. Perhaps if he could at least look inside the stables, he would know if Carmela and *don* Luis were hiding Rayo. Remembering *don* David's words of caution, he decided against it.

"*Vamos.*"

Rafe and Ricardo returned to *don* David's house. Frustrated, but encouraged with the day's findings, Rafe told Ricardo to return in the morning. He and *don* David discussed ideas long into the evening.

"You must be careful not to be recognized," *don* David told him. "I will send a note to Alirio Mansano and tell him I have been unable to locate Carmela. Perhaps he will respond."

"This is my problem and I appreciate your help, but do not get involved further. I do not want anything I do to reflect poorly on you." *Don* David waved his hand to dismiss the idea.

In the morning, Rafe came to breakfast dressed as a *peón*. He shaved his beard and mustache and wore a pair of dirty cotton *pantalones* and a baggy *camisa*. *Don* David looked up from his newspaper and almost did not recognize him.

"*¿Rafael, por qué estás vestido como peón?*" *don* David asked why he was dressed as a *peón*.

"I will not be recognized. Ricardo and I will try again to get into *don* Luis' home. It is better I look this way than as an *Americano*."

"That is true, but be careful. There is still unrest in the city between peasants and the Spanish. It is said Porfirio Díaz is fueling the unrest against our President Juárez to make it look like he is not caring for his people and his liberal ideas are not working." *Don* David pointed to the newspaper he was reading. "Porfirio lost the election to Juárez and wants to regain political control of the country for the aristocracy. You must be careful when you go to *don* Luis' today dressed in such a way and do not be out after dusk, it is dangerous," *don* David told him.

Rafe and Ricardo rode their horses to *don* Luis' street leaving them tethered in a side alley. Ricardo carried a heavy pack of blacksmithing tools and Rafe carried a sack of horseshoes. As they walked out to the street, several vendors were calling out to sell their wares. *"Manzanas!" "Verduras!" "Pasteles!"*

Stopping across the street from *don* Luis' they watched as a maid opened the gate to talk to the vendor selling vegetables.

"Come on," Rafe said and boldly strode across the street. As he and Ricardo walked up to the gate he mumbled at the maid and walked by her.

"*¡Alto!*" she shouted after them to stop.

"Keep walking," Rafe hissed to Ricardo who had stuck beside him and they walked with purpose toward the carriage barn. Walking through the barn doors Rafe was shocked at the disarray. Two stalls were completely ruined, with one gate torn off and the other a splintered mess.

"What happened in here?" Ricardo whispered to him.

"Rayo. Rayo did this," Rafe said.

"*¿Qué están haciendo aquí?*" an older man walked into the barn and asked them what they were doing. "*Voy a llamar a la policía,*" he finished by saying he would call the police.

"*Por favor,* we are hungry and looking for work. We will clean the horse stalls for a good price, *señor,*" Ricardo said.

"*Mi patrón* is not here, I cannot hire you," the man answered. "*Váyanse,*" he told them to leave.

"What happened here?" Rafe asked the man pointing to the debris.

"*Un loco Appaloosa salvaje y vicioso lo pateó toda la noche,*" he said a wild and vicious Appaloosa kicked it all night long. Rafe smiled under his straw sombrero, knowing Rayo tore the place up trying to escape.

"Where is the horse now?" Ricardo asked.

"*Lo llevaron a la hacienda en Jalisco,*" he said the horse had been taken to the *hacienda* in Jalisco.

"We are looking for permanent work. Do you think *el patrón* needs workers at his *hacienda?*" Rafe asked wanting more information.

"I cannot say. I only work here at his house and have never been to *el patrón's hacienda,*" he answered. "All I know is the *hacienda* is located near a small village called Las Lomas. Perhaps you can go there and ask," he answered.

Rafe heard all he needed to know. He muttered apologies for their intrusion and tugged on Ricardo's arm. Keeping his subservient posture, Rafe walked beside Ricardo as they left *don* Luis' courtyard with his sombrero tilted low on his face.

"Did your horse do all that damage?" Ricardo asked after they were well out of earshot.

"He is a blooded Appaloosa and he is tame for me, but he would not be so for someone else, especially if they mistreat him."

"I am going to Jalisco to find him," Rafe told Ricardo when they reached their horses tethered in the alley.

"We will go together," Ricardo answered.

CHAPTER 37

Doña Carmela stood on the veranda of the *hacienda* in Jalisco watching as two *vaqueros* tried to mount the wild Appaloosa. The first *vaquero* climbed up into the saddle while the other tried to hold the horse. At first it seemed as if they could control the horse, then suddenly with a lightning fast move the Appaloosa threw the man from its back. He landed with a thud about ten feet away. Watching the horse, Carmela thought Rayo, Spanish for thunderbolt, was an appropriate name and laughed.

The horse reared and bucked forcing the *vaqueros* to jump out of the way. Watching the seasoned *vaqueros* get thrown and kicked by the uncontrollable horse made her wonder how Rafael, the *pinche peón,* could have mastered the beast. Apparently, he had no trouble riding the Appaloosa. She smiled thinking how he was probably bitter at losing it. How she wished she had been able to see the look on his face when he realized she reclaimed the horse. Carmela saw Buck watching the show from the doorway of the barn. She did not like the *pinche gringo,* but the *don* said he was one of the best gunmen he had ever hired.

Life at *don* Luis' *hacienda* in Jalisco was not well suited for Buck. He was not a worker and as the *don's* bodyguard there was not much danger in this rural countryside. The closest town was Las Lomas and it was not much of a town. Its cantina had an old guitar player and two very worn out *putas*. Unlike the rioting in Mexico City, life in Jalisco was boring.

Buck missed the nightlife and his friend Salvador, but especially he missed Sayuri. Now, the only exciting thing at the *hacienda* was the crazy Appaloosa and the challenge of taming the stubborn horse. Several of the *hacienda's vaqueros* tried to ride the stallion. They prided themselves as expert horsemen, only to be thrown to the ground repeatedly by Rayo. Finally, they told Buck the horse was loco.

Every way Buck tried to calm the horse ended badly.

He used tricks to annoy the horse, beat him, and then he tried kindness and treats. Nothing he tried worked and the *doña* cursed at Buck's inability to train the horse and keep him quiet. She told him the horse was stolen by the *peón* who shot her husband *don* Bernardo; the same *peón* was her husband's bastard son who inherited her *hacienda* in Torreón. Buck struggled to understand her attachment to the horse and told her just to be rid of it. She staunchly refused and said someday the *peón* would come for him and then she would have him shot.

Even though he had yet to be successful in mounting the Appaloosa, Buck plotted so *doña* Carmela would just tell him to take the horse after she finally tired of its antics. He could tell the blooded horse was a breed above anything he ever saw. Buck noticed how the other horses responded to the big Appaloosa and followed him. Each night he made sure to feed the horse extra grains and talked to him. He thought Rayo was becoming more calm around him each day.

Upstairs in his bedroom in *don* David's house in Mexico City, Rafe was packing his satchel for the trip to Jalisco. He and Ricardo were leaving this morning. Dressing in a traveling suit, he wrapped his GSW pistols around his waist. If they encountered any trouble along the way, he would be ready.

He did not sleep well last night, waking often, and struggling to think of a plan where he could recover Rayo and not get killed in the process. He was sorry Carlos was not with him. Carlos always had good ideas, like the one to rescue Rafe's mother and sister from *don* Bernardo's *hacienda* last year. He woke last night thinking how he was going to miss Carlos and Bibiana's wedding next weekend. Carlos asked him to stand beside him during the ceremony. When he left on this journey, he was sure he would have already returned to Santa Fe and promised to be there.

While folding his more formal suit jacket he felt a piece of paper. It was the telegram from George and he had not yet responded. He unfolded it and reread the words. *Do not*

seek Rayo. Leave him and seek María. Go to Torreón. Please respond.
Rafe sat on the bed torn between two problems. If he did
not respond to George, his adopted parents would be frantic
with worry. If he responded he was leaving for Jalisco to find
Rayo, they would probably worry more. He stuffed the
telegram into his saddlebag.

Don David's servant loaded the packhorse and saddled
the brown mare. He was waiting in the courtyard with
Ricardo when Rafe walked out of the house. He shook
Ricardo's hand and took Rafe's shoulders in a hearty *abrazo.*

"God be with you on your journey," *don* David said to
him. "Please be careful."

"We will," Rafe responded. After he mounted, he
reached down and took the *don's* extended hand. "Can you
do me a favor?" he asked. "Send a telegram to Carlos and
tell him I am well, but will miss his wedding."

"Certainly." *Don* David watched the two men ride
from the courtyard. They rode off trailing the packhorse and
he said a prayer they could get out of the city without any
trouble. Then he said a prayer they would not get killed in
Jalisco.

As they rode out of Mexico City, Rafe wished he had
told Ricardo no, when he said he would go along. He was no
doubt putting Ricardo in danger. Now, as much as Rafe
appreciated his help, he worried about the older man's safety.

"Ricardo, you should turn back," Rafe said. "This is
not your fight and I do not want you to get hurt."

Ricardo smiled at him. "I am but a simple man. I have
worked in a livery and tended horses my entire life. It is time
for a little excitement."

"Have you been to Jalisco?" Rafe asked.

"Yes, once I went to Guadalajara, the capital. It was
Semana Santa, Holy Week. It is a beautiful city. I am hoping
we can go there after we get your horse," he answered.

"Tell me about Santa Fe?" Ricardo asked. "It is very
different in New Mexico?"

"In some ways it is much like the cities here in Mexico.
Spanish conquistadors settled New Mexico in 1598 and it
remained part of New Spain until Mexico won independence

from Spain in 1821. It was part of Mexico until 1848 when the United States took it. You would like it there Ricardo. You do not have to be an aristocrat there to own land or have your own business. Americans are free and are protected by a piece of paper called the Constitution," Rafe told him.

"Do they speak Spanish there?" Ricardo asked.

"Yes, Spanish is spoken in New Mexico, Texas, Arizona and California. It is changing now as many people from the eastern cities are moving west and speaking English. I learned to speak English. It is not so hard," Rafe continued.

"I would like to go there someday to visit, but I would not stay. I love my Mexico," Ricardo said.

CHAPTER 38

It took many days after the battle with Sancho, for Rodolfo and the small group to reach a point near the campsite just south and west of Torreón. They had no further trouble and Hector was feeling better, though was still riding in the wagon and not on a horse. The two soldiers were riding their horses. Maxorro stopped his mules at Rodolfo's signal.

Even at a fair distance Rodolfo saw a large plume of smoke rising in the evening sky. It rose near where he expected the campsite was located and it worried him. The smoke was noticeable from a great distance and *la policía* would surely have noticed it.

"What is wrong *jefe?*" Paco asked.

Rodolfo pointed to the smoke. "Perhaps *la policía* are setting a trap for us." The thought of losing the ill-gotten silver after all they went through to get it, made him extremely cautious. "Paco, go see if the camp is safe."

Paco returned in less than an hour. "It looks like they are having a fiesta," he told Rodolfo.

"A fiesta? What do you mean?"

"There is a big fire with a pig roasting. The children are running and laughing. There are more people than when we left *jefe.*"

"More! Did you see María?"

"No. But it does not look like they are worried about *la policía* finding them."

Rodolfo led the small procession toward the camp. Before they reached it, Javier came running down the path.

"Rodolfo," Javier called out. "Welcome back."

"Javier, why do you have such a big fire? I spotted the campsite from far away," Rodolfo asked him as he dismounted.

"It cannot be helped *jefe,*" he said.

"What do you mean it cannot be helped?" Rodolfo asked. "Look at me Javier, what do you mean?"

"When you left you know we had many new people. Now we have double as many, some with wives and children," he added.

"What! How can this be? Why are they coming to us? We cannot take care of so many people, especially children," Rodolfo sighed. He carried a small fortune on the mules, and yet none of that could be used to buy food for this growing group.

"I told you before; it is your fault *jefe*. You helped the *peóns* by sharing what we stole. You gave them hope for a future," Javier continued.

"Why haven't *la policía* arrested all of you," Rodolfo shot back. "Surely they see the smoke."

"You are not going to believe this *jefe*. *La policía* have found us, but the people protected us. Any of us who might be recognized as bandits hid in the hills. The people, especially María and the women, admonished the police sergeant for disturbing such poor innocent people. The sergeant backed down and apologized. Once they were gone we came out of hiding. The police sergeant came back several days ago. He brought a milk cow and the pig we are cooking. He said he will bring more food next week," Javier told him.

"Who are these people?" Javier asked seeing Maxorro and the two soldiers.

"Come I will tell everyone when we get to the camp." Rodolfo signaled the small procession to follow and with Javier leading them, they rode into the camp.

María looked up at the confusion on the trail heading into the camp. A joyous shout erupted. Behind Javier, she saw the top of Rodolfo's head. Screaming she ran down the path. Rodolfo jumped off his horse and she jumped into his arms.

"Querida," he whispered in her ear and they held each other tight.

"God has protected you my love and brought you back to us," María responded.

Maxorro and the soldiers waited patiently on the path. Maxorro smiled watching the scene unfold before his eyes.

At least fifty men, women, and children surrounded Rodolfo, Paco, and Hector. The scene was chaotic with children running and dogs barking in the middle, greeting the returning men.

"Javier, these are my new friends. Maxorro, Roberto, and Agustin. Introduce them to the men and make them feel at home. Find some clothes for Roberto and Agustin to replace those uniforms."

A small boy shyly came toward Maxorro and asked him if he could lead the mules back to the camp. The boy was about ten and Maxorro handed him the rope to the lead mule. Together they walked up the trail.

María pulled at Rodolfo. "You need a bath *querido,"* she poked at his dirty camisa. Following her to the nearby stream, María pulled off his dirty clothes and pushed him into the water throwing a bar of soap at him. He landed with a thud in the streambed and laughed.

"I have so much to tell you," María said.

"I have more to tell you. You have not even asked me about the silver?"

"What silver?"

"The silver in the saddle bags on the mules. We are rich beyond our wildest dreams *querida."*

"Rich?"

"There are fourteen bars of pure silver riding the backs of those mangy beasts. Maxorro is a muleteer. He helped us rob the muletrain from the mine.

"What about those soldiers?" María asked.

"They and Maxorro want to join our group. Our only problem now is how to use the silver bars to buy food and the guns and ammunition we need."

"Rodolfo we will not need more guns. We need plows and horses. Pablo came to the camp while you were gone. My brother Rafael has inherited the Reyes *hacienda* and he wants us and the people to live there and run it. He is giving it to us as a gift."

"Pablo must be mistaken. *Mestizos* cannot inherit land. He must be getting senile," Rodolfo said laughing at María's naïveté.

"You are wrong. There are new laws and a bastard son of a *haciendero* can inherit the property if there are no other heirs. *Don* Bernardo raped my mother and Rafael has proof he is truly the son of *don* Bernardo. Padre Andres documented his birth. It is all true." Rodolfo looked at her with disbelief at what she said.

"Rodolfo, this is a godsend. We do not have to live like *peóns*. We do not have to rob and steal for food anymore," she continued.

"But *querida,* we know nothing about running a *hacienda,*" he said wide eyed as reality began to set in. "Where and how do we get and pay workers?" he asked.

"Look at all the people we have here. They have been running a *hacienda* for years as the workers. We will take them with us and they can plant crops and now we can buy cattle with the silver you stole. This is the Lord taking care of us," she said and made the sign of the cross.

María stripped her skirt and blouse and jumped into the water splashing water at him as she approached.

A little while later, the people of the camp gathered around the roasted pig while two women cooked tortillas. Several pots of beans and root vegetables cooked over the fire. Rodolfo noticed the people looked both happy and healthy.

María wanted to tell the people to begin the packing and moving process, but Rodolfo asked her to wait. "Let me go talk to Pablo tomorrow. If it is what you say, then we will move the people. In the meantime, say nothing until we know for sure.

Maxorro was sitting amongst the people eating meat mixed with peppers wrapped in a tortilla and the soldiers sat near him. They were talking and eating with the *peóns* devouring a plate of the spicy food.

Rodolfo sat down beside the muleteer. "Maxorro, come with me tomorrow. We must go to the Reyes *hacienda* and talk to Pablo. María's believes her older brother has inherited the *hacienda* and is giving it to us. It is where we both grew up, so we know it well. If this is true, we can take the people and work the land for our profit. We would have a permanent place to live and we do not have to rob for our food," Rodolfo told him and paused to let it sink in.

"I do not believe it. How is it possible, you two are *peóns* just like me?" Maxorro asked.

"It is an incredible story, but María believes it is true," he answered.

"Say nothing, but tomorrow we will go talk to Pablo."

CHAPTER 39

George Summers sat at his desk going over the GSW accounting books. He tried to concentrate, but *don* David's telegram which Carlos shared with him, had him worried. He wondered why Rafe had not wired him directly. The wire said Rafe was well and was traveling to Jalisco. He told Carlos he would not make the wedding. It worried George and he could not get over the feeling thinking Rafe was heading into trouble in Mexico. Carlos seemed disappointed Rafe would not make the wedding, though otherwise did not seem worried.

There was a knock on the door. "George, yew in thar?" Mayor Billy Thornton called through the door to George's office.

"Come on in Billy," George called out.

"What you doing way out here Billy?" George asked. The mayor had never been to the foundry before and only once to the house for a Christmas party.

"Well George, I tell yew. I got most of the Santa Fe ristrocrats on my tail again bout yer boy killing that Diego feller. Theys lookin fer blood," the mayor said in his Missouri accent.

"I spoke to the sheriff several weeks ago, Billy. He says all the witnesses swear they saw Diego come after Rafe wielding a sword. I thought the investigation was over," George said.

"Yeah I know. He tol me the same thing as you say, but em ristrocrats, yew know who I'm talking bout, won't let it go. They want blood I tell yew. The sheriff and me think we need to have a formal hearing an git all the facts out to a federal judge. Maybe then em high and mighty Spaniards will let well nuff alone," the mayor reluctantly said.

George sighed wondering if this mess would ever be put right. "The sheriff should not let those *dons* push him around," George said.

"I hear you George, but the sheriff asked me to take

Rafe in iffin he's here or when he comes back."

"He's not here Billy," George replied.

"Now don't be diffcult George. We'll only keep him until the federal judge gets here week after next. I figger you might be a hiding im."

"I'm not being difficult Billy. Rafe is in Mexico taking care of family business and I don't know when he will be home. Maybe sometime later in September or October," George informed the mayor.

"Well awright George. I'll tell the sheriff, but therall be trouble with em ristrocrats. They ain't gonna like it."

"Tell the sheriff he needs to settle this himself. He shouldn't let the *dons* tell him what to do. We have laws here now, not a caste system where the *dons* can decide what they want," George said.

"I know, I know. I agrees with you, but the sheriff he don't like to take heat from the *dons*. Says he's justa trying to keep the peace."

"Well they burned down Rafe's house. That was not peaceful. The sheriff needs to get a spine. If Rafe was not *mestizo,* the *dons* would have called the fight a fair duel. It's time Santa Fe puts an end to this stupidity."

"You're probly right. Well, you be sure to tell us if young Rafe returns," the mayor said as he turned to leave.

After the mayor left George thanked God Rafe was safely in Mexico. Perhaps he was in less trouble there than he would be here in Santa Fe. The local Spaniards would not let Diego's death pass. George was sure time would dampen their anger after they had burned down Rafe's house and ran him out of town. Since Rafe's departure, the dandies had not attacked again. George worried they might also try to burn the barn, but all had been quiet.

What George told the mayor was true. The Santa Fe elites only wanted blood because Rafe was *mestizo*. The privileged Spaniards continued to believe in their superiority over mixed-race Mexicans. It was an ancient scheme started when the Spaniards came to the Americas. The church and the noblemen did not approve of the men intermixing with the native tribes. To squelch the behavior, the offspring of any mixed union was shunned, killed, or treated as a slave. Over time *mestizos* became the working slaves of New Spain. Even now though Mexico had an *Indio* president, the old ways did not die easily.

George shook his head. Rafe was a good man, a better man than most George had ever known. He deserved better than having to fight this stigma of his birth against men born to privilege. He deserved to be here living in Santa Fe, running his horse breeding business, and marrying Ana Teresa.

An idea formulated in George's brain. All the local *dons* and young dandies would be at Carlos' wedding. The wedding was the local talk of the town and anticipated to be the event of the year. George and his family were also invited. Perhaps George could talk to several of the older *dons*. Perhaps they would listen to him to call off this vendetta against Rafe. In the meantime, George knew it was better Rafe was still in Mexico.

CHAPTER 40

A week after he received the telegram from his uncle in Mexico City, saying Rafe was safe but would not be home soon, Carlos was preparing to marry Bibiana de Soto. The wedding was predicted to be the event of the season, an elaborate affair at the de Soto *hacienda* on the west side of Santa Fe. In Rafe's absence, Carlos asked George to stand in Rafe's place as his best man. Though Bibiana babbled to him for months about the plans and the details, Carlos was surprised by the lavish arrangements when he reached their *hacienda* the day of the wedding.

The de Soto courtyard was decorated with garlands of intertwined flowers and colorful paper streamers. Lace and flowers adorned tables of food and drink. An orchestra, positioned in the courtyard, was playing quietly. *Don* Pedro and *doña* Agustina de Soto greeted guests. *Doña* Agustina looked beautiful in her green and gold silk dress. Watching her, Carlos lost himself thinking how much Bibiana looked like her mother. He realized someday, even as Bibiana grew older, she too would remain lovely.

Bibiana refused to see Carlos for the past week. She told him it was bad luck. Instead she insisted Carlos visit the tailor and make sure his *traje* fit perfectly and he visited the barber yesterday for a haircut and shave. Bibiana's fussing annoyed him a bit, but now when he saw the wedding party coming to life, he understood her passion. The guests were dressed in their finest dresses and *trajes*. They brought wrapped presents and gifts. Carlos lost count after it seemed like over a hundred guests had arrived.

As Carlos looked around, he noticed several *dons* in their finest *trajes* standing together on one side of the yard. In another area several of the local young Spanish dandies congregated. He recognized Benjamin and Oscar, two of the local dandies who had accosted him. He wanted to go tell Bibiana to force them to leave, but then realized there was little chance of any trouble. Tonight was a night of fun and excitement, of music and wedding vows.

George and Josefina Summers arrived with their daughters, Lolo and Lizzy. Carlos could hardly believe how grownup the two girls looked in their fancy dresses. He saw one of the dandies take a long look at Lolo as she slowly stepped down from the carriage. Even he had to admit she had all the loveliness of a grown woman.

Carlos nervously stayed on the house's veranda. The only thing missing from this marvelous event was his best friend Rafe. He was stuck in Mexico after going to Mexico City to claim his legacy. Rafe's last telegram to George said Carmela stole Rayo. Carlos knew George was very worried Rafe could not let her action stand. Rafe had stolen the horse from the *hacienda* where Carmela was the mistress. Her revenge seemed obvious, especially since the Mexican government ruled in Rafe's favor and he inherited the Reyes *hacienda.*

As the sun reached its peak in the sky, the orchestra began to play. George joined Carlos near the stairs. Butterflies filled Carlos' stomach with anticipation. He was so much in love with Bibiana and had waited for this moment for the past year. He barely believed a woman such as she could love him.

As the music played, Carlos watched in astonishment as Bibiana stood with her father on the far side of the courtyard. She was a vision of magical beauty. Her white lace gown flowed behind her. A tall intricate *peineta* in her hair held a sheer lace veil over her face and it flowed down her back. Her arm was linked in her father's. Slowly *don* Pedro walked his eldest daughter toward him. Carlos tried to force himself to breath, though he found it hard. The beauty of his bride mesmerized him.

Suddenly the only sound Carlos could hear was the beating of his own heart as Bibiana reached about five feet from where he stood. He could only barely see her face under the veil, but he could see she was smiling. When Bibiana and her father reached Carlos, she turned to a woman behind her who was carrying the train of her dress. It was the first time Carlos noticed the woman. To his astonishment it was Ana Teresa, Bibiana's cousin from California and the woman Rafe loved.

Ana Teresa averted her eyes from Carlos, instead helping Bibiana lift her veil. Carefully smoothing the veil over the decorative *peineta* and down her back, Ana Teresa choked back tears. The only reason she had been allowed to attend Bibiana at the wedding was because Carlos' friend Rafe was not in Santa Fe. First her uncle, Bibiana's father, shipped her back to California, then Rafe was forced to leave town. The local *dons* and Diego's friends were set on revenge for Diego's death.

Ana Teresa picked up the heavy train of Bibiana's dress as her cousin placed a kiss on her father's cheek and then moved to take Carlos' hand. She was happy she came, though Ana Teresa now found keeping her emotions in check during the wedding rituals more difficult than she expected. In fact the entire wedding week had been thorny. Her uncle only begrudgingly allowed her to come to satisfy Bibiana's pleading. However, he was cold and still angry with her for falling in love with Rafe. Her uncle thought she brought a taint to their family, as Rafe was *mestizo,* especially after Rafe and Diego fought in the plaza and Diego died. According to Bibiana, Diego's friends planned to kill Rafe if he had stayed in town.

Carlos held out his hand and Bibiana took it. Ana Teresa adjusted the train of the dress and then stepped to the side. She found her mind wandering while the priest began the wedding with a prayer. She wondered if Rafe still loved and wanted to marry her. He had almost been killed by three dandies the day he asked her to marry him. She knew the fight with Diego was over her hand. Like her uncle, Diego detested *mestizos,* thinking anyone not a full-blooded Spaniard was inferior. Diego was loathsome, a man with no honor, and tried to violate her.

Before the priest began the wedding Mass, Carlos handed thirteen gold coins to the priest to be blessed. The coins represented Jesus and his twelve apostles and also represented Carlos' willingness to provide for his new bride. Symbolically, the coins reinforced the groom's love and admiration for his bride. When the bride accepted the coins, she was communicating her unconditional love, trust, and dedication to her new husband.

After they took their wedding vows, Carlos and Bibiana knelt together for a special prayer. As best man, George placed the *lazo,* a long cord of rosary beads, around the couple's shoulders to symbolize their commitment to one another. George wrapped it in the shape of the numeral eight or the infinity symbol to reinforce a lifetime commitment. The couple knelt with the *lazo* around their necks as the priest blessed them with a final wedding prayer.

After the wedding, the celebration became chaotic. Music played, people ate and drank, and Carlos' shoulder was sore from being slapped. Bibiana radiated. She and Carlos danced and greeted each of the guests cordially. Over the course of the evening, Carlos saw Ana Teresa dance with several of the dandies. She looked less than interested. Carlos tried to think of an excuse to talk to her privately, but Bibiana never gave him the chance. She kept his arm tightly linked in hers.

Bibiana told Carlos her father shipped Ana Teresa to Spain after the fiasco with Rafe. He accepted that information because Ana Teresa's parents were in Spain and had related it to Rafe. Carlos now wondered how that could have been true.

As tradition dictated, Carlos and Bibiana danced the Fandango to the delight of the crowd. As the band began the Fandango music, they put their hands up above their heads looking into each other's eyes. The dance started with a slow tempo, gradually increasing into a quick rhythm. They snapped their fingers and clicked their heels while they circled each other, never taking their eyes away. The Fandango was danced like a chase, where boy sees girl, girl snubs boy, girl chases boy, and then runs away. As the wedding dance, it depicted the courting ritual and ended in a kiss. Carlos and Bibiana promenaded from the dance floor and the crowd cheered and clapped.

Alvaro Gutierrez walked toward Ana Teresa. With Diego dead and Rafe out of the country, Alvaro thought the beautiful *señorita* available for his attention.

"A su servicio," Alvaro said, bowed, and kissed Ana Teresa's lace-gloved hand. He asked her to dance as the music for the Bolero began to play. Unable to refuse his request, Ana Teresa held out her hand to Alvaro and he led her out on the dance floor.

During the Bolero's slow tempo, the partners never turn, facing each other while taking slow steps forward and then long sideway steps. During the dance she pictured Rafe's face dancing with her, instead of Alvaro's. It had been the night they first met here in this same courtyard. Rafe's tone and demeanor was genuine and caring. Alvaro smirked at her showing his cracked front tooth. He was one of Diego's friends – one of Diego's friends who wanted Rafe dead. Ana Teresa only accepted his attention in the gracious obligation of social convention, however she detested everything he stood for. She wished she had stuck him with the sword the day they attacked Rafe at the abandoned *hacienda*.

As the evening neared the end, carriages began to line the driveway in front of the gate. Ana Teresa knew she needed to speak to Carlos before he and Bibiana departed. She boldly walked toward them as Carlos and Bibiana finished a dance.

"You have not allowed me a dance with my newest cousin," Ana Teresa said to Bibiana. As the music started to play, she did not give Bibiana a chance to refuse and Carlos willingly took her hand and led her away. The dance was one which did not give them a chance for any lengthy conversation. As they dipped and swayed toward each other, they exchanged short sentences.

"Is Rafe safe?" Ana Teresa asked. Carlos twirled her with the music.

"Yes, he is in Mexico," Carlos replied. "You are back from Spain?"

"I was not in Spain. I was sent back to California," she replied. "Is he coming home to Santa Fe?"

"I believe so, his business is here."

As the music played, Carlos bowed and handed Ana

Teresa's hand to another man. He took an older woman's hand and she curtsied to him. After a few turns of the music, Ana Teresa's partner returned her to him.

"Bibiana says Alvaro and his friends want revenge," she said resuming their conversation as they danced.

"Yes, there is trouble here over Diego's death."

"Diego was a *picaro*. I'm glad he's dead," she spit out the words.

"Nevertheless, his friends already burned Rafe's house and want him dead."

"Burned his house?"

"Yes, George is having it rebuilt."

They switched hands and Carlos twirled Ana Teresa twice to the music.

"Can you get a message to Rafe?" she asked.

"Maybe," Carlos replied.

"Tell him I still love him. Tell him I'm in Rancho Simi," she said.

The dance ended and Carlos bowed to Ana Teresa and led her by the arm back to where Bibiana stood waiting. A short time later Carlos and Bibiana left in a decorated carriage. Ana Teresa walked up the veranda steps and into the house.

CHAPTER 41

After five long days on the road to Jalisco, Rafe and Ricardo arrived at the village of Las Lomas. In sizing up the small village, they found only one cantina combined with a semblance of a restaurant. Next to the cantina was a pitiful looking hotel, but after sleeping on the ground, a real bed sounded good to them. Rafe was also hoping to be able to get a bath and a shave. Tying up the horses, they walked into the hotel. It was better than expected, with five rooms, clean beds, and a room in the back where they could pay for a tub of hot water. The proprietor was a friendly man and seemed happy to receive guests. Rafe checked in and Ricardo asked the man if he had a place to keep the horses.

"Yes, for a few pesos more, I will send for the livery boy."

"Very well, start the hot water as soon as you can," Rafe told him as he paid for the rooms and the extra pesos for the horses.

Rafe was surprised the room's door locks actually worked, as he needed to have a secure place for the supplies and his GSW pistols. He did not like leaving his weapons at this unknown location, but in this small village he had no choice.

"Ricardo, as soon as you clean up come get me and we'll go to the cantina and see what they have for food," Rafe told him.

Western shadows covered most of the sleepy village by the time Rafe and Ricardo got to the cantina. A single guitar sounded out a tune soured by old and frayed strings. Still, the skilled musician made up for the flawed instrument. At the bar were several *vaqueros,* two of the small tables were taken up by families having what looked like a child's birthday celebration. An elderly couple sat at another table eating. At the corner near the backdoor, four *peóns* quietly drank *pulque* and were no doubt wary of the *vaqueros* drinking at the bar. In this small town the cantina was for everyone, not just a drinking establishment for men.

Rafe went to the only empty table and Ricardo sat across from him. Rafe was dressed modestly, looking like a traveling businessman. Ricardo was dressed as a *peón*.

The man behind the bar came to their table and told them in Spanish, "Tonight we only have *pozole* and *birria.*" A traditional Mexican dish, *pozole* was a corn hominy soup made with pork and *birria* a spicy meat stew made of either goat or lamb.

"Pozole," Rafe ordered.

"I will take the *birria,*" Ricardo spoke up.

Rafe noticed the *vaqueros* gave them a quick look when they entered the cantina, but now mostly ignored them. The families were not interested with the two strangers at all. The *peóns* took no notice of them.

"Where are you strangers from?" the bartender asked as he served the food.

"We come from Mexico City. I am a salesman for farm equipment. This is my first trip to Jalisco. My helper and I are going to Guadalajara. I have been told there are many large *haciendas* in this area," Rafe lied but tried to sound convincing.

"Sí, there are many large *haciendas* in Jalisco," the bartender responded.

"What is the major crop?" Rafe asked.

"Well it used to be tobacco, coffee, and sugarcane. Now many of the *hacienderos* are growing agave for the tequila."

"Agave? How is it harvested?" Rafe asked.

"By hand, with a machete *señor,*" he replied. As the bartender walked away he wondered about the young salesman and his helper. Strangers did not come to this small town often. Shrugging his shoulders he walked behind the small bar and thought he should send a boy in the morning to tell several of the *hacienderos* of the strange pair.

Rafe tasted the *pozole.* It was a rich spicy red chili broth with pieces of pork and hominy. After the meal, Rafe ordered a beer for himself and a *pulque* for Ricardo.

"I will go and sit with the *peóns* and see what I can learn from them," Ricardo said and took the drink and headed to the corner of the cantina. Rafe sat with his back to the door casually watching the people. The bartender brought him another beer.

After a little while the *vaqueros* left and the families gathered leftovers and their children taking both as they departed to their homes. Rafe noticed the behavior of the *peóns* changed after the *vaqueros* were gone, becoming more rowdy and ordering more *pulque*. Ricardo sat with them, talking and laughing. Rafe watched the old blacksmith fit right in with the others as if he was their lifelong friend. One man started to sing an old drinking song and the others soon joined in. Another round of *pulque* sustained the singing. Finally the men began to leave, a few staggering as they tried to walk to the door.

Ricardo strolled over to Rafe and they headed for the hotel. "What did you learn?" Rafe asked him.

"Two of the men work at *don* Luis' *hacienda*. According to what I heard, it is the work in the agave fields which is backbreaking and they don't like it. *Don* Luis only has a small field of agave, but one man said he heard *don* Luis is planning on growing more. These men mostly clean the outside of the main house, work in the gardens, and take refuse out and burn it. I asked if we could go and help them for no cost. I told them all we wanted was to see how the *hacienda* is managed," Ricardo said.

"Were they suspicious?"

"They just do not care what we do for they hate their jobs, but it is all they have here for work."

"Where and what time do we go with them?" Rafe asked.

"They said to meet them on the road west out of the village before the sun is up."

"Ricardo, you don't have to go tomorrow. You have done enough by just coming with me. I don't want you to get hurt."

"We are amigos. Besides, they will not hurt me, a lowly *peón.*" Ricardo smiled under his sombrero and gave a throaty laugh. "Do you have a plan?"

"Not exactly. First I need to know if the Appaloosa is there. He is a remarkable horse, tall and lean. He has a white and brown rump with a dark tail. He will be the leader of the herd. If he is in a stall, he will be angry. He should not be hard to spot," Rafe described Rayo. "Tomorrow I just want to try to determine if he is at the *hacienda,* then I'll figure out a plan to get him back."

"We can sneak into the barn. *Haciendaros* mostly ignore *peóns* as long as they are working," Ricardo suggested.

"You don't know Carmela. She is vindictive and hates me, especially now that I have inherited the Reyes *hacienda.* If she recognizes me, there will be trouble."

"Ah, she is a woman and won't be in the barn or the fields. You should not worry so much. *Haciendaras* don't look at *peóns,* they only order them around."

"Regardless, once we get there stay away from me. Act as if you don't know me. If anything happens, you will find money in my saddlebags. There is plenty of money to pay for the hotel and keep you here for a while if need be. If I am killed, get a message to *don* David and tell him what happened. Keep the money and sell my packhorse and saddle. You deserve it for all your help," Rafe told him.

CHAPTER 42

It took more than an hour for the *peóns* along with Rafe and Ricardo to walk to *don* Luis' *hacienda*. Rafe wore typical dirty white cotton *pantalones* and *camisa,* a straw hat, and *huarache* sandals. He rubbed dirt on his clean feet and hands, so as not to give himself away. He noticed he was taller than all the other *peóns,* so he purposely stooped his shoulders and lowered his head hoping not to stand out. Ricardo also noticed his height and after Rafe stooped, he pushed Rafe to the middle of the pack of *peóns.*

The leader of the *peón* workers assigned the men to the various jobs he was hired to do for the day. Rafe and Ricardo were assigned to till the garden and were told to gather fertilizer from the fields for the garden. Rafe gladly accepted the job as it would give him a chance to look the pasture over and possibly look into the horse stalls. Rayo had to be in one of those two places, or so he hoped.

"Ricardo, I will take the wheelbarrow to the pasture to gather the manure. It will give me a chance to look for Rayo," Rafe insisted as they tilled the garden.

"You stay stooped and keep your hat low. You are taller than anyone else and will stand out," Ricardo warned him.

On the first trip to the pasture Rafe made a quick trip of it. He shoveled damp manure into the wheelbarrow and hurried back to the garden.

"Stop working so fast. Do you want to be noticed," Ricardo hissed at him. *Peóns* worked at one speed, slow. The slower they worked, the more *peóns* were needed at a *hacienda*. Local peasants earned next to nothing, but they made sure everyone shared in the work. Besides they were indentured servants and had no reason to work fast.

"I'm headed to the other field. I promise I'll go slow," Rafe said realizing what Ricardo said was true.

Rafe slowly pushed the rickety wheelbarrow from the garden. Stooping over it, he shuffled his sandals. The garden was on the east side of the horse barn. Slowly he walked as close to the barn as he thought he dared. Two *vaqueros* had a young horse roped and were running it in the corral. They looked up at him momentarily and Rafe lowered his head. He could not see into the barn.

Once past the barn, he slowly pushed the wheelbarrow toward the field. Both cows and horses grazed the open pasture. The horses were toward the far end of the field in a thicket of small trees. Cows grazed near him and left plenty of fresh manure scattered around. Filling the wheelbarrow with manure he gazed toward the horses. One horse stood taller than the rest, but Rafe could not see the markings in the shadow of the trees.

Rafe turned and slowly walked back to the garden.

"Did you find him?" Ricardo whispered.

"There are horses in the far pasture. I have to get closer," Rafe replied.

On the morning veranda in the back of the house, *don* Luis and *doña* Carmela were having breakfast. "You look lovely today *querida*," *don* Luis purred his affections. He and Carmela made love three times last night in fevered passion. He swore she might kill him one day with her lust.

"I saw Buck riding the Appaloosa yesterday," Carmela said. "I knew it would only take time before the horse would settle down."

"Yes he is not as wild. The other horses have made him the leader and follow him around. Your husband certainly bred fine horses. I'm glad we kept him. We will start breeding horses here from his sire as well as growing the agave," *don* Luis told her.

Carmela thought it ironic the only part of her life with *don* Bernardo which endured was a horse. He was magnificent and one of the best ever bred on the Reyes *hacienda*. She remembered Bernardo telling her so.

Rafe and Ricardo emptied the wheelbarrow in the garden. "I need to get closer to the horses," Rafe whispered.

"Be careful," Ricardo hissed. "You are the only *peón* going to the far field. Someone may notice."

On his next trip to gather manure, Rafe worked closer

to the small herd of horses in the thicket. He recognized Rayo standing in the middle surrounded by mares. Without thinking he instinctively was drawn toward his horse, leaving his wheelbarrow behind him. Rayo was healthy and did not look abused. A mare stood quietly by his side.

Rafe wanted to go to him, jump on his bare back as he had often done and ride like the wind away from the *hacienda*. He knew none of the horses here at *don* Luis' could catch him riding on Rayo, but it was a foolish plan. Now, at least he knew Rayo was here. A plan to rescue him was for another day.

As Rafe turned to leave, Rayo snorted. His ears perked as he spotted Rafe. The bond between this horse and owner was forged in the years of training Rafe spent when Rayo was just a colt. Rayo trotted toward Rafe as the rest of the herd followed their leader. As Rayo got closer, he came running to Rafe, whinnying and snorting. Rafe turned as he heard the hoofbeats coming behind him. The Appaloosa nudged his face at Rafe's chest and stomped around him pawing at the ground. He threw his head up and whinnied loudly.

"Shhh," Rafe tried to calm him rubbing down his nose and neck.

"Mira el appaloosa con el peón," *don* Luis told Carmela to look at the Appaloosa in the pasture. She noticed the tall Appaloosa in the field and the small herd following him were surrounding a *peón*.

Carmela watched the Appaloosa nuzzle the *peón*. The *vaqueros* were barely able to touch the horse. "It is the *peón* who took my *hacienda*," *doña* Carmela said emphatically. "Look at how the horse responds to him. I knew he would come!"

"Perhaps he is just good with horses. I have heard of such a thing," *don* Luis said.

"No. It must be him. The Appaloosa will not let anybody near it. Look how the horse is reacting," Carmela said.

As they watched, Rafe tried to walk away from Rayo. He retrieved the wheelbarrow and headed back across the field, a small herd of horses followed Rayo who followed Rafe. So much for not having a plan; what the hell was he thinking. Did he think he could just come here and grab the horse and simply ride off with it? Rafe kept his head down and hoped Rayo would stop following him.

"Stay here, I will take care of the *peón*," *don* Luis said wishing he had not sent Buck to Guadalajara to deliver money to *don* Cenobio. He picked up his pistol and stuffed it behind his *traje's* sash before stepping out the side door.

Don Luis casually strolled toward where his head *vaquero* worked tanning a cowhide. "Do you see the Appaloosa following that *peón?* Keep an eye on him and have your pistol ready." The *vaquero* stopped what he was doing and positioned himself behind a large cottonwood tree where he could see his *patrón* approach the *peón*. He pulled his pistol just in case there was trouble.

"*Manos arriba*," *don* Luis told Rafe to put his hands up. Rafe did not see the *don* come up behind him. He stopped and put the wheelbarrow handles down.

"Do not turn around *peón* or I will shoot you. Now, put your hands up like I told you." As soon as Rafe's hands were up, the *don* got behind Rafe and frisked his waist for weapons. He found none.

"What is the problem *jefe?*" Rafe asked. "I have only been collecting manure for the garden."

"Slowly, turn around and walk to the barn," he ordered with authority in his voice. Rafe did as he was told, knowing there were probably several pistols aimed at him.

Don Luis signaled the *vaquero* to follow him to the barn. The *vaquero* came out from behind the tree with pistol ready and walked behind *don* Luis. The trio made their way across the yard in front of the barn and *don* Luis told Rafe to keep walking.

In the garden one of the workers saw the new *peón* get marched into the barn. "*¿Que le ha pasado a tu amigo?*" he asked Ricardo what happened with his friend.

"I don't know. He was gathering manure in the far field," Ricardo said not wanting to tell the man why they came today. Ricardo watched the *don* and a *vaquero* push Rafe through the barn doorway and out of sight.

"Can you go to the barn and see why they took him?" Ricardo asked the man who described himself as the leader of the workers.

"No, I cannot do that. I only hope the *don* will not fire me and my men because your friend is in trouble," he grumbled. Ricardo knew the man was angry. He allowed two unknown men to come with him today who caused trouble and Ricardo knew it would be the last time.

Inside the barn the *don* ordered the *vaquero* to tie Rafe tightly to a stall post. As soon as he was secure, the *don* reared back and punched Rafe in his mid section knocking the air out of him. It was all Rafe could do to regain his breath.

"Why are you here *peón?*" the *don* asked.

Rafe fought for breath and could barely speak. "You . . . t . t . took my . . horse."

"The Appaloosa is not your horse *peón*. You stole it from *doña* Carmela," he said and hit Rafe again.

"I am not a *peón*. I am an American and the son of *don* Bernardo Reyes. The horse is rightfully mine."

"It is him!" *doña* Carmela screamed. They did not hear her approaching. She stepped around the *don* and slapped Rafe twice with all her might, surprising everyone.

"You stole the Appaloosa from my husband and now you stole the *hacienda* from me. Kill him Luis; I want this *peón* dead," she screamed at the *don*.

"Your husband raped my mother and my sister. My sister was only fifteen. Yes, I shot the *desgraciado* and rode the Appaloosa when I escaped. You knew your husband was violating young girls at the *hacienda* and you did nothing about it. You are to blame. What is wrong with you, why could you not keep him in your bed? Now I own all his property because you did nothing to stop him," Rafe blurted out looking directly into her eyes.

"How dare you speak to me," she screamed. "You stupid *peón*. You should have killed him, then I would have it all. You turned him into a *pinche* cripple. Why didn't you kill him?" She slapped Rafe over and over until her hands hurt.

Carmela seethed at how life wronged her. If only the *peón* had killed Bernardo all those years ago instead of crippling him, she would have inherited everything. Now she had nothing but the Appaloosa.

"Kill him! Give me your pistol I will kill him myself," she yelled hysterically grabbing at *don* Luis's gun.

"No Carmela, we cannot kill him here. Please go back to the house I will take care of him," the *don* said after he took her by her shoulders wanting to calm her down. *Don* Luis now saw a different perspective of his intended after listening to her tirade about her ex-husband and this young man. He was no *peón*, but an *Americano* and the legal owner of the Reyes *hacienda*. Luis did not want the *Americano's* blood on his hands here at the *hacienda*.

"You, you kill him," she screamed at the *vaquero*, but *don* Luis' trusted man did not move at the woman's outburst. He would kill the man, but only if the *don* commanded him.

"He will die today, but not here at my *hacienda*," *don* Luis told her calmly. "Now go Carmela, go back to the house and let me handle this."

"Make sure he suffers!" she screamed. She slapped Rafe several times more before she stormed out of the barn.

"Santino, go and get those two Otomí *Indios* you hired to build the stone wall around the main house," *don* Luis said turning to the *vaquero*.

Rafe squirmed against the tight ropes knowing his fate. It was foolish of him to think he and he alone could get Rayo back, especially without his pistols. They were neatly stowed with the rest of his gear in the saddlebags at the hotel in Las Lomas. Hearing the *don* saying he would not kill him here at his *hacienda* and calling for *Indios*, gave Rafe some small ray of hope. Perhaps he could bargain with the *Indios* or perhaps Ricardo would see what was happening and come to his rescue.

Shortly, the *vaquero* returned to the barn with two *Indios*. Rafe saw the two dressed in white cotton *pantalones* and *camisas*. They wore no hats and both had their heads shaved just above the forehead. Their faces and foreheads were tattooed with intricate designs and they had large holes on their earlobes. They were not tall, but looked fit and muscular and their skin was a deep bronze. Rafe was not familiar with the Otomí tribe. It was not one he and the Healer had visited. As they approached, the tattoos on their faces were geometric designs, but Rafe thought they represented animals.

Don Luis took them aside and spoke to them so Rafe could not hear what was said, though he could tell the *don* was speaking Spanish.

"Take this man far away from my *hacienda* and kill him. I will pay you when you return," he told them.

"No, you pay us now," one of them spoke up.

"Very well, I will give you fifty *pesos* now and fifty when you return. Leave him to the buzzards when you are done," the *don* told them.

Rafe watched as the *vaquero* named Santino backed a wagon into the barn. He untied Rafe from the stall and retied his feet and hands. The *Indios* climbed up on the wagon and Santino threw Rafe in the back and closed the tailgate. As soon as he was loaded, the *Indios* slapped the reins and Rafe felt the wagon move.

"Dios mande un milagro," he prayed for God to send him a miracle.

CHAPTER 43

The Otomí *Indios* drove the wagon away from the *hacienda* with Rafe tied in the back. As Rafe bounced against the wagon's wooden floor, his mind raced to formulate any type of plan to escape.

As the *Indios* drove, they spoke in a combination of Spanish and a native tongue Rafe did not understand, however, he could understand enough to know they were arguing about what to do with him. Rafe listened intently, wildly hoping he might be able to use their disagreement to his advantage.

"We have to kill him," the driver said. "The *don* is paying us."

"No we can sell him to the *haciendero,* the one looking for workers to harvest agave. It is not far from here. I have heard they are paying three hundred *pesos* for strong workers. This one looks young and healthy. Perhaps we can get more than three hundred," the other one said.

"If the *don* finds out we did not kill him, he will have our heads," the driver retorted.

"The *don* will not know. Men sold to the agave farms never leave until they are dead. The *don* only wants the *peón* to be gone, so he will be gone and we will be richer."

Rafe struggled with his tied feet and hands to twist into a sitting position.

"I am not a *peón*. I am an *Americano,*" Rafe spoke up.

"You are dressed as a *peón* and you work with the *peóns*. I think you are a *peón,*" the driver yelled back over his shoulder.

"I am not a *peón*. I was only here to find my horse the *don* and *doña* stole in Mexico City," Rafe yelled back at them. "If it is money you want I will give you five hundred *pesos* if you turn me lose," Rafe continued knowing he was bargaining for his life.

"Five hundred *pesos!* Where are you going to get five hundred *pesos,*" the driver yelled back at Rafe and both *Indios* laughed.

"I told you I am not a *peón*. I am an American businessman and I have money back in Las Lomas."

Rafe could see the *Indio* who was not driving pondering his words. "Perhaps he is telling the truth. I heard the *doña* yelling about the horse."

"Yes I am an *Americano* and others will come looking for me. Then you will have trouble," Rafe told the driver.

The driver pondered his words. "You are a *pendejo*. You will not fool me *peón*. If we can get three hundred *pesos* from the agave *haciendero* then you will live. If they do not pay we will kill you," the driver told him.

Rafe knew the *Indios* did not believe him. His money was at the hotel in Las Lomas along with his pistols. He cursed himself for his stupidity and arrogance. His mind wandered to Ana Teresa, thinking about her and how he would never see her again. Carlos, the Summers' family, and most of all his mother should curse his memory for this blatant foolhardiness. All this was his fault. He ignored George's warnings to leave the horse and go to Torreón.

It took several hours over a bumpy trail for them to arrive at the agave *hacienda*. At the main entrance the *Indio* on the passenger side jumped off the wagon and approached an armed guard. Rafe, still tied, waited in the back of the wagon. The *Indio* and the guard spoke briefly, then the guard waved the wagon on. When the wagon stopped again, a man pulled down the tailgate to inspect the human merchandise.

"He looks healthy enough," a man said. He carried a rifle and wore crossed bandoliers across his chest. He wore a large straw sombrero and a khaki colored uniform, but he was not a soldier.

"*Sí jefe,* and look at his size. He will make a good worker," the *Indios* spouted out. "We should get double for this one," the driver demanded.

"You will take the three hundred or I will shoot the both of you and take him for nothing. Nobody will care if they find two *Indios* full of holes and the coyotes will be happy to feast on your carcass," the man calmly said to the driver pointing the rifle at him.

"*Sí jefe,* three hundred is a good price," the driver said. He was visibly shaken by the man's disregard to his life.

"Untie him. I will get the money for you," the man told them and left.

When the guard returned he saw Rafe on the ground still tied up," I told you to untie him," he growled at the two.

Rafe wanted to reason with the guard, but doubted he would get a different response. He was dressed and looked like a *peón* and in this reality he was a *peón* in the eyes of *haciende002*. He was *mestizo,* regardless of his new legacy.

"He is a big man and might have hurt us and run away. We want our money, you untie him," the driver complained.

"Here is your money. Now go," he said handing them the three hundred *pesos.* As the two *Indios* were climbing up onto the wagon, the guard looked at Rafe. The *peón* looked to be over six foot and was well fed. He did not have the scrawny under-fed look of most peasants. The guard was impressed.

"If you find any more like this one, bring them to me," he called to the *Indios* as they left.

As the wagon drove off, the man whistled and several men dressed in khakis came running. One of them untied Rafe and led him to a hut made of adobe with a grass roof. Rafe saw smoke rising from a chimney and smelled roasting meat. "What is your name?" the guard asked Rafe.

"Rafael."

"Rafael, you have been sold to me as a slave for three hundred *pesos.* You will work in the agave fields until you can pay your debt or you die, whichever comes first. You will work hard or you will get the whip. You will not cause trouble and if you try to escape, I or one of the guards will shoot you. If you work hard, you will eat. If not, you will starve," the man told him.

"How do I pay my debt?" Rafe asked.

"We will pay you for your labor, but you have to pay us for your living quarters and for the food we supply you," the man answered and laughed. He knew the system and no man could ever save enough to leave the agave *hacienda.* The guard opened a door and shoved Rafe into a dilapidated shack.

"A new worker," the guard yelled to those inside.

Inside the shack it took almost a minute for Rafe's eyes to adjust from the sunlight outside to the dim lit room. Several wizened men were lying on cots and two men were cooking over a small fire. One man was roasting a slab of meat, chile peppers, and warming a pan of beans. Another man was making corn tortillas. It all smelled appetizing to Rafe. He had not eaten since daybreak this morning.

Only the men doing the cooking looked at Rafe when he was shoved inside. The men on the cots looked as if they could not move. The one man's skinny legs protruded from his body like sticks. His cheeks were sunken and shallow on his face.

"*Hola, me llamo Rafael,*" Rafe said to the man cooking the meat.

"You are a big man, but you will get no more food than anyone else," the man replied.

"What is expected of me? What will I be doing?" Rafe asked.

"They grow agave here. We harvest it and it is shipped to the Guadalajara distilleries," the tortilla man responded.

"Are you all slaves here?" Rafe asked.

"All of us here were sold to the *hacienda*. Some agreed to be sold instead of facing the gallows, others were sold just for the money. Most of us have been here for over a year," tortilla man said.

"What about those men?" Rafe asked about the two ill men on the cots.

"They can no longer work, so they no longer eat," the man replied. "Their time of pain is almost over." Rafe was shocked at the attitude of the cooker. Surely the man could slip a little food to the dying men.

"I am Alfonso; he is Juan," the tortilla man said. "You will have plenty of time to know everyone," he laughed. He pointed to an empty cot and said, "You can take that one. It belonged to Arturo. He is no longer with us."

Before sunset Rafe heard several wagons approaching the shack. Several minutes later eight more men were shoved into the hut and Rafe heard the door lock. They were dirty and obviously tired, but most had smiles on their faces.

"I am Pedro," one man introduced himself. "I am Rudy," another said. They asked Rafe where he was from.

"I'm from Torreón," Rafe replied. He thought it made more sense than telling these men he was an American.

"Torreón. You have come a long way my friend," one of the men said.

"Yes a long way to be stuck in this God forsaken place. Are you a murderer? Were you going to swing on the gallows?" a man with a missing tooth asked.

"No, I'm not a murderer," Rafe replied. He left it at that not knowing how to explain why he was here.

The meal was served and the men dug into the plates. Rafe was not fed.

"You only eat after you work," the cook said. "Tomorrow you will eat."

As the men ate, Rafe listened to them talk. He marveled at the amiable demeanor of the *peóns*. It reminded him of his youth at *don* Bernardo's *hacienda*. Peasants were treated as slaves, had little to eat, sometimes beaten, but still maintained a zest for good-natured camaraderie. Here was the same. These men had no hope of escape and yet they talked and laughed cheerfully.

CHAPTER 44

In the morning the door to the shack was unlocked. The men were given a half hour of freedom to relieve themselves and stretch. Rafe was given a small bowl of hot mush for breakfast and a cup of nasty tasting coffee. At least he thought it was coffee.

As three wagons rolled to a stop near the shack the guard yelled at the men, "Get loaded you filthy swine." He cracked his whip against the ground to emphasize his words.

Rafe climbed aboard one of the wagons with Pedro and several other men. The wagons rolled down a dirt path and in the distance Rafe saw hillsides covered in the tall spiky agave plants. As the wagons rolled by, Rafe could see agave fields of different sizes. One of the men in the wagon started singing a sad song about a girl. A few others chimed in.

Finally the wagon stopped near a field of tall agave plants. Each plant was about Rafe's height with a circumference of the spiky leaves more than five feet across.

A guard came up to Rafe and told him, "Your job is the simple one. See the man tipping the agave and using the machete; he is a *jimador*. You see how he trims the leaves before he goes to the next plant. Behind him a *rhizome* uses the *coa* blade to chop what is left of the leaves closer and chops away the roots, leaving the round ball of the heart of the agave. We call it the *piña*, or pineapple. All you have to do is pick up the *piña* and load it onto the wagon. When the wagon is full, follow it to the storage area and unload it. Then come back and do the same."

"How much do they weigh," Rafe asked looking at the large root balls left by the men trimming them.

"They weigh from eighty to one hundred-fifty pounds. You look strong enough to handle this simple job," the guard said laughing. "Here you will need these and they will come out of your pay," he said handing Rafe a pair of leather gloves.

Rafe did not bother asking the guard how much the

gloves were going to cost him. He already knew the system was rigged so the workers could never pay off their debt to escape this hell hole he was now in.

Following behind one of the cutters, Rafe waited for them to finish trimming the agave. The first *piña* Rafe picked up surprised him how dense and heavy it was. The large round ball of agave still had sharp edges from the cutting. Without gloves, his hands would have been a sliced mess and he suspected the gloves might not last a week.

Struggling to wrap his arms around the ball of agave, Rafe carried it to the waiting wagon. He noticed the workers kept a pace with each other, without signals or speaking. The *jimador* stripped the tall spiky leaves of the agave plant. He worked his way around starting at the bottom and working up to the taller leaves. When he finished, the agave looked as if it had a bad haircut. Behind him a *rhizome* wielded the razor-sharp *coa*. The *coa* had a long handle with a round flat blade. The blade sliced against the agave ball. Rafe saw how the *rhizome* used the *coa* knife to chop the ball from the roots underground. The finished ball looked somewhat like a large pineapple.

Rafe shook his shoulders between his work of picking up the large pineapples of agave. Though his hands were spared the sharpness of the cuts by the gloves, his arms were not spared. He noticed ribbons of blood seeping though his *camisa*.

After several hours of work, the guard signaled a break. Each man was given a mug of water and a tortilla wrapped around a meat and bean mixture. The tortilla was cold, but Rafe ate it in several bites. The rest period lasted about a half hour before the guard signaled the men to begin again.

Rafe watched the guard carefully. He was on horseback with his rifle across his lap or in his right hand. Wrapped around the pommel of the horse was a whip. Rafe doubted he would hesitate to use it.

On the first day in the afternoon, Rafe's arms screamed with fatigue. His arms were bloody from the jagged cuts made by the rough cut *piña*. He saw the guard with a ready whip look at him and he mustered all his strength and will power to continue without complaint.

Late in the afternoon the workers were returned to the small shack. Alfonso was cooking the evening meal in a pot over the fire. The cot where one of the wizened men laid this morning was empty. Rafe noticed the other workers looked at the empty cot and grew quiet.

After the meal Rafe fell exhausted onto his cot. While the others laughed and talked, he fell asleep.

On the second day, it was worse. Pain shot through every muscle in his arms, back, and legs when he lifted the first ball and dropped it. The guard with the whip watched him carefully, as if waiting for him to drop the *piña,* and let the whip fly against Rafe's back. The tip of the whip streaked across his back ripping his camisa and tearing his skin. His back screamed in pain.

"Now pick it up," the sadistic guard snarled. Rafe struggled with the weight of the ball, but managed to load it onto the wagon. His muscles felt like mush. The whip cuts on his back stung with the heat of the sun. He mustered every ounce of strength to continue working. The guard was watching him closely, probably expecting him to falter again.

He made it through to noon without dropping another ball and being whipped, however by mid afternoon he could barely lift. His arms had no strength. He was working with a *rhizome* on a row of agave. The *rhizome* hissed at him. "Use your legs more to lift," the man said. Rafe tried on the next *piña* to use more of his leg muscles, but lost his balance as the heavy ball shifted in his arms and both he and the ball fell to the ground.

The guard wasted no time snapping the whip and it caught him across his left shoulder. The guard let the whip fly twice at him.

"Once for the *piña,* and once for falling," he sneered.

That evening Rafe along with the other slaves stretched out on their cots from pure exhaustion. He ate whatever the cook made without asking what was in the stew or mush.

Rafe felt the guard's whip several times over the next day, twice for dropping a *piña* and once for being slow. That evening one of the men named Juan, walked to him and said, "Turn over. I'm going to put some sap from the agave on the cuts. It will help." Juan coated the cuts on Rafe's back and shoulder with a slimy clear gel.

At first the salve stung in the cuts, but about an hour later Rafe's back was in less pain. Another one of the men showed Rafe how to wrap his arms with rags to protect them from the spiky balls.

By the fourth day Rafe's muscles and stamina were building up and he had less trouble lifting the *piñas* and unloading the wagons. His arms and shoulders still ached from lifting the heavy balls, but luckily he was taller and in better shape from the years he worked at George's foundry in Santa Fe than some of the smaller and older men.

He was very impressed with the *jimadors* and *rhizomes*. They were fast and efficient at knocking down the agave plants and trimming them into balls. They made quick work of stripping the large plant of the spiky leaves. While he worked, Rafe scanned his surroundings looking for a way to escape. Though the men were not chained in any way, escape across the openness of the agave field was impossible. The guard on horseback with the whip and rifle could easily cut down a man on foot.

CHAPTER 45

"What are you going to do about Rafe?" Josefina asked her husband George as they readied for bed. She had tried to be patient, but her adopted son was missing and George was not talking to her about it. "Celiá is worried sick," she said.

George sighed knowing both Rafe's real mother and his wife were concerned.

"Actually I don't know what to do, my dear," he replied. Josefina found it an odd statement by her husband who always seemed to know how to handle any situation.

George Summers had not received a telegram from Rafe in almost two weeks. Five days ago he sent a wire to Carlos' uncle, *don* David, in Mexico City and received a reply that Rafe went with a man named Ricardo to Jalisco to try to retrieve Rayo. *Don* David knew nothing more.

Josefina stood up and wrapped her arms around George. He responded and held her tight. Rafe had become part of their family and they thought of him as their son.

"Don't worry. He is young and resourceful. You know how hard it is to send a telegram from Mexico, if he is not in a large town. He is probably sitting in a cantina drinking a beer right now," George said trying to appease his wife's worry.

"I hope so," she responded.

Several days later, Carlos found George in the foundry. Carlos, back from his wedding trip, was living at the de Soto *hacienda* with Bibiana until they found a home. It was the first time he made the trip back to the Summers' home since the day of the wedding.

"How are you George?" Carlos greeted him.

"Carlos! It is good to see you. You look as if married life agrees with you," George teased him.

"Yes I am happy. Bibiana and her mother are looking at houses today, so I slipped away for a little while. Have you heard from Rafe?"

George's stomach churned. Carlos knew Rafe was in Mexico and probably thought he was in Torreón.

Carlos saw George's face contort slightly at his question about Rafe. "George, what's happened?" Carlos asked.

"I'm not sure. Maybe nothing. Rafe followed Rayo's trail to Jalisco. He and a man named Ricardo left your uncle's house in Mexico City twelve days ago. We have heard nothing since, nor has your uncle."

"What are you going to do?" Carlos asked him.

"I'll send another telegram to both Mexico City and Torreón tomorrow. If I hear nothing by next week, I'm going to leave for Mexico," George said.

"I'll go with you," Carlos responded.

Later that evening Carlos waited until he and Bibiana were in their bedroom. Over dinner she was bubbly over a house she found. "It's perfect," she told him. "Mother liked it too and it is not very far from here."

In the bedroom he took her by the arms. *"Querida,* Rafe is missing in Mexico. *Don* Jorge and I need to find him if we have not heard anything by next week," Carlos told her.

"What do you mean you have to go to Mexico? Carlos, you cannot do that. We have so much to do here. I know you care for Rafe, but you are married now and you need to attend to our needs. You promised in your wedding vows to put me above all others," Bibiana told Carlos with tears welling in her eyes.

"Lo siento mi amor," Carlos apologized. "George is afraid something has happened. I cannot let him go down there alone. He needs my help. How can I say no to him?"

"How can you say no to me? I am afraid I will never see you again. I cannot live without you, *mi amor.* I need you here," she pleaded.

"Bibiana I love you very much, but without Rafael you know I would not be alive today. He and George are like family and it is my responsibility to help them or hopefully George is overreacting and I can talk him out of making the trip."

In the morning Bibiana told her father about Carlos'

plan to leave for Mexico to find Rafael. She was upset and *don* Pedro fumed at his son-in-law's stupidity. After supper Bibiana's father called Carlos into the parlor.

"I do not understand why you care so much about that lying *mestizo*. He has been nothing but trouble for you. Let him rot down there with his own people in Mexico," *don* Pedro de Soto, Bibiana's father, told Carlos. "Your duty is here with my daughter, Carlos. I should not have to remind you."

"I understand *don* Pedro, but you know I owe Rafael my life. It is a matter of honor," Carlos said adamantly, but respectfully.

Don Pedro seethed inside. The *mestizo* had been nothing but trouble to his family. His niece, Ana Teresa, almost ran off with the *mestizo* dog after he killed Diego de la Torre. It brought shame to the family with the other *dons*. Carlos' bond to the man who saved his life was honorable, but *don* Pedro would not allow him to abandon his daughter.

"I forbid you to go," *don* Pedro said. "You will not bring shame to my daughter and to the family again. Now go and console your bride and tell her you have abandoned this idea."

The *don* dismissed Carlos with a wave of his hand and Carlos knew the subject was closed. He owed Rafe his life, but he was a husband now. Bibiana was right, when she said it could be dangerous in Mexico. There was talk about a revolution all over Mexico, because the upper class did not like the liberal laws of the *Indio* President Juárez. It was Juárez' new laws that allowed Rafe to inherit the Reyes *hacienda.*

Carlos found Bibiana in the dining room helping her mother. He wrapped his arms around her in a tight *abrazo.* She knew without him saying, her father set him straight. His allegiance was here in Santa Fe and to her. He was not going on any foolish trip to Mexico.

CHAPTER 46

Mateo, the guard on the agave plantation, relished beating the new slaves. He knew how to make them understand he was the boss. Usually it was the second day when their muscles were aching that they started to falter. He could also recognize when the older, worn out men were not carrying their weight. Mateo would beat them until they could not work at all and then they would stop earning their food ration. Better to stop feeding them and let them die. In his mind it was somehow more humane.

Rafe kept to his work, lifting the heavy balls of agave into the wagons and then unloading them into a storage facility. Rafe started to track his days of captivity by making marks in the dirt under his cot. By the end of the first week, both of the wizened men who were lying on the cots when he first arrived were dead. When he asked one of the *peóns* if they were buried, the man laughed.

"Los dejan a los buitres," he said they were left for the buzzards. The thought tore at Rafe's heart. No one deserved to be treated like these men and they at least should be worthy of a burial.

In the evenings the men talked and laughed. Sometimes they would sing. Mostly they seemed resigned to their fate. Even watching their friends die, did not seem to affect them much. Only Raul seemed to rile about their situation. Raul told Rafe he was twenty-seven and agreed to come here to escape the firing squad. He joined the army when he was sixteen, rather than work on a *hacienda* near Guadalajara. His *capitán* was mean and deprived his troop adequate food and clothing. One day Raul attacked the *capitán* and he was sentenced to execution.

"Rafael, I have been studying the guard," Raul whispered to him one evening. "Several times a day he smokes his cigar."

"So, he still holds his rifle," Rafe replied.

"Yes but he is distracted," Raul continued. "Besides

the cigar smoke makes him calm. I have often seen him close his eyes while he smokes."

Raul was one of the larger and stronger workers. He learned tricks about warfare during his years in the Army and spoke often on how he had been good with a pistol.

"There is nowhere to run," Rafe told him. "Maybe if it was dark you could get away, but we are locked in here."

"If Mateo is smoking when we go with the wagon to the storage hut on the last load, he might not notice if we do not return with the wagon," Raul said. "We could hide and then escape later when it is dark."

Rafe noticed Raul used the term 'we' when he talked of the escape. "Where could you hide?" Rafe asked.

"Under the *piñas.*"

"You would be crushed," Rafe said. Each *piña* weighed almost a hundred pounds. He thought several would easily crush a man.

"We are young and strong. The *piñas* are round and we could curl between them to keep off some of their weight."

That night Rafe woke several times thinking about Raul's plan. The next day he watched Mateo carefully. Raul was right in saying he became engrossed in his cigars, seeming less attentive to the workers. Over the course of the next couple days, Rafe noticed Mateo never whipped a worker while he smoked, even if a worker dropped a *piña.* Later in the hut after dinner, Rafe spoke to Raul.

"I have been watching Mateo and you are right, he is distracted by the cigar. Raul spoke to him earnestly about the plan.´Rafe felt himself being consumed by the idea. He knew it was very risky, but watching the men here in the hut, he realized his fate. Ricardo, his money, and his old life were gone. He prayed María and Rodolfo could live at the Reyes *hacienda.* He prayed his mother and *don* Jorge would forgive him for being so stupid for trying to reclaim Rayo.

The next day Mateo was in a foul mood. He yelled and cracked his whip often. Rafe kept to his work trying to stay away from him. Late in the afternoon, Ignacio struggled and could not lift a very large *piña.* Waiting for his *rhizome* to finish with an agave, Rafe walked over to help Ignacio.

Mateo's whip hit the ground near his feet.

"Where are you going?" he sneered.

"To help Ignacio. The *piña* is too heavy for him," Rafe replied.

Mateo let his whip fly across Ignacio's back twice. "Now pick it up," he demanded. Ignacio struggled even more after the whipping to pick up the heavy agave ball. When he could not, the whip cracked again. Rafe stood helplessly near him. Ignacio worked his legs under the ball and started to lift it. About two feet off the ground, he wobbled falling backward. The heavy ball fell on top of him and Rafe heard a loud crack. Ignacio did not move.

Mateo looked at him and said, "So now you can pick it up." Rafe walked in front of the guard's horse. As he bent to wrap his arms around the agave ball, he heard the distinctive sound of the whip. It landed across his back, ripping his shirt and skin. Underneath the *piña,* Rafe could see life in Ignacio's eyes, but he knew if he lived it would not be for long.

Using his legs, Rafe picked the heavy *piña* off Ignacio's chest. While he carried it to the wagon, he heard the whip fly again. He readied himself as he knew it was aimed at his back. When the whip landed, he stumbled but did not drop the ball. He dumped it into the wagon and walked back to his spot. Mateo left Ignacio lying helpless on the ground.

It was only later in the hut when Rafe realized Raul was missing. He took the opportunity with the distraction of Ignacio to put his plan in action. That night, Rafe could barely sleep. Visions of Ignacio's eyes as he lay helpless burned through him. Mateo left him in the field as the coyote's dinner. When he was not thinking about Ignacio, he prayed for Raul to escape.

In the morning, the workers loaded into the wagons. The drivers drove the three wagons to the storage building where Mateo sat on his horse with his rifle in his arm. Raul was hanging by the neck from the hut's rafter. Rafe noticed his body looked bent as if he was badly beaten before he was hanged. His left leg stuck out in an odd position and blood dripped on his face and from his temple.

"Take a good look," Mateo growled. "There is no escape. Now get to work."

CHAPTER 47

For more than a week, Ricardo had been trying to figure out what happened to Rafael. He moved Rafael's belongings into his room and paid the bills. The leader of the *peón* workers at *don* Luis' *hacienda* was not helpful. He was mad at Ricardo because he and his friend caused a problem. Though it did not seem to affect the workers, the leader refused to allow Ricardo to join the group again or help in any way.

Without any ideas, Ricardo was thinking of giving up and going back to Mexico City. Rafael had told him to take the money, sell his saddle, and return the mare to *don* David, if he were dead. When Ricardo rummaged in Rafael's saddlebags, he found over a thousand *pesos*. He had no idea how an American could have so much money and though he thought most men would just take the money and leave Las Lomas immediately, he could not. He swore to himself he would only take the small fortune, if he found out Rafael was dead.

Tonight when Ricardo walked into the cantina, only one *peón* he recognized from *don* Luis' *hacienda* was sitting at a table with another man. Ricardo sat down.

"Hola," he greeted the men. "Can I buy you a *pulque?"*

The smile on the *peón's* face answered the question. After the three *pulques* were served, Ricardo asked the man if he had seen Rafael.

"I do not know where he is. I have not seen him at the *hacienda*. The last time I saw him, he was led into the barn by the *don* and a *vaquero*. Later I saw a wagon leave the barn. The two Otomí *Indios* were driving it."

"I need to talk to those *Indios*," Ricardo said.

"You cannot. The guard will kill you if you are caught snooping around," he warned him.

"Can you ask them. I have money and can pay you to take this chance," Ricardo said. "I need to know where they took him."

The man thought a few moments. "How much money?"

"Ten *pesos* now and ten for more information." Ricardo dug in his pocket and pulled out a two *cinco peso* coins and put them on the table. Ten pesos was a lot of money to a *peón,* especially for only asking a few questions. The man nodded in agreement.

"Be here tomorrow night," the *peón* said picking up the coins. Ricardo ordered another round of *pulque* for them.

Ricardo met with the *peón* worker at the cantina the following evening. He put two *cinco pesos* on the table when he sat down.

"I think your friend is alive," the man said, but it is confusing. "One of the workers said he heard the *don* order the Otomí *Indios* to take your friend away and kill him. They took him away in a wagon."

"You said you think he is alive?"

"I used one of the *cinco peso* coins and gave it to one of the *Indios.* He told me they were supposed to kill your friend, but they took him to the agave fields and sold him as a slave. He made me promise not to tell anyone, because they collected the money from *don* Luis for killing the *peón.*"

"Where did they take him?"

"He did not know the name of the place. It is a large *hacienda* growing agave and paying for workers. If they sold him to one of those *haciendas,* you will need to pay a lot of money to free him. He cannot be freed without paying his debt, and the debt grows bigger every day. Otherwise there is no escape. I'm afraid your friend is lost. No one escapes from the agave fields. They work until they die there."

Ricardo put twenty *pesos* on the table next to the two *cinco pesos.* "You have done well my friend. Tell no one of our conversation."

Ricardo walked back to the hotel with the information mulling in his mind. He needed to tell *don* David in Mexico City the news about Rafael. It was a six or seven day trip to Mexico City on horseback. The *peón* said with each day Rafael's debt was growing. Ricardo had no idea how much debt might be owed, though he thought the thousand *pesos* in Rafael's saddlebags should be enough.

What worried him more was attempting to free Rafael by himself. This was wild and treacherous territory. A man carrying a thousand *pesos* a target for thieves or worse yet he could be enslaved himself when he tried to buy out Rafael's debt. If *don* David would come, they could free Rafael. No one would dare question a man of *don* David's status.

Formulating his plan, Ricardo worried about Rafael's safety. It would take time to get a telegram to *don* David and for him to arrive here in Los Lomas. From the time he spent with the young man, Ricardo knew he was strong and healthy, but he was also resourceful and determined. It would not surprise him if Rafael attempted an escape, believing it his only chance for freedom. The *peón* worker told him escape was impossible and death was the only way out. Ricardo hoped he could bring *don* David before Rafael tried the impossible and was killed.

The following morning, Ricardo packed the saddlebags with the money and Rafael's belongings. He walked down the stairs and paid the desk clerk for the bill.

"What happened to your businessman friend?" the clerk asked him.

"I'm going to Guadalajara to meet up with him," Ricardo lied.

Ricardo walked to the livery and had both horses saddled. Climbing onto his horse he pulled Rafael's brown mare and the pack horse behind him. Guadalajara was much closer than Mexico City and the closest place he could send a telegram to *don* David.

CHAPTER 48

By the end of Rafe's second week of slavery, it already seemed an eternity. At first he tracked the days, hoping for a way to free himself. Now each day was the same and he stopped making marks under his cot to track the days. When his mind thought of escape, all he could see was Raul's beaten body hanging from the barn rafter. Instead of planning an escape, each night he tried to thank God for what he had.

His arms no longer ached at night, as his muscles adapted to the work. The guard had not beaten him for at least five or six days as Rafe learned to keep pace and gave him no cause. The whip cuts on his back were healing and physically he was in good shape. Two new men arrived several days ago, sold into this hellhole, giving the guards someone new to harass.

He and two other loaders were unloading the *piñas* at the alternate storage area near the main house of the *hacienda* when he saw a young girl on a red mare almost get thrown off. Something spooked the mare and it started bucking and kicking its hind legs. Rafe wasted no time as he rushed to the bucking mare and grabbed the reins just behind the mare's jaws. He held on tight bringing the mare's head down. Scared, the mare tried to bite him and shake him off, but Rafe held on. He talked to the mare trying to calm it down, just as he would any of his own horses when they acted spooked or hurt.

The guard pulled out his whip, thinking Rafe was trying to escape and rode toward the scene. When he saw Rafe grab the mare's reins trying to calm the horse, he backed off and watched the *peón* struggle with the mare. Rafe finally calmed the mare and helped a trembling young Chinese girl off the horse's back. He noticed the horse was favoring its right hind leg and then heard the distinctive sound of a rattlesnake.

Moving the girl to safety, Rafe grabbed a stick and beat

the snake twisting on the ground. The horse trampled it several times, but the snake was still dangerous. Finally, the rattlesnake stopped moving and Rafe picked it up with the stick and threw it away.

The frightened Chinese girl stood watching him, but Rafe could see she was unhurt. Rafe ran his hand down the horse's leg and noticed a trickle of blood just above the ankle.

Rafe pulled off his bandana and tied it just above the strike. He called out to the guard to bring a knife. The guard was watching amazed at the skill of the young *peón* and threw the knife into the dirt.

Rafe cut a large 'X' on top of the strike and pushed around the wound to release any poison, forcing it to bleed profusely. The mare snorted and huffed, but remained somewhat calm during the process.

"Go and bring me hot water and clean rags," Rafe called back to the guard. Instead, the girl ran to the main house of the *hacienda*.

"I will hold the mare," the guard said jumping off his horse and took hold of the reins. "The girl will get what you need," the guard said holding the horse steady, while Rafe inspected the wound.

Soon the girl arrived with clean rags and a bucket of hot water. Rafe wasted no time as he soaked one of the larger rags and used it to clean the wound and get a closer look at the snakebite.

"It does not look too bad. I don't think the poison traveled up the leg yet," Rafe told the guard.

"Here, my father said to use this on the wound before you wrap it," the young girl told Rafe and handed him a small glass jar containing a white paste.

Rafe sniffed it, but detected no odor. He applied the paste to the cut and wrapped it with a clean cloth and tied it as securely as he could. It was all he could do for the mare for now and hoped the snake had not gotten a clean strike. He patted the mare along her side until he grabbed her ear gently and spoke into it with a smooth gentle voice. The mare responded by lowering her head and then rubbed her face on Rafe's chest.

"You know about horses?" the guard asked.

"Yes, I grew up on a *hacienda* that raised blooded horses. I have been around them all my life. That one is a good mare. Take her back to her stall and keep an eye on her and if she has trouble come get me," Rafe told him.

"What is your name?" the guard asked him.

"Rafael," he answered.

"You are done for today *peón*. Go back to the shack and tell Alfonso you are to get an extra portion of food." The guard rode off leaving Rafe standing in the dusty area between the agave barn and the main house.

He was so busy doctoring the horse, he had not really looked at the young girl. She was not as young as he first thought, maybe in her early twenties. It surprised Rafe to see a Chinese girl here in the wilds of Jalisco.

"My name is Rafael. What is your name?" Rafe asked her speaking Spanish.

"Zhenzhen, it means precious," she replied in perfect Spanish.

"Very pretty name," he said.

"I must go now," the young girl said. *"Gracias, me salvaste la vida,"* she thanked Rafe for saving her life, then ran off to the main house and disappeared.

CHAPTER 49

As Rodolfo and Maxorro rode toward the Reyes *hacienda,* Rodolfo found himself telling Maxorro about his life as a child. He stopped his horse on top of a ridge overlooking the vast lands María told him were now owned by her brother Rafael.

"The land is fertile and over there is a lake," Rodolfo pointed to where the canyon dipped and they could see the edge of the lake. "The *don* raised blooded horses as well as crops. Pablo was the horse master and I remember times when many young horses roamed these canyons."

Maxorro sat looking out over the valley below. In the distance a road led up to a large house surrounded by a wall to create a huge courtyard. Numerous barns and corrals stretched behind the house. Dotted along the paths around the house were the small *jacals* where *peóns* had lived. On the other side of the house, fields stretched as far as he could see. The remnants of planted gardens still had wild shafts of corns popping up green against the blue sky. The property was a vast *hacienda* and Maxorro could not believe the story Rodolfo told him was true.

"When we were boys, Rafael and I were best friends. He often worked with Pablo in the horse barn and I worked in the fields. When we weren't needed or when we could just escape, he and I would scamper all over these hills hunting rabbits and doves," Rodolfo continued.

"It's much larger than I expected," Maxorro said.

"It is one of the larger *haciendas* around here. The lands stretch even further than you can see."

"I still do not believe a *peón* could own something like this," Maxorro said.

They turned the horses down the path and rode toward the buildings in the distance. As they rode into the courtyard of the Reyes estate, Pablo came out of the barn."

"Hola Pablo," Rodolfo called out.

"Rodolfo, you have returned. Who is this with you?"

Pablo asked walking up to them.

"This is Maxorro. He is a muleteer from Zacatecas."

"Ah welcome. So María has told you of Rafael's good fortune then?"

Rodolfo thought the house looked tired. Dead flowers hung from the window boxes and tumbleweeds gathered around the front porch. Pieces of the tile roof lay smashed in the courtyard dirt. The property showed years of neglect. Rodolfo could remember when it was splendid. The *don* and *doña* threw lavish parties in this courtyard for the elite of Torreón. Often he and Rafael climbed one of the large trees and watched as the people danced in their fancy dresses. Hundreds of candles lit the night as music filled the air.

It seemed impossible that Rafael could now own this property and more impossible that he wanted to give it to him and María.

"Pablo, is it not to be believed. Are you sure Rafael owns this land?"

"I talked to the lawyer in Torreón last week and all the paperwork has been completed. I have been fixing the barn. Come, I have a small pot of stew cooking."

Walking to the barn, Rodolfo saw where new wood was set into the barn's wall and it was obvious Pablo had been repairing the corrals. The interior of the barn was clean and a young colt stood in one of the stalls.

"I found him running alone in the canyon. There may be more of *don* Bernardo's stock still free and loose."

"Pablo, even if what you say is true, how do we run such a property. It is already September and the fields have been barren for the summer. The people will starve."

"They are not starving now and you have no fields. I saw the people in your camp. They know how to make something from nothing. They will plant gardens and make do with little until next year's harvest. Before I left Santa Fe, Rafael told me he will make money available for us to buy livestock and seeds to plant. Everything else God will provide."

Both Maxorro and Rodolfo knew of the small fortune of silver, which was still buried at the campsite, though neither told Pablo. It was all the money they needed to fix the *hacienda* and buy food. Unfortunately, any attempt to sell the silver bars would surely end in an arrest for the robbery. Each silver bar was stamped with the mine's insignia. Though he had known Pablo for all the years of his life, Rodolfo shied from telling him about the silver fortune.

"Pablo, where is Rafael? Is he coming here?" Rodolfo asked thinking perhaps Rafael, who was now a Santa Fe businessman might have an idea about the silver. Rodolfo thought Rafael could take the bars to New Mexico and exchange them for American money. It was one of the only ideas he thought might work.

"I received a telegram from Santa Fe last week. They are looking for him. They thought he might come here or perhaps he has already headed home to New Mexico."

Maxorro sat with Rodolfo and Pablo as they discussed the problems of the *hacienda*. Pablo assured Rodolfo he should bring the people and take over the houses. "María said there are women and young children at the camp. It will be getting colder soon, and they need to get settled in the *jacals* before it gets too cold. Bring them as soon as you can," Pablo told them.

As Pablo talked about the future here at the *hacienda*, Rodolfo realized the inheritance was true, even if it still seemed a dream. He could bring all the people at the camp and give them a real home, especially María. As he and Maxorro headed back to the camp, it was Maxorro who brought up the silver. "You did not mention the silver," he said.

"I now wish I never robbed your muletrain. *Peóns* can inherit a *hacienda*, but if we try to use the silver bars, we will be arrested. As long as we have the bars, we are in danger. What we need now is money to buy cows and horses and food for the people," Rodolfo mused about his dilemma.

Maxorro looked at Rodolfo. He understood their quandary and had pondered upon it for many days. "I might have an idea."

"What?"

"*Indios* have been using silver and gold for many

centuries. Even the Aztecs made trinkets and jewelry from gold and silver for hundreds of years. I have friends in my Cazcanes village who have worked with the metal. I can take a bar to their village and have them make it into buttons and jewelry. Could you then sell the items in the village market of Torreón?" he asked. He did not press Rodolfo when he did not answer knowing it was a complex problem.

When they arrived back to the campsite in the hills, Rodolfo gathered the people. He explained how María's brother inherited the abandoned Reyes *hacienda*.

"Gather your belongings," he told them.

On the ride back, he and Maxorro discussed how to organize the people. Families with small children would have first choice of the existing *jacals*. He and María would live in the main house along with several orphaned children. She wanted to use the large living room as a school for all the children. Maxorro said he was happy living in the barn and would build a small *jacal* near his mules and help Pablo with the horses.

"We will work together to rebuild the *hacienda*. We will share in everything. No one is a master and no one a slave," Rodolfo told everyone at the camp. "You are free to stay or leave at any time. If you have a skill, share that skill with the others. Go gather your things and we will leave in an hour."

The mood at the campsite escalated from disbelieving to excited chatter. The women orchestrated the move with efficiency. Within an hour each child had a small pack strapped to their backs and the women larger packs. The men loaded their horses with the heavier items. Maxorro and Rodolfo uncovered the silver bags and strapped them to Maxorro's mules. The two soldiers who arrived with Rodolfo had burned their uniforms and now were dressed in simple clothes. Rodolfo noticed Roberto, the younger man, was walking beside one of the single women.

María came to stand beside Rodolfo carrying a young child who could not walk the distance. Her face was radiant in the afternoon sun. Rodolfo signaled the group to move and like a caterpillar of humans, the group of *peóns* walked away from their remote campsite in the desert canyons to a new life.

CHAPTER 50

Into the third week, at least Rafe thought it was the third week, he had accepted his fate. During the day, he worked hard keeping up with the *jimadors* and *rhizomes* harvesting the agave. His muscles hardened from lifting and loading the *piñas* onto the wagons and the most recent whip cuts on his back were almost healed. At night he fell to sleep exhausted on his cot and slept dreamless nights. He tried to conjure Chiwiwi's or Ana Teresa's face in his mind, but he only saw dark images of nothingness.

Today they delivered the *piñas* to an alternate storage area some distance away from the main storage area. On the way, Rafe spotted a large field covered with red, purple, and white flowers. The beauty of the fields was mesmerizing in contrast to the brown terrain. As they rode closer, small dots became people in conical hats walking and bending amongst the flowers.

"What are those flowers?" Rafe asked one of the loaders.

"Flores de opio," the man said in a whisper, telling him the fields were opium flowers. "Do not ask questions and do not look. Mind your business."

Rafe tipped his head down under his sombrero, but could not help himself to wonder about the opium flowers. The presence of the young Chinese girl he saved from the bucking horse raised memories of El Paso, Texas. There the Chinese ran bathhouses and opium tents. Eldon Reynolds was high on the opium pipe the night Rafe killed him for shooting the sheriff. He remembered the sweet odor of opium smoke from that day and how the drug affected Eldon.

Since the day he saved the young girl and worked on the horse, Rafe thought the guard was more lenient toward him. He had not seen the young girl, but the guard told him the mare was doing well and the *jefe* appreciated him saving the girl.

The few days later all the workers were sitting in the shade of the main agave storage barn having the daily lunch which consisted of some beef mixed with onions and peppers wrapped in corn tortillas. Rafe thought the lunch was better than usual. As they ate, two wagons arrived to the main house from the road leading to the *hacienda*.

When the lunch break ended, the guards came up and ordered them to get back to work. "You, you, and you go to the main house and help unload those wagons," one of the guards yelled out pointing at Rafe and two other workers. One guard followed with his rifle ready if anyone of them tried to escape.

One of the wagons was loaded with food supplies. The other wagon was stacked with various sized wooden barrels. Rafe's nose detected a pungent aroma he did not recognize. He wondered if the barrels were for the agave or the opium processing.

On Rafe's fifth trip from the wagon to the storage area, he was surprised to see Zhenzhen talking to the guard. He nodded to her before she approached him.

"You must come with me to meet my father," she said and smiled. Rafe looked from Zhenzhen back to the guard. "The guard has allowed it," she said.

She led Rafe toward the gate of the main house. Typical of Spanish *haciendas,* the house was encircled by a high wall creating a hidden courtyard. Zhenzhen pushed on the gate and it swung open. They stepped inside and she closed the gate behind her. Much of the courtyard was a large pond. Zhenzhen walked across a narrow stone bridge toward the front of the house. A small pointed stone pillar was at each corner of the bridge.

Around the pond, lush flowers and small pruned bushes filled the garden. On the far end of the bridge, Rafe saw small green trees and flowers defining the pathway to the front door. The pond was alive with many different shades of golden and pale fish, some small and some more than a foot long. Small birds flitted in the trees, chirping at each other at the intrusion. Rafe had never seen anything to compare with the tranquility of the garden.

It was then he noticed the house was not typical of a Spanish *hacienda*. Though made of adobe, the tips of the red clay roofline were pointed, which gave the roof a bit of a look like it was ready to fly. The door was carved with dragons facing each other and he noticed the perfect details in the carvings as he and Zhenzhen approached. Without knocking, the door opened wide for them.

A small man dressed in loose black silk clothes opened the door and led them to what Rafe thought was a parlor. Around the room were many figurines made of beautiful green jade. Others were delicate porcelain with hand painted designs of flowers and birds. In the corner of the room stood a blue and white vase which was over five feet tall. The house had an intense presence of incense floating in the air.

"Go with Kang; there is a bath waiting for you," Zhenzhen told him. Rafe knew he reeked, but was accustomed to the smell of the men in the shack and hardly noticed it anymore. He had not bathed since the night before he and Ricardo went with the *peóns* to *don* Luis's *hacienda*. Zhenzhen stayed in the parlor as Rafe walked behind Kang to a small room.

Behind a silk curtain a large wooden tub steamed. Rafe disrobed, leaving his filthy clothes on the bench. Slipping into the tub brought back a memory of the bath in El Paso. He had saved George's life and George took him to the Chinese bathhouse. Rafe remembered how self-conscious he had been getting naked and letting the Chinese girls wash him. He could picture George roaring with laughter at his embarrassment.

As he relaxed in the scented water, he closed his eyes. He tried to forget the last several weeks of hell and imagined bathing at his home in Santa Fe. Soon he heard whispers and then hands washing him. Unlike his experience of being bathed in El Paso, Rafe relaxed and let the women clean him from head to toe. When they finished scrubbing his body and hair he was rinsed. They motioned to him to step out and they dried him.

Clean *pantalones* and a *camisa* were sitting on the bench and one of the women handed them to him. When he was dressed, Kang appeared and Rafe followed him. When they reached the parlor, Kang motioned Rafe to enter and closed the doors behind him.

"*Buenas taldes,*" an older Chinese man greeted Rafe speaking Spanish with an odd accent. It was an accent Rafe had heard in Santa Fe from Chinese storekeepers. Words with an 'r' were difficult for them to pronounce and it made the 'r' sound like an 'l.'

"*Buenas tardes,*" Rafe answered.

"My name is Longwei. My daughter Zhenzhen tells me your name is Rafael. I heard you saved her life the other day when the horse was bitten by a rattlesnake. I commended the guard for not shooting you when you ran to stop the horse. They have strict orders to control the workers in our service," Longwei told Rafe after he got up to face him.

Longwei was almost a foot shorter than Rafe. His silk pajamas-like clothes covered a slender body. Rafe thought he looked about George Summers' age and his stringy sparse beard showed strands of gray in the black hair.

"I was happy to be of service." Rafe found himself completely confused. Everything about the home and the man who stood in front of him was Chinese, yet he wondered where the *hacienda's* owner resided. Longwei and his daughter must be trusted servants to the *don* of the house. Zhenzhen sat quietly in a chair on the far side of the room. Her long dark hair flowed over a white tunic of silk embroidered with small birds.

"I am indebted to you for saving Zhenzhen's life and there is this Chinese proverb; if you save a life you are responsible for that life and your lives are bound together. Zhenzhen is now forever in your debt, as am I," he avowed.

Before Rafe could respond, Longwei continued, "You know about horses and I would guess you are not a *peón* like the others?" he asked.

"I am an American, not a *peón,* but I was raised on a *hacienda* in Torreón where they raised blooded horses. The horse master taught me how to care for and handle horses. I now have my own horse ranch in Santa Fe, New Mexico," Rafe explained to him.

"New Mexico? It is a long way from Jalisco. What are you doing here?" Longwei asked.

"*Señor,* it is a long story," Rafe stated.

"We have all the time in the world," Longwei said. He showed Rafe to a sofa and asked him to sit. Clapping his hands, the door opened and Longwei spoke to Kang in Chinese.

For several hours Rafe told Longwei the story of his life. How he had been raised as a *peón* on *don* Bernardo's *hacienda* near Torreón. He decided to tell Longwei everything, including shooting the *haciendero* for raping his sister and how he stole the Appaloosa and fled north. He described saving George Summers in the desert near El Paso and how he now owned a horse breeding business in Santa Fe.

From time to time Longwei interrupted him to ask questions, then allowed Rafe to continue. Twice Kang brought tea and Zhenzhen poured the small cups for her father and Rafe. Otherwise she listened intently to his tale.

Rafe explained how he inherited the Reyes *hacienda* and about Rodolfo and his sister. He ended the story explaining how he followed Carmela to Jalisco and was caught trying to reclaim the Appaloosa. He tried to explain to Longwei about his connection with Rayo and why he risked his life to retrieve him. *Doña* Carmela wanted him dead and *don* Luis told the two Otomí *Indios* to take him out to the wilderness and kill him. Instead the *Indios* decided to make some money and brought him here and sold him to this *hacienda.* They sold him to the *don* for three hundred *pesos.*

Longwei smiled broadly showing the tip of a gold tooth. "There is no *don* here. You were sold to me."

Rafe was dumbstruck and suddenly concerned he told the man too much information. "I am sorry I did not realize . . . " he stammered.

"You see life is not always as you see it," Longwei said. "I too was brought to this land as a slave. I was a child when my parents came from China to seek a better life here. They found mostly heartbreak and hard work.

"But, now you have all of this?" Rafe said as a

question. "How did that happen?"

"Ah amigo, I cannot tell you or you will never leave this place," Longwei said seriously. "Now let us talk business. Zhenzhen, I will call for you when we are finished speaking," he said to his daughter.

"Yes father," she said, bowed, and walked from the room closing the door behind her.

"I grow the agave because it is a good climate here and a legal crop. I also grow the poppy."

"I saw the flowered fields and one of the workers told me they were opium flowers. I know that much already. It is none of my business, but I thought opium flowers only grew in the highlands of Asia?" Rafe asked.

"Yes it is true, but I found this place and the climate is similar to Asia. It is not the best but it is good. I grow and process the poppies and it is making me very rich," Longwei said and gave a gold toothed smile.

"And the agave?"

"It too is a good crop. The *tequileros* are wanting more and more of the agave root, but it takes years to grow a plant to maturity. Luckily the agave is native to the region and requires no effort to grow. Nature provides everything it needs."

"What about Zhenzhen. Was she born here?"

"Yes. When I could not find a suitable woman here in Mexico, I bought a wife from China and we had Zhenzhen. She is the sunshine of my life."

"Where is your wife?" Rafe asked.

"She did not like it here, so she went back to China. I would not let her take Zhenzhen with her."

"Where do you sell the opium?" Rafe asked changing the subject back to the plantation.

"San Francisco. There is a Chinatown there and it is growing. I will not tell you how I get the opium there," Longwei told him.

A tap on the door interrupted them and Kang opened the door and spoke in Chinese to Longwei.

"Come supper is prepared," he said to Rafe. They followed Kang down a long hallway and onto a bright sun porch. The view from the open veranda was of the poppy fields in the distance, covering the hills in a flowery blanket. Zhenzhen was already seated at the table waiting for them. She had changed from the white floral silk pajama-like outfit to a pink silk dress with embroidered butterflies. Rafe bowed to her before he sat down.

Over supper Longwei talked to Rafe about Santa Fe and El Paso and the towns in Texas, Arizona, and New Mexico. Rafe discussed the changes to the area with the new American laws. Finally Longwei asked Rafe if he was interested in the opium business. He said he needed American contacts. Rafe noticed Longwei's attitude toward him seemed cordial and realized the fastest way out of his predicament would be to accept Longwei's offer, but it was not in his heart. Horse breeding was his passion. Besides, he had the *hacienda* in Torreón, the house to rebuild for his mother, his business in Santa Fe, and he still hoped he could find Ana Teresa.

"Opium is not my business. I have my own problems. I have to rescue my horse and get back to Santa Fe. I can repay you in horses or money, if you agree to let me go. I will have Zhenzhen in my heart always," Rafe said.

Longwei seemed disappointed though said nothing for several long moments. "It is against my better judgment to let you go, now that you know what I have here, but you did save my daughter and I owe you," Longwei said.

"You can trust me with your secrets. All I want is to get my horse and to return to my family in Santa Fe. I will repay my debt to you when I get to my saddlebags in Las Lomas," Rafe told him.

"I will sleep on my decision and we will talk more in the morning," Longwei said and signaled with his hand to Kang.

"Take Rafael to the guest room."

"Tell me what does Longwei mean in Chinese?" Rafe asked before he left.

"My father's name means Dragon Greatness," Zhenzhen spoke out and she giggled.

Rafe said goodnight and followed Kang to a spacious

room on the second floor. It was a good size bed and as Rafe sank on its softness, he thanked God for this small pleasure.

CHAPTER 51

Ricardo reached the Ciudad de Guadalajara and immediately sent a telegram to *don* David. In short sentences he tried to explain Rafael's situation. Then he checked into a hotel and took the horses to the livery.

The center of the city of Guadalajara was alive with activity. Across the plaza the Cathedral stood with two bell towers reaching high into the sky. The city center surrounded the central plaza in typical Spanish style. The Plaza de las Dos Copas was named for the two fountains on the east and west sides. The east fountain was surrounded by a walkway and flowers. A statue of the Archangel Michael stood in the center of the fountain.

Ricardo walked down the busy sidewalk. He passed by the Teatro Degollado which looked much newer than the Cathedral. As he turned the corner, a smaller plaza was active with people watching a puppet show. He strolled and watched as the papier-mâché puppets were orchestrated by men hiding behind the small facade. They made the puppets move by using attached sticks. The people laughed and clapped.

Behind the theater plaza a fountain dedicated to the city's founders was topped with a sculpture depicting Cristobal de Oñate. The Spanish conquistador was credited with founding the city and the plaque on the sculpture was dated 1532. Ricardo wandered through the plaza enjoying the excitement of the children and watching couples stroll, their arms linked together. Stopping at a cafe, he relaxed ordering a beer and his supper.

All day Ricardo wondered what to do about Rafael. Even when he sent the telegram to *don* David, he wondered what to say. He told Rafael he wanted some adventure in his life, but felt Rafael's predicament beyond his capability. Hopefully *don* David would reply tomorrow with a good idea how to find and save Rafael. In the meantime, he planned on enjoying an evening in the beautiful city.

Kang wakened and summoned Rafe the following morning to the sun porch. Longwei and Zhenzhen were waiting for him.

"Buenos días," they greeted each other.

"I assume you slept well," Longwei said.

"Yes, very well." Rafe was served coffee with rice and fruit.

"There is a supply wagon leaving this morning for Las Lomas. Zhenzhen has convinced me your debt has been more than paid. As soon as you have eaten, you may go on the wagon with my blessing."

"You are most kind, Longwei. If I can be of service . . . ." Rafe trailed off not knowing what to say.

"You must only promise me one thing," Longwei said. "Collect your belongings and leave Las Lomas immediately. You will forget your horse and not return to *don* Luis' *hacienda.* You will forget this place and speak to no one about it or about me. I am trusting you at your word."

Rafe's heart sank at the thought of leaving Rayo in Carmela's hands, but now knew his freedom and his life were more important.

"I give you my word," Rafe promised.

About an hour after wishing Longwei his gratitude and his best wishes to Zhenzhen, Rafe was riding in the back of a wagon on the road away from the agave plantation. As he rode away, the guard gave him a mean stare. Rafe wished he could help the poor men stuck working their lives for Longwei. While it riled him to think Longwei abused the men, he thanked God for his freedom. For now it was enough.

The trip to Las Lomas took most of the afternoon reaching the small village before supper. Rafe thanked the driver for the ride and jumped off the tailgate. Walking into the small hotel, he walked up to the desk clerk.

At first the clerk hardly recognized the American businessman. He was dark tan and wore the clothes of a *peón.* "You are back from Guadalajara!" the clerk said surprised to see him.

"Guadalajara?" Rafe said confused.

"Yes your man said he was meeting you there," the clerk replied.

"So he is not here?"

"No he left several days ago and took your horse and your things. He said he was meeting you there."

Suddenly Rafe realized his horse, his money, and his guns were gone. He had nothing but the clothes on his back. At least they were the clean clothes Longwei gave him yesterday.

"We must have missed each other. Did he say when he would return?" Rafe asked.

"No."

"Do you have a telegraph in this town?"

"No. You can send a letter with the stage from Guadalajara which stops every month."

"When is the next stage?" Rafe asked.

"It was here last week, so maybe three or four weeks time."

Rafe thanked the clerk and walked to the livery hoping Ricardo left the packhorse and planned to come back this way. Realizing it had been weeks since Rafe was enslaved at the plantation, he was beginning to think Ricardo most likely gave up on finding him, took the horses and money, and left. He did not blame him.

Walking into the livery, he greeted a thin man working in the back.

"*Hola,* I am looking for my brown mare and the packhorse. We brought them here several weeks ago."

"Ah yes, your friend took them both days ago," the man said. Rafe's shoulders sagged. "He paid me well, in fact he paid too much. Here," the man dug several *peso* coins from his pocket and gave them to Rafe.

"Thank you, but I need work. Do you know where I could find work in this town?"

"*Ah sí,* the *dons* are always looking for *peón* workers."

The ironic vicious circle almost made Rafe laugh. "Thank you for the coins, my friend. I'll come tomorrow and help you muck the stalls in repayment."

Don David received a telegram from Ricardo saying Rafael had been sold to a *hacienda* in Jalisco, but he was unsure which one or what to do. *Don* David replied to Ricardo to return to Las Lomas and he would meet him there as soon as possible. In the meantime, Ricardo was to continue trying to find Rafael. *Don* David also sent a telegram to George Summers. In it he wrote what he knew and told George he would seek the young man himself.

He departed Mexico City in a hurry the following day carrying a sack of money and trailing a packhorse. He had heard of the remote *haciendas* where *peóns* where enslaved for life. The practice was banned many years ago in the larger cities, but the law held little control over the vast reaches of rural Mexico. *Don* David rode hard and hoped he could reach Las Lomas in four or five days.

Having received *don* David's response, Ricardo was riding back to Las Lomas. He figured the *don* would arrive in a couple days. It was late in the afternoon when he finally reached the small village. He pulled the brown mare and packhorse behind him toward the livery and slid off the saddle when he got inside.

"*Hola,*" the man greeted him. "Your friend was looking for you," the thin liveryman said.

"My friend?"

"Yes he was looking for the brown mare and the packhorse. I think he went to the cantina."

Ricardo could not believe Rafael was here in Las Lomas. Quickly he left the horses with the liveryman and headed for the cantina. Dressed as a *peón,* thinner and a lot darker of skin, Rafael sat at a table near the back.

Rafe heard his name and looked up. Ricardo walked through the cantina doors. Relief swept over him. Now he could get away from this town, away from Carmela, and go home. He hated the thought of leaving Rayo, but he resigned himself to the reality.

After the two men greeted each other, Ricardo asked Rafe what happened. He made a promise to Longwei not to discuss anything about his time on the plantation. "I can't talk about it. Trust me, it was not pleasant."

Ricardo told him *don* David was on his way to Las Lomas and they should wait for him. "No, we'll leave in the morning," Rafe said shaking his head side to side. "We'll find *don* David on the road to Mexico City." Ricardo agreed it was a good plan. He ordered meals for them both and beer.

CHAPTER 52

Buck returned several days ago to *don* Luis' *hacienda* from Guadalajara. Carmela sent him for a list of supplies she could not get in Las Lomas. He brought everything she requested and she still griped. Buck decided it was time to request a sit down with his boss. *"Patrón,* it is time I return to my home in Kentucky," he came right out and said it.

"But I need you here, Buck. I am starting a new venture with the young *tequilero, don* Cenobio Sauza. I am investing a good amount of money with him and if all goes well we will be rich beyond our dreams. I will need your protection even more," *don* Luis protested.

Buck knew *don* Luis would protest and he was ready with an excuse.

"I would like nothing better than getting rich with you, *patrón,* but I have heard about carpetbaggers stealing Confederate land from those who cannot pay federal taxes. I must go and see about my family's properties," Buck pleaded his case. He knew the *don* could not keep him. He was not an indentured servant or *peón,* yet the *don* owed Buck money and Buck wanted the Appaloosa in exchange.

"Carmela and I are going back to Mexico City this week, so she can sell her house and we will marry. After you escort us home, you can leave. Can you help me find another bodyguard before you go?" the *don* asked, resigned to Buck's wishes.

"Mi amigo, Salvador Perez de Aguilar, will make a good bodyguard. He told me he was tired of working for his cousin the banker," Buck said. "I will talk to him in Mexico City."

"Get the horses ready. We are going to the village this afternoon during siesta. I have to see Margarita for the last time," *don* Luis said with a wink. Like most *hacienderos, don* Luis had a mistress. His was Margarita, a *mestiza* who owned the small mercantile. Luis bought and paid for the business to keep her happy many years before his first wife died.

Carmela was busy with the dresses and supplies Buck purchased in Guadalajara. *Don* Luis told her he and Buck were going to spend the day looking for more land and would take dinner in the village. "Do not wait up for me," he told her with a kiss.

Buck waited in the courtyard. He helped *don* Luis mount his horse and Buck rode Rayo. The Appaloosa finally relented and allowed Buck to ride him. Though Buck would not call the horse calm, he managed to keep the horse from bucking him off.

Don Luis rode toward Las Lomas taking a circuitous route. Several times he stopped and looked at the surrounding hillsides. "I can picture the agave growing on these hills," he told Buck. "Are you sure you do not want to stay and grow rich?"

"No. I think it is time I returned to Kentucky. The war is long over. It is time to rebuild my life there."

It was late afternoon when *don* Luis and Buck rode into Las Lomas. They tied the horses in front of the cantina. The *don* handed Buck several coins. "Stay here and I will return when I am finished with Margarita." Buck walked into the cantina, while the *don* walked down the sidewalk.

Rafe and Ricardo finished several beers and a good meal before they walked back to the livery. Rafe unstrapped his saddlebags from the mare and retrieved his GSW pistols, which were tucked into the bundles on the packhorse. He told the liveryman to have the horses brushed, fed, and ready in the morning. He gave the man twenty *pesos*.

"We should go to the mercantile and get some supplies for our trip. I used most of the bacon and coffee on the trip to Guadalajara," Ricardo said to Rafe. The two walked out of the livery and down the sidewalk to the small mercantile store.

A young man greeted them, "What can I do for you?"

Ricardo ordered supplies for the trip to Mexico City. Rafe was looking at the assortment of pistols in a case at the end of the counter while Ricardo was completing the order with the clerk when he heard the door.

"Buenas tardes don Luis," he heard the clerk say.

"Buenas tardes Juanito," don Luis replied. "Is Margarita upstairs?"

"Yes. She is upstairs *señor.* "

Rafe kept his head turned and moved further down the counter away from *don* Luis. He continued keeping his eyes averted until he heard a door close and the clerk resumed his conversation with Ricardo.

"Can you have the items taken to the livery so our packhorse can be readied?" Ricardo asked.

"Certainly. I will take care of it promptly. Will there be anything else?"

"No, gracias."

Rafe turned and walked out behind Ricardo. They walked out and into the street.

"That was *don* Luis," Rafe said. "I need to keep out of sight."

"Come, we'll go back to the hotel and you can stay in the room until morning. We'll leave very early, before the rooster crows."

Rafe agreed it was a good plan not wanting to be accidentally recognized by the old *don*. They walked toward the hotel.

"A bottle of tequila," Buck said to the bartender after taking a shot. Buck had only one job tonight. He had to wait for the *don* and ride back with him to the *hacienda.* The *don* usually spent two or three hours with Margarita. Buck figured he could drink the bottle before the *don* got back.

Rounding the corner of the street to the hotel and cantina, Rafe stopped midstride. Rayo stood quietly tied to the rail in front of the saloon. He grabbed Ricardo's arm. "Ricardo, that's my horse."

Rafe stopped. He did not want Rayo to recognize him, not yet. He thought about his promise to Longwei. He was not to seek the horse, but the horse was here in front of him.

"I see him," Ricardo said. "He is a remarkable horse. What are you going to do?"

"Come, follow me," Rafe whispered. Walking back

toward the livery, Ricardo followed Rafe through an alley and around to the back stairs of the hotel.

In their room, Rafe quickly changed from the *pantalones* and *camisa* into his traveling clothes from his saddlebags. He wrapped his gunbelt with his GSW pistols around his waist after checking their loads.

Ricardo was watching the street outside. From the window he could see the hind end of the Appaloosa standing by the rail.

"I assume you are taking your horse," Ricardo said while Rafe repacked his things. "You cannot ride that horse back to Mexico City. *Don* Luis will tell the authorities immediately. You will be spotted and shot."

Rafe did not respond to Ricardo's comments. Calmly he split his money and gave Ricardo more than five hundred *pesos.* "Here you have earned it. Take the brown mare and the packhorse and ride east tonight. Find *don* David and make sure he does not come to Las Lomas. Go back to Mexico City and have a good life. I owe you my friend, but I don't know if I will get to repay you more than this."

They grabbed their belongings and quietly walked down the hallway and back down the hotel's back stairs. Night had fallen over the small town of Las Lomas. Rafe could hear the guitar from the cantina. They walked around the side of the cantina through an alleyway and Rafe stopped short of the street.

"I need you to do one more thing," he whispered to Ricardo. "Untie Rayo, then head for the livery."

"Via con Dios, amigo," Ricardo said and they shook hands.

CHAPTER 53

Casually Ricardo strolled in front of the saloon. The streets of Las Lomas were quiet. He stopped near Rayo and lit a cigarette. As he struck the match, he nonchalantly untied Rayo's reins from the rail. As he did, he heard a series of sounds from the direction of the alley. Rayo perked his ears hearing Rafe's signal.

Rafe made several low clucking sounds with his tongue. Since Rayo had been a colt, Rafe trained him not only to respond to his touch, but to a series of clucks and clicks of his tongue. Rafe continued calling Rayo from the alley. Ricardo stood and watched the horse move from the railing following the sounds.

Buck stood up and stretched seeing the brief illumination of a match near the horses. Besides, he was tired of waiting for the *don*. The guitar player was strumming the off-key strings and Buck had enough of the screechy music. So much of Buck's time was like this – boring and waiting for the *don*. He longed for more action. In the Confederate Army he was in the Calvary. His job was to kill Yankees, as many as possible. He still could remember the first Yankee he killed. The Yankee was just a boy, maybe sixteen or seventeen at most. It bothered Buck a bit until the bullets started flying in his direction. After that, he began enjoying the killing of war.

Grabbing the tequila bottle, Buck headed for the door. He needed some fresh air and to see if the lights on the top floor of the mercantile were on. Pushing open the door, he stepped out into the night. A man smoking a cigarette stood near the railing. The Appaloosa was no longer tied next to *don* Luis' horse and was moving away from the rail and into the dark street.

The doors to the cantina clattered open. *"Oye peón, alejarse de esos caballos,"* a voice snarled at Ricardo telling him to get away from those horses. Buck stood in the doorway holding a bottle of tequila.

"Ah . . ah . " Ricardo stuttered not knowing what to say.

"You're trying to steal a horse?" Buck growled and dropped the tequila bottle.

"No señor, I am on my way home and saw a horse walk away," Ricardo lied.

Rafe heard smashing glass and an angry voice. Peeking out of the alley he saw Rayo heading his way. Under the dim light of the cantina he saw Ricardo and another man. The man was gesturing at Ricardo and Rafe could not tell if the man was brandishing a gun.

"The horse's reins must have come loose. Look, he is going down the street," Ricardo told the man. Ricardo noticed the man was dressed as a *caballero,* although he looked like a gringo.

Rayo was almost to the alley, his ears searching for the sounds which drew him toward a familiar voice.

"You stay here," Buck sneered at Ricardo not trusting the *peón.* Buck started down the street wavering a bit from the tequila.

When Buck got close to Rayo, Rafe stepped out of the shadows. "Don't touch that horse," he said calmly.

The voice shocked Buck as it seemed to come out of nowhere. He scanned the darkness finally seeing a shadow standing in the alley. He stood there trying to adjust his eyes toward the sound of the voice.

"What the fuck," Buck blurted in English out of instinct. Rafe saw him move his right hand to his pistol.

"I wouldn't do that," Rafe said. His hand rested on the butt of his GSW pistol. He had no fear he could kill the man, but he did not want to put Rayo in the crossfire. "You speak English," Rafe said after he heard the man curse.

"That's my horse and who the fuck are you," Buck replied.

"No it's not your horse, it's mine. Your mistress stole him in Mexico City," Rafe said.

With those words Buck knew the man in the shadow was the *peón* who inherited Carmela's land. His brain raced wondering how the *peón* had survived. The stupid Otomí

Indios don Luis hired had not killed him, but they took the
don's money. Buck growled thinking how he and the *don*
would take care of them after he disposed of this jasper.

"You have no proof. You are just a horse thief. People
around here have seen me riding the Appaloosa."

"And people saw you steal him in Mexico City from in
front of the land office the day of the hearing," Rafe
responded. It was neither true nor a lie, but Rafe thought it
might make the man think twice about his words.

Buck paused thinking it could be true. It bothered him
the day Carmela forced him to steal the horse. If anyone ever
found out, she would blame him. Numerous servants in the
don's household knew of the horse and knew it was not
Carmela's. He heard her bragging about stealing the horse
from the *peón* who inherited her land. Stupid woman could
not keep her mouth shut.

Ricardo stood quietly on the sidewalk in front of the
cantina thankful the man had not shot him. He saw Rafael
step out into the street and he was arguing with the man.
Ricardo wondered if he should position himself near the
man and distract him if he went for his gun to kill Rafael.

"I'll make this easy for you," Rafe said. "You let me
ride off on the horse and I will not kill you."

"Fuck you! You cannot kill me." Buck made a throaty
chuckle sure of his skills. He was quick on the draw and a
sure shot. As a gunfighter by trade he had never been bested
and the proof was many young *caballeros* in Mexico City who
died trying. Many *peóns* had tasted the lead from his six-
shooter who tried to rob his *patrón* here in Jalisco and Mexico
City. Now, this stupid *peón* thought he could best him. What
an arrogant fool.

"I can and I will if you do not give up the horse," Rafe
said. "I'm taking him one way or the other."

Anger and tequila mixed in Buck's head, with a rage
quickly building in him. No one challenged him, especially
not a bastard *peón*. His mind flashed with thoughts of
Kentucky. He should already be on his way riding the
blooded Appaloosa, but the *don* coaxed him to wait.

"Aarrgh," he growled as he went for his pistol.

Rafe's hand moved in a blur. Before Buck thumbed the hammer and squeezed the trigger, hot metal burned into his chest and it knocked him back. He tried to keep standing, but staggered to his right. The man was standing right in front of him, an easy shot. His gun hand was getting heavy. Buck tried to raise the pistol and used his last bit of strength to squeeze the trigger. The gun fired into the dirt in front of Rafe's feet then the pistol fell to the ground before Buck went to his knees and fell on his right side, his legs recoiling a couple of times.

Rafe walked over and said, "You did not have to die."

Buck groaned and then was quiet.

Ricardo rushed to the street to make sure Rafael was not injured

"I tried to talk him out of drawing on me," Rafe said.

The bartender and several patrons hurried out of the cantina hearing the shots. It was uncommon for gunfire to erupt in this sleepy little town. The bartender thought of himself as the constable, though he had no badge. Mostly he dealt with drunken *vaqueros* and sent *peóns* home when they had too much to drink. He hurried over to the two men standing in the street and another lying on the ground.

"What happened here?" he asked trying to sound official.

"He drew on me," Rafe said.

The bartender recognized Buck, *don* Luis' bodyguard and gun hand who lay not moving on the ground. Though the bartender never saw him draw, the talk was he was very fast. The gunman's pistol lay near the right hand of his outstretched body. Surely both men drew their guns; the young man must have been faster.

Don Luis heard the gunshots. *"Mierda,"* he cursed thinking Buck had probably gotten into trouble waiting for him. The hotheaded Kentuckian was always itching for trouble. Quickly pulling on his pants, he grabbed his pistol and tucked it into his waistband. He hurried down the back stairs of the mercantile and out to the street. Up ahead of him a little way from the cantina a group of people were gathered.

"What's going on here," he shouted as he walked up.

"Your man got himself shot," the bartender said. "He done it." His finger pointed to Rafael. *Don* Luis stared hard at the young man.

"He drew first," Rafe said. When he spoke, *don* Luis recognized the man's voice. He spoke Spanish, though with a slight accent.

"You, you are supposed to be dead," he growled.

"Yes, I remember when you told the *Indios* to take me out in the desert and kill me," Rafe responded. Everyone in the small crowd turned and stared at the *don*.

"He killed my man in cold blood, arrest him," the *don* blustered trying to ignore Rafe's comments.

"I shot a horse thief. He stole my horse in Mexico City. Carmela probably put him up to it. Then she ordered you to have me killed."

Don Luis grumbled knowing the man spoke the truth, but he was just a *peón* and nobody in this town would believe a *peón* over him, a *haciendero*.

"You stole Carmela's inheritance. She only wanted the horse. You should have left well enough alone," he growled.

"And you should not have let her steal the horse," Rafe spit back at him.

"Carmela said you stole the horse from the *hacienda* in Torreón. Her husband bred that horse. She was claiming rightful ownership."

"I am the rightful heir to the Reyes *hacienda*. I own the horse."

The bartender and people began to draw away from the two men as their argument became more heated. Both were armed and gunplay was feared. They knew *don* Luis' reputation and it was not affable. He was a shrewd man and the town believed he had killed a few neighbors to get control over their land.

Don Luis was getting agitated. He was going to have a hard time explaining to Carmela how Buck got shot and it would be worse if the *peón* took the horse. If somehow Carmela found out about his trip to see Margarita by busybodies in town, she probably would not marry him. He should have killed the *peón* as she asked and been done with him.

"This is my town *peón*. No one here believes you. Leave now or I will kill you," *don* Luis grumbled.

"I believe him," Ricardo spoke up. "I talked to your servants in Mexico City and they told me about the wild Appaloosa you stole."

Don Luis turned toward the speaker. He was an older man, maybe in his forties, and he was not a local *peón*. He felt the stares of the small group of people standing in the street. Rafe and Ricardo stood about ten feet from him. Buck's dead body lay between them. He heard the people muttering and all eyes were on him. *Don* Luis pulled at the gun at his waist and drew it out.

As he tried to raise it, Rafe's muzzle flashed. The *don's* gun jumped out of his hand and flew several feet away from him. He grabbed his right hand and stood there wide eyed, stunned at the quickness of the *peón's* handling of his pistol.

"I could have killed you," Rafe said calmly. "Go home and tell Carmela it is over."

Rafe whistled and Rayo walked over to where he stood. Rafe spoke to him softly. Quickly Rafe threw his saddlebags over Rayo's back and jumped on. He kept the horse to a walk as he turned toward the southern road leading out of from Las Lomas. As soon as he was out of the village, he clucked his tongue and Rayo jumped to a gallop. Rafe and Rayo flew into the night.

Chapter 54

George Summers pondered the telegram from *don* David Salazar. The telegram confirmed Rafe was missing somewhere in Jalisco. Carlos' uncle *don* David was heading to Jalisco to look for him. The telegram was cryptic as *don* David did not know any details.

He fretted for several days and would waken at night with a sour lump in his stomach. Tonight George sat by the crackling fireplace not paying attention to the dancing flames, as tiny cinders fizzled out above the burning logs into nothingness. His adopted son Rafe should be here in Santa Fe running his horse business and married to Ana Teresa. Instead he was lost in Mexico.

Even life here in Santa Fe was still perilous. The sheriff wanted Rafe to stand trial when he returned. Rafe was innocent and any jury should acquit him, but a jury of Spaniards could decide any fate, even hanging as they continued to call the death of Diego a murder.

Josefina found him smoking a cigar in his high back chair in the living room. She watched him fretting and wanted to tell him how afraid she was for Rafe's safety, but it would only make him worry more.

"Go look for him. I know you will not sleep until he is found," Josefina said as she stood beside him. She placed her hand on his shoulder as she spoke.

Two days later, it was a cool almost cold morning as Josefina and his two teenage daughters hugged him in the courtyard as George readied to leave for Mexico. Carlos and Celiá stood nearby.

"I will wire from El Paso and Torreón. If you hear anything from *don* David, wire ahead of me. Once I check on things in Torreón, I will go to Mexico City."

He and Carlos shook hands. "I wish I could go with you," Carlos said.

"Find Rafe, *Papá*. Bring him home," Lolo, George's oldest daughter said. Rafe was like an older brother to

George's two teenage girls. He had lived here with the family for over six years and the girls were distraught knowing he was missing in Mexico.

"I will find him." George hugged them again and mounted the horse. He trailed a packhorse and Carlos suggested taking a spare horse, but George said he could buy one if need be.

Traveling at a fast pace and only taking short breaks for the horses, George pushed harder than he normally would. In his younger years, George would have slept under the stars with a fire to keep him warm, but now in his fifties his body needed the rest of a real bed after a day on horseback.

Five days later he reached El Paso. His old body ached from the hours in the saddle and the horses needed rest. Reaching the Stratton Hotel, a place he frequented many times when he came to El Paso, was a relief.

"I need a room for a couple of days and a bath," George spoke to the desk clerk. "And my horses need taken to the livery, brushed and fed."

"Yes sir, Mr. Summers. We haven't seen you here for quite a spell."

"Yes it has been some time. Do you have a telegram for me?" he asked.

"No sir. Were you expecting one?"

"No, just hoping for one. I need you to get this over to the telegraph office."

George wrote out a telegram to Josefina. He told her he was safe in El Paso and would leave in two days for Torreón. She knew to wire him if she heard from either Rafe or *don* David. He was disappointed knowing the lack of information meant Rafe was still missing, but somewhat relieved it meant he could still be alive.

George placed a fifty-cent coin on the counter, thanked the clerk, and picked up the room key.

"Call for me when the bath is ready," George told him.

Don David was on his fourth day of riding toward Jalisco after sending the telegram to Carlos saying he would search for Rafael. The road to Jalisco from Mexico City was sparsely traveled. Stages did not run on any schedule and *don* David passed only three riders and two carriages over the last several days. He had never ridden to Jalisco and hoped he would reach the edge of the state later today.

All day yesterday he wondered why he was even attempting this trip. Rafael was not his concern. The young man was Carlos' friend and *don* David felt no special bond to him, however for some unexplained reason he found himself intrigued by Rafael's predicament. His was a rags to riches story, starting as a *peón* of a *haciendero* and becoming a horse breeder in Santa Fe. *Don* David thought he might one day like to visit New Mexico and see the United States for himself, perhaps visiting Carlos and his new bride.

He rode all day and finally stopped at a small stage stop built by local peasants. It was their home, which they opened to travelers providing food and shelter from the elements.

The wind picked up and the sun was setting behind him as Ricardo rode east from Las Lomas. It was the only road, so he was not concerned he would miss *don* David. Alone on the quiet road he found himself thinking of the gunfight in Las Lomas. He heard talk in the cantina about *don* Luis' gunman. They said he was deadly and fast, yet Rafael shot him dead with two shots before the gunman thumbed his pistol's hammer. Ricardo never saw anything like it.

Ricardo arrived late at the small stage stop. He woke the proprietor when he arrived. The man showed him to a small room behind the kitchen with a cot. The man told him his wife would make breakfast in the morning. Happy to have a roof over his head and something soft under his weary bones, Ricardo thanked the man. He removed his boots and was instantly asleep as soon as he stretched out on the cot.

The clanging of a pot in the kitchen woke Ricardo the next morning. Stretching, he put on his boots and walked into the kitchen.

"Buenos días," he greeted the woman.

"Buenos días, el desayuno estará listo pronto," she replied telling him breakfast would be ready soon. She told him to go take a seat in the front room with the other man.

Walking out of the kitchen, Ricardo was surprised to see *don* David sitting in a chair sipping a cup of coffee.

"Buenos días don David," he said.

"Ah Ricardo. What are you doing here? I thought we were to meet in Las Lomas?" *don* David asked surprised, but relieved to see him.

"It is a long story I will tell you over breakfast and then we will leave for Mexico City," Ricardo replied.

In El Paso, George had no reply from Josefina to his telegram. It meant she had heard nothing from *don* David in Mexico. After an early breakfast, George walked to the telegraph office and sent a wire to Pablo in Torreón. The wire said George was on his way and would arrive within the week. George also wrote saying to keep Rafe in Torreón, if he showed up, until George arrived. In his heart George knew Rafe was not headed to Torreón, but was still praying for a miracle.

CHAPTER 55

It was well into the night before Rodolfo and María washed up and were upstairs in the bedroom. During the day, María scrubbed the kitchen and organized the large main house's kitchen. Rodolfo worked with the families as they patched the adobe *jacals* and thatched the roofs for the coming winter. Several men with carpentry skills were building rough-hewn furniture for the rest of the people.

For the most part the people amiably decided which *jacal* was given to which family. One man suggested they pull lots, but the consensus was for the larger families to be given first choice of the *jacals*. A man with a pregnant young wife now lived in the *jacal* where Rodolfo had grown up.

Every one of the families living at the campsite chose to stay with Rodolfo and María at the *hacienda*. They were all doing their part tilling the fields, fixing the corrals, and making the *jacals* livable again. Rodolfo promised them they would have a place for their families to live as long as they wanted to work.

The mood around the *hacienda* was euphoric. For the most part the children played their madeup games all day long, while their parents worked. The work was hard and food was still an issue. One of the women harvested the few wild stalks of corn which had popped up in the old garden. She stripped and saved the kernels for next year's crop. She also found a few potatoes and wild onions.

As Rodolfo and María lay together on the mats in the upstairs bedroom María said, "Rodolfo, I'm worried about Rafael. Pablo said *don* Jorge is coming from Santa Fe. He'll stop here before he goes on to Mexico City. If they cannot find him, I am worried this *hacienda* might be in jeopardy." María thought of George Summers as *don* Jorge, having heard Rafael use George's Spanish name when he spoke to him.

I think I should go with him to search for Rafael," Rodolfo replied. "It is not safe for *Señor* Summers to be traveling in Mexico alone. Besides Rafael might need my help, too."

María paused before answering. "The people seem to be managing the work, but we need food. Perhaps you and *don* Jorge could take a bar of silver to Mexico City and exchange it for money."

Rodolfo and Maxorro buried the silver bars one night. Only the two soldiers knew of the silver besides them and they had been sworn to secrecy.

"*Querida,* I cannot put *Señor* Summers in peril. All the bars are marked with the mine's insignia. It would be foolhardy to be caught with one of them."

"What are we going to do? We need cows and pigs and chickens. The people will starve this winter without a stockpile of supplies," María responded.

"I will talk to *Señor* Summers when he arrives. Perhaps he can loan us money until we get the *hacienda* running properly."

Rodolfo lay his head back on his bent arm. Exhausted he fell asleep. María heard his breathing quiet and knew he was sleeping. Her arm rested over his bare chest. She had not told him she was pregnant and he was so consumed by the work he did not notice her swelling breasts and the small bump in her stomach.

A few days later Pablo found María in the kitchen. He held a telegram in his hand. "*Señor* Summers sent this telegram from El Paso. He will be here in a few days," Pablo told her.

"Where is he going to sleep?" María asked. She remembered George was a gentleman, used to more comforts. While the *hacienda* had been abandoned, most of the furniture and anything of value had been stolen. Only the very heavy dining room table and chest were still in good shape. The children were sleeping on blankets as were she and Rodolfo. It was warmer than sleeping under the stars, though not much softer.

"I will make him a mattress of hay. He will understand, María," Pablo said.

George Summers arrived in Torreón several days later.

He checked in at the Hotel Bilbao. It was mid afternoon and he decided to visit the *hacienda* before unpacking.

At the hotel's front desk, he asked for directions to the Reyes *hacienda*.

"Are you sure you want to go to the Reyes hacienda, *señor?* It has been abandoned since *don* Bernardo died," the clerk told him.

"Yes, the Reyes *hacienda.* I have business there with Pablo Medina," George told him.

The clerk gave him a confused glance then gave him instructions. George put several *pesos* on the counter.

It was after noon when George reached the *hacienda's* property line marked with stone pillars. As he rode down the lane toward the main house, people stopped working and stared at him. A few raised a hand to wave, while several of the men stopped and began walking behind him. Several children ran in front of him signaling his arrival. By the time he reached the courtyard, more than thirty men, women, and children were curiously following him.

"*Señor* Summers. I am glad to see you looking so well," Pablo said. Pablo helped him dismount and took the reins of the horse. "Come we must tell María you are here."

"Who are all these people?" George asked.

"These are the *peóns* who live with Rodolfo and María," Pablo explained.

A few minutes after sending a young boy to find María, she came running out of the front door of the main house.

"*Don* Jorge, welcome," she called to him as she ran to where he stood near Pablo. George could not believe it was the same girl who buried her baby son in their backyard in Santa Fe. That young girl was always sad and despondent with sunken eyes and dull lifeless hair. The young woman running up to him had a huge smile on her face. Her shiny dark hair cascaded down her back and flew as she ran. Her face and breasts were full and round.

"This is *don* Jorge from Santa Fe. He has come to help us," she announced to the crowd of people who gathered. Several of the men came to shake his hand while the children ran off to play. They were less curious than their parents.

George followed María into the main house. He was shocked at the lack of furniture. Pablo told him the *hacienda* had been vandalized, but George had not realized to what extent. Following her to the kitchen, George realized not only had the furniture been vandalized, the shelves were almost completely bare.

"Where is my brother?" María asked.

"He left Mexico City because Carmela stole Rayo after the land hearing concerning this *hacienda*. She was mad Rafael inherited it and took the horse. Rafe followed them to Jalisco and we have not heard from him since," George explained.

"Carmela is evil," María said. "Rafael should have let her have the horse. He has others."

"I agree with you, but Rafe has a very special bond with Rayo."

"Yes, Pablo said Rafael must be in trouble or something happened to him on the way to Torreón. What can we do?"

"I do not know. Rafe stayed with Carlos' uncle, who is headed to Jalisco following his trail. I am waiting to hear from him," George told her. "First, I need to go back to town and send several telegrams."

Just as he was standing to leave, a young man burst through the door. *"Bienvenidos,"* Rodolfo said as he strode over and shook George's hand in welcome. "I am Rodolfo. You are welcome here, *Señor* Summers. You are our honored guest."

George had heard a lot about Rodolfo from Rafe, some good and some bad. He was supposed to have been an outlaw, a bandit, but this young man did not appear to be threatening. In fact he reminded George of Rafe when George first met him – eager, smart, and humble.

"Don Jorge needs to ride back to Torreón to send some telegrams," María said.

"Have my horse saddled," Rodolfo told Pablo who was standing nearby. "I will ride with *Señor* Summers and make sure no harm comes to him."

"Please call me George," he said to Rodolfo, "or if you prefer, Rafael calls me *don* Jorge."

As they rode to Torreón, George questioned Rodolfo. "The people look happy, but where are the cows and chickens?"

"We need money to buy livestock and to finish fixing the house and guest *casita* as well as the *jacals* for the people," Rodolfo said. "The people came to us with only the clothes on their backs."

"You need milk cows for the children and goats and sheep. You need hay for the horses and food supplies," George continued to tell Rodolfo what he already knew.

"Yes, you are right. We are but *peóns, don* Jorge. I was hoping Rafael could loan us some money to get the *hacienda* started."

"If you had the money, could you purchase the livestock you need here in Torreón?" George asked.

"Yes. We could purchase the livestock from several of the other *haciendas* and buy the supplies here in town. We will need seed to plant for next year's harvest and God willing enough rain."

CHAPTER 56

When they arrived back in the town of Torreón, he thanked Rodolfo for accompanying him and said he would be spending most of the next day in town. George rode directly to the telegraph office, which was about a block down the sidewalk from the bank.

The telegraph clerk looked at the well-dressed stranger. He was an older man, maybe in his fifties with a bit of a hefty belly.

"Hola, me llamo Jorge Summers de Santa Fe, Nuevo Mexico," George said to the clerk. "I need to send several telegrams and may receive a response. I am staying at the Hotel Bilbao and wish to be notified immediately of a reply."

"Sí señor," the clerk replied.

George sent one telegram to Josefina to tell her he arrived safely. He sent another to *don* David in Mexico City wanting to know if he had found Rafe. Thanking the clerk, he walked down the sidewalk to the bank.

"Hola, me llamo Jorge Summers de Santa Fe, Nuevo Mexico," George said to the bank teller as he walked up to the cage. "I wish to speak to the manager. I have business here in Torreón." The clerk walked to an office behind the counter and shortly a well-dressed man walked toward George.

"Mi nombre es Gregorio Zamora. ¿Qué puedo hacer por usted Señor Summers?" The bank manager, Gregorio Zamora asked how he could be of service to George.

"The Reyes *hacienda* has been inherited by my adopted son, Rafael Reyes de Estrada. I wish to open an account to provide funding to allow him and the people who will be living there money to buy supplies in town."

Gregorio heard the news from Nicolás Jiménez when he returned from Mexico City. The banker was surprised to hear the news, but had little concern since the property was not mortgaged to the bank. Nicolás told him the inheritor was the bastard son of *don* Bernardo and a *peón* woman.

"It can be arranged, please follow me to my office,"

Gregorio said. Over the next hour George opened an account and hired Gregorio to provide a trustee service to the account. He would only provide access to Rafael, Rodolfo, María, and Pablo. Each month he would mail George an accounting. George opened the account with five hundred *pesos* in cash, and asked Gregorio to wire to his bank in Santa Fe for five thousand more.

"It is a large sum *señor,*" the banker said. "Surely you do not expect *peóns* to manage the money. They will squander it."

"I expect you to verify their needs, but I trust they will do a good job. They will need funds for cows, sheep, pigs, and chickens, as well as building supplies. I expect you to oversee that they do not get swindled by other local *hacienderos.* I will also open an account at the local mercantile for their supplies."

The sun was low in the sky as George left the bank and headed to the hotel. Checking in with the desk clerk, he explained he was to be notified immediately if a telegram was delivered.

"*Sí señor,*" the clerk replied.

"Can I get a bath in this hotel?"

"Certainly. I will send the woman to fill the tub at the end of the hallway. Will there be anything else *señor?*"

As George relaxed in the tub of hot water his mind wandered. He was stuck here in Torreón until he heard something about Rafe. He saw no reason to go to Mexico City. For sure Rafe was not there and obviously he was not here. If Rafe were able, George knew he would telegraph Santa Fe. George's thoughts continued to circle. He tried hard not to let himself believe Rafe was dead, but the thought nagged at him.

At about noon the next day a large wagon pulled by two horses arrived at the Reyes *hacienda.* In the back sacks of flour, lard, sugar, coffee, beans, potatoes, cornmeal, onions, and other essential foods covered the wagon's floor. Several slabs of pork belly were in canvas bags. In a large cage on top, six hens squawked and trailing the wagon was a milk cow and a pig. Several bushel baskets of apples perched precariously on top of the bulky sacks.

As the people saw the amazing site, they excitedly cheered and hugged each other.

"Esto es un milagro," they repeated it was a miracle.

María took charge of the unloading. All of the food was carried to the main house's kitchen. She ordered several of the women to begin separating portions and storing the rest. Two of the young boys untied the cow and walked it to the barn. Several older boys carried the chicken cages and one tugged on the pig.

María looked skyward crossing herself and thanked God, *"Gracias a Dios."* She thanked God but knew it was *don* Jorge who sent the food.

The *hacienda* was a flurry of activity all afternoon. María sent one of the teenage boys on a horse to find George at the hotel and tell him to come for a feast tonight at the *hacienda.* "Tell him everyone wants to show him their thanks," she told the boy.

After George arranged for the wagon of food to be sent to the *hacienda,* he walked to Nicolás Jiménez' office. The banker said Nicolás had arrived back to Torreón and George wanted to make sure the legality of the inheritance was secure.

"Buenos dias. Me llamo Jorge Summers de Santa Fe, Nuevo Mexico," George said to Nicolás when he arrived.

"Ah *Señor* Summers. Rafael has spoken so much about you. Welcome. Where is Rafael? Is he not with you?" the lawyer responded.

"No Rafael is not here. I am not exactly sure where he is," George said.

"What do you mean?"

"After the land hearing Carmela stole Rafael's horse, the Appaloosa. I suppose she was mad at losing the inheritance. Rafael has been trying to retrieve the horse and we have not heard from him in some time."

Nicolás bristled at the news. Carmela Reyes was an evil woman and he was not surprised she retaliated.

"Regardless, is all the inheritance paperwork in order?" George asked getting back to the point of his visit.

"Yes and no. Rafael is the legal and rightful owner. All the paperwork has been filed and accepted by the land officials. However, Rafael was to have completed the paperwork here to transfer the deed to his sister."

"I was afraid of that," George said, thinking it could get thorny if anything had happened to Rafe.

"Can anything be done? María, Rodolfo, and about fifty peasants are now living on the property. They are fixing it and I know Rafael wants them to continue to live there."

The lawyer leaned back in his chair. "You say you don't know where Rafael is. Is it possible he is . . . not alive?" Nicolás said the last part tactfully. If Rafael attempted to reclaim his horse from Carmela, the lawyer knew she could easily be ruthless, especially against the *peón* she believed stole her inheritance.

George sighed. "It is possible, though I am still hopeful."

"Does Rafael have any heirs? Wife or children?"

"No, just his mother, sister and his sister's two children."

"Good. In Mexico the inheritance could be claimed by his sister. She and her husband would have full rights to the property."

"She has no husband. The children are *don* Bernardo's. She is living with a man named Rodolfo, but they are not married."

"I suggest they marry as soon as possible. The courts would not look kindly on an unmarried woman inheriting such a large piece of land."

"I understand," George replied. "I will see that it happens quickly. In the meantime, you can reach me at the Hotel Bilbao. I will be here in Torreón until I get word about Rafael."

CHAPTER 57

George stopped by the telegraph office hoping word from Santa Fe or Mexico City had arrived. *"No, señor,"* was the clerk's answer. Disappointed, George walked back to the hotel. When he walked into the lobby the clerk told him a young boy was waiting.

"Señor, you are to come to the *hacienda.* María sent me to find you."

"Go back and tell her I will come later this afternoon," George told him.

George only knew María for the few months she lived in Santa Fe when she gave birth to her third child, baby Bernardo. After the baby died she left for El Paso. He only met Rodolfo yesterday, though Rafe told him about their friendship at the Reyes *hacienda* during their childhood. Rafe seemed comfortable allowing María and Rodolfo to live at the *hacienda.* He assumed they were in love, but wondered if he was meddling.

Stepping back to the plaza, George headed to the church at the far end. The double doors were closed, but as George tried the right handle the door easily swung open. Inside the church was quite elaborate. The afternoon light shone through large stained glass windows on either side of the altar. A large wooden image of the crucifixion hung on the wall behind it. On the left side, a sculpture of the Virgin Mary had many lighted candles at her feet. Elaborate candle-lit fixtures dimly lit the chapel on both sides. George dipped his fingers in the holy water and made the sign of the cross before walking down the aisle.

The church was empty except for a black veiled woman toward the front, who was on her knees. George sat in one of the pews about half way down the aisle. He knelt and said prayers for Carlos and Bibiana's marriage, for Josefina and his daughters. Then he asked God to protect Rafe. "Bring him back to us," George prayed.

A little bit later a padre walked up near the front altar.

He was preparing for the next Mass. George walked up to him and bowed his head slightly.

"Excuse me. I need your help," George asked.

"Yes, what can I do for you?"

"Padre, I am George Summers from Santa Fe. I need you to perform a marriage . . . tonight if possible," George said.

"Tonight? There is trouble I assume? Normally the intended need to see me for my blessing," the padre retorted.

"No it is not like that, padre. A young couple named María and Rodolfo need to be married to rightfully inherit the Reyes *hacienda*. Nicolás Jiménez believes María must marry Rodolfo to ensure she would be able to make a rightful claim. Nicolás suggested the sooner the better."

Hearing this man knew Nicolás Jiménez and Nicolás was suggesting the marriage, the padre softened. "I have a five o'clock Mass this afternoon. Afterwards I will ride to the *hacienda* and perform the marriage. Go now and tell them to prepare themselves. I will take their confessions before the ceremony."

George walked out of the church and back to the hotel. He asked the clerk to send a runner to the livery for his horse. He changed to his better business suit and combed his hair. About an hour after he talked to the padre, George arrived at the *hacienda*.

The courtyard was alive with activity. Obviously the wagon load of supplies arrived and a small deer was turning on a spit over a fire. The children swarmed his horse and he was careful not to let the horse trample any of them.

"*Gracias señor,*" was repeated over and over as the people greeted him. After a few minutes, Rodolfo and Pablo came out of the barn and walked toward where George stood in the courtyard.

"*Gracias don* Jorge," Rodolfo pumped his hand and gave him a huge hug. "You have provided a miracle for us."

"Rodolfo, come we must talk," George said. He put his arm around Rodolfo and led him off away from the noisy courtyard.

"I need to ask you a question," George started. "Do

you love María?"

"I love her with every breath of my soul *señor.*"

"And she you? I assume she loves you in return?"

"*Sí.* We would die for each other," Rodolfo said. "She told me several days ago she is carrying our child."

George sighed in relief. "The padre is coming here later tonight. He will marry you and María. It is necessary to maintain the *hacienda* if Rafael is not located. If Rafael cannot sign the proper papers over to you, his death could complicate your status here." It hurt George's soul to admit the possibility of Rafe's death, but he could not hide from the truth.

"I have wanted us to marry, but we have not made the time for the formality. I will go tell María, now. She has been working all day to prepare a feast for you. Tonight will be an even bigger celebration." Rodolfo pumped George's hand several times. The grin on his face was all George needed to know he loved María.

The evening feast was truly a celebration and the people cheered when Rodolfo and María were announced as husband and wife. One of the women put wildflowers in María's braided hair and she looked radiant. George wished María's mother could have been there to see her daughter so happy. After all the documents were signed, the padre told them all was legal and he would create the proper marriage record with the church.

"Bless you my children," he said.

As the padre departed for Torreón, George offered to ride with him. They left the peasants reveling in their new home, a bounty of food, and the marriage of their friends. Several of the men built a large bonfire in the courtyard and Paco and Hector sang. Even without any instruments, the men could carry a tune.

Chapter 58

Rafe rode hard away from Las Lomas. He was not a criminal and though the gunman was dead, he held his temper and did not kill *don* Luis. The old *don's* hand would heal with time, but Rafe doubted his pride would heal so quickly. He had told the *don* to tell Carmela it was over and while he hoped it would be true, he doubted Carmela would give up so easy.

He rode hard last night until he could tell Rayo was getting weary. There was no need to hurt the horse. He finally stopped after passing a small stage stop. The *casita* was dark and there was a small corral attached. Circling around, Rafe thought it better not to be seen. He thought Ricardo was right. Rayo was a remarkable horse and while Rafe might be able to blend into the *mestizo* population, Rayo would stand out.

This morning brought mostly sunny blue sky with a few patchy clouds. Knowing he was still probably in the state of Jalisco, Rafe pushed on. With the morning sun on his back, he could tell the road was heading southwest. Midday after seeing no one and no dust trails in any direction, he stopped, built a small fire, and made coffee and bacon.

Two days later Rafe rode into the town of Colima. He estimated he was more than one hundred miles from Las Lomas and had seen no one on his back trail. To the north several tall mountains rose into the cone shape of volcanoes. It was late afternoon when he arrived in the main part of Colima. It surprised him how much it reminded him of Santa Fe, except for some architecture which had a Moorish style with pointed archways. Rafe finally stopped on the far side of town in an area called Riviera where a cantina had a sign reading *"Cuartos Para Rentar,"* indicating rooms for rent. A small corral with a lean-to roof stood behind the cantina.

Rafe walked Rayo to the corral and stripped his saddlebags. A young boy heard him and came running.

"I keep your horse *señor.* I will brush him too."

"*¿Cómo te llamas?*" Rafe asked the boy his name.

"Chito." the boy replied.

Rafe flipped the young boy a *peso* coin. "Give him extra oats, Chito."

"*Sí señor.*"

The rooms for rent above the cantina were small and plain. The noise from the cantina filtered through the loosely fitting door and thin floorboards. After a beer and a bowl of spicy lamb stew, Rafe stretched on the cot and tried to sleep. The more he tried to relax the more the sounds from below seemed to increase. Music and laughter was occasionally interrupted by angry voices. Finally, he put his boots on and walked down the stairs. Having left his saddlebags upstairs in the small unlocked bedroom, Rafe took a seat at a table where he could watch the bedroom door and ordered a beer.

He was nursing his beer when two men sat across from him.

"*Hola,*" the one said.

"*Hola,*" Rafe greeted him in return.

The men ignored him, though Rafe heard them talking. They were carpenters and one wanted to go to Manzanillo. He told the other they could find work in the shipyards there. As they talked, Rafe became intrigued. He rode out of Las Lomas heading southwest not knowing where it would lead, though knew he would eventually reach the ocean. Several times he thought he should turn north, but a rugged mountain range was visible in the distance.

As the men talked of Manzanillo, Rafe heard them say it was a day's ride over the mountains. Apparently a large sheltered harbor and good wood from the neighboring mountain range had allowed the town to flourish in shipbuilding.

"Excuse me," Rafe said. The men stopped talking and looked at him. He was an obvious stranger and they seemed suspicious of him.

"This town, Manzanillo, is it a port?" Rafe asked.

"*Sí señor.* It is a port."

"What kind of ships? Where do the ships travel?"

"It is a cargo port *señor.* The ships travel to Sinaloa,

Sonora, and Acapulco to the south along the coast."

"Do some ships travel to California?" Rafe asked.

"I do not know *señor,* perhaps," the man replied.

Shortly thereafter the men stood and walked away leaving Rafe sitting alone, but not before Rafe knew where he was going.

He arrived in the busy harbor town of Manzanillo the following evening. It was not hard to find the wharf as the tall masts of sailing ships were visible for at least a mile. He directed Rayo toward the masts, until the sheltered wharf was fully visible. By the time he reached the marina, the ships were mostly quietly swaying in the water as nightfall overtook the port.

He tied Rayo to a post and pushed in the swinging doors of a portside restaurant and found a seat. The patrons of this restaurant were sailors and dockworkers. Their *pantalones* only reached to mid-calf and the *camisa* was tighter with a large collar. They wore long leggings and shoes, not *huarache* sandals. It was obvious their outfits were designed for the windy sea and not the heat of the interior of Mexico. As the waiter approached him, Rafe knew it was easy to tell he was a stranger.

"*Buenas tardes. Bienvenidos a Manzanillo,*" the waiter welcomed him.

"*Buenas tardes.* What is the specialty of the house?" Rafe asked.

"Grilled sailfish," the waiter answered. "Or perhaps spicy shrimp."

Rafe was not surprised the local fare was from the sea. He ordered the grilled sailfish and a beer. The meal was delightfully different. The dense fish, tender and simmered in tomatoes and butter, was delicious. When the waiter returned, Rafe asked him about the city.

"*Manzanillo is muy importante,*" the waiter replied. "We are the port for Colima. Our state is one of the smallest states in Mexico, but we have the harbor and shipping business. We build many ships here because of the wood from the mountains and the safe harbor," the waiter said puffed with pride. "You are not Mexican?" the waiter asked thinking any

Mexican should know the history of Colima.

Rafe thought it rather an odd question. He was Mexican and yet he was not. *"Soy Norteamericano,"* Rafe replied.

"Ah sí. Why are you here?"

"I seek a ship to go to California," Rafe replied.

"Ah, in the morning you can talk to the dock master. There are ships coming and going to California often."

Rafe thanked him and asked about a hotel nearby. The waiter told him of one near the dock. Checking into the hotel near the waterfront, Rafe secured Rayo in their small corral in the back. The rooms were small and clean with an overly soft bed, but he quickly fell fast asleep.

A loud mooing of a cow startled Rafe out of a deep sleep. It continued until he realized it was not a cow, but the sound of a foghorn waking him. The lowing of the horn continued and soon was joined by several others.

He lay there clearing his mind for a few minutes listening to the odd sounds of the sea. Intermixed with the foghorn, loud whistling in rhythmic bursts joined the eerie foghorn. He got up and quickly dressed in his American suit and gathered his belongings. He checked out of the hotel, collected Rayo, and asked directions to the dock master.

Last night at dinner he asked the waiter where he could go to seek passage on a boat headed to California. He was told there was a passenger boat company at the harbor and he could ask the dock master for passage. The waiter said it was a good way to travel and if he were willing to work, it would not cost anything. He said they always needed help.

"You do not have spaces for horses?" Rafe asked, irritated at the uninterested young man at the dock's passenger ship ticket window.

"That is correct *señor.* You cannot take your horse," the man answered and went back to reading the newspaper.

"Can you tell me if there is another passenger line here which will take horses?" Rafe asked.

"No señor, there is no other passenger line. This is the only one."

Rafe huffed away his frustration. He did not want to

travel by stage, as he worried *doña* Carmela would have the authorities after him. It did not matter he told *don* Luis to tell her to let it go. She could easily be searching for him still spiteful of his inheritance and more possibly horse thievery. Besides, the only stage went back to Mexico City. He could ride Rayo on the back trail of the countryside, though Rafe thought it a long and arduous journey for both he and the horse.

At this point he had little choice but to find a way to get on some ship heading north. Walking to the busy wharf, he stopped at a cafe and ordered coffee and breakfast. There were only a few sailors having breakfast at this later hour in the morning. The sailor's day started and ended with the sun. Rafe ate hurriedly and headed along the wharf to the Merchant Marine side of the harbor where large cargo ships were docked. Not familiar with ships and the ocean for that matter, Rafe felt like a child seeing a wondrous marvel for the very first time. The docks were a flurry of wagons and workers. The sailors nimbly jumped up the gangplanks with awkward bundles on their backs. One ship used a block and tackle for large pallets of wood.

As he watched the ships, he saw some being loaded and others were unloading cargo. Rafe could tell the ships which were heavily loaded, as they rode deep in the water. Two seemed to be sitting idle as they waited for cargo to arrive. Rafe tethered Rayo to a post and walked to a man who was walking down the plank of a ship being loaded.

"*Oye, ¿este barco va a California?*" Rafe asked the man if this boat was headed to California.

"*No, vamos al sur para Colombia,*" the man said they were going south to Colombia. Rafe thanked him and moved on.

The next man he asked said this ship was headed to Peru and another said they were bound to San Francisco, but were waiting a few days for cargo to arrive from Mexico City. Working his way along the docks, Rafe walked up to a man dressed in khakis with a pistol strapped around his hips. The man was carefully watching crates being carried from a wagon and taken onto the ship.

The ship was impressive, with three masts and the sails

were furled up. Rafe took a long look at the intricate rope rigging and wondered how the sailors managed to work the ropes to unfurl the sails and set them to catch the wind from any direction. He stood there studying the rigging wondering if he should even ask the armed man if they were heading to California. The waiter said some ships took on passengers who were willing to work for their passage. Rafe knew he could not even attempt to learn how to work as a sailor with the rigging so complex.

He was about to ask the man where they were going when he got a better look at the armed man in khakis. Rafe recognized him as one of the guards from the agave plantation owned by Longwei and Rafe knew the cargo they were loading contained hidden opium bound for San Francisco. Quickly he moved behind Rayo worried the man might recognize him and walked to the next ship. It was a steamer and was being loaded with lumber.

Rafe tethered Rayo and walked up to the loading ramp and was about to ask a sailor where the ship was headed when he heard the sailors speaking English.

"Is this ship going to California?" he asked one of the sailors.

"Yes we er, mate," he answered.

"Any chance my horse and I can get a ride to Los Angeles?"

"Cain't say mate. Ya hafta ask the cap'in,"

"Where can I find the captain?"

"He'll be here shortly; he's a having breakfast."

"Mind if I stay around and wait?" Rafe asked.

"Suit yerself mate," the sailor said and went about his work.

Rafe tethered Rayo to a hook and sat on a rusty cast iron rail just opposite the loading ramp of the steamship. A large smoke stack extended up from the center of the ship with two masts, one toward the bow and the other behind the smoke stack toward the stern. On the forward mast flew an American flag. On the bow of the ship just above the anchor, CALIFORNIA GOLD was painted in bold white letters.

He watched as the last of the lumber was loaded and the wagons cleared the area. Some of the sailors sat in the shade of the main cabin where the smoke stack was located. Others got off the ship and strolled to where small shops and street vendors were selling food and some were selling wood carvings, while others sold silver jewelry. Rafe laughed at the Americans trying to haggle with the vendors in broken and made up Spanish. The sailors headed back to the ship bragging to each other about how they outsmarted the Mexicans. The vendors laughed about how they sold inexpensive goods for a good price.

Soon Rafe spotted two men heading toward the ship. One was dressed in a navy blue uniform with ten gold buttons, five in a row from top to bottom on each side of the jacket. On his gold-trimmed hat were two oak leaves crossed at the bottom forming a U with an anchor in the center. The other was dressed in a gray business suit much like the one Rafe wore.

"Sir, I am looking for passage to California for myself and my horse," Rafe stepped up and spoke to the two men in English and pointed at Rayo. Both men looked at the magnificent Appaloosa stallion. "I can pay my way or am willing to work my way for my passage," Rafe continued not giving the captain a chance to answer right away.

The captain looked Rafe over seeing a well-dressed man looking Mexican, but speaking in English and it made him ponder a bit.

"Do you speak Spanish?" the other man asked.

"Yes sir, I do," Rafe answered. "I speak both English and Spanish."

"Captain, we could use a man like this to translate to the Mexicans I hired to help with the cargo. Like I told you, Manzanillo lumber is very delicate and needs to be moved so it won't develop rot from the ocean moisture."

"What do you say young man, will you translate what is needed to the Mexican sailors and make sure they do it properly?" the captain asked.

"Yes sir, I can to that. What about my horse?"

"We can take him, but you will have to go and buy feed

for him. It will take two to three weeks to get to Los Angeles. Do it quickly as we have a few more provisions to load and then we will be on our way."

Chapter 59

George spent the next two days in Torreón restlessly waiting for some word from *don* David. Each day seemed longer than the last. Trying to keep his spirits up, he spent most of the day at the Reyes *hacienda*. Each morning he had the mercantile load a wagon with supplies he knew were needed at the *hacienda*. This morning he brought wire for fence lines, shovels, picks, a wheel of braided rope, and two hand plows.

The joy and camaraderie of the people was inspiring. These peasants were anything but lazy. George watched them work hard from sun up to sun down. Even the children worked alongside their parents. The women were clearing patches beside the small *jacals* for gardens. The smaller children were carrying rocks to make the border.

He and Rodolfo rode to the Santos *hacienda* and George bought a bull and five cows. Three of the cows were already pregnant. *Señora* Santos promised Rodolfo five more calves by the end of the year.

The more George had a chance to get to know Rodolfo, the more impressed he became with the young man. Though not educated, Rodolfo had a way with people. They looked up to him as a leader. George knew it was an innate quality which could not be learned. He was a quiet man with an easy smile. As he and Rodolfo rode back pushing the small herd of cattle, Rodolfo began telling George of his plans.

"These cows will be the start of a large herd," he told George. "Over the winter I will have the men clear more acres for corn and hay. *Don* Bernardo let his horses graze the canyons, but these cattle will need more than the scratchy grass in these hills."

"Have you decided on a brand?"

"María wants an R with an upward arrow to symbolize a new beginning. What do you think?"

"I think it is a fine idea. Pablo wants to raise some

horses too," George said.

"Yes. He found one yearling mare running in the canyon and he has been scouting for more which might have been *don* Bernardo's. The others are good riding horses, but not blooded."

Yesterday María asked George to buy six children's books and six chalk tablets. One of the carpenters made her three rough benches. A woman named Carmen knew how to read a little and Rodolfo knew his numbers. María was determined to learn and wanted every child to get a basic education.

"Will you bring your children here," George asked her.

María looked at her sandaled feet. "I miss them terribly, *don* Jorge. Someday I hope they will forgive me, but I think they are better off in Santa Fe. There I know they will get a good education and a better life. We have high hopes and big plans here, but we are still *peóns* and I fear the government could take all of this away from us. Please tell my mother . . . " She did not finish the sentence as her voice choked with emotion.

George could not argue with her logic. The government of Mexico was struggling and many factions were at odds. Just like the *dons* of Santa Fe who were fighting the American laws, the elite ruling class was still strong in Mexico. Though he saw many encouraging signs, anything was possible.

George was in the barn when a rider came galloping down the lane. The young rider rode into the courtyard asking for *Señor* Summers. When George walked to meet the rider, he handed him a telegram. George pulled a *cinco peso* coin from his pocket and thanked the young rider. As he rode off, George's hand holding the telegram shook slightly. Rodolfo stood beside him knowing the telegram contained news of Rafael's fate.

"Open it. We must know," Rodolfo said to him. George unfolded the telegram and started reading aloud.

Don Jorge.

Rafael and Rayo alive and riding west from Jalisco.
My uncle has returned to Mexico City.
Carlos.

George could not stop tears from forming in his eyes. Rafe was alive and though he was not riding to Torreón it did not matter. Rodolfo grabbed George in a hearty *abrazo,* wrapping his strong arms around George's shoulders.

"I must go tell María," Rodolfo said and ran toward the main house.

George read the words again, 'Rafael and Rayo alive.' Carlos had not elaborated on where Rafe was going or why, or perhaps he knew nothing more. María came running from the house and ran to him. She wrapped her arms around him with tears on her cheeks. "We must thank God for this miracle," she said.

When George prepared to leave the *hacienda* in the evening, Rodolfo and María knew it was the last time he would come. He was heading home to Santa Fe tomorrow morning. They could not begin to thank him enough for all the things he had done to help them.

María threw her arms around George. "Bless you *don* Jorge. Tell my mother and the children I love them, when you get back to Santa Fe. Tell them I am well and happy and tell my mother about the new grandchild I carry. Tell her I will be a good mother to this child."

CHAPTER 60

As the California Gold steamship set sail, Rafe was enthralled as he watched the dark smoke rise from the smokestacks and the boat began to move. A flurry of activity unleashed the moorings as the engine started to grumble. Before the sun set, Rafe could no longer see the port of Manzanillo and the California Gold was well out to sea.

It took two days before Rafe began to get his sea legs. Several times a day he ventured down into the hold of the ship to feed and talk to Rayo. The horse seemed to be weathering the rocking of the ship with his four legs better than Rafe on two.

In the evening, Captain Edwards and Randolph Schelstrate invited him to dine with the officers in the aft dining room. Captain Edwards was originally from Sacramento, California and began his sailing career as a teenager. Randolph Schelstrate was a German immigrant to California. Randolph was a sailboat builder who imported Manzanillo lumber from Mexico to use for building his sailboats. He hired Rafe to translate his orders for the Mexican workers he hired to care for the lumber onboard ship.

"The workers must be very careful with the wood," Randolph told him. "The wood is naturally water-resistant, but the sap and the fruit are very poisonous."

"I'm confused. One of the tasks is to turn the wood so it will not get wood rot from the ocean moisture. How can it be water-resistant?" Rafe asked.

"While the wood is green, it is pliable and easily shaped, because it has a root system which draws water from the sandy soil of Manzanillo. This makes it good for shipbuilding. It takes time to dry the wood and only after it is dry does it become water resistant," Randolph explained.

Rafe took an instant liking to the shipbuilder and did his best to do a good job for him. Over the midday and evening meals they talked of ships and of sailing. Rafe told

Randolph about horse breeding and about bloodlines.

Rafe took extra care to follow Randolph's instructions about the wood. At times he even helped the Mexican workers care for the cargo of lumber finding the work invigorating. His biceps developed from lifting the agave balls made lifting the lumber an easy task.

About ten days after they left Manzanillo the calm waters of the Pacific churned and the sky became dark. The captain said an autumn storm was blowing their way and he ordered all the sailors to double-lash the cargo. Each passing hour the boat began to rock more wildly as the winds blowing from the southwest became stronger. Over dinner, the captain talked to Rafe and Randolph. I will cut our speed, but we must keep moving and keep the swells to our port side," the captain explained.

Randolph asked Rafe to double check the wood pallets and make sure they were lashed tight. After checking the wood, Rafe went to Rayo's stall. Rafe clung to the hold's timbers as the ship heaved in the storm swells. Even Rayo stepped and swayed unevenly. Rafe walked into Rayo's stall and spoke to the horse, urging Rayo to lie down. Finally the horse obeyed Rafe's commands. Rafe decided to stay with Rayo. Together in the small stall, Rafe heard the creaking of the ship as each wave took its toll. Rafe kept a hand on the horse's flank, fearing he would want to stand and might hurt himself.

Comforting Rayo, brought Rafe the comfort he also needed. His stomach churned and though it was not full-blown seasickness, it was unpleasant enough to keep him concentrating on holding onto his supper. The sudden storm made him think about traveling to Spain by ship to find Ana Teresa. As the storm battered the ship, Rafe's discomfort turned into fear and he wondered if he and Rayo were going to die at sea.

Rafe huddled with Rayo all night as the storm battered the boat. Finally, Rafe could tell the storm was passing. He found his legs and allowed Rayo to stand. After petting Rayo's big face, Rafe walked up to the deck. In the distance, he could see the edge of the cloudbank and behind it blue sky. He said a prayer of thanks.

That night at supper, the officers and captain talked about damage and repairs. Randolph asked Rafe about the Appaloosa.

"How did he weather the storm?" Randolph asked.

"Probably better than I," Rafe replied.

"This was your first storm at sea?" one of the officers asked.

"Yes, this is my first time at sea," Rafe responded.

The officers and captain fell into good natured talk of bad storms. The recent storm was typical and though it peaked Rafe's fear, apparently according to the sailors it was not that bad. Rafe wondered how bad it could get, but did not want to know.

The rest of the trip was uneventful, as good weather held. The captain told Rafe they would be docking at San Pedro, the port of Los Angeles. Randolph told Rafe about a new rail line from San Pedro to Los Angeles. He also told Rafe Los Angeles was a rowdy city and if he ran into any trouble to come to him for help.

"Get away from the docks immediately and do not stay there overnight. Men disappear, shanghai'd," he warned Rafe. "That horse of yours would be desirable. Take care not to leave him alone, even in a livery." Randolph suggested to Rafe to get further into the city before finding a hotel.

Rafe took an opportunity to demonstrate his GSW double action pistols. He shot them off the side of the ship into the sea.

"Amazing," Randolph said impressed enough to order a set for himself and told Rafe many of his friends in San Pedro would most likely want them.

It was before noon on the last day of November when the merchant ship California Gold docked at San Pedro Bay harbor. Rafe wasted no time finding the ticket office for the rail and he and Rayo took the next train north into Los Angeles. He got off on Wine Street and registered at a hotel called the Pico House.

"Do you have a stable and stable boy in back?" Rafe asked remembering Randolph's words.

"Yes sir. I will make sure your horse is safe and cared for properly," the clerk replied.

After putting his belongings in his room, Rafe went to send a wire to George Summers in Santa Fe. As he walked to the telegraph office, he noticed this part of Los Angeles was much like Santa Fe. Americans, Spanish *caballeros, mestizos,* and *Indios* milled along the street and market place. There were many booths and tables where people sold vegetables, meat, fruit, and some offered live chickens and goats. At one booth, a side of beef hung and the vendor sold pieces which he cut by request.

Reaching the telegraph office, he sent a message saying he was well and in Los Angeles and to wire money for him to the Farmers and Merchants Bank in Los Angeles. He told them to send the reply to the Pico House where he was staying. He then decided to go and check on Rayo.

On the way to the stables at the hotel, Rafe saw what looked like an Indian or *mestizo* hanging from a gas lamppost with a crude sign tacked to his pant leg. It read:

This savage tried to molest a woman. Hanged by the Citizens Security Patrol.

At the stables, Rafe saw Rayo was well taken care of and a young *mestizo* was brushing the horse. "What is the Citizens Security Patrol?" Rafe asked him.

"Do not be out at night without your guns *señor.* They are bad men who do not like Mexicans and will use any excuse to hang one. They are nothing but vigilantes who take the law into their own hands. The governor is trying to put a stop to it."

The young man stopped brushing and looked toward Rafe. Though Rafe looked prosperous and spoke flawless English, his heritage was unmistakable. "This is your horse? *Magnifico.* You must be careful when you ride this one. Those same men will accuse you of stealing it and take it away from you and hang you," the young man warned Rafe.

After seeing the man hanging on the gas lamppost, Rafe took the stable hand's advice to heart. He thanked him for taking care of Rayo and went to a nearby restaurant. He ordered a t-bone steak. Meals on the ship were good, but salted fish and bacon were the basis of most meals.

He devoured the steak quickly and found himself craving more. Taking the bone in his hands, he bit off all the sweet meat until the bone was clean. After a second cold beer, he noticed the late afternoon sun from the cloudless sky was creating long shadows. He followed the shadows back to the hotel to wait for a reply from Santa Fe.

Rafe was sitting in the hotel lobby as night fell, heeding the warnings about the city and the vigilantes. A boy came into the hotel and left a message at the desk. One of the clerks behind the counter called out, "Message for Mr. Reyes!"

"Thank you," Rafe said after he retrieved the envelope. He opened it and read:

Rafe,
Thank God you are safe in Los Angeles.
Money will be transferred.
Come home soon.
Love from us all.
George.
p.s. Carlos says Ana Teresa is in the Rancho Simi area staying with relatives.

Rafe's heart skipped a beat as he read the last part of the message. Ana Teresa was here in California, not Spain. All the angst and frustration of the last several months evaporated. He quickly went to the desk and asked for directions to Rancho Simi. The clerk brought out a map and spread it out on the counter. He showed Rafe how he could go north to the San Fernando Valley and then head west to Rancho Simi.

"You must either go over the mountains or along the coast. You cannot miss it. It has mostly large Spanish *haciendas* raising cattle, but some Americans now own ranches. There is a mercantile in the middle of the Rancho Simi valley. You can stop there and ask questions on how to find the ranch you are looking for," the clerk said happy to have helped.

"Thank you. I will be checking out in the morning," Rafe replied.

CHAPTER 61

Late the next morning, Rafe came to the top of a pass west of the San Fernando valley. The beautiful lush valley below sat between two mountain ranges, one to the south and one to the north.

He eased Rayo down the trail heading west until he reached the mercantile store. He dismounted and led Rayo to a water trough and let him get his fill, before he tethered him to a hitching rail.

Inside the store was a small restaurant with four tables. Around the walls the typical items for life were stacked neatly. At one of the tables, three *caballeros* sat having lunch. At another a man sat with a women and two children. Rafe sat at an empty table and waited for the server.

"Today we have a roasted hog with beans and tortillas," he told Rafe.

"Perfect and bring me water," Rafe ordered.

As Rafe ate, he pondered how to find Ana Teresa and how she might greet him. He wondered if she still loved him. His mind wandered from scenario to scenario – she threw herself into his arms or she was already promised to another. Rafe wondered if her father would let him court her.

By the time he finished his meal, the other patrons had left. He walked up to the counter and paid his bill. "I am looking for the de Soto family. Can you tell me where they live?" he asked the clerk.

"Yes, there is only one de Soto family left in the valley. You can find their ranch west from here. Follow the main trail for about two miles and then there is a small trail to the south. You will see a sign pointing to the de Soto ranch from there," he told Rafe.

"Thank you," Rafe said.

Rafe's stomach churned on his lunch, as he made the turn south from the main trail heading to the de Soto *hacienda* as the clerk described. Rayo spotted some mares grazing in the meadow and his ears perked up and he snorted and hastened his step.

"Whoa there boy. This is not our ranch and you cannot have those mares," Rafe tried to calm the Appaloosa and laughed.

He rode through the arch with the name de Soto painted on the face at the top telling him he was at the right place. An elderly man came out and held Rayo until Rafe dismounted. He walked up to the main door and knocked. A servant opened the door.

"Buenas tardes, ¿Ana Teresa está aquí?" Rafe said good afternoon and asked if Ana Teresa was here.

"Sí señor, please come in. Who will I tell her is calling?"

"Just tell her a friend from Santa Fe is here to see her."

She left and Rafe paced in the parlor nervously twirling his hat in hand. Suddenly he heard Ana Teresa's voice, "Rafael!"

She ran to him and hugged him tightly. It was a miracle. God had sent Rafael to her. She prayed every day since the day he asked for her hand and she accepted. The last she heard from Carlos he was in Mexico. Now by God's miracle, he was here.

"What are you doing here? How did you find me?" she trembled in his arms as tears flowed down her cheeks.

"How I got here is a very long story. When I reached Los Angeles, I received a wire which said you were here."

"I want to hear that very long story, but first kiss me and tell me you still love me," she said.

CHAPTER 62

The following day Rafe wired George. He wished he could talk to his adopted father and ask advice. Ana Teresa's cousin was not opposed to their marriage, but insisted on waiting until proper approval could be obtained from her parents.

"I am not her guardian," Francisco de Soto told Rafe. "Only her father can give such approval."

"But my father is in Spain. It will take months to reach him and for him to respond," Ana Teresa retorted. Ana Teresa had no plans to wait for her father's response, as she was sure her old-fashioned father would not approve of Rafe. He was a *mestizo*.

"California is a state. The laws of California prevail," Ana Teresa argued.

Yesterday morning, Rafe received a reply from George. In Rafe's telegram to Santa Fe, he wrote about finding Ana Teresa and their desire to wed. In George's reply he wrote:

Congratulations from all of us.
Your mother and the children are well.
Rodolfo and María living and married in Torreón.
Still unrest over Diego here in Santa Fe.
Love to you both.
George.

Yesterday afternoon they met with the local padre. He seemed torn when trying to counsel them.

"Yes the law allows you to marry," he told them. "But I know your father and he would expect to have the authority to grant his approval. Perhaps you should wait until he returns from Spain," the padre said to Ana Teresa.

"Padre, would you refuse to marry us without his blessing?" Rafe asked looking directly into the padre's eyes.

"No my son. I am bound by the church and by the laws of California, but the family would not look upon it favorably."

Late in the afternoon Rafe rode to the San Fernando valley to send George a reply.

Father.

Are my horses safe from Diego's friends?

Ana Teresa and I want to marry without approval from her father. Please advise.

Rafe.

Rafe stayed in the valley pondering their dilemma and waiting for replies from George. He wanted to know why Diego's friends could not accept what happened. They burned his almost completed house. It had been Diego who started the fight, attacking him and calling him a *peón.*

For the last several days, Rafe had felt torn. Santa Fe was his home and his mother and María's children were there, as well as his adopted family. Carlos and Bibiana were married. He wondered who was caring for his horses. No doubt George hired someone to manage the barn while he was lost in Mexico.

However, California was already a state of the United States of America. American laws prevailed here in California. New Mexico was a territory, still torn between the old ways and the new. The *dons* still maintained some control over the sheriff in Santa Fe and Diego's friends could get away with burning his house and probably worse, if they banded together.

Yet, he longed to take Ana Teresa back to Santa Fe and resume his life. He had nothing here – no land, no family, no connections. In the morning Rafe received a reply from George:

Rafe.

Two new colts. Hired a man to keep the barn.

Carlos and Bibiana send you their regards.

Josefina and I say to follow your heart.

George.

Later that afternoon Rafe and Ana Teresa took a ride into the foothills near her cousin's ranch. It was late November, though the air was warm and a gentle breeze blew. Rafe thought about Santa Fe and wondered if it was already covered in snow.

"If we are married, there is nothing my uncle or father can do. He will have to accept it. It is the law here in the United States. He cannot invoke an ancient Spanish law on us," Ana Teresa told Rafe. Her brash straightforwardness was one thing he admired about her. Any thoughts she might not love him were dispelled in the moment she kissed him and his heart was hers.

Rayo was tethered with her brown mare to a tree near a stream on the ranch's land. The terrain was starkly different than Santa Fe, where low scrub pines were set amongst brown soil and boulders. The field where Rafe's herd grazed was dotted with sparse wild grass. Here lush green stretched along the hills as far as he could see. Though they could not see it now, the ocean stretched away on the west side of the valley.

Staring out at the lush grass, Rafe could imagine his herd peacefully grazing here. He had Rayo and could easily move his herd here to Rancho Simi.

"We do not have to wait for my father's permission. I am of age," Ana Teresa argued.

"Yes, but I should ask for your hand and be accepted. Surely if we don't have permission, our marriage will never be recognized. Our children could be shunned by your family and this community," Rafe lamented.

Since Rafe arrived in Rancho Simi, the events of the last four months now seemed a blur. Whatever God's plan, it had led him here to her.

Ana Teresa pushed his shoulder. "Children? And how many children do you want?" she asked looking at him with a serious expression.

"Oh, maybe ten sons and ten daughters," he responded with a smile.

Teasing him she giggled. "We definitely better get started soon then." Rafe wrapped her in his arms.

FIN

Please continue reading a preview of the next Young Pistolero Series adventure by Robert J. Alvarado, *A Reckoning for the Young Pistolero* (Book 5) 2018 Sierra Press.

CHAPTER 1

Rumbling thunder rolled along the valley from the ocean toward the east into the San Fernando Valley threatening to pour a good December rain on Rancho Simi. Rafael Reyes de Estrada and Ana Teresa de Soto were sitting under an aged oak tree spending time alone together. They heard the thunder, but subconsciously ignored it. All they cared about was being alone. It was a ritual now, where after lunch they saddled their horses and rode to this remote spot, secluded by the shade of the old oak tree. It was a quiet spot and their horses grazed on green grass nearby. Today the thunder threatened they might get wet, but it did not sway them to leave.

"We can't wait for permission from my father," Ana Teresa said. "It will take too long for a letter to get to Spain and for my father to answer back to us here in California," she continued the conversation about their dilemma.

"I agree my love, but I worry your family will shun you and our children. I do not want that to happen. Believe me, family is very important and we must respect them. Your father will be insulted if he is not allowed to give us his blessing," Rafael told her.

"Of course you are right, but remember what happened to us in Santa Fe. My father is stuck in the old ways, just like my uncle Pedro. He will never give us permission and most likely he'll have you run out of this valley because you are *mestizo*. Then what?" She pulled away from him. There seemed no solution. They were in love and had every right to marry. It was a legal right, not a right according to Spanish traditions.

Rafael had been in the valley of Rancho Simi, near the California coast north of Los Angeles for almost two weeks. After escaping from the hellhole of the opium fields in Jalisco, Mexico, Rafael miraculously found her living with a cousin. Her parents were in Spain trying to obtain proof of their rightful land grant for their ranch here in this fertile valley.

Ana Teresa was a pure-blooded Spanish woman born in California and Rafael was considered a *mestizo* from Mexico, a man of mixed bloodlines, both Spanish and Mexican Indian. Old Spanish traditions forbade this type of marriage, regardless of the fact Rafael was a successful American businessman and Ana Teresa penniless.

Over the past week, he viewed several available parcels of land in the Simi Valley area. The land here in California was expensive, more than three times what he paid for his land in Santa Fe, New Mexico. However, the land was lush and his horses could graze on the hillsides year round. Though it was December, the weather was mild and temperate and the grass on the hillsides was still green. Ana Teresa told him it never snowed in Rancho Simi. It would be a good place for a horse breeding business to flourish.

Unfortunately, Rafael's family and his business in Santa Fe nagged at him. He could not abandon his mother and his sister María's children. In a recent telegram, his adopted father George Summers wrote the builder had reframed the ranchhouse and would continue working until the colder winter weather stopped progress. The original home he was building for his mother and Ana Teresa had been burned to the ground last spring by Diego de la Torre's friends as an act of revenge.

George's telegram also alluded to continuing anger toward him over Diego's death. Apparently, the sheriff wanted to have a formal trial to finally put the matter to rest. Rafael knew he was innocent and had many witnesses to that fact. However, the Spanish aristocrats of Santa Fe still had clout and he worried they could pay off or intimidate a judge or jury. Diego's friends were another matter. He felt confident he could best them in any fair fight. It was the part about fair, which troubled him. Diego's friends traveled together and would most likely catch him alone, as they did last year surrounding him with their swords at the abandoned *hacienda*. It would make living in Santa Fe perilous for both he and Ana Teresa.

He pondered what Ana Teresa told him about her father. If her father refused him just because of his heritage, Rafael feared how he would react. If her father was anything like his brother, *don* Pedro in Santa Fe, things would get ugly. The last thing he wanted was to come between Ana Teresa and her family. He wanted to avoid trouble or confront it before they got married, but in his heart he knew she was right. Her father would never accept him.

A loud clap of thunder shook the earth around them as big fat drops began hitting the ground. He pulled her close under the protective canopy of the oak tree. There was no course of action for them not fraught with some peril, which both angered him and pushed him to action. It would be Christmas soon and he wanted to share the holiday with his family in Santa Fe, and he wanted to take Ana Teresa with him as his wife.

"Ana Teresa, I love you and I will not leave here without you. You are probably right to believe your father will never accept me. All I can promise you is my love forever. Let's go to the padre and ask him to marry us today," he suggested having decided on a course of action.

"No, he will summon my cousin, Francisco, and he will put a stop to it," she warned him.

"Then let's go to Los Angeles and be married there. We will find a church and they will not know of your family. Then we can take the stage to Santa Fe to spend Christmas with my family. After that, well, after that we'll make plans for our future," he said holding her hands in his.

She threw her arms around him and kissed him as her response. Yes she would go with him. It was what she wanted with all her heart.

"Everything I own is in my saddlebags or in Santa Fe. What things do you have at your cousin's house?" he asked.

"Nothing worth much. All my clothes are old and well worn. I have no money and have been living off my cousin's kindness," she answered as tears trickled down her cheeks. As the rain poured around them, they plotted their escape. Ana Teresa thought her cousin, Francisco, might try to stop her from leaving. Though he had no real authority, he might feel compelled to take action.

"We must just go and not look back," she told him.

"If you do not at least tell Francisco we are leaving, he will call the sheriff when you do not return tonight," Rafael responded.

They waited until the rain subsided, cuddling near the trunk of the oak tree until the first hint of sunlight peeked through the clouds. He helped her up on her horse and mounted the Appaloosa he called Rayo. They decided Ana Teresa would leave a letter at the mercantile in Rancho Simi. It would be delivered to her cousin later in the afternoon. The letter would explain her disappearance.

They rode from the secluded spot toward the main part of Simi. Making the quick stop at the mercantile, they then headed east out of the valley of Rancho Simi toward Los Angeles. It was nearly seven o'clock Monday night when they reached the Pico House in mid-town Los Angeles. Rafael led them to the stables where he gave the liveryman two dollars to feed and brush both horses well. At the desk of the hotel, he paid for two rooms.

"First thing tomorrow, we'll go to the Farmers and Merchants Bank to retrieve the funds George wired for me. Then we'll go and buy clothes for you and a new suit for me. After that, we'll find a padre who will marry us. Good night my love," he told her taking her in his arms.

Ana Teresa clung to him not wanting to let go. She knew what they were planning would be frowned on by her family and by Spanish aristocrats both here and in Santa Fe. It had been the world she grew up in, but not the world she believed in.

The following morning was cool and sunny. All remnants of yesterday's storm were gone. They rode to the bank and Rafael retrieved the funds from the teller. He asked the teller where to find a dress shop nearby. Ana Teresa chose a simple cream dress for the wedding, three other dresses, sleeping gowns, undergarments, and a winter coat as traveling attire for their trip to Santa Fe.

"We'll go talk to the padre while the dresses are being altered," he said as they left the dress shop. Towing their horses, they walked across the plaza to a small Catholic church where they found an elderly priest tending a nativity scene to the side of the front steps. The wood carved statue of one of the three kings had fallen over and he was trying to anchor it with some large rocks. It was the fourteenth of December and only ten days before Christmas. Rafael stepped up and helped the padre with his task.

"Padre, my name is Rafael and this is Ana Teresa. Is it possible you can marry us today?" Rafael asked after the statue was stable.

The padre got slowly up off his knees and adjusted his eyeglasses taking a closer look. The young couple standing in front of him was definitely old enough to get married. The woman was obviously Spanish, with long brown hair and her eyes shone a soft golden brown. The young man was darker of skin with a handsome face framing white teeth. His Mexican-Indian heritage was apparent, though he was over six feet tall and broad shouldered.

"You say you want to get married today?" he asked in a raspy voice and Rafael noticed his hands trembled slightly. "You are not from my parish. Where is your family?"

"Padre, we have no family near here. Ana Teresa's family is in Spain and my family is in Santa Fe, New Mexico. I will tell you her family would not allow us to marry because I am a *mestizo,* but we do not believe in those old traditions. They do not fit into the ways of the United States. We will marry, even if we do it with a civil judge, but we would rather be married here by you padre, in the sight of God," Rafael told him as he took Ana Teresa's hand in his.

"And how do you feel, my daughter?" he asked Ana Teresa after he slowly turned and adjusted his eyeglasses again.

"Padre, I love Rafael. Nothing will stop me from

marrying him," she replied.

"Very well my children come back after evening Mass and I will hear your confessions before I marry you. Do you have any witnesses?"

"No padre we are alone here," Ana Teresa answered.

"Not to worry, I will have one of the brothers witness for you," he said and shuffled off into the church.

They looked at each other and smiled. "Let's go back to the hotel and have some lunch," Rafael said. They walked back to where they left the horses tied near the front of the church. He helped her mount her horse and they rode across the plaza toward the hotel. Two cowboys lounged near the hotel, but Rafael only gave them a brief glance. Jumping off Rayo, he was tying him to the rail on the left side of the wide steps in front of the hotel.

"Hey thar Mex, whard ja steal that Paloose," a gruff voice stopped him.

"Who wants to know?" Rafael asked instinctively keeping his left hand on Rayo's reins. He backed away from Rayo and pulled his coat away from his guns. He had heard the same question and tone of voice when the Reynolds' boys confronted him like this in El Paso and it would not happen again.

"The Citizens Security Patrol wants to know. Ain't rat a Mex like yew cud own a hoss like that," one of the two men answered. Rafael's instincts heightened seeing the two cowboys glaring at him. They stepped along the sidewalk nearer him. Both men wore western hats and boots with leather vests over checkered flannel shirts. The one who spoke wore a dusty black Stetson.

The speaker and the other man stood just off the sidewalk. Rafael knew he could take both of them before they could thumb the hammers on their holstered pistols. Another man stood nearby, dressed in a black business suit and no hat. Rafael was not sure if the man was part of this group or just an interested bystander.

"This is my horse mister," he responded not taking his eyes off them. "I'm here in Los Angeles from Santa Fe where I breed blooded horses." He took another step away from

Rayo keeping his view of the two men clear.

"Doncha yew lie ta me Mex. I know yew stole it. Now, step away from that hoss," the bold one wearing the black Stetson raised his voice at Rafael.

"Mister, I want no trouble with you. I said this is my horse and I plan to keep it," he replied.

"The Appaloosa is his horse. You need to let it go," Ana Teresa interrupted.

"Yew stay outta this sen'o'rita," the other man sneered at her. "What yew doing with this Mex anyaways?"

"Im'a takin that hoss. Yew keep yer hands away from them guns," the man wearing the black Stetson warned.

By now a crowd gathered near the confrontation along the sidewalk. People were whispering to each other and women grabbed their children, holding them close. A few hurried away down the street. Rafael sized up his competition and had no concerns except was still not sure about the third man. He was standing at the front of the crowd and was wearing a gun, though not dressed as the cowboys.

"If you come for this horse you better come shooting," Rafael warned him right back.

"Why yew uppity Mex. Who the hell yew think yew are," Black Stetson growled as he went for his gun.

Rafael pulled both of his GSW double-action revolvers out and shot Black Stetson in the right shoulder before the man's pistol cleared the holster. He held the two pistols on the other cowboy and the third man before they could react, but did not shoot. Ana Teresa's horse gave a small buck from the report of Rafael's pistol, before she got it under control.

"I'm warning you, don't go for your guns. I could have killed him and I have no problem killing you. Now you better take your friend to a doctor before he bleeds to death," Rafael told the other cowboy.

The wounded cowboy was standing holding his arm and groaning. "Yew fuckin Mex. Yew gonna pay fer this. Yew gonna pay," Black Stetson cried out.

"This is your own fault. I told you this is my horse and I will fight to keep it. Now take him to the doctor," Rafael retorted.

The third man stepped toward the wounded man. "You'll be hearing from the Citizens Security Patrol," the man in the business suit said. He and the cowboy shouldered the injured man and helped him to the sidewalk. Rafael knew these men were part of the local vigilantes who targeted Mexicans.

He walked over to Ana Teresa and put his hand on her thigh. "Do you still want to marry me?"

SPANISH GLOSSARY

Italicized Spanish words used repeatedly throughout the series which do not have an English counterpart, such as important = *importante* or Mama = *Mamá*. Other infrequently used words, phrases, and sentences written in Spanish are immediately explained within the text itself.

abogado: a lawyer, attorney at law
abrazo: a hug
abuelo; abuela: grandfather; grandmother (m;f)
adios: goodbye
alcalde: the mayor of a town or city
amigo(s); amiga(s): friend (m;f)
anglo(s): a word to mean a white man, an American
ayúdame: help, asking for help
baboso(s): drooling idiot (a slang or curse word)
bandido(s): a bandit or outlaw
bueno: good
buenos días; tardes; noches: good day; evening; night
bienvenido(s): welcome
cabrón: asshole or bastard (a curse word)
caballo(s); caballero(s): horse; horseman or gentleman
cállate: shutup or be quiet
cálmate; cálmese: be calm or calm down
camisa: a blouse or top
casita; casa: small home, home
chaqueta(s): jacket or suit coat
chico(s); chica(s); chiquita: young boy or young girl (m;f)
chingado: shit or fuck (a curse word)
cojones: slang for a man's testicles
compañero(s): companion, friends
criollo(s): pure-blooded Spaniard born in the New World
ciudad: a town or city
culón: a chickenshit (a curse word)
desgraciado(s): a miserable wretch or terrible person
Dios: God
don; doña: title for nobleman/woman
gachupín(s): pure-blooded Spaniards born in Spain
garrancha: means sword, slang for penis
gracias; muchas gracias: thank you; many thanks
grandee: Spanish nobleman, aristocrat (i.e. dandy)

hermano; hermana: brother; sister (m;f)

hacienda: a large plantation or estate

haciendero(s): the nobleman owning the hacienda

hola: hello greeting

Indio(s); India(s): means Indian (m;f)

jacal(s): small ramshakle house of mud and sticks

jefe: the boss man

mañana: tomorrow or the sometime later

mestizo(s); person of mixed Spanish and Indian (m)

mestiza(s): person of mixed Spanish and Indian (f)

mierda: same as shit (a curse word)

mi hijito; hijo; mijo; hijita; hija; mija: my son; daughter

muchacho(s); muchacha(s): like saying 'the guys' (m;f)

nada: no or nothing

Nana; Tata: nickname for grandmother; grandfather

padre: head friar, monk, minister, priest

pantalones: pants

paseo: the road, boulevard; place to stroll or ride

patrón; patróna: formal for a boss; a mistress (m;f)

pendejo(s); pendeja(s): slang for asshole (a curse)

pene(s): slang for a penis

peninsulares: pure-blooded Spaniards born in Spain

peón(s): a peasant

peso(s): Mexican money

picaro: a womanizer

pinche: fucking (a curse word)

plata: silver

primo(s); prima(s): cousin (m;f)

pulque; pulqueria: a poor man's drink in Mexico

puta(s): a whore (a slang or curse word)

que?: what or why

querido; querida: affectionate meaning my dear (m;f)

rayo: thunderbolt

sarape: cape, loose coat or blanket

señor(es); señora(s): like saying Mr. or Mrs.

señorita(s): like saying Miss (young woman or girl)

sí: yes

tío; tía: uncle; aunt (m;f)

traje(s): ornate Spanish aristocrat's style of suit

vaquero(s): livestock herder or cowboy

vámonos or vamos: let's go, get out of here